Stephen Crane (November 1, 1871 – June 5, 1900) was an American poet, novelist, and short story writer. Prolific throughout his short life, he wrote notable works in the Realist tradition as well as early examples of American Naturalism and Impressionism. He is recognized by modern critics as one of the most innovative writers of his generation. The ninth surviving child of Methodist parents, Crane began writing at the age of four and had published several articles by the age of 16. Having little interest in university studies though he was active in a fraternity, he left Syracuse University in 1891 to work as a reporter and writer. Crane's first novel was the 1893 Bowery tale Maggie: A Girl of the Streets, generally considered by critics to be the first work of American literary Naturalism. He won international acclaim in 1895 for his Civil War novel The Red Badge of Courage, which he wrote without having any battle experience. (Source: Wikipedia)

Literary works:
Maggie: A Girl of the Streets (1893)
The Red Badge of Courage (1895)
The Black Riders and Other Lines (1895)
George's Mother (1896)
The Third Violet (1897)
The Open Boat and Other Tales of Adventure (1898)
War is Kind (1899)
Active Service (1899)
The Monster and Other Stories (1899)
Wounds in the Rain (1900)
Great Battles of the World
The O'Ruddy (1903)
The Monster. London
Last Words. London
Whilomville Stories

PRINCE CLASSICS

WAR IS KIND,
WHILOMVILLE
STORIES
&
THE MONSTER
AND OTHER STORIES

STEPHEN CRANE

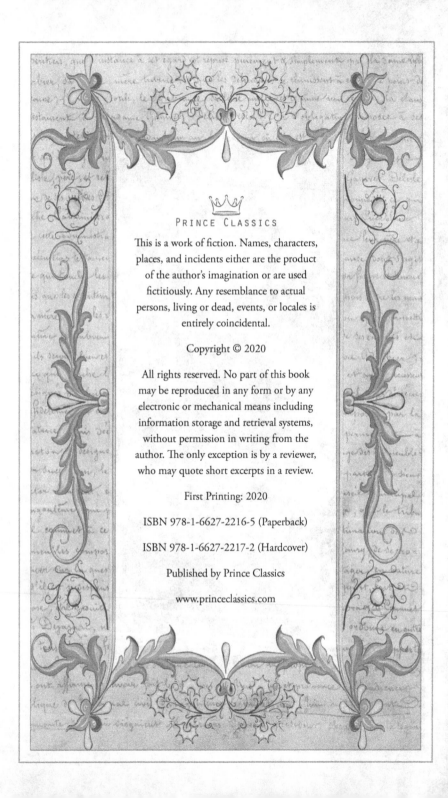

PRINCE CLASSICS

First Printing: 2020

ISBN 978-1-6627-2216-5 (Paperback)

ISBN 978-1-6627-2217-2 (Hardcover)

Published by Prince Classics

www.princeclassics.com

Contents

WAR IS KIND,
WHILOMVILLE
STORIES
&
THE MONSTER
AND OTHER STORIES

WAR IS KIND

WAR IS KIND

Do not weep, maiden, for war is kind.

Because your lover threw wild hands toward the sky

And the affrighted steed ran on alone,

Do not weep.

War is kind.

     Hoarse, booming drums of the

          regiment,

     Little souls who thirst for fight,

     These men were born to drill and die.

     The unexplained glory files above

          them,

     Great is the battle-god, great, and his

          kingdom—;

     A field where a thousand corpses lie.

Do not weep, babe, for war is kind.

Because your father tumbled in the yellow

     trenches,

Raged at his breast, gulped and died,

Do not weep.

War is kind.

Swift blazing flag of the regiment,

Eagle with crest of red and gold,

These men were born to drill and die.

Point for them the virtue of the slaughter,

Make plain to them the excellence of killing

And a field where a thousand corpses

lie.

Mother whose heart hung humble as a button

On the bright splendid shroud of your son,

Do not weep.

War is kind.

What says the sea, little shell?

"What says the sea?

"Long has our brother been silent to us,

"Kept his message for the ships,

"Awkward ships, stupid ships."

"The sea bids you mourn, O Pines,

"Sing low in the moonlight.

"He sends tale of the land of doom,

"Of place where endless falls

"A rain of women's tears,

"And men in grey robes—

"Men in grey robes—

"Chant the unknown pain."

"What says the sea, little shell?

"What says the sea?

"Long has our brother been silent to us,

"Kept is message for the ships,

"Puny ships, silly ships."

"The sea bids you teach, O Pines,

"Sing low in the moonlight;

"Teach the gold of patience,

"Cry gospel of gentle hands,

"Cry a brotherhood of hearts.

"The sea bids you teach, O Pines."

"And where is the reward, little shell?

"What says the sea?

"Long has our brother been silent to us,

"Kept his message for the ships,

"Puny ships, silly ships."

"No word says the sea, O Pines,

"No word says the sea.

"Long will your brother be silent to you,

"Keep his message for the ships,

"O puny ships, silly pines."

To the maiden

The sea was blue meadow,

Alive with little froth-people

Singing.

To the sailor, wrecked,

The sea was dead grey walls

Superlative in vacancy,

Upon which nevertheless at fateful time

Was written

The grim hatred of nature.

A little ink more or less!

It surely can't matter?

Even the sky and the opulent sea,

The plains and the hills, aloof,

Hear the uproar of all these books.

But it is only a little ink more or less.

What?

You define me God with these trinkets?

Can my misery meal on an ordered walking

Of surpliced numskulls?

And a fanfare of lights?

Or even upon the measured pulpitings

Of the familiar false and true?

Is this God?

Where, then is hell?

Show me some bastard mushrooms

Sprung from a pollution of blood.

It is better.

Where is God?

"Have you ever made a just man?"

"Oh, I have made three," answered

  God,

"But two of them are dead,

"And the third—

"Listen! Listen!

"And you will hear the thud of his defeat."

I explain the silvered passing of a ship

  at night,

The sweep of each sad lost wave,

The dwindling boom of the steel thing's striving,

The little cry of a man to a man,

A shadow falling across the greyer night,

And the sinking of the small star;

Then the waste, the far waste of waters,

And the soft lashing of black waves

For long and in loneliness.

Remember, thou, O ship of love,

Thou leavest a far waste of waters,

And the soft lashing of black waves

For long and in loneliness.

"I have heard the sunset song of the
     birches,

"A white melody in the silence,

"I have seen a quarrel of the pines.

"At nightfall

"The little grasses have rushed by me

"With the wind men.

"These things have I lived," quoth the
     maniac,

"Possessing only eyes and ears.

"But you—

"You don green spectacles before you look at roses."

Fast rode the knight

With spurs, hot and reeking,

Ever waving an eager sword,

"To save my lady!"

Fast rode the knight,

And leaped from saddle to war.

Men of steel flickered and gleamed

Like riot of silver lights,

And the gold of the knight's good banner

Still waved on a castle wall.

.   .   .   .

A horse,

Blowing, staggering, bloody thing,

Forgotten at foot of castle wall.

A horse

Dead at foot of castle wall.

Forth went the candid man

And spoke freely to the wind—

When he looked about him he was in a far

      strange country.

Forth went the candid man

And spoke freely to the stars—

Yellow light tore sight from his eye.

"My good fool," said a learned bystander,

"Your operations are mad."

"You are too candid," cried the candid man.

And when his stick left the head of the

    learned bystander

It was two sticks.

You tell me this is God?

I tell you this is a printed list,

A burning candle and an ass.

On the desert

A silence from the moon's deepest

    valley.

Fire rays fall athwart the robes

Of hooded men, squat and dumb.

Before them, a woman

Moves to the blowing of shrill whistles

And distant thunder of drums,

While mystic things, sinuous, dull with

    terrible color,

Sleepily fondle her body

Or move at her will, swishing stealthily over

    the sand.

The snakes whisper softly;

The whispering, whispering snakes,

Dreaming and swaying and staring,

But always whispering, softly whispering.

The wind streams from the lone reaches

Of Arabia, solemn with night,

And the wild fire makes shimmer of blood

Over the robes of the hooded men

Squat and dumb.

Bands of moving bronze, emerald, yellow,

Circle the throat and arms of her,

And over the sands serpents move warily

Slow, menacing and submissive,

Swinging to the whistles and drums,

The whispering, whispering snakes,

Dreaming and swaying and staring,

But always whispering, softly whispering.

The dignity of the accursed;

The glory of slavery, despair, death,

Is in the dance of the whispering snakes.

A newspaper is a collection of half-injustices

Which, bawled by boys from mile to mile,

Spreads its curious opinion

To a million merciful and sneering men,

While families cuddle the joys of the fireside

When spurred by tale of dire lone agony.

A newspaper is a court

Where every one is kindly and unfairly tried

By a squalor of honest men.

A newspaper is a market

Where wisdom sells its freedom

And melons are crowned by the crowd.

A newspaper is a game

Where his error scores the player victory

While another's skill wins death.

A newspaper is a symbol;

It is fetless life's chronical,

A collection of loud tales

Concentrating eternal stupidities,

That in remote ages lived unhaltered,

Roaming through a fenceless world.

The wayfarer,

Perceiving the pathway to truth,

Was struck with astonishment.

It was thickly grown with weeds.

"Ha," he said,

"I see that none has passed here

"In a long time."

Later he saw that each weed

Was a singular knife.

"Well," he mumbled at last,

"Doubtless there are other roads."

A slant of sun on dull brown walls,

A forgotten sky of bashful blue.

Toward God a mighty hymn,

A song of collisions and cries,

Rumbling wheels, hoof-beats, bells,

Welcomes, farewells, love-calls, final moans,

Voices of joy, idiocy, warning, despair,

The unknown appeals of brutes,

The chanting of flowers,

The screams of cut trees,

The senseless babble of hens and wise men—

A cluttered incoherency that says at the

stars;

"O God, save us!"

Once a man clambering to the housetops

Appealed to the heavens.

With a strong voice he called to the deaf

    spheres;

A warrior's shout he raised to the suns.

Lo, at last, there was a dot on the clouds,

And—at last and at last—

—God—the sky was filled with armies.

There was a man with tongue of wood

Who essayed to sing,

And in truth it was lamentable.

But there was one who heard

The clip-clapper of this tongue of wood

And knew what the man

Wished to sing,

And with that the singer was content.

The successful man has thrust himself

Through the water of the years,

Reeking wet with mistakes,—

Bloody mistakes;

Slimed with victories over the lesser,

A figure thankful on the shore of money.

Then, with the bones of fools

He buys silken banners

Limned with his triumphant face;

With the skins of wise men

He buys the trivial bows of all.

Flesh painted with marrow

Contributes a coverlet,

A coverlet for his contented slumber.

In guiltless ignorance, in ignorant guilt,

He delivered his secrets to the riven multitude.

    "Thus I defended: Thus I wrought."

Complacent, smiling,

He stands heavily on the dead.

Erect on a pillar of skulls

He declaims his trampling of babes;

Smirking, fat, dripping,

He makes speech in guiltless ignorance,

Innocence.

In the night

Grey heavy clouds muffled the valleys,

And the peaks looked toward God alone.

"O Master that movest the wind with a

finger,

"Humble, idle, futile peaks are we.

"Grant that we may run swiftly across

the world

"To huddle in worship at Thy feet."

In the morning

A noise of men at work came the clear blue miles,

And the little black cities were apparent.

"O Master that knowest the meaning of raindrops,

"Humble, idle, futile peaks are we.

"Give voice to us, we pray, O Lord,

"That we may sing Thy goodness to the sun."

In the evening

The far valleys were sprinkled with tiny lights.

"O Master,

"Thou that knowest the value of kings and birds,

"Thou hast made us humble, idle, futile peaks.

"Thous only needest eternal patience;

"We bow to Thy wisdom, O Lord—

"Humble, idle, futile peaks."

In the night

Grey heavy clouds muffles the valleys,

And the peaks looked toward God alone.

The chatter of a death-demon from a tree-top.

Blood—blood and torn grass—

Had marked the rise of his agony—

This lone hunter.

The grey-green woods impassive

Had watched the threshing of his limbs.

A canoe with flashing paddle,

A girl with soft searching eyes,

A call: "John!"

.   .   .   .

Come, arise, hunter!

Can you not hear?

The chatter of a death-demon from a tree-top.

The impact of a dollar upon the heart

Smiles warm red light,

Sweeping from the hearth rosily upon the

      white table,

With the hanging cool velvet shadows

Moving softly upon the door.

The impact of a million dollars

Is a crash of flunkys,

And yawning emblems of Persia

Cheeked against oak, France and a sabre,

The outcry of old beauty

Whored by pimping merchants

To submission before wine and chatter.

Silly rich peasants stamp the carpets of men,

Dead men who dreamed fragrance and light

Into their woof, their lives;

The rug of an honest bear

Under the feet of a cryptic slave

Who speaks always of baubles,

Forgetting state, multitude, work, and state,

Champing and mouthing of hats,

Making ratful squeak of hats,

Hats.

A man said to the universe:

"Sir, I exist!"

"However," replied the universe,

"The fact has not created in me

"A sense of obligation."

When the prophet, a complacent fat

      man,

Arrived at the mountain-top,

He cried: "Woe to my knowledge!

"I intended to see good white lands

"And bad black lands,

"But the scene is grey."

There was a land where lived no

      violets.

A traveller at once demanded: "Why?"

The people told him:

"Once the violets of this place spoke thus:

"'Until some woman freely give her lover

"'To another woman

"'We will fight in bloody scuffle.'"

Sadly the people added:

"There are no violets here."

There was one I met upon the road

Who looked at me with kind eyes.

He said: "Show me of your wares."

And I did,

Holding forth one,

He said: "It is a sin."

Then I held forth another.

He said: "It is a sin."

Then I held forth another.

He said: "It is a sin."

And so to the end.

Always He said: "It is a sin."

At last, I cried out:

"But I have non other."

He looked at me

With kinder eyes.

"Poor soul," he said.

Aye, workman, make me a dream,

A dream for my love.

Cunningly weave sunlight,

Breezes, and flowers.

Let it be of the cloth of meadows.

And—good workman—

And let there be a man walking thereon.

Each small gleam was a voice,

A lantern voice—

In little songs of carmine, violet, green, gold.

A chorus of colors came over the water;

The wondrous leaf-shadow no longer wavered,

No pines crooned on the hills,

The blue night was elsewhere a silence,

When the chorus of colors came over the

      water,

Little songs of carmine, violet, green, gold.

Small glowing pebbles

Thrown on the dark plane of evening

Sing good ballads of God

And eternity, with soul's rest.

Little priests, little holy fathers,

None can doubt the truth of hour hymning.

When the marvellous chorus comes over the
    water,

Songs of carmine, violet, green, gold.

The trees in the garden rained flowers.

Children ran there joyously.

They gathered the flowers

Each to himself.

Now there were some

Who gathered great heaps—

Having opportunity and skill—

Until, behold, only chance blossoms

Remained for the feeble.

Then a little spindling tutor

Ran importantly to the father, crying:

"Pray, come hither!

"See this unjust thing in your garden!"

But when the father had surveyed,

He admonished the tutor:

"Not so, small sage!

"This thing is just.

"For, look you,

"Are not they who possess the flowers

"Stronger, bolder, shrewder

"Than they who have none?

"Why should the strong—

"The beautiful strong—

"Why should they not have the flowers?

Upon reflection, the tutor bowed to the
        ground.

"My lord," he said,

"The stars are displaced

"By this towering wisdom."

INTRIGUE

Thou art my love,

And thou art the peace of sundown

When the blue shadows soothe,

And the grasses and the leaves sleep

To the song of the little brooks,

Woe is me.

Thou art my love,

And thou art a strorm

That breaks black in the sky,

And, sweeping headlong,

Drenches and cowers each tree,

And at the panting end

There is no sound

Save the melancholy cry of a single owl—

Woe is me!

Thou are my love,

And thou art a tinsel thing,

And I in my play

Broke thee easily,

And from the little fragments

Arose my long sorrow—

Woe is me.

Thou art my love,

And thou art a wary violet,

Drooping from sun-caresses,

Answering mine carelessly—

Woe is me.

Thou art my love,

And thou art the ashes of other men's love,

And I bury my face in these ashes,

And I love them—

Woe is me.

Thou art my love,

And thou art the beard

On another man's face—

Woe is me.

Thou art my love,

And thou art a temple,

And in this temple is an altar,

And on this altar is my heart—

Woe is me.

Thou art my love,

And thou art a wretch.

Let these sacred love-lies choke thee,

From I am come to where I know your lies

     as truth

And you truth as lies—

Woe is me.

Thou art my love,

And thou art a priestess,

And in they hand is a bloody dagger,

And my doom comes to me surely—

Woe is me.

Thou art my love,

And thou art a skull with ruby eyes,

And I love thee—

Woe is me.

Thou art my love,

And I doubt thee.

And if peace came with thy murder

Then would I murder—

Woe is me.

Thou art my love,

And thou art death,

Aye, thou art death

Black and yet black,

But I love thee,

I love thee—

Woe, welcome woe, to me.

Love, forgive me if I wish you grief,

For in your grief

You huddle to my breast,

And for it

Would I pay the price of your grief.

You walk among men

And all men do not surrender,

And thus I understand

That love reaches his hand

In mercy to me.

He had your picture in his room,

A scurvy traitor picture,

And he smiled

—Merely a fat complacence of men who

    know fine women—

And thus I divided with him

A part of my love.

Fool, not to know that thy little shoe

Can make men weep!

—Some men weep.

I weep and I gnash,

And I love the little shoe,

The little, little shoe.

God give me medals,

God give me loud honors,

That I may strut before you, sweetheart,

And be worthy of—

The love I bear you.

Now let me crunch you

With full weight of affrighted love.

I doubted you

—I doubted you—

And in this short doubting

My love grew like a genie

For my further undoing.

Beware of my friends,

Be not in speech too civil,

For in all courtesy

My weak heart sees spectres,

Mists of desire

Arising from the lips of my chosen;

Be not civil.

The flower I gave thee once

Was incident to a stride,

A detail of a gesture,

But search those pale petals

And see engraven thereon

A record of my intention.

Ah, God, the way your little finger moved,

As you thrust a bare arm backward

And made play with your hair

And a comb, a silly gilt comb

—Ah, God—that I should suffer

Because of the way a little finger moved.

Once I saw thee idly rocking

—Idly rocking—

And chattering girlishly to other girls,

Bell-voiced, happy,

Careless with the stout heart of unscarred

    womanhood,

And life to thee was all light melody.

I thought of the great storms of love as I

    knew it,

Torn, miserable, and ashamed of my open

    sorrow,

I thought of the thunders that lived in my

    head,

And I wish to be an ogre,

And hale and haul my beloved to a castle,

And make her mourn with my mourning.

Tell me why, behind thee,

I see always the shadow of another lover?

Is it real,

Or is this the thrice damned memory of a

　　better happiness?

Plague on him if he be dead,

Plague on him if he be alive—

A swinish numskull

To intrude his shade

Always between me and my peace!

And yet I have seen thee happy with me.

I am no fool

To poll stupidly into iron.

I have heard your quick breaths

And seen your arms writhe toward me;

At those times

—God help us—

I was impelled to be a grand knight,

And swagger and snap my fingers,

And explain my mind finely.

Oh, lost sweetheart,

I would that I had not been a grand knight.

I said: "Sweetheart."

Thou said'st: "Sweetheart."

And we preserved an admirable mimicry

Without heeding the drip of the blood

From my heart.

I heard thee laugh,

And in this merriment

I defined the measure of my pain;

I knew that I was alone,

Alone with love,

Poor shivering love,

And he, little sprite,

Came to watch with me,

And at midnight,

We were like two creatures by a dead camp-

      fire.

I wonder if sometimes in the dusk,

When the brave lights that gild thy

      evenings

Have not yet been touched with flame,

I wonder if sometimes in the dusk

Thou rememberest a time,

A time when thou loved me

And our love was to thee thy all?

Is the memory rubbish now?

An old gown

Worn in an age of other fashions?

Woe is me, oh, lost one,

For that love is now to me

A supernal dream,

White, white, white with many suns.

Love met me at noonday,

—Reckless imp,

To leave his shaded nights

And brave the glare,—

And I saw him then plainly

For a bungler,

A stupid, simpering, eyeless bungler,

Breaking the hearts of brave people

As the snivelling idiot-boy cracks his bowl,

And I cursed him,

Cursed him to and fro, back and forth,

Into all the silly mazes of his mind,

But in the end

He laughed and pointed to my breast,

Where a heart still beat for thee, beloved.

I have seen thy face aflame

For love of me,

Thy fair arms go mad,

Thy lips tremble and mutter and rave.

And—surely—

This should leave a man content?

Thou lovest not me now,

But thou didst love me,

And in loving me once

Thou gavest me an eternal privilege,

For I can think of thee.

WHILOMVILLE STORIES

I. THE ANGEL CHILD

I

ALTHOUGH Whilomville was in no sense a summer resort, the advent of the warm season meant much to it, for then came visitors from the city—people of considerable confidence—alighting upon their country cousins. Moreover, many citizens who could afford to do so escaped at this time to the sea-side. The town, with the commercial life quite taken out of it, drawled and drowsed through long months, during which nothing was worse than the white dust which arose behind every vehicle at blinding noon, and nothing was finer than the cool sheen of the hose sprays over the cropped lawns under the many maples in the twilight.

One summer the Trescotts had a visitation. Mrs. Trescott owned a cousin who was a painter of high degree. I had almost said that he was of national reputation, but, come to think of it, it is better to say that almost everybody in the United States who knew about art and its travail knew about him. He had picked out a wife, and naturally, looking at him, one wondered how he had done it. She was quick, beautiful, imperious, while he was quiet, slow, and misty. She was a veritable queen of health, while he, apparently, was of a most brittle constitution. When he played tennis, particularly, he looked every minute as if he were going to break.

They lived in New York, in awesome apartments wherein Japan and Persia, and indeed all the world, confounded the observer. At the end was a cathedral-like studio. They had one child. Perhaps it would be better to say that they had one CHILD. It was a girl. When she came to Whilomville with her parents, it was patent that she had an inexhaustible store of white frocks, and that her voice was high and commanding. These things the town knew quickly. Other things it was doomed to discover by a process.

Her effect upon the children of the Trescott neighborhood was singular.

They at first feared, then admired, then embraced. In two days she was a Begum. All day long her voice could be heard directing, drilling, and compelling those free-born children; and to say that they felt oppression would be wrong, for they really fought for records of loyal obedience.

All went well until one day was her birthday.

On the morning of this day she walked out into the Trescott garden and said to her father, confidently, "Papa, give me some money, because this is my birthday."

He looked dreamily up from his easel. "Your birthday?" he murmured. Her envisioned father was never energetic enough to be irritable unless some one broke through into that place where he lived with the desires of his life. But neither wife nor child ever heeded or even understood the temperamental values, and so some part of him had grown hardened to their inroads. "Money?" he said. "Here." He handed her a five-dollar bill. It was that he did not at all understand the nature of a five-dollar bill. He was deaf to it. He had it; he gave it; that was all.

She sallied forth to a waiting people—Jimmie Trescott, Dan Earl, Ella Earl, the Margate twins, the three Phelps children, and others. "I've got some pennies now," she cried, waving the bill, "and I am going to buy some candy." They were deeply stirred by this announcement. Most children are penniless three hundred days in the year, and to another possessing five pennies they pay deference. To little Cora waving a bright green note these children paid heathenish homage. In some disorder they thronged after her to a small shop on Bridge Street hill. First of all came ice-cream. Seated in the comic little back parlor, they clamored shrilly over plates of various flavors, and the shopkeeper marvelled that cream could vanish so quickly down throats that seemed wide open, always, for the making of excited screams.

These children represented the families of most excellent people. They were all born in whatever purple there was to be had in the vicinity of Whilomville. The Margate twins, for example, were out-and-out prize-winners. With their long golden curls and their countenances of similar vacuity, they shone upon the front bench of all Sunday-school functions, hand in hand, while their uplifted mother felt about her the envy of a hundred other parents, and less heavenly children scoffed from near the door.

Then there was little Dan Earl, probably the nicest boy in the world, gentle, fine-grained, obedient to the point where he obeyed anybody. Jimmie Trescott himself was, indeed, the only child who was at all versed in villany, but in these particular days he was on his very good behavior. As a matter of fact, he was in love. The beauty of his regal little cousin had stolen his manly heart.

Yes, they were all most excellent children, but, loosened upon this candy-shop with five dollars, they resembled, in a tiny way, drunken revelling soldiers within the walls of a stormed city. Upon the heels of ice-cream and cake came chocolate mice, butter-scotch, "everlastings," chocolate cigars, taffy-on-a-stick, taffy-on-a-slate-pencil, and many semi-transparent devices resembling lions, tigers, elephants, horses, cats, dogs, cows, sheep, tables, chairs, engines (both railway and for the fighting of fire), soldiers, fine ladies, odd-looking men, clocks, watches, revolvers, rabbits, and bedsteads. A cent was the price of a single wonder.

Some of the children, going quite daft, soon had thought to make fight over the spoils, but their queen ruled with an iron grip. Her first inspiration was to satisfy her own fancies, but as soon as that was done she mingled prodigality with a fine justice, dividing, balancing, bestowing, and sometimes taking away from somebody even that which he had.

It was an orgy. In thirty-five minutes those respectable children looked as if they had been dragged at the tail of a chariot. The sacred Margate twins, blinking and grunting, wished to take seat upon the floor, and even the most durable Jimmie Trescott found occasion to lean against the counter, wearing at the time a solemn and abstracted air, as if he expected something to happen to him shortly.

Of course their belief had been in an unlimited capacity, but they found there was an end. The shopkeeper handed the queen her change.

"Two seventy-three from five leaves two twenty-seven, Miss Cora," he said, looking upon her with admiration.

She turned swiftly to her clan. "O-oh!" she cried, in amazement. "Look how much I have left!" They gazed at the coins in her palm. They knew then that it was not their capacities which were endless; it was the five dollars.

The queen led the way to the street. "We must think up some way of spending more money," she said, frowning. They stood in silence, awaiting her further speech.

Suddenly she clapped her hands and screamed with delight. "Come on!" she cried. "I know what let's do." Now behold, she had discovered the red and white pole in front of the shop of one William Neeltje, a barber by trade.

It becomes necessary to say a few words concerning Neeltje. He was new to the town. He had come and opened a dusty little shop on dusty Bridge Street hill, and although the neighborhood knew from the courier winds that his diet was mainly cabbage, they were satisfied with that meagre data. Of course Riefsnyder came to investigate him for the local Barbers' Union, but he found in him only sweetness and light, with a willingness to charge any price at all for a shave or a haircut. In fact, the advent of Neeltje would have made barely a ripple upon the placid bosom of Whilomville if it were not that his name was Neeltje.

At first the people looked at his sign-board out of the eye corner, and wondered lazily why any one should bear the name of Neeltje; but as time went on, men spoke to other men, saying, "How do you pronounce the name of that barber up there on Bridge Street hill?" And then, before any could prevent it, the best minds of the town were splintering their lances against William Neeltje's sign-board. If a man had a mental superior, he guided him seductively to this name, and watched with glee his wrecking. The clergy of the town even entered the lists. There was one among them who had taken a collegiate prize in Syriac, as well as in several less opaque languages, and the other clergymen—at one of their weekly meetings—sought to betray him into this ambush. He pronounced the name correctly, but that mattered little, since none of them knew whether he did or did not; and so they took triumph according to their ignorance. Under these arduous circumstances it was certain that the town should look for a nickname, and at this time the nickname was in process of formation. So William Neeltje lived on with his secret, smiling foolishly towards the world.

"Come on," cried little Cora. "Let's all get our hair cut. That's what let's do. Let's all get our hair cut! Come on! Come on! Come on!" The others were carried off their feet by the fury of this assault. To get their hair cut! What joy! Little did they know if this were fun; they only knew that their small leader said it was fun. Chocolate-stained but confident, the band marched into William Neeltje's barber shop.

"We wish to get our hair cut," said little Cora, haughtily.

Neeltje, in his shirt-sleeves, stood looking at them with his half-idiot smile.

"Hurry, now!" commanded the queen. A dray-horse toiled step by step, step by step, up Bridge Street hill; a far woman's voice arose; there could be heard the ceaseless hammers of shingling carpenters; all was summer peace. "Come on, now. Who's goin' first? Come on, Ella; you go first. Gettin' our hair cut! Oh what fun!"

Little Ella Earl would not, however, be first in the chair. She was drawn towards it by a singular fascination, but at the same time she was afraid of it, and so she hung back, saying: "No! You go first! No! You go first!" The question was precipitated by the twins and one of the Phelps children. They made simultaneous rush for the chair, and screamed and kicked, each pair preventing the third child. The queen entered this mêlée, and decided in favor of the Phelps boy. He ascended the chair. Thereat an awed silence fell upon the band. And always William Neeltje smiled fatuously.

He tucked a cloth in the neck of the Phelps boy, and taking scissors, began to cut his hair. The group of children came closer and closer. Even the queen was deeply moved. "Does it hurt any?" she asked, in a wee voice.

"Naw," said the Phelps boy, with dignity. "Anyhow, I've had m' hair cut afore."

When he appeared to them looking very soldierly with his cropped little head, there was a tumult over the chair. The Margate twins howled; Jimmie Trescott was kicking them on the shins. It was a fight.

But the twins could not prevail, being the smallest of all the children. The queen herself took the chair, and ordered Neeltje as if he were a lady's-maid. To the floor there fell proud ringlets, blazing even there in their humiliation with a full fine bronze light. Then Jimmie Trescott, then Ella Earl (two long ash-colored plaits), then a Phelps girl, then another Phelps girl; and so on from head to head. The ceremony received unexpected check when the turn came to Dan Earl. This lad, usually docile to any rein, had suddenly grown mulishly obstinate. No, he would not, he would not. He himself did not seem to know why he refused to have his hair cut, but, despite the shrill derision of the company, he remained obdurate. Anyhow, the twins, long held in check, and now feverishly eager, were already struggling for the chair.

And so to the floor at last came the golden Margate curls, the heart treasure and glory of a mother, three aunts, and some feminine cousins.

All having been finished, the children, highly elate, thronged out into the street. They crowed and cackled with pride and joy, anon turning to scorn the cowardly Dan Earl.

Ella Earl was an exception. She had been pensive for some time, and now the shorn little maiden began vaguely to weep. In the door of his shop William Neeltje stood watching them, upon his face a grin of almost inhuman idiocy.

II

It now becomes the duty of the unfortunate writer to exhibit these children to their fond parents. "Come on, Jimmie," cried little Cora, "let's go show mamma." And they hurried off, these happy children, to show mamma.

The Trescotts and their guests were assembled indolently awaiting the luncheon-bell. Jimmie and the angel child burst in upon them. "Oh, mamma," shrieked little Cora, "see how fine I am! I've had my hair cut! Isn't it splendid? And Jimmie too!"

The wretched mother took one sight, emitted one yell, and fell into a chair. Mrs. Trescott dropped a large lady's journal and made a nerveless mechanical clutch at it. The painter gripped the arms of his chair and leaned forward, staring until his eyes were like two little clock faces. Dr. Trescott did not move or speak.

To the children the next moments were chaotic. There was a loudly wailing mother, and a pale-faced, aghast mother; a stammering father, and a grim and terrible father. The angel child did not understand anything of it save the voice of calamity, and in a moment all her little imperialism went to the winds. She ran sobbing to her mother. "Oh, mamma! mamma! mamma!"

The desolate Jimmie heard out of this inexplicable situation a voice which he knew well, a sort of colonel's voice, and he obeyed like any good soldier. "Jimmie!"

He stepped three paces to the front. "Yes, sir."

"How did this—how did this happen?" said Trescott.

Now Jimmie could have explained how had happened anything which had happened, but he did not know what had happened, so he said, "I—I—nothin'."

"And, oh, look at her frock!" said Mrs. Trescott, brokenly.

The words turned the mind of the mother of the angel child. She looked up, her eyes blazing. "Frock!" she repeated. "Frock! What do I care for her frock? Frock!" she choked out again from the depths of her bitterness. Then she arose suddenly, and whirled tragically upon her husband. "Look!" she declaimed. "All—her lovely—hair—all her lovely hair—gone—gone!" The painter was apparently in a fit; his jaw was set, his eyes were glazed, his body was stiff and straight. "All gone—all—her lovely hair—all gone—my poor little darlin'—my—poor—little—darlin'!" And the angel child added her heart-broken voice to her mother's wail as they fled into each other's arms.

In the mean time Trescott was patiently unravelling some skeins of Jimmie's tangled intellect. "And then you went to this barber's on the hill.

Yes. And where did you get the money? Yes. I see. And who besides you and Cora had their hair cut? The Margate twi—Oh, lord!"

Over at the Margate place old Eldridge Margate, the grandfather of the twins, was in the back garden picking pease and smoking ruminatively to himself. Suddenly he heard from the house great noises. Doors slammed, women rushed up-stairs and down-stairs calling to each other in voices of agony. And then full and mellow upon the still air arose the roar of the twins in pain.

Old Eldridge stepped out of the pea-patch and moved towards the house, puzzled, staring, not yet having decided that it was his duty to rush forward. Then around the corner of the house shot his daughter Mollie, her face pale with horror.

"What's the matter?" he cried.

"Oh, father," she gasped, "the children! They—"

Then around the corner of the house came the twins, howling at the top of their power, their faces flowing with tears. They were still hand in hand, the ruling passion being strong even in this suffering. At sight of them old Eldridge took his pipe hastily out of his mouth. "Good God!" he said.

And now what befell one William Neeltje, a barber by trade? And what was said by angry parents of the mother of such an angel child? And what was the fate of the angel child herself?

There was surely a tempest. With the exception of the Margate twins, the boys could well be eliminated from the affair. Of course it didn't matter if their hair was cut. Also the two little Phelps girls had had very short hair, anyhow, and their parents were not too greatly incensed. In the case of Ella Earl, it was mainly the pathos of the little girl's own grieving; but her mother played a most generous part, and called upon Mrs. Trescott, and condoled with the mother of the angel child over their equivalent losses. But the Margate contingent! They simply screeched.

Trescott, composed and cool-blooded, was in the middle of a giddy whirl. He was not going to allow the mobbing of his wife's cousins, nor was he going to pretend that the spoliation of the Margate twins was a virtuous and beautiful act. He was elected, gratuitously, to the position of a buffer.

But, curiously enough, the one who achieved the bulk of the misery was old Eldridge Margate, who had been picking pease at the time. The feminine Margates stormed his position as individuals, in pairs, in teams, and *en masse*. In two days they may have aged him seven years. He must destroy the utter Neeltje. He must midnightly massacre the angel child and her mother. He must dip his arms in blood to the elbows.

Trescott took the first opportunity to express to him his concern over the affair, but when the subject of the disaster was mentioned, old Eldridge, to the doctor's great surprise, actually chuckled long and deeply. "Oh, well, look-a-here," he said. "I never was so much in love with them there damn curls. The curls was purty—yes—but then I'd a darn sight rather see boys look more like boys than like two little wax figgers. An', ye know, the little cusses like it themselves. *They* never took no stock in all this washin' an' combin' an' fixin' an' goin' to church an' paradin' an' showin' off. They stood it because they were told to. That's all. Of course this here Neel-te-gee, er whatever his name is, is a plumb dumb ijit, but I don't see what's to be done, now that the kids is full well cropped. I might go and burn his shop over his head, but that wouldn't bring no hair back onto the kids. They're even kicking on sashes now, and that's all right, 'cause what fer does a boy want a sash?"

Whereupon Trescott perceived that the old man wore his brains above his shoulders, and Trescott departed from him rejoicing greatly that it was only women who could not know that there was finality to most disasters, and that when a thing was fully done, no amount of door-slammings, rushing up-stairs and down-stairs, calls, lamentations, tears, could bring back a single hair to the heads of twins.

But the rains came and the winds blew in the most biblical way when a certain fact came to light in the Trescott household. Little Cora, corroborated by Jimmie, innocently remarked that five dollars had been given her by her father on her birthday, and with this money the evil had been wrought. Trescott had known it, but he—thoughtful man—had said nothing. For her part, the mother of the angel child had up to that moment never reflected that the consummation of the wickedness must have cost a small sum of money. But now it was all clear to her. He was the guilty one—he! "My angel child!"

The scene which ensued was inspiriting. A few days later, loungers at the railway station saw a lady leading a shorn and still undaunted lamb. Attached to them was a husband and father, who was plainly bewildered, but still more plainly vexed, as if he would be saying: "Damn 'em! Why can't they leave me alone?"

II. LYNX-HUNTING

JIMMIE lounged about the dining-room and watched his mother with large, serious eyes. Suddenly he said, "Ma—now—can I borrow pa's gun?"

She was overcome with the feminine horror which is able to mistake preliminary words for the full accomplishment of the dread thing. "Why, Jimmie!" she cried. "Of al-l wonders! Your father's gun! No indeed you can't!"

He was fairly well crushed, but he managed to mutter, sullenly, "Well, Willie Dalzel, he's got a gun." In reality his heart had previously been beating with such tumult—he had himself been so impressed with the daring and sin of his request—that he was glad that all was over now, and his mother could do very little further harm to his sensibilities. He had been influenced into the venture by the larger boys.

"Huh!" the Dalzel urchin had said; "your father's got a gun, hasn't he? Well, why don't you bring that?"

Puffing himself, Jimmie had replied, "Well, I can, if I want to." It was a black lie, but really the Dalzel boy was too outrageous with his eternal bill-posting about the gun which a beaming uncle had intrusted to him. Its possession made him superior in manfulness to most boys in the neighborhood—or at least they enviously conceded him such position—but he was so overbearing, and stuffed the fact of his treasure so relentlessly down their throats, that on this occasion the miserable Jimmie had lied as naturally as most animals swim.

Willie Dalzel had not been checkmated, for he had instantly retorted, "Why don't you get it, then?"

"Well, I can, if I want to."

"Well, get it, then!"

"Well, I can, if I want to."

Thereupon Jimmie had paced away with great airs of surety as far as the door of his home, where his manner changed to one of tremulous misgiving as it came upon him to address his mother in the dining-room. There had happened that which had happened.

When Jimmie returned to his two distinguished companions he was blown out with a singular pomposity. He spoke these noble words: "Oh, well, I guess I don't want to take the gun out to-day."

They had been watching him with gleaming ferret eyes, and they detected his falsity at once. They challenged him with shouted gibes, but it was not in the rules for the conduct of boys that one should admit anything whatsoever, and so Jimmie, backed into an ethical corner, lied as stupidly, as desperately, as hopelessly as ever lone savage fights when surrounded at last in his jungle.

Such accusations were never known to come to any point, for the reason that the number and kind of denials always equalled or exceeded the number of accusations, and no boy was ever brought really to book for these misdeeds.

In the end they went off together, Willie Dalzel with his gun being a trifle in advance and discoursing upon his various works. They passed along a maple-lined avenue, a highway common to boys bound for that free land of hills and woods in which they lived in some part their romance of the moment, whether it was of Indians, miners, smugglers, soldiers, or outlaws. The paths were their paths, and much was known to them of the secrets of the dark green hemlock thickets, the wastes of sweet-fern and huckleberry, the cliffs of gaunt bluestone with the sumach burning red at their feet. Each boy had, I am sure, a conviction that some day the wilderness was to give forth to him a marvellous secret. They felt that the hills and the forest knew much, and they heard a voice of it in the silence. It was vague, thrilling, fearful, and altogether fabulous. The grown folk seemed to regard these wastes merely as so much distance between one place and another place, or as a rabbit-cover, or as a district to be judged according to the value of the timber; but to the boys it spoke some great inspiring word, which they knew even as those who pace the shore know the enigmatic speech of the surf. In the mean time they lived there, in season, lives of ringing adventure—by dint of imagination.

The boys left the avenue, skirted hastily through some private grounds, climbed a fence, and entered the thickets. It happened that at school the previous day Willie Dalzel had been forced to read and acquire in some part a solemn description of a lynx. The meagre information thrust upon him had caused him grimaces of suffering, but now he said, suddenly, "I'm goin' to shoot a lynx."

The other boys admired this statement, but they were silent for a time. Finally Jimmie said, meekly, "What's a lynx?" He had endured his ignorance as long as he was able.

The Dalzel boy mocked him. "Why, don't you know what a lynx is? A lynx? Why, a lynx is a animal somethin' like a cat, an' it's got great big green eyes, and it sits on the limb of a tree an' jus' glares at you. It's a pretty bad animal, I tell you. Why, when I—"

"Huh!" said the third boy. "Where'd you ever see a lynx?"

"Oh, I've seen 'em—plenty of 'em. I bet you'd be scared if you seen one once."

Jimmie and the other boy each demanded, "How do you know I would?"

They penetrated deeper into the wood. They climbed a rocky zigzag path which led them at times where with their hands they could almost touch the tops of giant pines. The gray cliffs sprang sheer towards the sky. Willie Dalzel babbled about his impossible lynx, and they stalked the mountain-side like chamois-hunters, although no noise of bird or beast broke the stillness of the hills. Below them Whilomville was spread out somewhat like the cheap green and black lithograph of the time—"A Bird's-eye View of Whilomville, N. Y."

In the end the boys reached the top of the mountain and scouted off among wild and desolate ridges. They were burning with the desire to slay large animals. They thought continually of elephants, lions, tigers, crocodiles. They discoursed upon their immaculate conduct in case such monsters confronted them, and they all lied carefully about their courage.

The breeze was heavy with the smell of sweet-fern. The pines and hemlocks sighed as they waved their branches. In the hollows the leaves of the laurels were lacquered where the sunlight found them. No matter the weather, it would be impossible to long continue an expedition of this kind without a fire, and presently they built one, snapping down for fuel the brittle under-branches of the pines. About this fire they were willed to conduct a sort of play, the Dalzel boy taking the part of a bandit chief, and the other boys being his trusty lieutenants. They stalked to and fro, long-strided, stern yet devil-may-care, three terrible little figures.

Jimmie had an uncle who made game of him whenever he caught him in this kind of play, and often this uncle quoted derisively the following classic: "Once aboard the lugger, Bill, and the girl is mine. Now to burn the château and destroy all evidence of our crime. But, hark'e, Bill, no wiolence." Wheeling abruptly, he addressed these dramatic words to his comrades. They were impressed; they decided at once to be smugglers, and in the most ribald fashion they talked about carrying off young women.

At last they continued their march through the woods. The smuggling *motif* was now grafted fantastically upon the original lynx idea, which Willie Dalzel refused to abandon at any price.

Once they came upon an innocent bird who happened to be looking another way at the time. After a great deal of manœvering and big words, Willie Dalzel reared his fowling-piece and blew this poor thing into a mere rag of wet feathers, of which he was proud.

Afterwards the other big boy had a turn at another bird. Then it was plainly Jimmie's chance. The two others had, of course, some thought of cheating him out of this chance, but of a truth he was timid to explode such a thunderous weapon, and as soon as they detected this fear they simply overbore him, and made it clearly understood that if he refused to shoot he would lose his caste, his scalp-lock, his girdle, his honor.

They had reached the old death-colored snake-fence which marked the limits of the upper pasture of the Fleming farm. Under some hickory-trees the path ran parallel to the fence. Behold! a small priestly chipmonk came to a rail, and folding his hands on his abdomen, addressed them in his own tongue. It was Jimmie's shot. Adjured by the others, he took the gun. His face was stiff with apprehension. The Dalzel boy was giving forth fine words. "Go ahead. Aw, don't be afraid. It's nothin' to do. Why, I've done it a million times. Don't shut both your eyes, now. Jus' keep one open and shut the other one. He'll get away if you don't watch out. Now you're all right. Why don't you let'er go? Go ahead."

Jimmie, with his legs braced apart, was in the centre of the path. His back was greatly bent, owing to the mechanics of supporting the heavy gun. His companions were screeching in the rear. There was a wait.

Then he pulled trigger. To him there was a frightful roar, his cheek and his shoulder took a stunning blow, his face felt a hot flush of fire, and opening his two eyes, he found that he was still alive. He was not too dazed to instantly adopt a becoming egotism. It had been the first shot of his life.

But directly after the well-mannered celebration of this victory a certain cow, which had been grazing in the line of fire, was seen to break wildly across the pasture, bellowing and bucking. The three smugglers and lynx-hunters looked at each other out of blanched faces. Jimmie had hit the cow. The first evidence of his comprehension of this fact was in the celerity with which he returned the discharged gun to Willie Dalzel.

They turned to flee. The land was black, as if it had been overshadowed suddenly with thick storm-clouds, and even as they fled in their horror a gigantic Swedish farm-hand came from the heavens and fell upon them, shrieking in eerie triumph. In a twinkle they were clouted prostrate. The Swede was elate and ferocious in a foreign and fulsome way. He continued to beat them and yell.

From the ground they raised their dismal appeal. "Oh, please, mister, we didn't do it! He did it! I didn't do it! We didn't do it! We didn't mean to do it! Oh, please, mister!"

In these moments of childish terror little lads go half-blind, and it is possible that few moments of their after-life made them suffer as they did when the Swede flung them over the fence and marched them towards the farm-house. They begged like cowards on the scaffold, and each one was for himself. "Oh, please let me go, mister! I didn't do it, mister! He did it! Oh, p-l-ease let me go, mister!"

The boyish view belongs to boys alone, and if this tall and knotted laborer was needlessly without charity, none of the three lads questioned it. Usually when they were punished they decided that they deserved it, and the more they were punished the more they were convinced that they were criminals of a most subterranean type. As to the hitting of the cow being a pure accident, and therefore not of necessity a criminal matter, such reading never entered their heads. When things happened and they were caught, they commonly paid dire consequences, and they were accustomed to measure the probabilities of woe utterly by the damage done, and not in any way by the culpability. The shooting of the cow was plainly heinous, and undoubtedly their dungeons would be knee-deep in water.

"He did it, mister!" This was a general outcry. Jimmie used it as often as did the others. As for them, it is certain that they had no direct thought of betraying their comrade for their own salvation. They thought themselves guilty because they were caught; when boys were not caught they might possibly be innocent. But captured boys were guilty. When they cried out that Jimmie was the culprit, it was principally a simple expression of terror.

Old Henry Fleming, the owner of the farm, strode across the pasture towards them. He had in his hand a most cruel whip. This whip he flourished. At his approach the boys suffered the agonies of the fire regions. And yet anybody with half an eye could see that the whip in his hand was a mere accident, and that he was a kind old man—when he cared.

When he had come near he spoke crisply. "What you boys ben doin' to my cow?" The tone had deep threat in it. They all answered by saying that none of them had shot the cow. Their denials were tearful and clamorous, and they crawled knee by knee. The vision of it was like three martyrs being dragged towards the stake. Old Fleming stood there, grim, tight-lipped. After a time he said, "Which boy done it?"

There was some confusion, and then Jimmie spake. "I done it, mister."

Fleming looked at him. Then he asked, "Well, what did you shoot 'er fer?"

Jimmie thought, hesitated, decided, faltered, and then formulated this: "I thought she was a lynx."

Old Fleming and his Swede at once lay down in the grass and laughed themselves helpless.

III. THE LOVER AND THE TELLTALE

WHEN the angel child returned with her parents to New York, the fond heart of Jimmie Trescott felt its bruise greatly. For two days he simply moped, becoming a stranger to all former joys. When his old comrades yelled invitation, as they swept off on some interesting quest, he replied with mournful gestures of disillusion.

He thought often of writing to her, but of course the shame of it made him pause. Write a letter to a girl? The mere enormity of the idea caused him shudders. Persons of his quality never wrote letters to girls. Such was the occupation of mollycoddles and snivellers. He knew that if his acquaintances and friends found in him evidences of such weakness and general milkiness, they would fling themselves upon him like so many wolves, and bait him beyond the borders of sanity.

However, one day at school, in that time of the morning session when children of his age were allowed fifteen minutes of play in the school-grounds, he did not as usual rush forth ferociously to his games. Commonly he was of the worst hoodlums, preying upon his weaker brethren with all the cruel disregard of a grown man. On this particular morning he stayed in the school-room, and with his tongue stuck from the corner of his mouth, and his head twisting in a painful way, he wrote to little Cora, pouring out to her all the poetry of his hungry soul, as follows: "My dear Cora I love thee with all my hart oh come bac again, bac, bac gain for I love thee best of all oh come bac again When the spring come again we'l fly and we'l fly like a brid."

As for the last word, he knew under normal circumstances perfectly well how to spell "bird," but in this case he had transposed two of the letters through excitement, supreme agitation.

Nor had this letter been composed without fear and furtive glancing. There was always a number of children who, for the time, cared more for the quiet of the school-room than for the tempest of the play-ground, and there was always that dismal company who were being forcibly deprived of their recess—who were being "kept in." More than one curious eye was turned upon the desperate and lawless Jimmie Trescott suddenly taken to ways of peace, and as he felt these eyes he flushed guiltily, with felonious glances from side to side.

It happened that a certain vigilant little girl had a seat directly across the aisle from Jimmie's seat, and she had remained in the room during the intermission, because of her interest in some absurd domestic details concerning her desk. Parenthetically it might be stated that she was in the habit of imagining this desk to be a house, and at this time, with an important little frown, indicative of a proper matron, she was engaged in dramatizing her ideas of a household.

But this small Rose Goldege happened to be of a family which numbered few males. It was, in fact, one of those curious middle-class families that hold much of their ground, retain most of their position, after all their visible means of support have been dropped in the grave. It contained now only a collection of women who existed submissively, defiantly, securely, mysteriously, in a pretentious and often exasperating virtue. It was often too triumphantly clear that they were free of bad habits. However, bad habits is a term here used in a commoner meaning, because it is certainly true that the principal and indeed solitary joy which entered their lonely lives was the joy of talking wickedly and busily about their neighbors. It was all done without dream of its being of the vulgarity of the alleys. Indeed it was simply a constitutional but not incredible chastity and honesty expressing itself in its ordinary superior way of the whirling circles of life, and the vehemence of the criticism was not lessened by a further infusion of an acid of worldly defeat, worldly suffering, and worldly hopelessness.

Out of this family circle had sprung the typical little girl who discovered Jimmie Trescott agonizingly writing a letter to his sweetheart. Of course all the children were the most abandoned gossips, but she was peculiarly adapted to the purpose of making Jimmie miserable over this particular point. It was her life to sit of evenings about the stove and hearken to her mother and a lot of spinsters talk of many things. During these evenings she was never licensed to utter an opinion either one way or the other way. She was then simply a very little girl sitting open-eyed in the gloom, and listening to many things which she often interpreted wrongly. They on their part kept up a kind of a smug-faced pretence of concealing from her information in detail of the widespread crime, which pretence may have been more elaborately dangerous than no pretence at all. Thus all her home-teaching fitted her to recognize at once in Jimmie Trescott's manner that he was concealing something that would properly interest the world. She set up a scream. "Oh! Oh! Oh! Jimmie Trescott's writing to his girl! Oh! Oh!"

Jimmie cast a miserable glance upon her—a glance in which hatred mingled with despair. Through the open window he could hear the boisterous cries of his friends—his hoodlum friends—who would no more understand the utter poetry of his position than they would understand an ancient tribal sign-language. His face was set in a truer expression of horror than any of the romances describe upon the features of a man flung into a moat, a man shot in the breast with an arrow, a man cleft in the neck with a battle-axe. He was suppedaneous of the fullest power of childish pain. His one course was to rush upon her and attempt, by an impossible means of strangulation, to keep her important news from the public.

The teacher, a thoughtful young woman at her desk upon the platform, saw a little scuffle which informed her that two of her scholars were larking. She called out sharply. The command penetrated to the middle of an early world struggle. In Jimmie's age there was no particular scruple in the minds of the male sex against laying warrior hands upon their weaker sisters. But, of course, this voice from the throne hindered Jimmie in what might have been a berserk attack.

Even the little girl was retarded by the voice, but, without being unlawful, she managed soon to shy through the door and out upon the play-ground, yelling, "Oh, Jimmie Trescott's been writing to his girl!"

The unhappy Jimmie was following as closely as he was allowed by his knowledge of the decencies to be preserved under the eye of the teacher.

Jimmie himself was mainly responsible for the scene which ensued on the play-ground. It is possible that the little girl might have run, shrieking his infamy, without exciting more than a general but unmilitant interest. These barbarians were excited only by the actual appearance of human woe; in that event they cheered and danced. Jimmie made the strategic mistake of pursuing little Rose, and thus exposed his thin skin to the whole school. He had in his cowering mind a vision of a hundred children turning from their play under the maple-trees and speeding towards him over the gravel with sudden wild taunts. Upon him drove a yelping demoniac mob, to which his words were futile. He saw in this mob boys that he dimly knew, and his deadly enemies, and his retainers, and his most intimate friends. The virulence of his deadly enemy was no greater than the virulence of his intimate friend. From the outskirts the little informer could be heard still screaming the news, like a toy parrot with clock-work inside of it. It broke up all sorts of games, not so much because of the mere fact of the letter-writing, as because the children knew that some sufferer was at the last point, and, like little blood-fanged wolves, they thronged to the scene of his destruction. They galloped about him shrilly chanting insults. He turned from one to another, only to meet with howls. He was baited.

Then, in one instant, he changed all this with a blow. Bang! The most pitiless of the boys near him received a punch, fairly and skilfully, which made him bellow out like a walrus, and then Jimmie laid desperately into the whole world, striking out frenziedly in all directions. Boys who could handily whip him, and knew it, backed away from this onslaught. Here was intention—serious intention. They themselves were not in frenzy, and their cooler judgment respected Jimmie's efforts when he ran amuck. They saw that it really was none of their affair. In the mean time the wretched little girl who had caused the bloody riot was away, by the fence, weeping because boys were fighting.

Jimmie several times hit the wrong boy—that is to say, he several times hit a wrong boy hard enough to arouse also in him a spirit of strife. Jimmie wore a little shirt-waist. It was passing now rapidly into oblivion. He was sobbing, and there was one blood stain upon his cheek. The school-ground sounded like a pinetree when a hundred crows roost in it at night.

Then upon the situation there pealed a brazen bell. It was a bell that these children obeyed, even as older nations obey the formal law which is printed in calf-skin. It smote them into some sort of inaction; even Jimmie was influenced by its potency, although, as a finale, he kicked out lustily into the legs of an intimate friend who had been one of the foremost in the torture.

When they came to form into line for the march into the school-room it was curious that Jimmie had many admirers. It was not his prowess; it was the soul he had infused into his gymnastics; and he, still panting, looked about him with a stern and challenging glare.

And yet when the long tramping line had entered the school-room his status had again changed. The other children then began to regard him as a boy in disrepair, and boys in disrepair were always accosted ominously from the throne. Jimmie's march towards his seat was a feat. It was composed partly of a most slinking attempt to dodge the perception of the teacher and partly of pure braggadocio erected for the benefit of his observant fellow-men.

The teacher looked carefully down at him. "Jimmie Trescott," she said.

"Yes'm," he answered, with businesslike briskness, which really spelled out falsity in all its letters.

"Come up to the desk."

He rose amid the awe of the entire school-room. When he arrived she said,

"Jimmie, you've been fighting."

"Yes'm," he answered. This was not so much an admission of the fact as it was a concessional answer to anything she might say.

"Who have you been fighting?" she asked.

"I dunno', 'm."

Whereupon the empress blazed out in wrath. "You don't know who you've been fighting?"

Jimmie looked at her gloomily. "No, 'm."

She seemed about to disintegrate to mere flaming fagots of anger. "You don't know who you've been fighting?" she demanded, blazing. "Well, you stay in after school until you find out."

As he returned to his place all the children knew by his vanquished air that sorrow had fallen upon the house of Trescott. When he took his seat he saw gloating upon him the satanic black eyes of the little Goldege girl.

IV. "SHOWIN' OFF"

JIMMIE TRESCOTT'S new velocipede had the largest front wheel of any velocipede in Whilomville. When it first arrived from New York he wished to sacrifice school, food, and sleep to it. Evidently he wished to become a sort of a perpetual velocipede-rider. But the powers of the family laid a number of judicious embargoes upon him, and he was prevented from becoming a fanatic. Of course this caused him to retain a fondness for the three-wheeled thing much longer than if he had been allowed to debauch himself for a span of days. But in the end it was an immaterial machine to him. For long periods he left it idle in the stable.

One day he loitered from school towards home by a very circuitous route. He was accompanied by only one of his retainers. The object of this détour was the wooing of a little girl in a red hood. He had been in love with her for some three weeks. His desk was near her desk in school, but he had never spoken to her. He had been afraid to take such a radical step. It was not customary to speak to girls. Even boys who had school-going sisters seldom addressed them during that part of a day which was devoted to education.

The reasons for this conduct were very plain. First, the more robust boys considered talking with girls an unmanly occupation; second, the greater part of the boys were afraid; third, they had no idea of what to say, because they esteemed the proper sentences should be supernaturally incisive and eloquent. In consequence, a small contingent of blue-eyed weaklings were the sole intimates of the frail sex, and for it they were boisterously and disdainfully called "girl-boys."

But this situation did not prevent serious and ardent wooing. For instance, Jimmie and the little girl who wore the red hood must have exchanged glances at least two hundred times in every school-hour, and this exchange of glances accomplished everything. In them the two children renewed their curious inarticulate vows.

Jimmie had developed a devotion to school which was the admiration of his father and mother. In the mornings he was so impatient to have it made known to him that no misfortune had befallen his romance during the night that he was actually detected at times feverishly listening for the "first bell." Dr. Trescott was exceedingly complacent of the change, and as for Mrs. Trescott, she had ecstatic visions of a white-haired Jimmie leading the nations in knowledge, comprehending all from bugs to comets. It was merely the doing of the little girl in the red hood.

When Jimmie made up his mind to follow his sweetheart home from school, the project seemed such an arbitrary and shameless innovation that he hastily lied to himself about it. No, he was not following Abbie. He was merely making his way homeward through the new and rather longer route of Bryant Street and Oakland Park. It had nothing at all to do with a girl. It was a mere eccentric notion.

"Come on," said Jimmie, gruffly, to his retainer. "Let's go home this way."

"What fer?" demanded the retainer.

"Oh, b'cause."

"Huh?"

"Oh, it's more fun—goin' this way."

The retainer was bored and loath, but that mattered very little. He did not know how to disobey his chief. Together they followed the trail of red-hooded Abbie and another small girl. These latter at once understood the object of the chase, and looking back giggling, they pretended to quicken their pace. But they were always looking back. Jimmie now began his courtship in earnest. The first thing to do was to prove his strength in battle. This was transacted by means of the retainer. He took that devoted boy and flung him heavily to the ground, meanwhile mouthing a preposterous ferocity.

The retainer accepted this behavior with a sort of bland resignation. After his overthrow he raised himself, coolly brushed some dust and dead leaves from his clothes, and then seemed to forget the incident.

"I can jump farther'n you can," said Jimmie, in a loud voice.

"I know it," responded the retainer, simply.

But this would not do. There must be a contest.

"Come on," shouted Jimmie, imperiously. "Let's see you jump."

The retainer selected a footing on the curb, balanced and calculated a moment, and jumped without enthusiasm. Jimmie's leap of course was longer.

"There!" he cried, blowing out his lips. "I beat you, didn't I? Easy. I beat you." He made a great hubbub, as if the affair was unprecedented.

"Yes," admitted the other, emotionless.

Later, Jimmie forced his retainer to run a race with him, held more jumping matches, flung him twice to earth, and generally behaved as if a retainer was indestructible. If the retainer had been in the plot, it is conceivable that he would have endured this treatment with mere whispered, half-laughing protests. But he was not in the plot at all, and so he became enigmatic. One cannot often sound the profound well in which lie the meanings of boyhood.

Following the two little girls, Jimmie eventually passed into that suburb of Whilomville which is called Oakland Park. At his heels came a badly battered retainer. Oakland Park was a somewhat strange country to the boys. They were dubious of the manners and customs, and of course they would have to meet the local chieftains, who might look askance upon this invasion.

Jimmie's girl departed into her home with a last backward glance that almost blinded the thrilling boy. On this pretext and that pretext, he kept his retainer in play before the house. He had hopes that she would emerge as soon as she had deposited her school-bag.

A boy came along the walk. Jimmie knew him at school. He was Tommie Semple, one of the weaklings who made friends with the fair sex. "Hello, Tom," said Jimmie. "You live round here?"

"Yeh," said Tom, with composed pride. At school he was afraid of Jimmie, but he did not evince any of this fear as he strolled well inside his own frontiers. Jimmie and his retainer had not expected this boy to display the manners of a minor chief, and they contemplated him attentively. There was a silence. Finally Jimmie said:

"I can put you down." He moved forward briskly. "Can't I?" he demanded.

The challenged boy backed away. "I know you can," he declared, frankly and promptly.

The little girl in the red hood had come out with a hoop. She looked at Jimmie with an air of insolent surprise in the fact that he still existed, and began to trundle her hoop off towards some other little girls who were shrilly playing near a nurse-maid and a perambulator.

Jimmie adroitly shifted his position until he too was playing near the perambulator, pretentiously making mince-meat out of his retainer and Tommie Semple.

Of course little Abbie had defined the meaning of Jimmie's appearance in Oakland Park. Despite this nonchalance and grand air of accident, nothing could have been more plain. Whereupon she of course became insufferably vain in manner, and whenever Jimmie came near her she tossed her head and turned away her face, and daintily swished her skirts as if he were contagion itself. But Jimmie was happy. His soul was satisfied with the mere presence of the beloved object so long as he could feel that she furtively gazed upon him from time to time and noted his extraordinary prowess, which he was proving upon the persons of his retainer and Tommie Semple. And he was making an impression. There could be no doubt of it. He had many times caught her eye fixed admiringly upon him as he mauled the retainer. Indeed, all the little girls gave attention to his deeds, and he was the hero of the hour.

Presently a boy on a velocipede was seen to be tooling down towards them. "Who's this comin'?" said Jimmie, bluntly, to the Semple boy.

"That's Horace Glenn," said Tommie, "an' he's got a new velocipede, an' he can ride it like anything."

"Can you lick him?" asked Jimmie.

"I don't—I never fought with 'im," answered the other. He bravely tried to appear as a man of respectable achievement, but with Horace coming towards them the risk was too great. However, he added, *"Maybe* I could."

The advent of Horace on his new velocipede created a sensation which he haughtily accepted as a familiar thing. Only Jimmie and his retainer remained silent and impassive. Horace eyed the two invaders.

"Hello, Jimmie!"

"Hello, Horace!"

After the typical silence Jimmie said, pompously, "I got a velocipede."

"Have you?" asked Horace, anxiously. He did not wish anybody in the world but himself to possess a velocipede.

"Yes," sang Jimmie. "An' it's a bigger one than that, too! A good deal bigger! An' it's a better one, too!"

"Huh!" retorted Horace, sceptically.

"'Ain't I, Clarence? 'Ain't I? 'Ain't I got one bigger'n that?"

The retainer answered with alacrity:

"Yes, he has! A good deal bigger! An' it's a dindy, too!"

This corroboration rather disconcerted Horace, but he continued to scoff at any statement that Jimmie also owned a velocipede. As for the contention that this supposed velocipede could be larger than his own, he simply wouldn't hear of it.

Jimmie had been a very gallant figure before the coming of Horace, but the new velocipede had relegated him to a squalid secondary position. So he affected to look with contempt upon it. Voluminously he bragged of the velocipede in the stable at home. He painted its virtues and beauty in loud and extravagant words, flaming words. And the retainer stood by, glibly endorsing everything.

The little company heeded him, and he passed on vociferously from extravagance to utter impossibility. Horace was very sick of it. His defence was reduced to a mere mechanical grumbling: "Don't believe you got one 'tall. Don't believe you got one 'tall."

Jimmie turned upon him suddenly. "How fast can you go? How fast can you go?" he demanded. "Let's see. I bet you can't go fast."

Horace lifted his spirits and answered with proper defiance. "Can't I?" he mocked. "Can't I?"

"No, you can't," said Jimmie. "You can't go fast."

Horace cried: "Well, you see me now! I'll show you! I'll show you if I can't go fast!" Taking a firm seat on his vermilion machine, he pedalled furiously up the walk, turned, and pedalled back again. "There, now!" he shouted, triumphantly. "Ain't that fast? There, now!" There was a low murmur of appreciation from the little girls. Jimmie saw with pain that even his divinity was smiling upon his rival. "There! Ain't that fast? Ain't that fast?" He strove to pin Jimmie down to an admission. He was exuberant with victory.

Notwithstanding a feeling of discomfiture, Jimmie did not lose a moment of time. "Why," he yelled, "that ain't goin' fast 'tall! That ain't goin' fast 'tall! Why, I can go almost *twice* as fast as that! Almost twice as fast! Can't I, Clarence?"

The royal retainer nodded solemnly at the wide-eyed group. "Course you can!"

"Why," spouted Jimmie, "you just ought to see me ride once! You just ought to see me! Why, I can go like the wind! Can't I, Clarence? And I can ride far, too—oh, awful far! Can't I, Clarence? Why, I wouldn't have that one! 'Tain't any good! You just ought to see mine once!"

The overwhelmed Horace attempted to reconstruct his battered glories. "I can ride right over the curb-stone—at some of the crossin's," he announced, brightly.

Jimmie's derision was a splendid sight. "'*Right over the curb-stone*!' Why, that wouldn't be *nothin'* for me to do! I've rode mine down Bridge Street hill. Yessir! 'Ain't I, Clarence? Why, it ain't nothin' to ride over a curb-stone—not for *me*! Is it, Clarence?"

"Down Bridge Street hill? You never!" said Horace, hopelessly.

"Well, didn't I, Clarence? Didn't I, now?"

The faithful retainer again nodded solemnly at the assemblage.

At last Horace, having fallen as low as was possible, began to display a spirit for climbing up again. "Oh, you can do wonders!" he said, laughing. "You can do wonders! I s'pose you could ride down that bank there?" he asked, with art. He had indicated a grassy terrace some six feet in height which bounded one side of the walk. At the bottom was a small ravine in which the reckless had flung ashes and tins. "I s'pose you could ride down that bank?"

All eyes now turned upon Jimmie to detect a sign of his weakening, but he instantly and sublimely arose to the occasion. "That bank?" he asked, scornfully. "Why, I've ridden down banks like that many a time. 'Ain't I, Clarence?"

This was too much for the company. A sound like the wind in the leaves arose; it was the song of incredulity and ridicule. "O—o—o—o—o!" And on the outskirts a little girl suddenly shrieked out, "Story-teller!"

Horace had certainly won a skirmish. He was gleeful. "Oh, you can do wonders!" he gurgled. "You can do wonders!" The neighborhood's superficial hostility to foreigners arose like magic under the influence of his sudden success, and Horace had the delight of seeing Jimmie persecuted in that manner known only to children and insects.

Jimmie called angrily to the boy on the velocipede, "If you'll lend me yours, I'll show you whether I can or not."

Horace turned his superior nose in the air. "Oh no! I don't ever lend it." Then he thought of a blow which would make Jimmie's humiliation complete. "Besides," he said, airily, "'tain't really anything hard to do. I could do it—easy—if I wanted to."

But his supposed adherents, instead of receiving this boast with cheers, looked upon him in a sudden blank silence. Jimmie and his retainer pounced like cats upon their advantage.

"Oh," they yelled, "you *could*, eh? Well, let's see you do it, then! Let's see you do it! Let's see you do it! Now!" In a moment the crew of little spectators were gibing at Horace.

The blow that would make Jimmie's humiliation complete! Instead, it had boomeranged Horace into the mud. He kept up a sullen muttering:

"'Tain't really anything! I could if I wanted to!"

"Dare you to!" screeched Jimmie and his partisans. "Dare you to! Dare you to! Dare you to!"

There were two things to be done—to make gallant effort or to retreat. Somewhat to their amazement, the children at last found Horace moving through their clamor to the edge of the bank. Sitting on the velocipede, he looked at the ravine, and then, with gloomy pride, at the other children. A hush came upon them, for it was seen that he was intending to make some kind of an ante-mortem statement.

"I—" he began. Then he vanished from the edge of the walk. The start had been unintentional—an accident.

The stupefied Jimmie saw the calamity through a haze. His first clear vision was when Horace, with a face as red as a red flag, arose bawling from his tangled velocipede. He and his retainer exchanged a glance of horror and fled the neighborhood. They did not look back until they had reached the top of the hill near the lake. They could see Horace walking slowly under the maples towards his home, pushing his shattered velocipede before him. His chin was thrown high, and the breeze bore them the sound of his howls.

V. MAKING AN ORATOR

IN the school at Whilomville it was the habit, when children had progressed to a certain class, to have them devote Friday afternoon to what was called elocution. This was in the piteously ignorant belief that orators were thus made. By process of school law, unfortunate boys and girls were dragged up to address their fellow-scholars in the literature of the mid-century. Probably the children who were most capable of expressing themselves, the children who were most sensitive to the power of speech, suffered the most wrong. Little blockheads who could learn eight lines of conventional poetry, and could get up and spin it rapidly at their classmates, did not undergo a single pang. The plan operated mainly to agonize many children permanently against arising to speak their thought to fellow-creatures.

Jimmie Trescott had an idea that by exhibition of undue ignorance he could escape from being promoted into the first class room which exacted such penalty from its inmates. He preferred to dwell in a less classic shade rather than venture into a domain where he was obliged to perform a certain duty which struck him as being worse than death. However, willy-nilly, he was somehow sent ahead into the place of torture.

Every Friday at least ten of the little children had to mount the stage beside the teacher's desk and babble something which none of them understood. This was to make them orators. If it had been ordered that they should croak like frogs, it would have advanced most of them just as far towards oratory.

Alphabetically Jimmie Trescott was near the end of the list of victims, but his time was none the less inevitable. "Tanner, Timmens, Trass, Trescott—" He saw his downfall approaching.

He was passive to the teacher while she drove into his mind the incomprehensible lines of "The Charge of the Light Brigade":

Half a league, half a league,

Half a league onward—

He had no conception of a league. If in the ordinary course of life somebody had told him that he was half a league from home, he might have been frightened that half a league was fifty miles; but he struggled manfully with the valley of death and a mystic six hundred, who were performing something there which was very fine, he had been told. He learned all the verses.

But as his own Friday afternoon approached he was moved to make known to his family that a dreadful disease was upon him, and was likely at any time to prevent him from going to his beloved school.

On the great Friday when the children of his initials were to speak their pieces Dr. Trescott was away from home, and the mother of the boy was alarmed beyond measure at Jimmie's curious illness, which caused him to lie on the rug in front of the fire and groan cavernously.

She bathed his feet in hot mustard water until they were lobster-red. She also placed a mustard plaster on his chest.

He announced that these remedies did him no good at all—no good at all. With an air of martyrdom he endured a perfect downpour of motherly attention all that day. Thus the first Friday was passed in safety.

With singular patience he sat before the fire in the dining-room and looked at picture-books, only complaining of pain when he suspected his mother of thinking that he was getting better.

The next day being Saturday and a holiday, he was miraculously delivered from the arms of disease, and went forth to play, a blatantly healthy boy.

He had no further attack until Thursday night of the next week, when he announced that he felt very, very poorly. The mother was already chronically alarmed over the condition of her son, but Dr. Trescott asked him questions which denoted some incredulity. On the third Friday Jimmie was dropped at the door of the school from the doctor's buggy. The other children, notably those who had already passed over the mountain of distress, looked at him with glee, seeing in him another lamb brought to butchery. Seated at his desk in the school-room, Jimmie sometimes remembered with dreadful distinctness every line of "The Charge of the Light Brigade," and at other times his mind was utterly empty of it. Geography, arithmetic, and spelling—usually great tasks—quite rolled off him. His mind was dwelling with terror upon the time when his name should be called and he was obliged to go up to the platform, turn, bow, and recite his message to his fellow-men.

Desperate expedients for delay came to him. If he could have engaged the services of a real pain, he would have been glad. But steadily, inexorably, the minutes marched on towards his great crisis, and all his plans for escape blended into a mere panic fear.

The maples outside were defeating the weakening rays of the afternoon sun, and in the shadowed school-room had come a stillness, in which, nevertheless, one could feel the complacence of the little pupils who had already passed through the flames. They were calmly prepared to recognize as a spectacle the torture of others.

Little Johnnie Tanner opened the ceremony. He stamped heavily up to the platform, and bowed in such a manner that he almost fell down. He blurted out that it would ill befit him to sit silent while the name of his fair Ireland was being reproached, and he appealed to the gallant soldier before him if every British battle-field was not sown with the bones of sons of the Emerald Isle. He was also heard to say that he had listened with deepening surprise and scorn to the insinuation of the honorable member from North Glenmorganshire that the loyalty of the Irish regiments in her Majesty's service could be questioned. To what purpose, then, he asked, had the blood of Irishmen flowed on a hundred fields? To what purpose had Irishmen gone to their death with bravery and devotion in every part of the world where the victorious flag of England had been carried? If the honorable member for North Glenmorganshire insisted upon construing a mere pothouse row between soldiers in Dublin into a grand treachery to the colors and to her Majesty's uniform, then it was time for Ireland to think bitterly of her dead sons, whose graves now marked every step of England's progress, and yet who could have their honors stripped from them so easily by the honorable member for North Glenmorganshire. Furthermore, the honorable member for North Glenmorganshire—

It is needless to say that little Johnnie Tanner's language made it exceedingly hot for the honorable member for North Glenmorganshire. But Johnnie was not angry. He was only in haste. He finished the honorable member for North Glenmorganshire in what might be called a gallop.

Susie Timmens then went to the platform, and with a face as pale as death whisperingly reiterated that she would be Queen of the May. The child represented there a perfect picture of unnecessary suffering. Her small lips were quite blue, and her eyes, opened wide, stared with a look of horror at nothing.

The phlegmatic Trass boy, with his moon face only expressing peasant parentage, calmly spoke some undeniably true words concerning destiny.

In his seat Jimmie Trescott was going half blind with fear of his approaching doom. He wished that the Trass boy would talk forever about destiny. If the school-house had taken fire he thought that he would have felt simply relief. Anything was better. Death amid the flames was preferable to a recital of "The Charge of the Light Brigade."

But the Trass boy finished his remarks about destiny in a very short time. Jimmie heard the teacher call his name, and he felt the whole world look at him. He did not know how he made his way to the stage. Parts of him seemed to be of lead, and at the same time parts of him seemed to be light as air, detached. His face had gone as pale as had been the face of Susie Timmens. He was simply a child in torment; that is all there is to be said specifically about it; and to intelligent people the exhibition would have been not more edifying than a dog-fight.

He bowed precariously, choked, made an inarticulate sound, and then he suddenly said,

"Half a leg—"

"*League*," said the teacher, coolly.

"Half a leg—"

"*League*," said the teacher.

"*League*," repeated Jimmie, wildly.

"Half a league, half a league, half a league onward."

He paused here and looked wretchedly at the teacher.

"Half a league," he muttered—"half a league—"

He seemed likely to keep continuing this phrase indefinitely, so after a time the teacher said, "Well, go on."

"Half a league," responded Jimmie.

The teacher had the opened book before her, and she read from it:

"'All in the valley of Death

Rode the—'

Go on," she concluded.

Jimmie said,

"All in the valley of Death

Rode the—the—the—"

He cast a glance of supreme appeal upon the teacher, and breathlessly whispered, "Rode the what?"

The young woman flushed with indignation to the roots of her hair.

"Rode the six hundred,"

she snapped at him.

The class was arustle with delight at this cruel display. They were no better than a Roman populace in Nero's time.

Jimmie started off again:

"Half a leg—league, half a league, half a league onward.

All in the valley of death rode the six hundred.

Forward—forward—forward—"

"The Light Brigade," suggested the teacher, sharply.

"The Light Brigade," said Jimmie. He was about to die of the ignoble pain of his position.

As for Tennyson's lines, they had all gone grandly out of his mind, leaving it a whited wall.

The teacher's indignation was still rampant. She looked at the miserable wretch before her with an angry stare.

"You stay in after school and learn that all over again," she commanded. "And be prepared to speak it next Friday. I am astonished at you, Jimmie. Go to your seat."

If she had suddenly and magically made a spirit of him and left him free to soar high above all the travail of our earthly lives she could not have overjoyed him more. He fled back to his seat without hearing the low-toned gibes of his schoolmates. He gave no thought to the terrors of the next Friday. The evils of the day had been sufficient, and to a childish mind a week is a great space of time.

With the delightful inconsistency of his age he sat in blissful calm, and watched the sufferings of an unfortunate boy named Zimmerman, who was the next victim of education. Jimmie, of course, did not know that on this day there had been laid for him the foundation of a finished incapacity for public speaking which would be his until he died.

VI. SHAME

DON'T come in here botherin' me," said the cook, intolerantly. "What with your mother bein' away on a visit, an' your father comin' home soon to lunch, I have enough on my mind—and that without bein' bothered with *you*. The kitchen is no place for little boys, anyhow. Run away, and don't be interferin' with my work." She frowned and made a grand pretence of being deep in herculean labors; but Jimmie did not run away.

"Now—they're goin' to have a picnic," he said, half audibly.

"What?"

"Now—they're goin' to have a picnic."

"Who's goin' to have a picnic?" demanded the cook, loudly. Her accent could have led one to suppose that if the projectors did not turn out to be the proper parties, she immediately would forbid this picnic.

Jimmie looked at her with more hopefulness. After twenty minutes of futile skirmishing, he had at least succeeded in introducing the subject. To her question he answered, eagerly:

"Oh, everybody! Lots and lots of boys and girls. Everybody."

"Who's everybody?"

According to custom, Jimmie began to singsong through his nose in a quite indescribable fashion an enumeration of the prospective picnickers: "Willie Dalzel an' Dan Earl an' Ella Earl an' Wolcott Margate an' Reeves Margate an' Walter Phelps an' Homer Phelps an' Minnie Phelps an'—oh—lots more girls an'—everybody. An' their mothers an' big sisters too." Then he announced a new bit of information: "They're goin' to have a picnic."

"Well, let them," said the cook, blandly.

Jimmie fidgeted for a time in silence. At last he murmured, "I—now—I thought maybe you'd let me go."

The cook turned from her work with an air of irritation and amazement that Jimmie should still be in the kitchen. "Who's stoppin' you?" she asked, sharply. "I ain't stoppin' you, am I?"

"No," admitted Jimmie, in a low voice.

"Well, why don't you go, then? Nobody's stoppin' you."

"But," said Jimmie, "I—you—now—each fellow has got to take somethin' to eat with 'm."

"Oh ho!" cried the cook, triumphantly. "So that's it, is it? So that's what you've been shyin' round here fer, eh? Well, you may as well take yourself off without more words. What with your mother bein' away on a visit, an' your father comin' home soon to his lunch, I have enough on my mind—an' that without being bothered with *you*!"

Jimmie made no reply, but moved in grief towards the door. The cook continued: "Some people in this house seem to think there's 'bout a thousand cooks in this kitchen. Where I used to work b'fore, there was some reason in 'em. I ain't a horse. A picnic!"

Jimmie said nothing, but he loitered.

"Seems as if I had enough to do, without havin' you come round talkin' about picnics. Nobody ever seems to think of the work I have to do. Nobody ever seems to think of it. Then they come and talk to me about picnics! What do I care about picnics?"

Jimmie loitered.

"Where I used to work b'fore, there was some reason in 'em. I never heard tell of no picnics right on top of your mother bein' away on a visit an' your father comin' home soon to his lunch. It's all foolishness."

Little Jimmie leaned his head flat against the wall and began to weep. She stared at him scornfully. "Cryin', eh? Cryin'? What are you cryin' fer?"

"N-n-nothin'," sobbed Jimmie.

There was a silence, save for Jimmie's convulsive breathing. At length the cook said: "Stop that blubberin', now. Stop it! This kitchen ain't no place fer it. Stop it!... Very well! If you don't stop, I won't give you nothin' to go to the picnic with—there!"

For the moment he could not end his tears. "You never said," he sputtered—"you never said you'd give me anything."

"An' why would I?" she cried, angrily. "Why would I—with you in here a-cryin' an' a-blubberin' an' a-bleatin' round? Enough to drive a woman crazy! I don't see how you could expect me to! The idea!"

Suddenly Jimmie announced: "I've stopped cryin'. I ain't goin' to cry no more 'tall."

"Well, then," grumbled the cook—"well, then, stop it. I've got enough on my mind." It chanced that she was making for luncheon some salmon croquettes. A tin still half full of pinky prepared fish was beside her on the table. Still grumbling, she seized a loaf of bread and, wielding a knife, she cut from this loaf four slices, each of which was as big as a six-shilling novel. She profligately spread them with butter, and jabbing the point of her knife into the salmon-tin, she brought up bits of salmon, which she flung and flattened upon the bread. Then she crashed the pieces of bread together in pairs, much as one would clash cymbals. There was no doubt in her own mind but that she had created two sandwiches.

"There," she cried. "That'll do you all right. Lemme see. What 'll I put 'em in? There—I've got it." She thrust the sandwiches into a small pail and jammed on the lid. Jimmie was ready for the picnic. "Oh, thank you, Mary!" he cried, joyfully, and in a moment he was off, running swiftly.

The picnickers had started nearly half an hour earlier, owing to his inability to quickly attack and subdue the cook, but he knew that the rendezvous was in the grove of tall, pillarlike hemlocks and pines that grew on a rocky knoll at the lake shore. His heart was very light as he sped, swinging his pail. But a few minutes previously his soul had been gloomed in despair; now he was happy. He was going to the picnic, where privilege of participation was to be bought by the contents of the little tin pail.

When he arrived in the outskirts of the grove he heard a merry clamor, and when he reached the top of the knoll he looked down the slope upon a scene which almost made his little breast burst with joy. They actually had two camp-fires! Two camp-fires! At one of them Mrs. Earl was making something—chocolate, no doubt—and at the other a young lady in white duck and a sailor hat was dropping eggs into boiling water. Other grown-up people had spread a white cloth and were laying upon it things from baskets. In the deep cool shadow of the trees the children scurried, laughing. Jimmie hastened forward to join his friends.

Homer Phelps caught first sight of him. "Ho!" he shouted; "here comes Jimmie Trescott! Come on, Jimmie; you be on our side!" The children had divided themselves into two bands for some purpose of play. The others of Homer Phelps's party loudly endorsed his plan. "Yes, Jimmie, you be on our side." Then arose the usual dispute. "Well, we got the weakest side."

"'Tain't any weaker'n ours."

Homer Phelps suddenly started, and looking hard, said, "What you got in the pail, Jim?"

Jimmie answered, somewhat uneasily, "Got m' lunch in it."

Instantly that brat of a Minnie Phelps simply tore down the sky with her shrieks of derision. "Got his *lunch* in it! In a *pail!*" She ran screaming to her mother. "Oh, mamma! Oh, mamma! Jimmie Trescott's got his picnic in a pail!"

Now there was nothing in the nature of this fact to particularly move the others—notably the boys, who were not competent to care if he had brought his luncheon in a coal-bin; but such is the instinct of childish society that they all immediately moved away from him. In a moment he had been made a social leper. All old intimacies were flung into the lake, so to speak. They dared not compromise themselves. At safe distances the boys shouted, scornfully: "Huh! Got his picnic in a pail!" Never again during that picnic did the little girls speak of him as Jimmie Trescott. His name now was Him.

His mind was dark with pain as he stood, the hangdog, kicking the gravel, and muttering as defiantly as he was able, "Well, I can have it in a pail if I want to." This statement of freedom was of no importance, and he knew it, but it was the only idea in his head.

He had been baited at school for being detected in writing a letter to little Cora, the angel child, and he had known how to defend himself, but this situation was in no way similar. This was a social affair, with grown people on all sides. It would be sweet to catch the Margate twins, for instance, and hammer them into a state of bleating respect for his pail; but that was a matter for the jungles of childhood, where grown folk seldom penetrated. He could only glower.

The amiable voice of Mrs. Earl suddenly called: "Come, children! Everything's ready!" They scampered away, glancing back for one last gloat at Jimmie standing there with his pail.

He did not know what to do. He knew that the grown folk expected him at the spread, but if he approached he would be greeted by a shameful chorus from the children—more especially from some of those damnable little girls. Still, luxuries beyond all dreaming were heaped on that cloth. One could not forget them. Perhaps if he crept up modestly, and was very gentle and very nice to the little girls, they would allow him peace. Of course it had been dreadful to come with a pail to such a grand picnic, but they might forgive him.

Oh no, they would not! He knew them better. And then suddenly he remembered with what delightful expectations he had raced to this grove, and self-pity overwhelmed him, and he thought he wanted to die and make every one feel sorry.

The young lady in white duck and a sailor hat looked at him, and then spoke to her sister, Mrs. Earl. "Who's that hovering in the distance, Emily?"

Mrs. Earl peered. "Why, it's Jimmie Trescott! Jimmie, come to the picnic! Why don't you come to the picnic, Jimmie?" He began to sidle towards the cloth.

But at Mrs. Earl's call there was another outburst from many of the children. "He's got his picnic in a pail! In a *pail!* Got it in a pail!"

Minnie Phelps was a shrill fiend. "Oh, mamma, he's got it in that pail! See! Isn't it funny? Isn't it dreadful funny?"

"What ghastly prigs children are, Emily!" said the young lady. "They are spoiling that boy's whole day, breaking his heart, the little cats! I think I'll go over and talk to him."

"Maybe you had better not," answered Mrs. Earl, dubiously. "Somehow these things arrange themselves. If you interfere, you are likely to prolong everything."

"Well, I'll try, at least," said the young lady.

At the second outburst against him Jimmie had crouched down by a tree, half hiding behind it, half pretending that he was not hiding behind it. He turned his sad gaze towards the lake. The bit of water seen through the shadows seemed perpendicular, a slate-colored wall. He heard a noise near him, and turning, he perceived the young lady looking down at him. In her hand she held plates. "May I sit near you?" she asked, coolly.

Jimmie could hardly believe his ears. After disposing herself and the plates upon the pine needles, she made brief explanation. "They're rather crowded, you see, over there. I don't like to be crowded at a picnic, so I thought I'd come here. I hope you don't mind."

Jimmie made haste to find his tongue. "Oh, I don't mind! I *like* to have you here." The ingenuous emphasis made it appear that the fact of his liking to have her there was in the nature of a law-dispelling phenomenon, but she did not smile.

"How large is that lake?" she asked.

Jimmie, falling into the snare, at once began to talk in the manner of a proprietor of the lake. "Oh, it's almost twenty miles long, an' in one place it's almost four miles wide! an' it's *deep* too—awful deep—an' it's got real steamboats on it, an'—oh—lots of other boats, an'—an'—an'—"

"Do you go out on it sometimes?"

"Oh, lots of times! My father's got a boat," he said, eying her to note the effect of his words.

She was correctly pleased and struck with wonder. "Oh, has he?" she cried, as if she never before had heard of a man owning a boat.

Jimmie continued: "Yes, an' it's a grea' big boat, too, with sails, real sails; an' sometimes he takes me out in her, too; an' once he took me fishin', an' we had sandwiches, plenty of 'em, an' my father he drank beer right out of the bottle—*right out of the bottle!*"

The young lady was properly overwhelmed by this amazing intelligence. Jimmie saw the impression he had created, and he enthusiastically resumed his narrative: "An' after, he let me throw the bottles in the water, and I throwed 'em 'way, 'way, 'way out. An' they sank, an'—never comed up," he concluded, dramatically.

His face was glorified; he had forgotten all about the pail; he was absorbed in this communion with a beautiful lady who was so interested in what he had to say.

She indicated one of the plates, and said, indifferently: "Perhaps you would like some of those sandwiches. I made them. Do you like olives? And there's a deviled egg. I made that also."

"Did you really?" said Jimmie, politely. His face gloomed for a moment because the pail was recalled to his mind, but he timidly possessed himself of a sandwich.

"Hope you are not going to scorn my deviled egg," said his goddess. "I am very proud of it." He did not; he scorned little that was on the plate.

Their gentle intimacy was ineffable to the boy. He thought he had a friend, a beautiful lady, who liked him more than she did anybody at the picnic, to say the least. This was proved by the fact that she had flung aside the luxuries of the spread cloth to sit with him, the exile. Thus early did he fall a victim to woman's wiles.

"Where do you live?" he asked, suddenly.

"Oh, a long way from here! In New York."

His next question was put very bluntly. "Are you married?"

"Oh no!" she answered, gravely.

Jimmie was silent for a time, during which he glanced shyly and furtively up at her face. It was evident that he was somewhat embarrassed. Finally he said, "When I grow up to be a man—"

"Oh, that is some time yet!" said the beautiful lady.

"But when I *do*, I—I should like to marry you."

"Well, I will remember it," she answered; "but don't talk of it now, because it's such a long time; and—I wouldn't wish you to consider yourself bound." She smiled at him.

He began to brag. "When I grow up to be a man, I'm goin' to have lots an' lots of money, an' I'm goin' to have a grea' big house, an' a horse an' a shot-gun, an' lots an' lots of books 'bout elephants an' tigers, an' lots an' lots of ice-cream an' pie an'—caramels." As before, she was impressed; he could see it. "An' I'm goin' to have lots an' lots of children—'bout three hundred, I guess—an' there won't none of 'em be girls. They'll all be boys—like me."

"Oh, my!" she said.

His garment of shame was gone from him. The pail was dead and well buried. It seemed to him that months elapsed as he dwelt in happiness near the beautiful lady and trumpeted his vanity.

At last there was a shout. "Come on! we're going home." The picnickers trooped out of the grove. The children wished to resume their jeering, for Jimmie still gripped his pail, but they were restrained by the circumstances. He was walking at the side of the beautiful lady.

During this journey he abandoned many of his habits. For instance, he never travelled without skipping gracefully from crack to crack between the stones, or without pretending that he was a train of cars, or without some mumming device of childhood. But now he behaved with dignity. He made no more noise than a little mouse. He escorted the beautiful lady to the gate of the Earl home, where he awkwardly, solemnly, and wistfully shook hands in good-by. He watched her go up the walk; the door clanged.

On his way home he dreamed. One of these dreams was fascinating. Supposing the beautiful lady was his teacher in school! Oh, my! wouldn't he be a good boy, sitting like a statuette all day long, and knowing every lesson to perfection, and—everything. And then supposing that a boy should sass her. Jimmie painted himself waylaying that boy on the homeward road, and the fate of the boy was a thing to make strong men cover their eyes with their hands. And she would like him more and more—more and more. And he— he would be a little god.

But as he was entering his father's grounds an appalling recollection came to him. He was returning with the bread-and-butter and the salmon untouched in the pail! He could imagine the cook, nine feet tall, waving her fist. "An' so that's what I took trouble for, is it? So's you could bring it back? So's you could bring it back?" He skulked towards the house like a marauding bushranger. When he neared the kitchen door he made a desperate rush past it, aiming to gain the stables and there secrete his guilt. He was nearing them, when a thunderous voice hailed him from the rear:

"Jimmie Trescott, where you goin' with that pail?"

It was the cook. He made no reply, but plunged into the shelter of the stables. He whirled the lid from the pail and dashed its contents beneath a heap of blankets. Then he stood panting, his eyes on the door. The cook did not pursue, but she was bawling:

"Jimmie Trescott, what you doin' with that pail?"

He came forth, swinging it. "Nothin'," he said, in virtuous protest.

"I know better," she said, sharply, as she relieved him of his curse.

In the morning Jimmie was playing near the stable, when he heard a shout from Peter Washington, who attended Dr. Trescott's horse:

"Jim! Oh, Jim!"

"What?"

"Come yah."

Jimmie went reluctantly to the door of the stable, and Peter Washington asked:

"Wut's dish yere fish an' brade doin' unner dese yer blankups?"

"I don't know. I didn't have nothin' to do with it," answered Jimmie, indignantly.

"Don' tell *me*!" cried Peter Washington, as he flung it all away—"don' tell *me*! When I fin' fish an' brade unner dese yer blankups, I don' go an' think dese yer ho'ses er yer pop's put 'em. I *know*. An' if I caitch enny more dish yer fish an' brade in dish yer stable, I'*ll* tell yer pop."

VII. THE CARRIAGE-LAMPS

IT was the fault of a small nickel-plated revolver, a most incompetent weapon, which, wherever one aimed, would fling the bullet as the devil willed, and no man, when about to use it, could tell exactly what was in store for the surrounding country. This treasure had been acquired by Jimmie Trescott after arduous bargaining with another small boy. Jimmie wended homeward, patting his hip pocket at every three paces.

Peter Washington, working in the carriage-house, looked out upon him with a shrewd eye. "Oh, Jim," he called, "wut you got in yer hind pocket?"

"Nothin'," said Jimmie, feeling carefully under his jacket to make sure that the revolver wouldn't fall out.

Peter chuckled. "S'more foolishness, I raikon. You gwine be hung one day, Jim, you keep up all dish yer nonsense."

Jimmie made no reply, but went into the back garden, where he hid the revolver in a box under a lilac-bush. Then he returned to the vicinity of Peter, and began to cruise to and fro in the offing, showing all the signals of one wishing to open treaty. "Pete," he said, "how much does a box of cartridges cost?"

Peter raised himself violently, holding in one hand a piece of harness, and in the other an old rag. "Ca'tridgers! *Ca'tridgers!* Lan'sake! wut the kid want with ca'tridgers? Knew it! Knew it! Come home er-holdin' on to his hind pocket like he got money in it. An' now he want ca'tridgers."

Jimmie, after viewing with dismay the excitement caused by his question, began to move warily out of the reach of a possible hostile movement.

"Ca'tridgers!" continued Peter, in scorn and horror. "Kid like you! No bigger'n er minute! Look yah, Jim, you done been swappin' round, an' you done got hol' of er pistol!" The charge was dramatic.

The wind was almost knocked out of Jimmie by this display of Peter's terrible miraculous power, and as he backed away his feeble denials were more convincing than a confession.

"I'll tell yer pop!" cried Peter, in virtuous grandeur. "I'll tell yer pop!"

In the distance Jimmie stood appalled. He knew not what to do. The dread adult wisdom of Peter Washington had laid bare the sin, and disgrace stared at Jimmie.

There was a whirl of wheels, and a high, lean trotting-mare spun Doctor Trescott's buggy towards Peter, who ran forward busily. As the doctor climbed out, Peter, holding the mare's head, began his denunciation:

"Docteh, I gwine tell on Jim. He come home er-holdin' on to his hind pocket, an' proud like he won a tuhkey-raffle, an' I sure know what he been up to, an' I done challenge him, an' he nev' say he didn't."

"Why, what do you mean?" said the doctor. "What's this, Jimmie?"

The boy came forward, glaring wrathfully at Peter. In fact, he suddenly was so filled with rage at Peter that he forgot all precautions. "It's about a pistol," he said, bluntly. "I've got a pistol. I swapped for it."

"I done tol' 'im his pop wouldn' stand no fiah-awms, an' him a kid like he is. I done tol' 'im. Lan' sake! he strut like he was a soldier! Come in yere proud, an' er-holdin' on to his hind pocket. He think he was Jesse James, I raikon. But I done tol' 'im his pop stan' no sech foolishness. First thing— *blam*—he shoot his haid off. No, seh, he too tinety t' come in yere er-struttin' like he jest bought Main Street. I tol' 'im. I done tol' 'im—shawp. I don' wanter be loafin' round dis yer stable if Jim he gwine go shootin' round an' shootin' round—*blim—blam—blim—blam*! No, seh. I retiahs. I retiahs. It's all right if er grown man got er gun, but ain't no kids come foolishin' round *me* with fiah-awms. No, seh. I retiahs."

"Oh, be quiet, Peter!" said the doctor. "Where is this thing, Jimmie?"

The boy went sulkily to the box under the lilac-bush and returned with the revolver. "Here 'tis," he said, with a glare over his shoulder at Peter. The doctor looked at the silly weapon in critical contempt.

"It's not much of a thing, Jimmie, but I don't think you are quite old enough for it yet. I'll keep it for you in one of the drawers of my desk."

Peter Washington burst out proudly: "I done tol' 'im th' docteh wouldn' stan' no traffickin' round yere with fiah-awms. I done tol' 'im."

Jimmie and his father went together into the house, and as Peter unharnessed the mare he continued his comments on the boy and the revolver. He was not cast down by the absence of hearers. In fact, he usually talked better when there was no one to listen save the horses. But now his observations bore small resemblance to his earlier and public statements. Admiration and the keen family pride of a Southern negro who has been long in one place were now in his tone.

"That boy! He's er devil! When he get to be er man—wow! He'll jes take an' make things whirl round yere. Raikon we'll all take er back seat when he come erlong er-raisin' Cain."

He had unharnessed the mare, and with his back bent was pushing the buggy into the carriage-house.

"Er pistol! An' him no bigger than er minute!"

A small stone whizzed past Peter's head and clattered on the stable. He hastily dropped all occupation and struck a curious attitude. His right knee was almost up to his chin, and his arms were wreathed protectingly about his head. He had not looked in the direction from which the stone had come, but he had begun immediately to yell:

"You Jim! Quit! Quit, I tell yer, Jim! Watch out! You gwine break somethin', Jim!"

"Yah!" taunted the boy, as with the speed and ease of a light-cavalryman he manœuvred in the distance. "Yah! Told on me, did you! Told on me, hey! There! How do you like that?" The missiles resounded against the stable.

"Watch out, Jim! You gwine break something, Jim, I tell yer! Quit yer foolishness, Jim! Ow! Watch out, boy! I—"

There was a crash. With diabolic ingenuity, one of Jimmie's pebbles had entered the carriage-house and had landed among a row of carriage-lamps on a shelf, creating havoc which was apparently beyond all reason of physical law. It seemed to Jimmie that the racket of falling glass could have been heard in an adjacent county.

Peter was a prophet who after persecution was suffered to recall everything to the mind of the persecutor. "*There!* Knew it! Knew it! *Now* I raikon you'll quit. Hi! jes look ut dese yer lamps! Fer lan' sake! Oh, now yer pop jes break ev'ry bone in yer body!"

In the doorway of the kitchen the cook appeared with a startled face. Jimmie's father and mother came suddenly out on the front veranda. "What was that noise?" called the the doctor.

Peter went forward to explain. "Jim he was er-heavin' rocks at me, docteh, an' erlong come one rock an' go *blam* inter all th' lamps an' jes skitter 'em t' bits. I declayah—"

Jimmie, half blinded with emotion, was nevertheless aware of a lightning glance from his father, a glance which cowed and frightened him to the ends of his toes. He heard the steady but deadly tones of his father in a fury: "Go into the house and wait until I come."

Bowed in anguish, the boy moved across the lawn and up the steps. His mother was standing on the veranda still gazing towards the stable. He loitered in the faint hope that she might take some small pity on his state. But she could have heeded him no less if he had been invisible. He entered the house.

When the doctor returned from his investigation of the harm done by Jimmie's hand, Mrs. Trescott looked at him anxiously, for she knew that he was concealing some volcanic impulses. "Well?" she asked.

"It isn't the lamps," he said at first. He seated himself on the rail. "I don't know what we are going to do with that boy. It isn't so much the lamps as it is the other thing. He was throwing stones at Peter because Peter told me about the revolver. What are we going to do with him?"

"I'm sure I don't know," replied the mother. "We've tried almost everything. Of course much of it is pure animal spirits. Jimmie is not naturally vicious—"

"Oh, I know," interrupted the doctor, impatiently. "Do you suppose, when the stones were singing about Peter's ears, he cared whether they were flung by a boy who was naturally vicious or a boy who was not? The question might interest him afterward, but at the time he was mainly occupied in dodging these effects of pure animal spirits."

"Don't be too hard on the boy, Ned. There's lots of time yet. He's so young yet, and—I believe he gets most of his naughtiness from that wretched Dalzel boy. That Dalzel boy—well, he's simply awful!" Then, with true motherly instinct to shift blame from her own boy's shoulders, she proceeded to sketch the character of the Dalzel boy in lines that would have made that talented young vagabond stare. It was not admittedly her feeling that the doctor's attention should be diverted from the main issue and his indignation divided among the camps, but presently the doctor felt himself burn with wrath for the Dalzel boy.

"Why don't you keep Jimmie away from him?" he demanded. "Jimmie has no business consorting with abandoned little predestined jail-birds like him. If I catch him on the place I'll box his ears."

"It is simply impossible, unless we kept Jimmie shut up all the time," said Mrs. Trescott. "I can't watch him every minute of the day, and the moment my back is turned, he's off."

"I should think those Dalzel people would hire somebody to bring up their child for them," said the doctor. "They don't seem to know how to do it themselves."

Presently you would have thought from the talk that one Willie Dalzel had been throwing stones at Peter Washington because Peter Washington had told Doctor Trescott that Willie Dalzel had come into possession of a revolver.

In the mean time Jimmie had gone into the house to await the coming of his father. He was in a rebellious mood. He had not intended to destroy the carriage-lamps. He had been merely hurling stones at a creature whose perfidy deserved such action, and the hitting of the lamps had been merely another move of the great conspirator Fate to force one Jimmie Trescott into dark and troublous ways. The boy was beginning to find the world a bitter place. He couldn't win appreciation for a single virtue; he could only achieve quick, rigorous punishment for his misdemeanors. Everything was an enemy. Now there were those silly old lamps—what were they doing up on that shelf, anyhow? It would have been just as easy for them at the time to have been in some other place. But no; there they had been, like the crowd that is passing under the wall when the mason for the first time in twenty years lets fall a brick. Furthermore, the flight of that stone had been perfectly unreasonable. It had been a sort of freak in physical law. Jimmie understood that he might have thrown stones from the same fatal spot for an hour without hurting a single lamp. He was a victim—that was it. Fate had conspired with the detail of his environment to simply hound him into a grave or into a cell.

But who would understand? Who would understand? And here the boy turned his mental glance in every direction, and found nothing but what was to him the black of cruel ignorance. Very well; some day they would—

From somewhere out in the street he heard a peculiar whistle of two notes. It was the common signal of the boys in the neighborhood, and judging from the direction of the sound, it was apparently intended to summon him. He moved immediately to one of the windows of the sitting-room. It opened upon a part of the grounds remote from the stables and cut off from the veranda by a wing. He perceived Willie Dalzel loitering in the street. Jimmie whistled the signal after having pushed up the window-sash some inches. He saw the Dalzel boy turn and regard him, and then call several other boys. They stood in a group and gestured. These gestures plainly said: "Come out. We've got something on hand." Jimmie sadly shook his head.

But they did not go away. They held a long consultation. Presently Jimmie saw the intrepid Dalzel boy climb the fence and begin to creep among the shrubbery, in elaborate imitation of an Indian scout. In time he arrived under Jimmie's window, and raised his face to whisper: "Come on out! We're going on a bear-hunt."

A bear-hunt! Of course Jimmie knew that it would not be a real bear-hunt, but would be a sort of carouse of pretension and big talking and preposterous lying and valor, wherein each boy would strive to have himself called Kit Carson by the others. He was profoundly affected. However, the parental word was upon him, and he could not move. "No," he answered, "I can't. I've got to stay in."

"Are you a prisoner?" demanded the Dalzel boy, eagerly.

"No-o—yes—I s'pose I am."

The other lad became much excited, but he did not lose his wariness. "Don't you want to be rescued?"

"Why—no—I dun'no'," replied Jimmie, dubiously.

Willie Dalzel was indignant. "Why, of course you want to be rescued! We'll rescue you. I'll go and get my men." And thinking this a good sentence, he repeated, pompously, "I'll go and get my men." He began to crawl away, but when he was distant some ten paces he turned to say: "Keep up a stout heart. Remember that you have friends who will be faithful unto death. The time is not now far off when you will again view the blessed sunlight."

The poetry of these remarks filled Jimmie with ecstasy, and he watched eagerly for the coming of the friends who would be faithful unto death. They delayed some time, for the reason that Willie Dalzel was making a speech.

"Now, men," he said, "our comrade is a prisoner in yon—in yond—in that there fortress. We must to the rescue. Who volunteers to go with me?" He fixed them with a stern eye.

There was a silence, and then one of the smaller boys remarked,

"If Doc Trescott ketches us trackin' over his lawn—"

Willie Dalzel pounced upon the speaker and took him by the throat. The two presented a sort of a burlesque of the wood-cut on the cover of a dime novel which Willie had just been reading—*The Red Captain: A Tale of the Pirates of the Spanish Main.*

"You are a coward!" said Willie, through his clinched teeth.

"No, I ain't, Willie," piped the other, as best he could.

"I say you are," cried the great chieftain, indignantly. "Don't tell me I'm a liar." He relinquished his hold upon the coward and resumed his speech. "You know me, men. Many of you have been my followers for long years. You saw me slay Six-handed Dick with my own hand. You know I never falter. Our comrade is a prisoner in the cruel hands of our enemies. Aw, Pete Washington? He dassent. My pa says if Pete ever troubles me he'll brain 'im. Come on! To the rescue! Who will go with me to the rescue? Aw, come on! What are you afraid of?"

It was another instance of the power of eloquence upon the human mind. There was only one boy who was not thrilled by this oration, and he was a boy whose favorite reading had been of the road-agents and gun-fighters of the great West, and he thought the whole thing should be conducted in the Deadwood Dick manner. This talk of a "comrade" was silly; "pard" was the proper word. He resolved that he would make a show of being a pirate, and keep secret the fact that he really was Hold-up Harry, the Terror of the Sierras.

But the others were knit close in piratical bonds. One by one they climbed the fence at a point hidden from the house by tall shrubs. With many a low-breathed caution they went upon their perilous adventure.

Jimmie was grown tired of waiting for his friends who would be faithful unto death. Finally he decided that he would rescue himself. It would be a gross breach of rule, but he couldn't sit there all the rest of the day waiting for his faithful-unto-death friends. The window was only five feet from the ground. He softly raised the sash and threw one leg over the sill. But at the same time he perceived his friends snaking among the bushes. He withdrew his leg and waited, seeing that he was now to be rescued in an orthodox way. The brave pirates came nearer and nearer.

Jimmie heard a noise of a closing door, and turning, he saw his father in the room looking at him and the open window in angry surprise. Boys never faint, but Jimmie probably came as near to it as may the average boy.

"What's all this?" asked the doctor, staring. Involuntarily Jimmie glanced over his shoulder through the window. His father saw the creeping figures. "What are those boys doing?" he said, sharply, and he knit his brows.

"Nothin'."

"Nothing! Don't tell me that. Are they coming here to the window?"

"Y-e-s, sir."

"What for?"

"To—to see me."

"What about?"

"About—about nothin'."

"What about?"

Jimmie knew that he could conceal nothing.

He said, "They're comin' to—to—to rescue me." He began to whimper.

The doctor sat down heavily.

"What? To rescue you?" he gasped.

"Y-yes, sir."

The doctor's eyes began to twinkle. "Very well," he said presently. "I will sit here and observe this rescue. And on no account do you warn them that I am here. Understand?"

Of course Jimmie understood. He had been mad to warn his friends, but his father's mere presence had frightened him from doing it. He stood trembling at the window, while the doctor stretched in an easy-chair near at hand. They waited. The doctor could tell by his son's increasing agitation that the great moment was near. Suddenly he heard Willie Dalzel's voice hiss out a word: "S-s-silence!" Then the same voice addressed Jimmie at the window: "Good cheer, my comrade. The time is now at hand. I have come. Never did the Red Captain turn his back on a friend. One minute more and you will be free. Once aboard my gallant craft and you can bid defiance to your haughty enemies. Why don't you hurry up? What are you standin' there lookin' like a cow for?"

"I—er—now—you—" stammered Jimmie.

Here Hold-up Harry, the Terror of the Sierras, evidently concluded that Willie Dalzel had had enough of the premier part, so he said:

"Brace up, pard. Don't ye turn white-livered now, fer ye know that Hold-up Harry, the Terrar of the Sarahs, ain't the man ter—"

"Oh, stop it!" said Willie Dalzel. "He won't understand that, you know. He's a pirate. Now, Jimmie, come on. Be of light heart, my comrade. Soon you—"

"I 'low arter all this here long time in jail ye thought ye had no friends mebbe, but I tell ye Hold-up Harry, the Terrar of the Sarahs—"

"A boat is waitin'—"

"I have ready a trusty horse—"

Willie Dalzel could endure his rival no longer.

"Look here, Henry, you're spoilin' the whole thing. We're all pirates, don't you see, and you're a pirate too."

"I ain't a pirate. I'm Hold-up Harry, the Terrar of the Sarahs."

"You ain't, I say," said Willie, in despair. "You're spoilin' everything, you are. All right, now. You wait. I'll fix you for this, see if I don't! Oh, come on, Jimmie. A boat awaits us at the foot of the rocks. In one short hour you'll be free forever from your ex—exewable enemies, and their vile plots. Hasten, for the dawn approaches."

The suffering Jimmie looked at his father, and was surprised at what he saw. The doctor was doubled up like a man with the colic. He was breathing heavily. The boy turned again to his friends. "I—now—look here," he began, stumbling among the words. "You—I—I don't think I'll be rescued to-day."

The pirates were scandalized. "What?" they whispered, angrily. "Ain't you goin' to be rescued? Well, all right for you, Jimmie Trescott. That's a nice way to act, that is!" Their upturned eyes glowered at Jimmie.

Suddenly Doctor Trescott appeared at the window with Jimmie. "Oh, go home, boys!" he gasped, but they did not hear him. Upon the instant they had whirled and scampered away like deer. The first lad to reach the fence was the Red Captain, but Hold-up Harry, the Terror of the Sierras, was so close that there was little to choose between them.

Doctor Trescott lowered the window, and then spoke to his son in his usual quiet way. "Jimmie, I wish you would go and tell Peter to have the buggy ready at seven o'clock."

"Yes, sir," said Jimmie, and he swaggered

out to the stables. "Pete, father wants the buggy ready at seven o'clock."

Peter paid no heed to this order, but with the tender sympathy of a true friend he inquired, "Hu't?"

"Hurt? Did what hurt?"

"Yer trouncin'."

"Trouncin'!" said Jimmie, contemptuously. "I didn't get any trouncin'."

"No?" said Peter. He gave Jimmie a quick shrewd glance, and saw that he was telling the truth. He began to mutter and mumble over his work. "Ump! Ump! Dese yer white folks act like they think er boy's made er glass. No trouncin'! Ump!" He was consumed with curiosity to learn why Jimmie had not felt a heavy parental hand, but he did not care to lower his dignity by asking questions about it. At last, however, he reached the limits of his endurance, and in a voice pretentiously careless he asked, "Didn' yer pop take on like mad er-bout dese yer cay'ge-lamps?"

"Carriage-lamps?" inquired Jimmie.

"Ump."

"No, he didn't say anything about carriage-lamps—not that I remember. Maybe he did, though. Lemme see.... No, he never mentioned 'em."

VIII. THE KNIFE

I

SI BRYANT'S place was on the shore of the lake, and his garden-patch, shielded from the north by a bold little promontory and a higher ridge inland, was accounted the most successful and surprising in all Whilomville township. One afternoon Si was working in the garden-patch, when Doctor Trescott's man, Peter Washington, came trudging slowly along the road, observing nature. He scanned the white man's fine agricultural results. "Take your eye off them there mellons, you rascal," said Si, placidly.

The negro's face widened in a grin of delight. "Well, Mist' Bryant, I raikon I ain't on'y make m'se'f covertous er-lookin' at dem yere mellums, sure 'nough. Dey suhtainly is grand."

"That's all right," responded Si, with affected bitterness of spirit. "That's all right. Just don't you admire 'em too much, that's all." Peter chuckled and chuckled. "Ma Lode! Mist' Bryant, y-y-you don' think I'm gwine come prowlin' in dish yer gawden?"

"No, I know you hain't," said Si, with solemnity. "B'cause, if you did, I'd shoot you so full of holes you couldn't tell yourself from a sponge."

"Um—no, seh! No, seh! I don' raikon you'll get chance at Pete, Mist' Bryant. No, seh. I'll take an' run 'long an' rob er bank 'fore I'll come foolishin' 'round *your* gawden, Mist' Bryant."

Bryant, gnarled and strong as an old tree, leaned on his hoe, and laughed a Yankee laugh. His mouth remained tightly closed, but the sinister lines which ran from the sides of his nose to the meetings of his lips developed to form a comic oval, and he emitted a series of grunts, while his eyes gleamed merrily and his shoulders shook. Pete, on the contrary, threw back his head and guffawed thunderously. The effete joke in regard to an American negro's fondness for watermelons was still an admirable pleasantry to them, and this was not the first time they had engaged in badinage over it. In fact, this venerable survival had formed between them a friendship of casual roadside quality.

Afterwards Peter went on up the road. He continued to chuckle until he was far away. He was going to pay a visit to old Alek Williams, a negro who lived with a large family in a hut clinging to the side of a mountain. The scattered colony of negroes which hovered near Whilomville was of interesting origin, being the result of some contrabands who had drifted as far north as Whilomville during the great civil war. The descendants of these adventurers were mainly conspicuous for their bewildering number, and the facility which they possessed for adding even to this number. Speaking, for example, of the Jacksons—one couldn't hurl a stone into the hills about Whilomville without having it land on the roof of a hut full of Jacksons. The town reaped little in labor from these curious suburbs. There were a few men who came in regularly to work in gardens, to drive teams, to care for horses, and there were a few women who came in to cook or to wash. These latter had usually drunken husbands. In the main the colony loafed in high spirits, and the industrious minority gained no direct honor from their fellows, unless they spent their earnings on raiment, in which case they were naturally treated with distinction. On the whole, the hardships of these people were the wind, the rain, the snow, and any other physical difficulties which they could cultivate. About twice a year the lady philanthropists of Whilomville went up against them, and came away poorer in goods but rich in complacence. After one of these attacks the colony would preserve a comic air of rectitude for two days, and then relapse again to the genial irresponsibility of a crew of monkeys.

Peter Washington was one of the industrious class who occupied a position of distinction, for he surely spent his money on personal decoration. On occasion he could dress better than the Mayor of Whilomville himself, or at least in more colors, which was the main thing to the minds of his admirers. His ideal had been the late gallant Henry Johnson, whose conquests in Watermelon Alley, as well as in the hill shanties, had proved him the equal if not the superior of any Pullman-car porter in the country. Perhaps Peter had too much Virginia laziness and humor in him to be a wholly adequate successor to the fastidious Henry Johnson, but, at any rate, he admired his memory so attentively as to be openly termed a dude by envious people.

On this afternoon he was going to call on old Alek Williams because Alek's eldest girl was just turned seventeen, and, to Peter's mind, was a triumph of beauty. He was not wearing his best clothes, because on his last visit Alek's half-breed hound Susie had taken occasion to forcefully extract a quite large and valuable part of the visitor's trousers. When Peter arrived at the end of the rocky field which contained old Alek's shanty he stooped and provided himself with several large stones, weighing them carefully in his hand, and finally continuing his journey with three stones of about eight ounces each. When he was near the house, three gaunt hounds, Rover and Carlo and Susie, came sweeping down upon him. His impression was that they were going to climb him as if he were a tree, but at the critical moment they swerved and went growling and snapping around him, their heads low, their eyes malignant. The afternoon caller waited until Susie presented her side to him, then he heaved one of his eight-ounce rocks. When it landed, her hollow ribs gave forth a drumlike sound, and she was knocked sprawling, her legs in the air. The other hounds at once fled in horror, and she followed as soon as she was able, yelping at the top of her lungs. The afternoon caller resumed his march.

At the wild expressions of Susie's anguish old Alek had flung open the door and come hastily into the sunshine. "Yah, you Suse, come erlong outa dat now. What fer you—Oh, how do, how do, Mist' Wash'ton—how do?"

"How do, Mist' Willums? I done foun' it necessa'y fer ter damnearkill dish yer dawg a yourn, Mist' Willums."

"Come in, come in, Mist' Wash'ton. Dawg no 'count, Mist' Wash'ton." Then he turned to address the unfortunate animal. "Hu't, did it? Hu't? 'Pears like you gwine dun some saince by time somebody brek yer back. 'Pears like I gwine club yer inter er frazzle 'fore you fin' out some saince. Gw'on 'way f'm yah!"

As the old man and his guest entered the shanty a body of black children spread out in crescent-shape formation and observed Peter with awe. Fat old Mrs. Williams greeted him turbulently, while the eldest girl, Mollie, lurked in a corner and giggled with finished imbecility, gazing at the visitor with eyes that were shy and bold by turns. She seemed at times absurdly over-confident, at times foolishly afraid; but her giggle consistently endured. It was a giggle on which an irascible but right-minded judge would have ordered her forthwith to be buried alive.

Amid a great deal of hospitable gabbling, Peter was conducted to the best chair out of the three that the house contained. Enthroned therein, he made himself charming in talk to the old people, who beamed upon him joyously. As for Mollie, he affected to be unaware of her existence. This may have been a method for entrapping the sentimental interest of that young gazelle, or it may be that the giggle had worked upon him.

He was absolutely fascinating to the old people. They could talk like rotary snow-ploughs, and he gave them every chance, while his face was illumined with appreciation. They pressed him to stay for supper, and he consented, after a glance at the pot on the stove which was too furtive to be noted.

During the meal old Alek recounted the high state of Judge Oglethorpe's kitchen-garden, which Alek said was due to his unremitting industry and fine intelligence. Alek was a gardener, whenever impending starvation forced him to cease temporarily from being a lily of the field.

"Mist' Bryant he suhtainly got er grand gawden," observed Peter.

"Dat so, dat so, Mist' Wash'ton," assented Alek. "He got fine gawden."

"Seems like I nev' *did* see sech mellums, big as er bar'l, layin' dere. I don't raikon an'body in dish yer county kin hol' it with Mist' Bryant when comes ter mellums."

"Dat so, Mist' Wash'ton."

They did not talk of watermelons until their heads held nothing else, as the phrase goes. But they talked of watermelons until, when Peter started for home that night over a lonely road, they held a certain dominant position in his mind. Alek had come with him as far as the fence, in order to protect him from a possible attack by the mongrels. There they had cheerfully parted, two honest men.

The night was dark, and heavy with moisture. Peter found it uncomfortable to walk rapidly. He merely loitered on the road. When opposite Si Bryant's place he paused and looked over the fence into the garden. He imagined he could see the form of a huge melon lying in dim stateliness not ten yards away. He looked at the Bryant house. Two windows, down-stairs, were lighted. The Bryants kept no dog, old Si's favorite child having once been bitten by a dog, and having since died, within that year, of pneumonia.

Peering over the fence, Peter fancied that if any low-minded night-prowler should happen to note the melon, he would not find it difficult to possess himself of it. This person would merely wait until the lights were out in the house, and the people presumably asleep. Then he would climb the fence, reach the melon in a few strides, sever the stem with his ready knife, and in a trice be back in the road with his prize. There need be no noise, and, after all, the house was some distance.

Selecting a smooth bit of turf, Peter took a seat by the road-side. From time to time he glanced at the lighted window.

II

When Peter and Alek had said good-bye, the old man turned back in the rocky field and shaped a slow course towards that high dim light which marked the little window of his shanty. It would be incorrect to say that Alek could think of nothing but watermelons. But it was true that Si Bryant's watermelon-patch occupied a certain conspicuous position in his thoughts.

He sighed; he almost wished that he was again a conscienceless pickaninny, instead of being one of the most ornate, solemn, and look-at-me-sinner deacons that ever graced the handle of a collection-basket. At this time it made him quite sad to reflect upon his granite integrity. A weaker man might perhaps bow his moral head to the temptation, but for him such a fall was impossible. He was a prince of the church, and if he had been nine princes of the church he could not have been more proud. In fact, religion was to the old man a sort of personal dignity. And he was on Sundays so obtrusively good that you could see his sanctity through a door. He forced it on you until you would have felt its influence even in a forecastle.

It was clear in his mind that he must put watermelon thoughts from him, and after a moment he told himself, with much ostentation, that he had done so. But it was cooler under the sky than in the shanty, and as he was not sleepy, he decided to take a stroll down to Si Bryant's place and look at the melons from a pinnacle of spotless innocence. Reaching the road, he paused to listen. It would not do to let Peter hear him, because that graceless rapscallion would probably misunderstand him. But, assuring himself that Peter was well on his way, he set out, walking briskly until he was within four hundred yards of Bryant's place. Here he went to the side of the road, and walked thereafter on the damp, yielding turf. He made no sound.

He did not go on to that point in the main road which was directly opposite the water-melon-patch. He did not wish to have his ascetic contemplation disturbed by some chance wayfarer. He turned off along a short lane which led to Si Bryant's barn. Here he reached a place where he could see, over the fence, the faint shapes of the melons.

Alek was affected. The house was some distance away, there was no dog, and doubtless the Bryants would soon extinguish their lights and go to bed. Then some poor lost lamb of sin might come and scale the fence, reach a melon in a moment, sever the stem with his ready knife, and in a trice be back in the road with his prize. And this poor lost lamb of sin might even be a bishop, but no one would ever know it. Alek singled out with his eye a very large melon, and thought that the lamb would prove his judgment if he took that one.

He found a soft place in the grass, and arranged himself comfortably. He watched the lights in the windows.

III

It seemed to Peter Washington that the Bryants absolutely consulted their own wishes in regard to the time for retiring; but at last he saw the lighted windows fade briskly from left to right, and after a moment a window on the second floor blazed out against the darkness. Si was going to bed. In five minutes this window abruptly vanished, and all the world was night.

Peter spent the ensuing quarter-hour in no mental debate. His mind was fixed. He was here, and the melon was there. He would have it. But an idea of being caught appalled him. He thought of his position. He was the beau of his community, honored right and left. He pictured the consternation of his friends and the cheers of his enemies if the hands of the redoubtable Si Bryant should grip him in his shame.

He arose, and going to the fence, listened. No sound broke the stillness, save the rhythmical incessant clicking of myriad insects, and the guttural chanting of the frogs in the reeds at the lake-side. Moved by sudden decision, he climbed the fence and crept silently and swiftly down upon the melon. His open knife was in his hand. There was the melon, cool, fair to see, as pompous in its fatness as the cook in a monastery.

Peter put out a hand to steady it while he cut the stem. But at the instant he was aware that a black form had dropped over the fence lining the lane in front of him and was coming stealthily towards him. In a palsy of terror he dropped flat upon the ground, not having strength enough to run away. The next moment he was looking into the amazed and agonized face of old Alek Williams.

There was a moment of loaded silence, and then Peter was overcome by a mad inspiration. He suddenly dropped his knife and leaped upon Alek. "I got che!" he hissed. "I got che! I got che!" The old man sank down as limp as rags. "I got che! I got che! Steal Mist' Bryant's mellums, hey?"

Alek, in a low voice, began to beg. "Oh, Mist' Peter Wash'ton, don' go fer ter be too ha'd on er ole man! I nev' come yere fer ter steal 'em. 'Deed

I didn't, Mist' Wash'ton! I come yere jes fer ter *feel* 'em. Oh, please, Mist' Wash'ton—"

"Come erlong outa yere, you ol' rip," said Peter, "an' don' trumple on dese yer baids. I gwine put you wah you won' ketch col'."

Without difficulty he tumbled the whining Alek over the fence to the roadway, and followed him with sheriff-like expedition! He took him by the scruff. "Come erlong, deacon. I raikon I gwine put you wah you kin pray, deacon. Come erlong, deacon."

The emphasis and reiteration of his layman's title in the church produced a deadly effect upon Alek. He felt to his marrow the heinous crime into which this treacherous night had betrayed him. As Peter marched his prisoner up the road towards the mouth of the lane, he continued his remarks: "Come erlong, deacon. Nev' see er man so anxious like erbout er mellum-paitch, deacon. Seem like you jes must see'em er-growin' an' *feel* 'em, deacon. Mist' Bryant he'll be s'prised, deacon, findin' out you come fer ter *feel* his mellums. Come erlong, deacon. Mist' Bryant he expectin' some ole rip like you come soon."

They had almost reached the lane when Alek's cur Susie, who had followed her master, approached in the silence which attends dangerous dogs; and seeing indications of what she took to be war, she appended herself swiftly but firmly to the calf of Peter's left leg. The mêlée was short, but spirited. Alek had no wish to have his dog complicate his already serious misfortunes, and went manfully to the defence of his captor. He procured a large stone, and by beating this with both hands down upon the resounding skull of the animal, he induced her to quit her grip. Breathing heavily, Peter dropped into the long grass at the road-side. He said nothing.

"Mist' Wash'ton," said Alek at last, in a quavering voice, "I raikon I gwine wait yere see what you gwine do ter me."

Whereupon Peter passed into a spasmodic state, in which he rolled to and fro and shook.

"Mist' Wash'ton, I hope dish yer dog 'ain't gone an' give you fitses?"

Peter sat up suddenly. "No, she 'ain't," he answered; "but she gin me er big skeer; an' fer yer 'sistance with er cobblestone, Mist' Willums, I tell you what I gwine do—I tell you what I gwine do." He waited an impressive moment. "I gwine 'lease you!"

Old Alek trembled like a little bush in a wind. "Mist' Wash'ton?"

Quoth Peter, deliberately, "I gwine 'lease you."

The old man was filled with a desire to negotiate this statement at once, but he felt the necessity of carrying off the event without an appearance of haste. "Yes, seh; thank 'e, seh; thank 'e, Mist' Wash'ton. I raikon I ramble home pressenly." He waited an interval, and then dubiously said, "Good-evenin', Mist' Wash'ton."

"Good-evenin', deacon. Don' come foolin' roun' *feelin'* no mellums, and I say troof. Good-evenin', deacon."

Alek took off his hat and made three profound bows. "Thank 'e, seh. Thank 'e, seh. Thank 'e, seh."

Peter underwent another severe spasm, but the old man walked off towards his home with a humble and contrite heart.

IV

The next morning Alek proceeded from his shanty under the complete but customary illusion that he was going to work. He trudged manfully along until he reached the vicinity of Si Bryant's place. Then, by stages, he relapsed into a slink. He was passing the garden-patch under full steam, when, at some distance ahead of him, he saw Si Bryant leaning casually on the garden fence.

"Good-mornin', Alek."

"Good-mawnin', Mist' Bryant," answered Alek, with a new deference. He was marching on, when he was halted by a word—"Alek!"

He stopped. "Yes, seh."

"I found a knife this mornin' in th' road," drawled Si, "an' I thought maybe it was yourn."

Improved in mind by this divergence from the direct line of attack, Alek stepped up easily to look at the knife. "No, seh," he said, scanning it as it lay in Si's palm, while the cold steel-blue eyes of the white man looked down into his stomach, "'tain't no knife er mine." But he knew the knife. He knew it as if it had been his mother. And at the same moment a spark flashed through his head and made wise his understanding. He knew everything. "'Tain't much of er knife, Mist' Bryant," he said, deprecatingly.

"'Tain't much of a knife, I know that," cried Si, in sudden heat, "but I found it this mornin' in my watermelon-patch—hear?"

"Watahmellum-paitch?" yelled Alek, not astounded.

"Yes, in my watermelon-patch," sneered Si, "an' I think you know something about it, too!"

"Me?" cried Alek. "Me?"

"Yes—you!" said Si, with icy ferocity. "Yes—you!" He had become convinced that Alek was not in any way guilty, but he was certain that the old man knew the owner of the knife, and so he pressed him at first on criminal lines. "Alek, you might as well own up now. You've been meddlin' with my watermelons!"

"Me?" cried Alek again. "Yah's *ma* knife. I done cah'e it foh yeahs."

Bryant changed his ways. "Look here, Alek," he said, confidentially: "I know you and you know me, and there ain't no use in any more skirmishin'. *I* know that *you* know whose knife that is. Now whose is it?"

This challenge was so formidable in character that Alek temporarily quailed and began to stammer. "Er—now—Mist' Bryant—you—you—frien' er mine—"

"I know I'm a friend of yours, but," said Bryant, inexorably, "who owns this knife?"

118

Alek gathered unto himself some remnants of dignity and spoke with reproach: "Mist' Bryant, dish yer knife ain' mine."

"No," said Bryant, "it ain't. But you know who it belongs to, an' I want you to tell me—quick."

"Well, Mist' Bryant," answered Alek, scratching his wool, "I won't say 's I *do* know who b'longs ter dish yer knife, an' I won't say 's I *don't*."

Bryant again laughed his Yankee laugh, but this time there was little humor in it. It was dangerous.

Alek, seeing that he had gotten himself into hot water by the fine diplomacy of his last sentence, immediately began to flounder and totally submerge himself. "No, Mist' Bryant," he repeated, "I won't say 's I *do* know who b'longs ter dish yer knife, an' I won't say 's I *don't*." And he began to parrot this fatal sentence again and again. It seemed wound about his tongue. He could not rid himself of it. Its very power to make trouble for him seemed to originate the mysterious Afric reason for its repetition.

"Is he a very close friend of yourn?" said Bryant, softly.

"F-frien'?" stuttered Alek. He appeared to weigh this question with much care. "Well, seems like he *was* er frien', an' then agin, it seems like he—"

"It seems like he *wasn't*?" asked Bryant.

"Yes, seh, jest so, jest so," cried Alek. "Sometimes it seems like he wasn't. Then agin—" He stopped for profound meditation.

The patience of the white man seemed inexhaustible. At length his low and oily voice broke the stillness. "Oh, well, of course if he's a friend of yourn, Alek! You know I wouldn't want to make no trouble for a friend of yourn."

"Yes, seh," cried the negro at once. "He's er frien' er mine. He is dat."

"Well, then, it seems as if about the only thing to do is for you to tell me his name so's I can send him his knife, and that's all there is to it."

Alek took off his hat, and in perplexity ran his hand over his wool. He studied the ground. But several times he raised his eyes to take a sly peep at the imperturbable visage of the white man. "Y—y—yes, Mist' Bryant. ...I raikon dat's erbout all what kin be done. I gwine tell you who b'longs ter dish yer knife."

"Of course," said the smooth Bryant, "it ain't a very nice thing to have to do, but—"

"No, seh," cried Alek, brightly; "I'm gwine tell you, Mist' Bryant. I gwine tell you erbout dat knife. Mist' Bryant," he asked, solemnly, "does you know who b'longs ter dat knife?"

"No, I—"

"Well, I gwine tell. I gwine tell who, Mr Bryant—" The old man drew himself to a stately pose and held forth his arm. "I gwine tell who, Mist' Bryant, *dish yer knife b'longs ter Sam Jackson!*"

Bryant *was* startled into indignation. "Who in hell is Sam Jackson?" he growled.

"He's a nigger," said Alek, impressively, "and he wuks in er lumber-yawd up yere in Hoswego."

IX. THE STOVE

I

THEY'LL bring her," said Mrs. Trescott, dubiously. Her cousin, the painter, the bewildered father of the angel child, had written to say that if they were asked, he and his wife would come to the Trescotts for the Christmas holidays. But he had not officially stated that the angel child would form part of the expedition. "But of course they'll bring her," said Mrs. Trescott to her husband.

The doctor assented. "Yes, they'll have to bring her. They wouldn't dare leave New York at her mercy."

"Well," sighed Mrs. Trescott, after a pause, "the neighbors will be pleased. When they see her they'll immediately lock up their children for safety."

"Anyhow," said Trescott, "the devastation of the Margate twins was complete. She can't do that particular thing again. I shall be interested to note what form her energy will take this time."

"Oh yes! that's it!" cried the wife. "You'll be interested. You've hit it exactly. You'll be interested to note what form her energy will take this time. And then, when the real crisis comes, you'll put on your hat and walk out of the house and leave me to straighten things out. This is not a scientific question; this is a practical matter."

"Well, as a practical man, I advocate chaining her out in the stable," answered the doctor.

When Jimmie Trescott was told that his old flame was again to appear, he remained calm. In fact, time had so mended his youthful heart that it was a regular apple of oblivion and peace. Her image in his thought was as the track of a bird on deep snow—it was an impression, but it did not concern the depths. However, he did what befitted his state. He went out and bragged in the street: "My cousin is comin' next week f'om New York." ..."My cousin is comin' to-morrow f'om New York."

"Girl or boy?" said the populace, bluntly; but, when enlightened, they speedily cried, "Oh, we remember *her!*" They were charmed, for they thought of her as an outlaw, and they surmised that she could lead them into a very ecstasy of sin. They thought of her as a brave bandit, because they had been whipped for various pranks into which she had led them. When Jimmie made his declaration, they fell into a state of pleased and shuddering expectancy.

Mrs. Trescott pronounced her point of view: "The child is a nice child, if only Caroline had some sense. But she hasn't. And Willis is like a wax figure. I don't see what can be done, unless—unless you simply go to Willis and put the whole thing right at him." Then, for purposes of indication, she improvised a speech: "Look here, Willis, you've got a little daughter, haven't you? But, confound it, man, she is not the only girl child ever brought into the sunlight. There are a lot of children. Children are an ordinary phenomenon. In China they drown girl babies. If you wish to submit to this frightful impostor and tyrant, that is all very well, but why in the name of humanity do you make us submit to it?"

Doctor Trescott laughed. "I wouldn't dare say it to him."

"Anyhow," said Mrs. Trescott, determinedly, "that is what you *should* say to him."

"It wouldn't do the slightest good. It would only make him very angry, and I would lay myself perfectly open to a suggestion that I had better attend to my own affairs with more rigor."

"Well, I suppose you are right," Mrs. Trescott again said.

"Why don't you speak to Caroline?" asked the doctor, humorously.

"Speak to Caroline! Why, I wouldn't for the *world*! She'd fly through the roof. She'd snap my head off! Speak to Caroline! You must be mad!"

One afternoon the doctor went to await his visitors on the platform of the railway station. He was thoughtfully smiling. For some quaint reason he was convinced that he was to be treated to a quick manifestation of little Cora's peculiar and interesting powers. And yet, when the train paused at the station, there appeared to him only a pretty little girl in a fur-lined hood, and with her nose reddening from the sudden cold, and—attended respectfully by her parents. He smiled again, reflecting that he had comically exaggerated the dangers of dear little Cora. It amused his philosophy to note that he had really been perturbed.

As the big sleigh sped homeward there was a sudden shrill outcry from the angel child: "Oh, mamma! mamma! They've forgotten my stove!"

"Hush, dear; hush!" said the mother. "It's all right."

"Oh, but, mamma, they've forgotten my stove!"

The doctor thrust his chin suddenly out of his top-coat collar. "Stove?" he said. "Stove? What stove?"

"Oh, just a toy of the child's," explained the mother. "She's grown so fond of it, she loves it so, that if we didn't take it everywhere with her she'd suffer dreadfully. So we always bring it."

"Oh!" said the doctor. He pictured a little tin trinket. But when the stove was really unmasked, it turned out to be an affair of cast iron, as big as a portmanteau, and, as the stage people say, practicable. There was some trouble that evening when came the hour of children's bedtime. Little Cora burst into a wild declaration that she could not retire for the night unless the stove was carried up-stairs and placed, at her bedside. While the mother was trying to dissuade the child, the Trescott's held their peace and gazed with awe. The incident closed when the lamb-eyed father gathered the stove in his arms and preceded the angel child to her chamber.

In the morning, Trescott was standing with his back to the dining room fire, awaiting breakfast, when he heard a noise of descending guests. Presently the door opened, and the party entered in regular order. First came the angel child, then the cooing mother, and last the great painter with his arm full of the stove. He deposited it gently in a corner, and sighed. Trescott wore a wide grin.

"What are you carting that thing all over the house for?" he said, brutally. "Why don't you put it some place where she can play with it, and leave it there?"

The mother rebuked him with a look. "Well, if it gives her pleasure, Ned?" she expostulated, softly. "If it makes the child happy to have the stove with her, why shouldn't she have it?"

"Just so," said the doctor, with calmness.

Jimmie's idea was the roaring fireplace in the cabin of the lone mountaineer. At first he was not able to admire a girl's stove built on well-known domestic lines. He eyed it and thought it was very pretty, but it did not move him immediately. But a certain respect grew to an interest, and he became the angel child's accomplice. And even if he had not

had an interest grow upon him, he was certain to have been implicated sooner or later, because of the imperious way of little Cora, who made a serf of him in a few swift sentences. Together they carried the stove out into the desolate garden and squatted it in the snow. Jimmie's snug little muscles had been pitted against the sheer nervous vigor of this little golden-haired girl, and he had not won great honors. When the mind blazed inside the small body, the angel child was pure force. She began to speak: "Now, Jim, get some paper. Get some wood-little sticks at first. Now we want a match. You got a match? Well, go get a match. Get some more wood. Hurry up, now! No. *No!* I'll light it my own self. You get some more wood. There! Isn't that splendid? You get a whole lot of wood an' pile it up here by the stove. An' now what'll we cook? We must have somethin' to cook, you know, else it ain't like the real."

"Potatoes," said Jimmie, at once.

The day was clear, cold, bright. An icy wind sped from over the waters of the lake. A grown person would hardly have been abroad save on compulsion of a kind, and yet, when they were called to luncheon, the two little simpletons protested with great cries.

II

The ladies of Whilomville were somewhat given to the pagan habit of tea parties. When a tea party was to befall a certain house one could read it in the manner of the prospective hostess, who for some previous days would go about twitching this and twisting that, and dusting here and polishing there; the ordinary habits of the household began then to disagree with her, and her unfortunate husband and children fled to the lengths of their tethers. Then there was a hush. Then there was a tea party. On the fatal afternoon a small picked company of latent enemies would meet. There would be a fanfare of affectionate greetings, during which everybody would measure to an inch the importance of what everybody else was wearing. Those who wore old dresses would wish then that they had not come; and those who saw that, in the company, they were well clad, would be pleased or exalted, or filled with the joys of cruelty. Then they had tea, which was a habit and a delight with none of them, their usual beverage being coffee with milk.

Usually the party jerked horribly in the beginning, while the hostess strove and pulled and pushed to make its progress smooth. Then suddenly it would be off like the wind, eight, fifteen, or twenty-five tongues clattering, with a noise like a cotton-mill combined with the noise of a few penny whistles. Then the hostess had nothing to do but to look glad, and see that everybody had enough tea and cake. When the door was closed behind the last guest, the hostess would usually drop into a chair and say: "Thank Heaven! They're gone!" There would be no malice in this expression. It simply would be that, womanlike, she had flung herself headlong at the accomplishment of a pleasure which she could not even define, and at the end she felt only weariness.

The value and beauty, or oddity, of the tea-cups was another element which entered largely into the spirit of these terrible enterprises. The quality of the tea was an element which did not enter at all. Uniformly it was rather bad. But the cups! Some of the more ambitious people aspired to have cups each of a different pattern, possessing, in fact, the sole similarity that with their odd curves and dips of form they each resembled anything but a teacup. Others of the more ambitious aspired to a quite severe and godly "set," which, when viewed, appalled one with its austere and rigid family resemblances, and made one desire to ask the hostess if the teapot was not the father of all the little cups, and at the same time protesting gallantly that such a young and charming cream-jug surely could not be their mother.

But of course the serious part is that these collections so differed in style and the obvious amount paid for them that nobody could be happy. The poorer ones envied; the richer ones feared; the poorer ones continually striving to overtake the leaders; the leaders always with their heads turned back to hear overtaking footsteps. And none of these things here written did they know. Instead of seeing that they were very stupid, they thought they were very fine. And they gave and took heart-bruises—fierce, deep heart-bruises—under the clear impression that of such kind of rubbish was the kingdom of nice people. The characteristics of outsiders of course emerged in shreds from these tea parties, and it is doubtful if the characteristics of insiders escaped entirely. In fact, these tea parties were in the large way the result of a conspiracy of certain unenlightened people to make life still more uncomfortable.

Mrs. Trescott was in the circle of tea-fighters largely through a sort of artificial necessity—a necessity, in short, which she had herself created in a spirit of femininity.

When the painter and his family came for the holidays, Mrs. Trescott had for some time been feeling that it was her turn to give a tea party, and she was resolved upon it now that she was reinforced by the beautiful wife of the painter, whose charms would make all the other women feel badly. And Mrs. Trescott further resolved that the affair should be notable in more than one way. The painter's wife suggested that, as an innovation, they give the people good tea; but Mrs. Trescott shook her head; she was quite sure they would not like it.

It was an impressive gathering. A few came to see if they could not find out the faults of the painter's wife, and these, added to those who would have attended even without that attractive prospect, swelled the company to a number quite large for Whilomville. There were the usual preliminary jolts, and then suddenly the tea party was in full swing, and looked like an unprecedented success.

Mrs. Trescott exchanged a glance with the painter's wife. They felt proud and superior. This tea party was almost perfection.

III

Jimmie and the angel child, after being oppressed by innumerable admonitions to behave correctly during the afternoon, succeeded in reaching the garden, where the stove awaited them. They were enjoying themselves grandly, when snow began to fall so heavily that it gradually dampened their ardor as well as extinguished the fire in the stove. They stood ruefully until the angel child devised the plan of carrying the stove into the stable, and there, safe from the storm, to continue the festivities. But they were met at the door of the stable by Peter Washington.

"What you 'bout, Jim?"

"Now—it's snowin' so hard, we thought we'd take the stove into the stable."

"An' have er fiah in it? No, seh! G'w'on 'way f'm heh!—g'w'on! Don' 'low no sech foolishin' round yer. No, seh!"

"Well, we ain't goin' to hurt your old stable, are we?" asked Jimmie, ironically.

"Dat you ain't, Jim! Not so long's I keep my two eyes right plumb squaah pinted at ol' Jim. No, seh!" Peter began to chuckle in derision.

The two vagabonds stood before him while he informed them of their iniquities as well as their absurdities, and further made clear his own masterly grasp of the spirit of their devices. Nothing affects children so much as rhetoric. It may not involve any definite presentation of common-sense, but if it is picturesque they surrender decently to its influence. Peter was by all means a rhetorician, and it was not long before the two children had dismally succumbed to him. They went away.

Depositing the stove in the snow, they straightened to look at each other. It did not enter either head to relinquish the idea of continuing the game. But the situation seemed invulnerable.

The angel child went on a scouting tour. Presently she returned, flying. "I know! Let's have it in the cellar! In the cellar! Oh, it'll be lovely!"

The outer door of the cellar was open, and they proceeded down some steps with their treasure. There was plenty of light; the cellar was high-walled, warm, and dry. They named it an ideal place. Two huge cylindrical furnaces were humming away, one at either end. Overhead the beams detonated with the different emotions which agitated the tea party.

Jimmie worked like a stoker, and soon there was a fine bright fire in the stove. The fuel was of small brittle sticks which did not make a great deal of smoke.

"Now what'll we cook?" cried little Cora. "What'll we cook, Jim? We must have something to cook, you know."

"Potatoes?" said Jimmie.

But the angel child made a scornful gesture. "No. I've cooked 'bout a million potatoes, I guess. Potatoes aren't nice any more."

Jimmie's mind was all said and done when the question of potatoes had been passed, and he looked weakly at his companion.

"Haven't you got any turnips in your house?" she inquired, contemptuously. "In my house we have *turnips*."

"Oh, turnips!" exclaimed Jimmie, immensely relieved to find that the honor of his family was safe. "Turnips? Oh, bushels an' bushels an' bushels! Out in the shed."

"Well, go an' get a whole lot," commanded the angel child. "Go an' get a whole lot. Grea' big ones. *We* always have grea' big ones."

Jimmie went to the shed and kicked gently at a company of turnips which the frost had amalgamated. He made three journeys to and from the cellar, carrying always the very largest types from his father's store. Four of them filled the oven of little Cora's stove. This fact did not please her, so they placed three rows of turnips on the hot top. Then the angel child, profoundly moved by an inspiration, suddenly cried out,

"Oh, Jimmie, let's play we're keepin' a hotel, an' have got to cook for 'bout a thousand people, an' those two furnaces will be the ovens, an' I'll be the chief cook—"

"No; I want to be chief cook some of the time," interrupted Jimmie.

"No; I'll be chief cook my own self. You must be my 'sistant. Now I'll prepare 'em—see? An' then you put 'em in the ovens. Get the shovel. We'll play that's the pan. I'll fix 'em, an' then you put 'em in the oven. Hold it still now."

Jim held the coal-shovel while little Cora, with a frown of importance, arranged turnips in rows upon it. She patted each one daintily, and then backed away to view it, with her head critically sideways.

"There!" she shouted at last. "That'll do, I guess. Put 'em in the oven."

Jimmie marched with his shovelful of turnips to one of the furnaces. The door was already open, and he slid the shovel in upon the red coals.

"Come on," cried little Cora. "I've got another batch nearly ready."

"But what am I goin' to do with these?" asked Jimmie. "There ain't only one shovel."

"Leave 'm in there," retorted the girl, passionately. "Leave 'm in there, an' then play you're comin' with another pan. 'Tain't right to stand there an' *hold* the pan, you goose."

So Jimmie expelled all his turnips from his shovel out upon the furnace fire, and returned obediently for another batch.

"These are puddings," yelled the angel child, gleefully. "Dozens an' dozens of puddings for the thousand people at our grea' big hotel."

129

IV

At the first alarm the painter had fled to the doctor's office, where he hid his face behind a book and pretended that he did not hear the noise of feminine revelling. When the doctor came from a round of calls, he too retreated upon the office, and the men consoled each other as well as they were able. Once Mrs. Trescott dashed in to say delightedly that her tea party was not only the success of the season, but it was probably the very nicest tea party that had ever been held in Whilomville. After vainly beseeching them to return with her, she dashed away again, her face bright with happiness.

The doctor and the painter remained for a long time in silence, Trescott tapping reflectively upon the window-pane. Finally he turned to the painter, and sniffing, said: "What is that, Willis? Don't you smell something?"

The painter also sniffed. "Why, yes! It's like—it's like turnips."

"Turnips? No; it can't be."

"Well, it's very much like it."

The puzzled doctor opened the door into the hall, and at first it appeared that he was going to give back two paces. A result of frizzling turnips, which was almost as tangible as mist, had blown in upon his face and made him gasp. "Good God! Willis, what can this be?" he cried.

"Whee!" said the painter. "It's awful, isn't it?"

The doctor made his way hurriedly to his wife, but before he could speak with her he had to endure the business of greeting a score of women. Then he whispered, "Out in the hall there's an awful—"

But at that moment it came to them on the wings of a sudden draught. The solemn odor of burning turnips rolled in like a sea-fog, and fell upon that dainty, perfumed tea party. It was almost a personality; if some unbidden and extremely odious guest had entered the room, the effect would have been much the same. The sprightly talk stopped with a jolt, and people looked at each other. Then a few brave and considerate persons made the usual attempt to talk away as if nothing had happened. They all looked at their hostess, who wore an air of stupefaction.

The odor of burning turnips grew and grew. To Trescott it seemed to make a noise. He thought he could hear the dull roar of this outrage. Under some circumstances he might have been able to take the situation from a point of view of comedy, but the agony of his wife was too acute, and, for him, too visible. She was saying: "Yes, we saw the play the last time we were in New York. I liked it very much. That scene in the second act—the gloomy church, you know, and all that—and the organ playing—and then when the four singing little girls came in—" But Trescott comprehended that she did not know if she was talking of a play or a parachute.

He had not been in the room twenty seconds before his brow suddenly flushed with an angry inspiration. He left the room hastily, leaving behind him an incoherent phrase of apology, and charged upon his office, where he found the painter somnolent.

"Willis!" he cried, sternly, "come with me. It's that damn kid of yours!"

The painter was immediately agitated. He always seemed to feel more than any one else in the world the peculiar ability of his child to create resounding excitement, but he seemed always to exhibit his feelings very late. He arose hastily, and hurried after Trescott to the top of the inside cellar stairway. Trescott motioned him to pause, and for an instant they listened.

"Hurry up, Jim," cried the busy little Cora. "Here's another whole batch of lovely puddings. Hurry up now, an' put 'em in the oven."

Trescott looked at the painter; the painter groaned. Then they appeared violently in the middle of the great kitchen of the hotel with a thousand people in it. "Jimmie, go up-stairs!" said Trescott, and then he turned to watch the painter deal with the angel child.

With some imitation of wrath, the painter stalked to his daughter's side and grasped her by the arm.

"Oh, papa! papa!" she screamed. "You're pinching me! You're pinching me! You're pinching me, papa!"

At first the painter had seemed resolved to keep his grip, but suddenly he let go her arm in a panic. "I've hurt her," he said, turning to Trescott.

Trescott had swiftly done much towards the obliteration of the hotel kitchen, but he looked up now and spoke, after a short period of reflection. "You've hurt her, have you? Well, hurt her again. Spank her!" he cried, enthusiastically. "Spank her, confound you, man! She needs it. Here's your chance. Spank her, and spank her good. Spank her!"

The painter naturally wavered over this incendiary proposition, but at last, in one supreme burst of daring, he shut his eyes and again grabbed his precious offspring.

The spanking was lamentably the work of a perfect bungler. It couldn't have hurt at all; but the angel child raised to heaven a loud, clear soprano howl that expressed the last word in even mediæval anguish. Soon the painter was aghast. "Stop it, darling! I didn't mean—I didn't mean to—to hurt you so much, you know." He danced nervously. Trescott sat on a box, and devilishly smiled.

But the pasture call of suffering motherhood came down to them, and a moment later a splendid apparition appeared on the cellar stairs. She understood the scene at a glance. "Willis! What have you been doing?"

Trescott sat on his box, the painter guiltily moved from foot to foot, and the angel child advanced to her mother with arms outstretched, making a piteous wail of amazed and pained pride that would have moved Peter the Great. Regardless of her frock, the panting mother knelt on the stone floor and took her child to her bosom, and looked, then, bitterly, scornfully, at the cowering father and husband.

The painter, for his part, at once looked reproachfully at Trescott, as if to say: "There! You see?"

Trescott arose and extended his hands in a quiet but magnificent gesture

132

of despair and weariness. He seemed about to say something classic, and, quite instinctively, they waited. The stillness was deep, and the wait was longer than a moment. "Well," he said, "we can't live in the cellar. Let's go up-stairs."

X. THE TRIAL, EXECUTION, AND BURIAL OF HOMER PHELPS

FROM time to time an enwearied pine bough let fall to the earth its load of melting snow, and the branch swung back glistening in the faint wintry sunlight. Down the gulch a brook clattered amid its ice with the sound of a perpetual breaking of glass. All the forest looked drenched and forlorn.

The sky-line was a ragged enclosure of gray cliffs and hemlocks and pines. If one had been miraculously set down in this gulch one could have imagined easily that the nearest human habitation was hundreds of miles away, if it were not for an old half-discernible wood-road that led towards the brook.

"Halt! Who's there?"

This low and gruff cry suddenly dispelled the stillness which lay upon the lonely gulch, but the hush which followed it seemed even more profound. The hush endured for some seconds, and then the voice of the challenger was again raised, this time with a distinctly querulous note in it.

"Halt! Who's there? Why don't you answer when I holler? Don't you know you're likely to get shot?"

A second voice answered, "Oh, you knew who I was easy enough."

"That don't make no diff'rence." One of the Margate twins stepped from a thicket and confronted Homer Phelps on the old wood-road. The majestic scowl of official wrath was upon the brow of Reeves Margate, a long stick was held in the hollow of his arm as one would hold a rifle, and he strode grimly to the other boy. "That don't make no diff'rence. You've got to answer when I holler, anyhow. Willie says so."

At the mention of the dread chieftain's name the Phelps boy daunted a trifle, but he still sulkily murmured, "Well, you knew it was me."

He started on his way through the snow, but the twin sturdily blocked the path. "You can't pass less'n you give the countersign."

"Huh?" said the Phelps boy. "Countersign?"

"Yes—countersign," sneered the twin, strong in his sense of virtue.

But the Phelps boy became very angry. "Can't I, hey? Can't I, hey? I'll show you whether I can or not! I'll show you, Reeves Margate!"

There was a short scuffle, and then arose the anguished clamor of the sentry: "Hey, fellers! Here's a man tryin' to run a-past the guard. Hey, fellers! Hey!"

There was a great noise in the adjacent underbrush. The voice of Willie could be heard exhorting his followers to charge swiftly and bravely. Then they appeared—Willie Dalzel, Jimmie Trescott, the other Margate twin, and Dan Earl. The chieftain's face was dark with wrath. "What's the matter? Can't you play it right? 'Ain't you got any sense?" he asked the Phelps boy.

The sentry was yelling out his grievance. "Now—he came along an' I hollered at 'im, an' he didn't pay no 'tention, an' when I ast 'im for the countersign, he wouldn't say nothin'. That ain't no way."

"Can't you play it right?" asked the chief again, with gloomy scorn.

"He knew it was me easy enough," said the Phelps boy.

"That 'ain't got nothin' to do with it," cried the chief, furiously. "That 'ain't got nothin' to do with it. If you're goin' to play, you've got to play it right. It ain't no fun if you go spoilin' the whole thing this way. Can't you play it right?"

"I forgot the countersign," lied the culprit, weakly.

Whereupon the remainder of the band yelled out, with one triumphant voice: "War to the knife! War to the knife! I remember it, Willie. Don't I, Willie?"

The leader was puzzled. Evidently he was trying to develop in his mind a plan for dealing correctly with this unusual incident. He felt, no doubt, that he must proceed according to the books, but unfortunately the books did not cover the point precisely. However, he finally said to Homer Phelps, "You are under arrest." Then with a stentorian voice he shouted, "Seize him!"

His loyal followers looked startled for a brief moment, but directly they began to move upon the Phelps boy. The latter clearly did not intend to be seized. He backed away, expostulating wildly. He even seemed somewhat frightened. "No, no; don't you touch me, I tell you; don't you dare touch me."

The others did not seem anxious to engage. They moved slowly, watching the desperate light in his eyes. The chieftain stood with folded arms, his face growing darker and darker with impatience. At length he burst out: "Oh, seize him, I tell you! Why don't you seize him? Grab him by the leg, Dannie! Hurry up, all of you! Seize him, I keep a-say-in'!"

Thus adjured, the Margate twins and Dan Earl made another pained effort, while Jimmie Trescott manœuvred to cut off a retreat. But, to tell the truth, there was a boyish law which held them back from laying hands of violence upon little Phelps under these conditions. Perhaps it was because they were only playing, whereas he was now undeniably serious. At any rate, they looked very sick of their occupation.

"Don't you dare!" snarled the Phelps boy, facing first one and then the other; he was almost in tears—"don't you dare touch me!"

The chieftain was now hopping with exasperation. "Oh, seize him, can't you? You're no good at all!" Then he loosed his wrath upon the Phelps boy: "Stand still, Homer, can't you? You've got to be seized, you know. That ain't the way. It ain't any fun if you keep a-dodgin' that way. Stand still, can't you! You've got to be seized."

"I don't want to be seized," retorted the Phelps boy, obstinate and bitter.

"But you've *got* to be seized!" yelled the maddened chief. "Don't you see? That's the way to play it."

The Phelps boy answered, promptly, "But I don't want to play that way."

"But that's the *right* way to play it. Don't you see? You've got to play it the right way. You've got to be seized, an' then we'll hold a trial on you, an'— an' all sorts of things."

But this prospect held no illusions for the Phelps boy. He continued doggedly to repeat, "I don't want to play that way!"

Of course in the end the chief stooped to beg and beseech this unreasonable lad. "Oh, come on, Homer! Don't be so mean. You're a-spoilin' everything. We won't hurt you any. Not the tintiest bit. It's all just playin'. What's the matter with you?"

The different tone of the leader made an immediate impression upon the other. He showed some signs of the beginning of weakness. "Well," he asked, "what you goin' to do?"

"Why, first we're goin' to put you in a dungeon, or tie you to a stake, or something like that—just pertend, you know," added the chief, hurriedly, "an' then we'll hold a trial, awful solemn, but there won't be anything what'll hurt you. Not a thing."

And so the game was readjusted. The Phelps boy was marched off between Dan Earl and a Margate twin. The party proceeded to their camp, which was hidden some hundred feet back in the thickets. There was a miserable little hut with a pine-bark roof, which so frankly and constantly leaked that existence in the open air was always preferable. At present it was noisily dripping melted snow into the black mouldy interior. In front of this hut a feeble fire was flickering through its unhappy career. Underfoot, the watery snow was of the color of lead.

The party having arrived at the camp, the chief leaned against a tree, and balancing on one foot, drew off a rubber boot. From this boot he emptied about a quart of snow. He squeezed his stocking, which had a hole from which protruded a lobster-red toe. He resumed his boot. "Bring up the prisoner," said he. They did it. "Guilty or not guilty?" he asked.

"Huh?" said the Phelps boy.

"Guilty or not guilty?" demanded the chief,

peremptorily. "Guilty or not guilty? Don't you understand?"

Homer Phelps looked profoundly puzzled. "Guilty or not guilty?" he asked, slowly and weakly.

The chief made a swift gesture, and turned in despair to the others. "Oh,

137

he don't do it right! He does it all wrong!" He again faced the prisoner with an air of making a last attempt, "Now look-a-here, Homer, when I say, 'Guilty or not guilty?' you want to up an' say, 'Not Guilty.' Don't you see?"

"Not guilty," said Homer, at once.

"No, no, no. Wait till I ask you. Now wait." He called out, pompously, "Pards, if this prisoner before us is guilty, what shall be his fate?"

All those well-trained little infants with one voice sung out, "*Death!*"

"Prisoner," continued the chief, "are you guilty or not guilty?"

"But look-a-here," argued Homer, "you said it wouldn't be nothin' that would hurt. I—"

"Thunder an' lightnin'!" roared the wretched chief. "Keep your mouth shut, can't ye? What in the mischief—"

But there was an interruption from Jimmie Trescott, who shouldered a twin aside and stepped to the front. "Here," he said, very contemptuously, "let me be the prisoner. I'll show 'im how to do it."

"All right, Jim," cried the chief, delighted; "you be the prisoner, then. Now all you fellers with guns stand there in a row! Get out of the way, Homer!" He cleared his throat, and addressed Jimmie. "Prisoner, are you guilty or not guilty?"

"Not guilty," answered Jimmie, firmly. Standing there before his judge— unarmed, slim, quiet, modest—he was ideal.

The chief beamed upon him, and looked aside to cast a triumphant and withering glance upon Homer Phelps. He said: "There! That's the way to do it."

The twins and Dan Earl also much admired Jimmie.

"That's all right so far, anyhow," said the satisfied chief. "An' now we'll— now we'll—we'll perceed with the execution."

"That ain't right," said the new prisoner, suddenly. "That ain't the next thing. You've got to have a trial first. You've got to fetch up a lot of people first who'll say I done it."

"That's so," said the chief. "I didn't think. Here, Reeves, you be first witness. Did the prisoner do it?"

The twin gulped for a moment in his anxiety to make the proper reply. He was at the point where the roads forked. Finally he hazarded, "Yes."

"There," said the chief, "that's one of 'em. Now, Dan, you be a witness. Did he do it?"

Dan Earl, having before him the twin's example, did not hesitate. "Yes," he said.

"Well, then, pards, what shall be his fate?"

Again came the ringing answer, "*Death!*"

With Jimmie in the principal rôle, this drama, hidden deep in the hemlock thicket neared a kind of perfection. "You must blind-fold me," cried the condemned lad, briskly, "an' then I'll go off an' stand, an' you must all get in a row an' shoot me."

The chief gave this plan his urbane countenance, and the twins and Dan Earl were greatly pleased. They blindfolded Jimmie under his careful directions. He waded a few paces into snow, and then turned and stood with quiet dignity, awaiting his fate. The chief marshalled the twins and Dan Earl in line with their sticks. He gave the necessary commands: "Load! Ready! Aim! Fire!" At the last command the firing party all together yelled, "Bang!"

Jimmie threw his hands high, tottered in agony for a moment, and then crashed full length into the snow—into, one would think, a serious case of pneumonia. It was beautiful.

He arose almost immediately and came back to them, wondrously pleased with himself. They acclaimed him joyously.

The chief was particularly grateful. He was always trying to bring off these little romantic affairs, and it seemed, after all, that the only boy who could ever really help him was Jimmie Trescott. "There," he said to the others, "that's the way it ought to be done."

They were touched to the heart by the whole thing, and they looked at Jimmie with big, smiling eyes. Jimmie, blown out like a balloon-fish with pride of his performance, swaggered to the fire and took seat on some wet hemlock boughs. "Fetch some more wood, one of you kids," he murmured, negligently. One of the twins came fortunately upon a small cedar-tree the lower branches of which were dead and dry. An armful of these branches flung upon the sick fire soon made a high, ruddy, warm blaze, which was like an illumination in honor of Jimmie's success.

The boys sprawled about the fire and talked the regular language of the game. "Waal, pards," remarked the chief, "it's many a night we've had together here in the Rockies among the b'ars an' the Indyuns, hey?"

"Yes, pard," replied Jimmie Trescott, "I reckon you're right. Our wild, free life is—there ain't nothin' to compare with our wild, free life."

Whereupon the two lads arose and magnificently shook hands, while the others watched them in an ecstasy. "I'll allus stick by ye, pard," said Jimmie, earnestly. "When yer in trouble, don't forget that Lightnin' Lou is at yer back."

"Thanky, pard," quoth Willie Dalzel, deeply affected. "I'll not forgit it, pard. An' don't you forget, either, that Dead-shot Demon, the leader of the Red Raiders, never forgits a friend."

But Homer Phelps was having none of this great fun. Since his disgraceful refusal to be seized and executed he had been hovering unheeded on the outskirts of the band. He seemed very sorry; he cast a wistful eye at the romantic scene. He knew too well that if he went near at that particular time he would be certain to encounter a pitiless snubbing. So he vacillated modestly in the background.

At last the moment came when he dared venture near enough to the fire to gain some warmth, for he was now bitterly suffering with the cold. He sidled close to Willie Dalzel. No one heeded him. Eventually he looked at his chief, and with a bright face said,

"Now—if I was seized now to be executed, I could do it as well as Jimmie Trescott, I could."

The chief gave a crow of scorn, in which he was followed by the other'boys. "Ho!" he cried, "why didn't you do it, then? Why didn't you do it?" Homer Phelps felt upon him many pairs of disdainful eyes. He wagged his shoulders in misery.

"You're dead," said the chief, frankly. "That's what you are. We executed you, we did."

"When?" demanded the Phelps boy, with some spirit.

"Just a little while ago. Didn't we, fellers? Hey, fellers, didn't we?"

The trained chorus cried: "Yes, of course we did. You're dead, Homer. You can't play any more. You're dead."

"That wasn't me. It was Jimmie Trescott," he said, in a low and bitter voice, his eyes on the ground. He would have given the world if he could have retracted his mad refusals of the early part of the drama.

"No," said the chief, "it was you. We're playin' it was you, an' it *was* you. You're dead, you are." And seeing the cruel effect of his words, he did not refrain from administering some advice: "The next time, don't be such a chuckle-head."

Presently the camp imagined that it was attacked by Indians, and the boys dodged behind trees with their stick-rifles, shouting out, "Bang!" and encouraging each other to resist until the last. In the mean time the dead lad hovered near the fire, looking moodily at the gay and exciting scene. After the fight the gallant defenders returned one by one to the fire, where they grandly clasped hands, calling each other "old pard," and boasting of their deeds.

Parenthetically, one of the twins had an unfortunate inspiration. "I killed the Indy-un chief, fellers. Did you see me kill the Indy-un chief?"

But Willie Dalzel, his own chief, turned upon him wrathfully: "*You* didn't kill no chief. *I* killed 'im with me own hand."

"Oh!" said the twin, apologetically, at once. "It must have been some other Indy-un."

"Who's wounded?" cried Willie Dalzel. "Ain't anybody wounded?" The party professed themselves well and sound. The roving and inventive eye of the chief chanced upon Homer Phelps. "Ho! Here's a dead man! Come on, fellers, here's a dead man! We've got to bury him, you know." And at his bidding they pounced upon the dead Phelps lad. The unhappy boy saw clearly his road to rehabilitation, but mind and body revolted at the idea of burial, even as they had revolted at the thought of execution. "No!" he said, stubbornly. "No! I don't want to be buried! I don't want to be buried!"

"You've *got* to be buried!" yelled the chief, passionately. "'Tain't goin' to hurt ye, is it? Think you're made of glass? Come on, fellers, get the grave ready!"

They scattered hemlock boughs upon the snow in the form of a rectangle, and piled other boughs near at hand. The victim surveyed these preparations with a glassy eye. When all was ready, the chief turned determinedly to him: "Come on now, Homer. We've got to carry you to the grave. Get him by the legs, Jim!"

Little Phelps had now passed into that state which may be described as a curious and temporary childish fatalism. He still objected, but it was only feeble muttering, as if he did not know what he spoke. In some confusion

they carried him to the rectangle of hemlock boughs and dropped him. Then they piled other boughs upon him until he was not to be seen. The chief stepped forward to make a short address, but before proceeding with it he thought it expedient, from certain indications, to speak to the grave itself. "Lie still, can't ye? Lie still until I get through." There was a faint movement of the boughs, and then a perfect silence.

The chief took off his hat. Those who watched him could see that his face was harrowed with emotion. "Pards," he began, brokenly—"pards, we've got one more debt to pay them murderin' red-skins. Bowie-knife Joe was a brave man an' a good pard, but—he's gone now—gone." He paused for a moment, overcome, and the stillness was only broken by the deep manly grief of Jimmie Trescott.

XI. THE FIGHT

I

THE child life of the neighborhood was sometimes moved in its deeps at the sight of wagon-loads of furniture arriving in front of some house which, with closed blinds and barred doors, had been for a time a mystery, or even a fear. The boys often expressed this fear by stamping bravely and noisily on the porch of the house, and then suddenly darting away with screams of nervous laughter, as if they expected to be pursued by something uncanny. There was a group who held that the cellar of a vacant house was certainly the abode of robbers, smugglers, assassins, mysterious masked men in council about the dim rays of a candle, and possessing skulls, emblematic bloody daggers, and owls. Then, near the first of April, would come along a wagon-load of furniture, and children would assemble on the walk by the gate and make serious examination of everything that passed into the house, and taking no thought whatever of masked men.

One day it was announced in the neighborhood that a family was actually moving into the Hannigan house, next door to Dr. Trescott's. Jimmie was one of the first to be informed, and by the time some of his friends came dashing up he was versed in much.

"Any boys?" they demanded, eagerly.

"Yes," answered Jimmie, proudly. "One's a little feller, and one's most as big as me. I saw 'em, I did."

"Where are they?" asked Willie Dalzel, as if under the circumstances he could not take Jimmie's word, but must have the evidence of his senses.

"Oh, they're in there," said Jimmie, carelessly. It was evident he owned these new boys.

Willie Dalzel resented Jimmie's proprietary way.

"Ho!" he cried, scornfully. "Why don't they come out, then? Why don't they come out?"

"How d' I know?" said Jimmie.

"Well," retorted Willie Dalzel, "you seemed to know so thundering much about 'em."

At the moment a boy came strolling down the gravel walk which led from the front door to the gate. He was about the height and age of Jimmie Trescott, but he was thick through the chest and had fat legs. His face was round and rosy and plump, but his hair was curly black, and his brows were naturally darkling, so that he resembled both a pudding and a young bull.

He approached slowly the group of older inhabitants, and they had grown profoundly silent. They looked him over; he looked them over. They might have been savages observing the first white man, or white men observing the first savage. The silence held steady.

As he neared the gate the strange boy wandered off to the left in a definite way, which proved his instinct to make a circular voyage when in doubt. The motionless group stared at him. In time this unsmiling scrutiny worked upon him somewhat, and he leaned against the fence and fastidiously examined one shoe.

In the end Willie Dalzel authoritatively broke the stillness. "What's your name?" said he, gruffly.

"Johnnie Hedge 'tis," answered the new boy. Then came another great silence while Whilomville pondered this intelligence.

Again came the voice of authority—"Where'd you live b'fore?"

"Jersey City."

These two sentences completed the first section of the formal code. The second section concerned itself with the establishment of the new-comer's exact position in the neighborhood.

"I kin lick you," announced Willie Dalzel, and awaited the answer.

The Hedge boy had stared at Willie Dalzel, but he stared at him again. After a pause he said, "I know you kin."

"Well," demanded Willie, "kin *he* lick you?" And he indicated Jimmie Trescott with a sweep which announced plainly that Jimmie was the next in prowess.

Whereupon the new boy looked at Jimmie respectfully but carefully, and at length said, "I dun'no'."

This was the signal for an outburst of shrill screaming, and everybody pushed Jimmie forward. He knew what he had to say, and, as befitted the occasion, he said it fiercely: "Kin you lick me?"

The new boy also understood what he had to say, and, despite his unhappy and lonely state, he said it bravely: "Yes."

"Well," retorted Jimmie, bluntly, "come out and do it, then! Jest come out and do it!" And these words were greeted with cheers. These little rascals yelled that there should be a fight at once. They were in bliss over the prospect. "Go on, Jim! Make 'im come out. He said he could lick you. Aw-aw-aw! He said he could lick you!" There probably never was a fight among this class in Whilomville which was not the result of the goading and guying of two proud lads by a populace of urchins who simply wished to see a show.

Willie Dalzel was very busy. He turned first to the one and then to the other. "You said you could lick him. Well, why don't you come out and do it, then? You said you could lick him, didn't you?"

"Yes," answered the new boy, dogged and dubious.

Willie tried to drag Jimmie by the arm. "Aw, go on, Jimmie! You ain't afraid, are you?"

"No," said Jimmie.

The two victims opened wide eyes at each other. The fence separated them, and so it was impossible for them to immediately engage; but they seemed to understand that they were ultimately to be sacrificed to the ferocious aspirations of the other boys, and each scanned the other to learn something of his spirit. They were not angry at all. They were merely two little gladiators who were being clamorously told to hurt each other. Each displayed hesitation and doubt without displaying fear. They did not exactly understand what were their feelings, and they moodily kicked the ground and made low and sullen answers to Willie Dalzel, who worked like a circus-manager.

"Aw, go on, Jim! What's the matter with you? You ain't afraid, are you? Well, then, say something." This sentiment received more cheering from the abandoned little wretches who wished to be entertained, and in this cheering there could be heard notes of derision of Jimmie Trescott. The latter had a position to sustain; he was well known; he often bragged of his willingness and ability to thrash other boys; well, then, here was a boy of his size who said that he could not thrash him. What was he going to do about it? The crowd made these arguments very clear, and repeated them again and again.

Finally Jimmie, driven to aggression, walked close to the fence and said to the new boy, "The first time I catch you out of your own yard I'll lam the head off'n you!" This was received with wild plaudits by the Whilomville urchins.

But the new boy stepped back from the fence. He was awed by Jimmie's formidable mien. But he managed to get out a semi-defiant sentence. "Maybe you will, and maybe you won't," said he.

However, his short retreat was taken as a practical victory for Jimmie, and the boys hooted him bitterly. He remained inside the fence, swinging one foot and scowling, while Jimmie was escorted off down the street amid acclamations. The new boy turned and walked back towards the house, his face gloomy, lined deep with discouragement, as if he felt that the new environment's antagonism and palpable cruelty were sure to prove too much for him.

II

The mother of Johnnie Hedge was a widow, and the chief theory of her life was that her boy should be in school on the greatest possible number of days. He himself had no sympathy with this ambition, but she detected the truth of his diseases with an unerring eye, and he was required to be really ill before he could win the right to disregard the first bell, morning and noon. The chicken-pox and the mumps had given him vacations—vacations of misery, wherein he nearly died between pain and nursing. But bad colds in the head did nothing for him, and he was not able to invent a satisfactory hacking cough. His mother was not consistently a tartar. In most things he swayed her to his will. He was allowed to have more jam, pickles, and pie than most boys; she respected his profound loathing of Sunday-school; on summer evenings he could remain out-of-doors until 8.30; but in this matter of school she was inexorable. This single point in her character was of steel.

The Hedges arrived in Whilomville on a Saturday, and on the following Monday Johnnie wended his way to school with a note to the principal and his Jersey City school-books. He knew perfectly well that he would be told to buy new and different books, but in those days mothers always had an idea that old books would "do," and they invariably sent boys off to a new school with books which would not meet the selected and unchangeable views of the new administration. The old books never would "do." Then the boys brought them home to annoyed mothers and asked for ninety cents or sixty cents or eighty-five cents or some number of cents for another outfit. In the garret of every house holding a large family there was a collection of effete school-books, with mother rebellious because James could not inherit his books from Paul, who should properly be Peter's heir, while Peter should be a beneficiary under Henry's will.

But the matter of the books was not the measure of Johnnie Hedge's unhappiness. This whole business of changing schools was a complete torture. Alone he had to go among a new people, a new tribe, and he apprehended his serious time. There were only two fates for him. One meant victory. One meant a kind of serfdom in which he would subscribe to every word of some superior boy and support his every word. It was not anything like an English system of fagging, because boys invariably drifted into the figurative service of other boys whom they devotedly admired, and if they were obliged to subscribe to everything, it is true that they would have done so freely in any case. One means to suggest that Johnnie Hedge had to find his place. Willie Dalzel was a type of the little chieftain, and Willie was a master, but he was not a bully in a special physical sense. He did not drag little boys by the ears until they cried, nor make them tearfully fetch and carry for him. They fetched and carried, but it was because of their worship of his prowess and genius. And so all through the strata of boy life were chieftains and subchieftains and assistant subchieftains. There was no question of little Hedge being towed about by the nose; it was, as one has said, that he had to find his place in a new school. And this in itself was a problem which awed his boyish heart. He was a stranger cast away upon the moon. None knew him, understood him, felt for him. He would be surrounded for this initiative time by a horde of jackal creatures who might turn out in the end to be little boys like himself, but this last point his philosophy could not understand in its fulness.

He came to a white meeting-house sort of a place, in the squat tower of which a great bell was clanging impressively. He passed through an iron gate into a play-ground worn bare as the bed of a mountain brook by the endless runnings and scufflings of little children. There was still a half-hour before the final clangor in the squat tower, but the play-ground held a number of frolicsome imps. A loitering boy espied Johnnie Hedge, and he howled: "Oh! oh! Here's a new feller! Here's a new feller!" He advanced upon the strange arrival. "What's your name?" he demanded, belligerently, like a particularly offensive custom-house officer.

"Johnnie Hedge," responded the new-comer, shyly.

This name struck the other boy as being very comic. All new names strike boys as being comic. He laughed noisily.

"Oh, fellers, he says his name is Johnnie Hedge! Haw! haw! haw!"

The new boy felt that his name was the most disgraceful thing which had ever been attached to a human being.

"Johnnie Hedge! Haw! haw! What room you in?" said the other lad.

"I dun'no'," said Johnnie. In the mean time a small flock of interested vultures had gathered about him. The main thing was his absolute strangeness. He even would have welcomed the sight of his tormentors of Saturday; he had seen them before at least. These creatures were only so many incomprehensible problems. He diffidently began to make his way towards the main door of the school, and the other boys followed him. They demanded information.

"Are you through subtraction yet? We study jogerfre—did you, ever? You live here now? You goin' to school here now?"

To many questions he made answer as well as the clamor would permit, and at length he reached the main door and went quaking unto his new kings. As befitted them, the rabble stopped at the door. A teacher strolling along a corridor found a small boy holding in his hand a note. The boy palpably did not know what to do with the note, but the teacher knew, and took it. Thereafter this little boy was in harness.

A splendid lady in gorgeous robes gave him a seat at a double desk, at the end of which sat a hoodlum with grimy finger-nails, who eyed the inauguration with an extreme and personal curiosity. The other desks were gradually occupied by children, who first were told of the new boy, and then turned upon him a speculative and somewhat derisive eye. The school opened; little classes went forward to a position in front of the teacher's platform and tried to explain that they knew something. The new boy was not requisitioned a great deal; he was allowed to lie dormant until he became used to the scenes and until the teacher found, approximately, his mental position. In the mean time he suffered a shower of stares and whispers and giggles, as if he were a man-ape, whereas he was precisely like other children. From time to time he made funny and pathetic little overtures to other boys, but these overtures could not yet be received; he was not known; he was a foreigner. The village school was like a nation. It was tight. Its amiability or friendship must be won in certain ways.

At recess he hovered in the school-room around the weak lights of society and around the teacher, in the hope that somebody might be good to him, but none considered him save as some sort of a specimen. The teacher of course had a secondary interest in the fact that he was an additional one to a class of sixty-three.

At twelve o'clock, when the ordered files of boys and girls marched towards the door, he exhibited—to no eye—the tremblings of a coward in a charge. He exaggerated the lawlessness of the play-ground and the street.

But the reality was hard enough. A shout greeted him:

"Oh, here's the new feller! Here's the new feller!"

Small and utterly obscure boys teased him. He had a hard time of it to get to the gate. There never was any actual hurt, but everything was competent to smite the lad with shame. It was a curious, groundless shame, but nevertheless it was shame. He was a new-comer, and he definitely felt the disgrace of the fact. In the street he was seen and recognized by some lads who had formed part of the group of Saturday. They shouted:

"Oh, Jimmie! Jimmie! Here he is! Here's that new feller!"

Jimmie Trescott was going virtuously towards his luncheon when he heard these cries behind him. He pretended not to hear, and in this deception he was assisted by the fact that he was engaged at the time in a furious argument with a friend over the relative merits of two "Uncle Tom's Cabin" companies. It appeared that one company had only two bloodhounds, while the other had ten. On the other hand, the first company had two Topsys and two Uncle Toms, while the second had only one Topsy and one Uncle Tom.

But the shouting little boys were hard after him. Finally they were even pulling at his arms.

"Jimmie—"

"What?" he demanded, turning with a snarl. "What d'you want? Leggo my arm!"

"Here he is! Here's the new feller! Here's the new feller! Now!"

"I don't care if he is," said Jimmie, with grand impatience. He tilted his chin. "I don't care if he is."

150

Then they reviled him. "Thought you was goin' to lick him first time you caught him! Yah! You're a 'fraid-cat!" They began to sing "'Fraid-cat! 'Fraidcat! 'Fraid-cat!" He expostulated hotly, turning from one to the other, but they would not listen. In the mean time the Hedge boy slunk on his way, looking with deep anxiety upon this attempt to send Jimmie against him. But Jimmie would have none of the plan.

III

When the children met again on the play-ground, Jimmie was openly challenged with cowardice. He had made a big threat in the hearing of comrades, and when invited by them to take advantage of an opportunity, he had refused. They had been fairly sure of their amusement, and they were indignant. Jimmie was finally driven to declare that as soon as school was out for the day, he would thrash the Hedge boy.

When finally the children came rushing out of the iron gate, filled with the delights of freedom, a hundred boys surrounded Jimmie in high spirits, for he had said that he was determined. They waited for the lone lad from Jersey City. When he appeared, Jimmie wasted no time. He walked straight to him and said, "Did you say you kin lick me?"

Johnnie Hedge was cowed, shrinking, affrighted, and the roars of a hundred boys thundered in his ears, but again he knew what he had to say. "Yes," he gasped, in anguish.

"Then," said Jimmie, resolutely, "you've got to fight." There was a joyous clamor by the mob. The beleaguered lad looked this way and that way for succor, as Willie Dalzel and other officious youngsters policed an irregular circle in the crowd. He saw Jimmie facing him; there was no help for it; he dropped his books—the old books which would not "do."

Now it was the fashion among tiny Whilomville belligerents to fight much in the manner of little bear cubs. Two boys would rush upon each other, immediately grapple, and—the best boy having probably succeeded in getting the coveted "under hold"—there would presently be a crash to the earth of the inferior boy, and he would probably be mopped around in the dust, or the mud, or the snow, or whatever the material happened to be, until the engagement was over. Whatever havoc was dealt out to him was ordinarily the result of his wild endeavors to throw off his opponent and arise. Both infants wept during the fight, as a common thing, and if they wept very hard, the fight was a harder fight. The result was never very bloody, but the complete dishevelment of both victor and vanquished was extraordinary. As for the spectacle, it more resembled a collision of boys in a fog than it did the manly art of hammering another human being into speechless inability.

The fight began when Jimmie made a mad, bear-cub rush at the new boy, amid savage cries of encouragement. Willie Dalzel, for instance, almost howled his head off. Very timid boys on the outskirts of the throng felt their hearts leap to their throats. It was a time when certain natures were impressed that only man is vile.

But it appeared that bear-cub rushing was no part of the instruction received by boys in Jersey City. Boys in Jersey City were apparently schooled curiously. Upon the onslaught of Jimmie, the stranger had gone wild with rage—boylike. Some spark had touched his fighting-blood, and in a moment he was a cornered, desperate, fire-eyed little man. He began to swing his arms, to revolve them so swiftly that one might have considered him a small, working model of an extra-fine patented windmill which was caught in a gale. For a moment this defence surprised Jimmie more than it damaged him, but two moments later a small, knotty fist caught him squarely in the eye, and with a shriek he went down in defeat. He lay on the ground so stunned that he could not even cry; but if he had been able to cry, he would have cried over his prestige—or something—not over his eye.

There was a dreadful tumult. The boys cast glances of amazement and terror upon the victor, and thronged upon the beaten Jimmie Trescott. It was a moment of excitement so intense that one cannot say what happened. Never before had Whilomville seen such a thing—not the little tots. They were aghast, dumfounded, and they glanced often over their shoulders at the new boy, who stood alone, his clinched fists at his side, his face crimson, his lips still working with the fury of battle.

But there was another surprise for Whilomville. It might have been seen that the little victor was silently debating against an impulse.

But the impulse won, for the lone lad from Jersey City suddenly wheeled, sprang like a demon, and struck another boy.

A curtain should be drawn before this deed. A knowledge of it is really too much for the heart to bear. The other boy was Willie Dalzel. The lone lad from Jersey City had smitten him full sore.

There is little to say of it. It must have been that a feeling worked gradually to the top of the little stranger's wrath that Jimmie Trescott had been a mere tool, that the front and centre of his persecutors had been Willie Dalzel, and being rendered temporarily lawless by his fighting-blood, he raised his hand and smote for revenge.

Willie Dalzel had been in the middle of a vandal's cry, which screeched out over the voices of everybody. The new boy's fist cut it in half, so to say. And then arose the howl of an amazed and terrorized walrus.

One wishes to draw a second curtain. Without discussion or inquiry or brief retort, Willie Dalzel ran away. He ran like a hare straight for home, this redoubtable chieftain. Following him at a heavy and slow pace ran the impassioned new boy. The scene was long remembered.

Willie Dalzel was no coward; he had been panic-stricken into running away from a new thing. He ran as a man might run from the sudden appearance of a vampire or a ghoul or a gorilla. This was no time for academics—he ran.

Jimmie slowly gathered himself and came to his feet. "Where's Willie?" said he, first of all. The crowd sniggered. "Where's Willie?" said Jimmie again.

"Why, he licked him *too*!" answered a boy suddenly.

"He did?" said Jimmie. He sat weakly down on the roadway. "He did?" After allowing a moment for the fact to sink into him, he looked up at the crowd with his one good eye and his one bunged eye, and smiled cheerfully

XII. THE CITY URCHIN AND THE CHASTE VILLAGERS

AFTER the brief encounters between the Hedge boy and Jimmie Trescott and the Hedge boy and Willie Dalzel, the neighborhood which contained the homes of the boys was, as far as child life is concerned, in a state resembling anarchy. This was owing to the signal overthrow and shameful retreat of the boy who had for several years led a certain little clan by the nose. The adherence of the little community did not go necessarily to the boy who could whip all the others, but it certainly could not go to a boy who had run away in a manner that made his shame patent to the whole world. Willie Dalzel found himself in a painful position. This tiny tribe which had followed him with such unwavering faith was now largely engaged in whistling and catcalling and hooting. He chased a number of them into the sanctity of their own yards, but from these coigns they continued to ridicule him.

But it must not be supposed that the fickle tribe went over in a body to the new light. They did nothing of the sort. They occupied themselves with avenging all which they had endured—gladly enough, too—for many months. As for the Hedge boy, he maintained a curious timid reserve, minding his own business with extreme care, and going to school with that deadly punctuality of which his mother was the genius. Jimmie Trescott suffered no adverse criticism from his fellows. He was entitled to be beaten by a boy who had made Willie Dalzel bellow like a bull-calf and run away. Indeed, he received some honors. He had confronted a very superior boy and received a bang in the eye which for a time was the wonder of the children, and he had not bellowed like a bull-calf. As a matter of fact, he was often invited to tell how it had felt, and this he did with some pride, claiming arrogantly that he had been superior to any particular pain.

Early in the episode he and the Hedge boy had patched up a treaty. Living next door to each other, they could not fail to have each other often in sight. One afternoon they wandered together in the strange indefinite diplomacy of boyhood. As they drew close the new boy suddenly said, "Napple?"

"Yes," said Jimmie, and the new boy bestowed upon him an apple. It was one of those green-coated winter-apples which lie for many months in safe and dry places, and can at any time be brought forth for the persecution of the unwary and inexperienced. An older age would have fled from this apple, but to the unguided youth of Jimmie Trescott it was a thing to be possessed and cherished. Wherefore this apple was the emblem of something more than a truce, despite the fact that it tasted like wet Indian meal; and Jimmie looked at the Hedge boy out of one good eye and one bunged eye. The long-drawn animosities of men have no place in the life of a boy. The boy's mind is flexible; he readjusts his position with an ease which is derived from the fact—simply—that he is not yet a man.

But there were other and more important matters. Johnnie Hedge's exploits had brought him into such prominence among the school-boys that it was necessary to settle a number of points once and for all. There was the usual number of boys in the school who were popularly known to be champions in their various classes. Among these Johnnie Hedge now had to thread his way, every boy taking it upon himself to feel anxious that Johnnie's exact position should be soon established. His fame as a fighter had gone forth to the world, but there were other boys who had fame as fighters, and the world was extremely anxious to know where to place the new-comer. Various heroes were urged to attempt this classification. Usually it was not accounted a matter of supreme importance, but in this boy life it was essential.

In all cases the heroes were backward enough. It was their followings who agitated the question. And so Johnnie Hedge was more or less beset.

He maintained his bashfulness. He backed away from altercation. It was plain that to bring matters to a point he must be forced into a quarrel. It was also plain that the proper person for the business was some boy who could whip Willie Dalzel, and these formidable warriors were distinctly averse to undertaking the new contract. It is a kind of a law in boy life that a quiet, decent, peace-loving lad is able to thrash a wide-mouthed talker. And so it had transpired that by a peculiar system of elimination most of the real chiefs were quiet, decent, peace-loving boys, and they had no desire to engage in a fight with a boy on the sole grounds that it was not known who could whip. Johnnie Hedge attended his affairs, they attended their affairs, and around them waged this discussion of relative merit. Jimmie Trescott took a prominent part in these arguments. He contended that Johnnie Hedge could thrash any boy in the world. He was certain of it, and to any one who opposed him he said, "You just get one of those smashes in the eye, and then you'll see." In the mean time there was a grand and impressive silence in the direction of Willie Dalzel. He had gathered remnants of his clan, but the main parts of his sovereignty were scattered to the winds. He was an enemy.

Owing to the circumspect behavior of the new boy, the commotions on the school grounds came to nothing. He was often asked, "Kin you lick him?" And he invariably replied, "I dun'no'." This idea of waging battle with the entire world appalled him.

A war for complete supremacy of the tribe which had been headed by Willie Dalzel was fought out in the country of the tribe. It came to pass that a certain half-dime blood-and-thunder pamphlet had a great vogue in the tribe at this particular time. This story relates the experience of a lad who began his career as cabin-boy on a pirate ship. Throughout the first fifteen chapters he was rope's-ended from one end of the ship to the other end, and very often he was felled to the deck by a heavy fist. He lived through enough hardships to have killed a battalion of Turkish soldiers, but in the end he rose upon them. Yes, he rose upon them. Hordes of pirates fell before his intrepid arm, and in the last chapters of the book he is seen jauntily careering on his own hook as one of the most gallous pirate captains that ever sailed the seas.

Naturally, when this tale was thoroughly understood by the tribe, they had to dramatize it, although it was a dramatization that would gain no royalties for the author. Now it was plain that the urchin who was cast for the cabin-boy's part would lead a life throughout the first fifteen chapters which would attract few actors. Willie Dalzel developed a scheme by which some small lad would play cabin-boy during this period of misfortune and abuse, and then, when the cabin-boy came to the part where he slew all his enemies and reached his zenith, that he, Willie Dalzel, should take the part.

This fugitive and disconnected rendering of a great play opened in

Jimmie Trescott's back garden. The path between the two lines of gooseberry-bushes was elected unanimously to be the ship. Then Willie Dalzel insisted that Homer Phelps should be the cabin-boy. Homer tried the position for a time, and then elected that he would resign in favor of some other victim. There was no other applicant to succeed him, whereupon it became necessary to press some boy. Jimmie Trescott was a great actor, as is well known, but he steadfastly refused to engage for the part. Ultimately they seized upon little Dan Earl, whose disposition was so milky and docile that he would do whatever anybody asked of him. But Dan Earl made the one firm revolt of his life after trying existence as cabin-boy for some ten minutes. Willie Dalzel was in despair. Then he suddenly sighted the little brother of Johnnie Hedge, who had come into the garden, and in a poor-little-stranger sort of fashion was looking wistfully at the play. When he was invited to become the cabin-boy he accepted joyfully, thinking that it was his initiation into the tribe. Then they proceeded to give him the rope's end and to punch him with a realism which was not altogether painless. Directly he began to cry out. They exhorted him not to cry out, not to mind it, but still they continued to hurt him.

There was a commotion among the gooseberry-bushes, two branches were swept aside, and Johnnie Hedge walked down upon them. Every boy stopped in his tracks. Johnnie was boiling with rage.

"Who hurt him?" he said, ferociously. "Did *you*?" He had looked at Willie Dalzel.

Willie Dalzel began to mumble: "We was on'y playin'. Wasn't nothin' fer him to cry fer."

The new boy had at his command some big phrases, and he used them. "I am goin' to whip you within an inch of your life. I am goin' to tan the hide off'n you." And immediately there was a mixture—an infusion of two boys which looked as if it had been done by a chemist. The other children stood back, stricken with horror. But out of this whirl they presently perceived the figure of Willie Dalzel seated upon the chest of the Hedge boy.

"Got enough?" asked Willie, hoarsely.

"No," choked out the Hedge boy. Then there was another flapping and floundering, and finally another calm.

"Got enough?" asked Willie.

"No," said the Hedge boy. A sort of war-cloud again puzzled the sight of the observers. Both combatants were breathless, bloodless in their faces, and very weak.

"Got enough?" said Willie.

"No," said the Hedge boy. The carnage was again renewed. All the spectators were silent but Johnnie Hedge's little brother, who shrilly exhorted him to continue the struggle. But it was not plain that the Hedge boy needed any encouragement, for he was crying bitterly, and it has been explained that when a boy cried it was a bad time to hope for peace. He had managed to wriggle over upon his hands and knees. But Willie Dalzel was tenaciously gripping him from the back, and it seemed that his strength would spend itself in futility. The bear cub seemed to have the advantage of the working model of the windmill. They heaved, uttered strange words, wept, and the sun looked down upon them with steady, unwinking eye.

Peter Washington came out of the stable and observed this tragedy of the back garden. He stood transfixed for a moment, and then ran towards it, shouting: "Hi! What's all dish yere? Hi! Stopper dat, stopper dat, you two! For lan' sake, what's all dish yere?" He grabbed the struggling boys and pulled them apart. He was stormy and fine in his indignation. "For lan' sake! You two kids act like you gwine mad dogs. Stopper dat!" The whitened, tearful, soiled combatants, their clothing all awry, glared fiercely at each other as Peter stood between them, lecturing. They made several futile attempts to circumvent him and again come to battle. As he fended them off with his open hands he delivered his reproaches at Jimmie. "I's s'prised at you! I suhtainly is!"

"Why?" said Jimmie. "I 'ain't done nothin'. What have I done?"

"Y-y-you done 'courage dese yere kids ter scrap," said Peter, virtuously.

"Me?" cried Jimmie. "I 'ain't had nothin' to do with it."

"I raikon you 'ain't," retorted Peter, with heavy sarcasm. "I raikon you been er-prayin', 'ain't you?" Turning to Willie Dalzel, he said, "You jest take an' run erlong outer dish yere or I'll jest nachually take an' damnearkill you." Willie Dalzel went. To the new boy Peter said: "You look like you had some saince, but I raikon you don't know no more'n er rabbit. You jest take an' trot erlong off home, an' don' lemme caitch you round yere er-fightin' or I'll break yer back." The Hedge boy moved away with dignity, followed by his little brother. The latter, when he had placed a sufficient distance between himself and Peter, played his fingers at his nose and called out:

"Nig-ger-r-r! Nig-ger-r-r!"

Peter Washington's resentment poured out upon Jimmie.

"'Pears like you never would understan' you ain't reg'lar common trash. You take an' 'sociate with an'body what done come erlong."

"Aw, go on," retorted Jimmie, profanely. "Go soak your head, Pete."

The remaining boys retired to the street, whereupon they perceived Willie Dalzel in the distance. He ran to them.

"I licked him!" he shouted, exultantly. "I licked him! Didn't I, now?"

From the Whilomville point of view he was entitled to a favorable answer. They made it. "Yes," they said, "you did."

"I run in," cried Willie, "an' I grabbed 'im, an' afore he knew what it was I throwed 'im. An' then it was easy." He puffed out his chest and smiled like an English recruiting-sergeant. "An' now," said he, suddenly facing Jimmie Trescott, "whose side were you on?"

The question was direct and startling. Jimmie gave back two paces. "He licked you once," he explained, haltingly.

"He never saw the day when he could lick one side of me. I could lick him with my left hand tied behind me. Why, I could lick him when I was asleep." Willie Dalzel was magnificent.

A gate clicked, and Johnnie Hedge was seen to be strolling towards them.

"You said," he remarked, coldly, "you licked me, didn't you?"

Willie Dalzel stood his ground. "Yes," he said, stoutly.

"Well, you're a liar," said the Hedge boy.

"You're another," retorted Willie.

"No, I ain't, either, but you're a liar."

"You're another," retorted Willie.

"Don't you dare tell me I'm a liar, or I'll smack your mouth for you," said the Hedge boy.

"Well, I did, didn't I?" barked Willie. "An' whatche goin' to do about it?"

"I'm goin' to lam you," said the Hedge boy.

He approached to attack warily, and the other boys held their breaths. Willie Dalzel winced back a pace. "Hol' on a minute," he cried, raising his palm. "I'm not—"

But the comic windmill was again in motion, and between gasps from his exertions Johnnie Hedge remarked, "I'll show—you—whether—you kin—lick me—or not."

The first blows did not reach home on Willie, for he backed away with expedition, keeping up his futile cry, "Hol' on a minute." Soon enough a swinging fist landed on his cheek. It did not knock him down, but it hurt him a little and frightened him a great deal. He suddenly opened his mouth to an amazing and startling extent, tilted back his head, and howled, while his eyes, glittering with tears, were fixed upon this scowling butcher of a Johnnie Hedge. The latter was making slow and vicious circles, evidently intending to renew the massacre.

But the spectators really had been desolated and shocked by the terrible thing which had happened to Willie Dalzel. They now cried out: "No, no; don't hit 'im any more! Don't hit 'im any more!"

Jimmie Trescott, in a panic of bravery, yelled, "We'll all jump on you if you do."

The Hedge boy paused, at bay. He breathed angrily, and flashed his glance from lad to lad.

They still protested: "No, no; don't hit 'im any more. Don't hit 'im no more."

"I'll hammer him until he can't stand up," said Johnnie, observing that they all feared him. "I'll fix him so he won't know hisself, an' if any of you kids bother with me—"

Suddenly he ceased, he trembled, he collapsed. The hand of one approaching from behind had laid hold upon his ear, and it was the hand of one whom he knew.

The other lads heard a loud, iron-filing voice say, "Caught ye at it again, ye brat, ye." They saw a dreadful woman with gray hair, with a sharp red nose, with bare arms, with spectacles of such magnifying quality that her eyes shone through them like two fierce white moons. She was Johnnie Hedge's mother. Still holding Johnnie by the ear, she swung out swiftly and dexterously, and succeeded in boxing the ears of two boys before the crowd regained its presence of mind and stampeded. Yes, the war for supremacy was over, and the question was never again disputed. The supreme power was Mrs. Hedge.

XIII. A LITTLE PILGRIMAGE

ONE November it became clear to childish minds in certain parts of Whilomville that the Sunday-school of the Presbyterian church would not have for the children the usual tree on Christmas eve. The funds free for that ancient festival would be used for the relief of suffering among the victims of the Charleston earthquake.

The plan had been born in the generous head of the superintendent of the Sunday-school, and during one session he had made a strong plea that the children should forego the vain pleasures of a tree and, in glorious application of the Golden Rule, refuse a local use of the fund, and will that it be sent where dire pain might be alleviated. At the end of a tearfully eloquent speech the question was put fairly to a vote, and the children in a burst of virtuous abandon carried the question for Charleston. Many of the teachers had been careful to preserve a finely neutral attitude, but even if they had cautioned the children against being too impetuous they could not have checked the wild impulses.

But this was a long time before Christmas.

Very early, boys held important speech together. "Huh! you ain't goin' to have no Christmas tree at the Presbyterian Sunday-school."

Sullenly the victim answered, "No, we ain't."

"Huh!" scoffed the other denomination, "we are goin' to have the all-firedest biggest tree that you ever saw in the world."

The little Presbyterians were greatly downcast.

It happened that Jimmie Trescott had regularly attended the Presbyterian Sunday-school. The Trescotts were consistently undenominational, but they had sent their lad on Sundays to one of the places where they thought he would receive benefits. However, on one day in December, Jimmie appeared before his father and made a strong spiritual appeal to be forthwith attached to the Sunday-school of the Big Progressive church. Doctor Trescott mused this question considerably. "Well, Jim," he said, "why do you conclude that the Big Progressive Sunday-school is better for you than the Presbyterian Sunday-school?"

"Now—it's nicer," answered Jimmie, looking at his father with an anxious eye.

"How do you mean?"

"Why—now—some of the boys what go to the Presbyterian place, they ain't very nice," explained the flagrant Jimmie.

Trescott mused the question considerably once more. In the end he said: "Well, you may change if you wish, this one time, but you must not be changing to and fro. You decide now, and then you must abide by your decision."

"Yessir," said Jimmie, brightly. "Big Progressive."

"All right," said the father. "But remember what I've told you."

On the following Sunday morning Jimmie presented himself at the door of the basement of the Big Progressive church. He was conspicuously washed, notably raimented, prominently polished. And, incidentally, he was very uncomfortable because of all these virtues.

A number of acquaintances greeted him contemptuously. "Hello, Jimmie! What you doin' here? Thought you was a Presbyterian?"

Jimmie cast down his eyes and made no reply. He was too cowed by the change. However, Homer Phelps, who was a regular patron of the Big Progressive Sunday-school, suddenly appeared and said, "Hello, Jim!" Jimmie seized upon him. Homer Phelps was amenable to Trescott laws, tribal if you like, but iron-bound, almost compulsory.

"Hello, Homer!" said Jimmie, and his manner was so good that Homer felt a great thrill in being able to show his superior a new condition of life.

"You 'ain't never come here afore, have you?" he demanded, with a new arrogance.

"No, I 'ain't," said Jimmie. Then they stared at each other and manœuvred.

"You don't know my teacher," said Homer.

"No, I don't know her" admitted Jimmie, but in a way which contended, modestly, that he knew countless other Sunday-school teachers.

"Better join our class," said Homer, sagely. "She wears spectacles; don't see very well. Sometimes we do almost what we like."

"All right," said Jimmie, glad to place himself in the hands of his friends. In due time they entered the Sunday-school room, where a man with benevolent whiskers stood on a platform and said, "We will now sing No. 33—'Pull for the Shore, Sailor, Pull for the Shore.'" And as the obedient throng burst into melody the man on the platform indicated the time with a fat, white, and graceful hand. He was an ideal Sunday-school superintendent—one who had never felt hunger or thirst or the wound of the challenge of dishonor; a man, indeed, with beautiful flat hands who waved them in greasy victorious beneficence over a crowd of children.

Jimmie, walking carefully on his toes, followed Homer Phelps. He felt that the kingly superintendent might cry out and blast him to ashes before he could reach a chair. It was a desperate journey. But at last he heard Homer muttering to a young lady, who looked at him through glasses which greatly magnified her eyes. "A new boy," she said, in an oily and deeply religious voice.

"Yes'm," said Jimmie, trembling. The five other boys of the class scanned him keenly and derided his condition.

"We will proceed to the lesson," said the young lady. Then she cried sternly, like a sergeant, "The seventh chapter of Jeremiah!"

There was a swift fluttering of leaflets. Then the name of Jeremiah, a wise man, towered over the feelings of these boys. Homer Phelps was doomed to read the fourth verse. He took a deep breath, he puffed out his lips, he gathered his strength for a great effort. His beginning was childishly explosive. He hurriedly said:

"Trust ye not in lying words, saying The temple of the Lord, the temple of the Lord, the temple of the Lord, are these."

"Now," said the teacher, "Johnnie Scanlan, tell us what these words mean." The Scanlan boy shamefacedly muttered that he did not know. The teacher's countenance saddened. Her heart was in her work; she wanted to make a success of this Sunday-school class. "Perhaps Homer Phelps can tell us," she remarked.

Homer gulped; he looked at Jimmie. Through the great room hummed a steady hum. A little circle, very near, was being told about Daniel in the lion's den. They were deeply moved. At the moment they liked Sunday-school.

"Why—now—it means," said Homer, with a grand pomposity born of a sense of hopeless ignorance—"it means—why it means that they were in the wrong place."

"No," said the teacher, profoundly; "it means that we should be good, very good indeed. That is what it means. It means that we should love the Lord and be good. Love the Lord and be good. That is what it means."

The little boys suddenly had a sense of black wickedness as their teacher looked austerely upon them. They gazed at her with the wide-open eyes of simplicity. They were stirred again. This thing of being good—this great business of life—apparently it was always successful. They knew from the fairy tales. But it was difficult, wasn't it? It was said to be the most heart-breaking task to be generous, wasn't it? One had to pay the price of one's eyes in order to be pacific, didn't one? As for patience, it was tortured martyrdom to be patient, wasn't it? Sin was simple, wasn't it? But virtue was so difficult that it could only be practised by heavenly beings, wasn't it?

And the angels, the Sunday-school superintendent, and the teacher swam in the high visions of the little boys as beings so good that if a boy scratched his shin in the same room he was a profane and sentenced devil.

"And," said the teacher, "'The temple of the Lord'—what does that mean? I'll ask the new boy. What does that mean?"

"I dun'no'," said Jimmie, blankly.

But here the professional bright boy of the class suddenly awoke to his obligations. "Teacher," he cried, "it means church, same as this."

"Exactly," said the teacher, deeply satisfied with this reply. "You know your lesson well, Clarence. I am much pleased."

The other boys, instead of being envious, looked with admiration upon Clarence, while he adopted an air of being habituated to perform such feats every day of his life. Still, he was not much of a boy. He had the virtue of being able to walk on very high stilts, but when the season of stilts had passed he possessed no rank save this Sunday-school rank, this clever-little-Clarence business of knowing the Bible and the lesson better than the other boys. The other boys, sometimes looking at him meditatively, did not actually decide to thrash him as soon as he cleared the portals of the church, but they certainly decided to molest him in such ways as would re-establish their self-respect. Back of the superintendent's chair hung a lithograph of the martyrdom of St. Stephen.

Jimmie, feeling stiff and encased in his best clothes, waited for the ordeal to end. A bell pealed: the fat hand of the superintendent had tapped a bell. Slowly the rustling and murmuring dwindled to silence. The benevolent man faced the school. "I have to announce," he began, waving his body from side to side in the conventional bows of his kind, "that—" Bang went the bell. "Give me your attention, please, children. I have to announce that the Board has decided that this year there will be no Christmas tree, but the—"

Instantly the room buzzed with the subdued clamor of the children. Jimmie was speechless. He stood morosely during the singing of the closing hymn. He passed out into the street with the others, pushing no more than was required.

Speedily the whole idea left him. If he remembered Sunday-school at all, it was to remember that he did not like it.

THE MONSTER AND
OTHER STORIES

THE MONSTER

I

Little Jim was, for the time, engine Number 36, and he was making the run between Syracuse and Rochester. He was fourteen minutes behind time, and the throttle was wide open. In consequence, when he swung around the curve at the flower-bed, a wheel of his cart destroyed a peony. Number 36 slowed down at once and looked guiltily at his father, who was mowing the lawn. The doctor had his back to this accident, and he continued to pace slowly to and fro, pushing the mower.

Jim dropped the tongue of the cart. He looked at his father and at the broken flower. Finally he went to the peony and tried to stand it on its pins, resuscitated, but the spine of it was hurt, and it would only hang limply from his hand. Jim could do no reparation. He looked again towards his father.

He went on to the lawn, very slowly, and kicking wretchedly at the turf. Presently his father came along with the whirring machine, while the sweet, new grass blades spun from the knives. In a low voice, Jim said, "Pa!"

The doctor was shaving this lawn as if it were a priest's chin. All during the season he had worked at it in the coolness and peace of the evenings after supper. Even in the shadow of the cherry-trees the grass was strong and healthy. Jim raised his voice a trifle. "Pa!"

The doctor paused, and with the howl of the machine no longer occupying the sense, one could hear the robins in the cherry-trees arranging their affairs. Jim's hands were behind his back, and sometimes his fingers clasped and unclasped. Again he said, "Pa!" The child's fresh and rosy lip was lowered.

The doctor stared down at his son, thrusting his head forward and frowning attentively. "What is it, Jimmie?"

"Pa!" repeated the child at length. Then he raised his finger and pointed at the flowerbed. "There!"

"What?" said the doctor, frowning more. "What is it, Jim?"

After a period of silence, during which the child may have undergone a severe mental tumult, he raised his finger and repeated his former word—"There!" The father had respected this silence with perfect courtesy. Afterwards his glance carefully followed the direction indicated by the child's finger, but he could see nothing which explained to him. "I don't understand what you mean, Jimmie," he said.

It seemed that the importance of the whole thing had taken away the boy's vocabulary, He could only reiterate, "There!"

The doctor mused upon the situation, but he could make nothing of it. At last he said, "Come, show me."

Together they crossed the lawn towards the flower-bed. At some yards from the broken peony Jimmie began to lag. "There!" The word came almost breathlessly.

"Where?" said the doctor.

Jimmie kicked at the grass. "There!" he replied.

The doctor was obliged to go forward alone. After some trouble he found the subject of the incident, the broken flower. Turning then, he saw the child lurking at the rear and scanning his countenance.

The father reflected. After a time he said, "Jimmie, come here." With an infinite modesty of demeanor the child came forward. "Jimmie, how did this happen?"

The child answered, "Now—I was playin' train—and—now—I runned over it."

"You were doing what?"

"I was playin' train."

The father reflected again. "Well, Jimmie," he said, slowly, "I guess you had better not play train any more to-day. Do you think you had better?"

"No, sir," said Jimmie.

During the delivery of the judgment the child had not faced his father, and afterwards he went away, with his head lowered, shuffling his feet.

II

It was apparent from Jimmie's manner that he felt some kind of desire to efface himself. He went down to the stable. Henry Johnson, the negro who cared for the doctor's horses, was sponging the buggy. He grinned fraternally when he saw Jimmie coming. These two were pals. In regard to almost everything in life they seemed to have minds precisely alike. Of course there were points of emphatic divergence. For instance, it was plain from Henry's talk that he was a very handsome negro, and he was known to be a light, a weight, and an eminence in the suburb of the town, where lived the larger number of the negroes, and obviously this glory was over Jimmie's horizon; but he vaguely appreciated it and paid deference to Henry for it mainly because Henry appreciated it and deferred to himself. However, on all points of conduct as related to the doctor, who was the moon, they were in complete but unexpressed understanding. Whenever Jimmie became the victim of an eclipse he went to the stable to solace himself with Henry's crimes. Henry, with the elasticity of his race, could usually provide a sin to place himself on a footing with the disgraced one. Perhaps he would remember that he had forgotten to put the hitching-strap in the back of the buggy on some recent occasion, and had been reprimanded by the doctor. Then these two would commune subtly and without words concerning their moon, holding themselves sympathetically as people who had committed similar treasons. On the other hand, Henry would sometimes choose to absolutely repudiate this idea, and when Jimmie appeared in his shame would bully him most virtuously, preaching with assurance the precepts of the doctor's creed, and pointing out to Jimmie all his abominations. Jimmie did not discover that this was odious in his comrade. He accepted it and lived in its shadow with

173

humility, merely trying to conciliate the saintly Henry with acts of deference. Won by this attitude, Henry would sometimes allow the child to enjoy the felicity of squeezing the sponge over a buggy-wheel, even when Jimmie was still gory from unspeakable deeds.

Whenever Henry dwelt for a time in sackcloth, Jimmie did not patronize him at all. This was a justice of his age, his condition. He did not know. Besides, Henry could drive a horse, and Jimmie had a full sense of this sublimity. Henry personally conducted the moon during the splendid journeys through the country roads, where farms spread on all sides, with sheep, cows, and other marvels abounding.

"Hello, Jim!" said Henry, poising his sponge. Water was dripping from the buggy. Sometimes the horses in the stalls stamped thunderingly on the pine floor. There was an atmosphere of hay and of harness.

For a minute Jimmie refused to take an interest in anything. He was very downcast. He could not even feel the wonders of wagon washing. Henry, while at his work, narrowly observed him.

"Your pop done wallop yer, didn't he?" he said at last.

"No," said Jimmie, defensively; "he didn't."

After this casual remark Henry continued his labor, with a scowl of occupation. Presently he said: "I done tol' yer many's th' time not to go a-foolin' an' a-projjeckin' with them flowers. Yer pop don' like it nohow." As a matter of fact, Henry had never mentioned flowers to the boy.

Jimmie preserved a gloomy silence, so Henry began to use seductive wiles in this affair of washing a wagon. It was not until he began to spin a wheel on the tree, and the sprinkling water flew everywhere, that the boy was visibly moved. He had been seated on the sill of the carriage-house door, but at the beginning of this ceremony he arose and circled towards the buggy, with an interest that slowly consumed the remembrance of a late disgrace.

Johnson could then display all the dignity of a man whose duty it was to protect Jimmie from a splashing. "Look out, boy! look out! You done gwi' spile yer pants. I raikon your mommer don't 'low this foolishness, she know it. I ain't gwi' have you round yere spilin' yer pants, an' have Mis' Trescott light on me pressen'ly. 'Deed I ain't." He spoke with an air of great irritation, but he was not annoyed at all. This tone was merely a part of his importance. In reality he was always delighted to have the child there to witness the business of the stable. For one thing, Jimmie was invariably overcome with reverence when he was told how beautifully a harness was polished or a horse groomed. Henry explained each detail of this kind with unction, procuring great joy from the child's admiration.

III

After Johnson had taken his supper in the kitchen, he went to his loft in the carriage house and dressed himself with much care. No belle of a court circle could bestow more mind on a toilet than did Johnson. On second thought, he was more like a priest arraying himself for some parade of the church. As he emerged from his room and sauntered down the carriage-drive, no one would have suspected him of ever having washed a buggy.

It was not altogether a matter of the lavender trousers, nor yet the straw hat with its bright silk band. The change was somewhere, far in the interior of Henry. But there was no cake-walk hyperbole in it. He was simply a quiet, well-bred gentleman of position, wealth, and other necessary achievements out for an evening stroll, and he had never washed a wagon in his life.

In the morning, when in his working-clothes, he had met a friend—"Hello, Pete!" "Hello, Henry!" Now, in his effulgence, he encountered this same friend. His bow was not at all haughty. If it expressed anything, it expressed consummate generosity—"Good-evenin', Misteh Washington." Pete, who was very dirty, being at work in a potato-patch, responded in a mixture of abasement and appreciation—Good-evenin', Misteh Johnsing."

The shimmering blue of the electric arc lamps was strong in the main street of the town. At numerous points it was conquered by the orange glare of the outnumbering gaslights in the windows of shops. Through this radiant lane moved a crowd, which culminated in a throng before the post-office, awaiting the distribution of the evening mails. Occasionally there came into it a shrill electric street-car, the motor singing like a cageful of grasshoppers, and possessing a great gong that clanged forth both warnings and simple noise. At the little theatre, which was a varnish and red plush miniature of one of the famous New York theatres, a company of strollers was to play "East Lynne." The young men of the town were mainly gathered at the corners, in distinctive groups, which expressed various shades and lines of chumship, and had little to do with any social gradations. There they discussed everything with critical insight, passing the whole town in review as it swarmed in the street. When the gongs of the electric cars ceased for a moment to harry the ears, there could be heard the sound of the feet of the leisurely crowd on the bluestone pavement, and it was like the peaceful evening lashing at the shore of a lake. At the foot of the hill, where two lines of maples sentinelled the way, an electric lamp glowed high among the embowering branches, and made most wonderful shadow-etchings on the road below it.

When Johnson appeared amid the throng a member of one of the profane groups at a corner instantly telegraphed news of this extraordinary arrival to his companions. They hailed him. "Hello, Henry! Going to walk for a cake to-night?"

"Ain't he smooth?"

"Why, you've got that cake right in your pocket, Henry!"

"Throw out your chest a little more."

Henry was not ruffled in any way by these quiet admonitions and compliments. In reply he laughed a supremely good-natured, chuckling laugh, which nevertheless expressed an underground complacency of superior metal.

Young Griscom, the lawyer, was just emerging from Reifsnyder's barber shop, rubbing his chin contentedly. On the steps he dropped his hand and looked with wide eyes into the crowd. Suddenly he bolted back into the shop. "Wow!" he cried to the parliament; "you ought to see the coon that's coming!"

Reifsnyder and his assistant instantly poised their razors high and turned towards the window. Two belathered heads reared from the chairs. The electric shine in the street caused an effect like water to them who looked through the glass from the yellow glamour of Reifsnyder's shop. In fact, the people without resembled the inhabitants of a great aquarium that here had a square pane in it. Presently into this frame swam the graceful form of Henry Johnson.

"Chee!" said Reifsnyder. He and his assistant with one accord threw their obligations to the winds, and leaving their lathered victims helpless, advanced to the window. "Ain't he a taisy?" said Reifsnyder, marvelling.

But the man in the first chair, with a grievance in his mind, had found a weapon. "Why, that's only Henry Johnson, you blamed idiots! Come on now, Reif, and shave me. What do you think I am—a mummy?"

Reifsnyder turned, in a great excitement. "I bait you any money that vas not Henry Johnson! Henry Johnson! Rats!" The scorn put into this last word made it an explosion. "That man was a Pullman-car porter or someding. How could that be Henry Johnson?" he demanded, turbulently. "You vas crazy."

The man in the first chair faced the barber in a storm of indignation. "Didn't I give him those lavender trousers?" he roared.

And young Griscom, who had remained attentively at the window, said: "Yes, I guess that was Henry. It looked like him."

"Oh, vell," said Reifsnyder, returning to his business, "if you think so! Oh, vell!" He implied that he was submitting for the sake of amiability.

Finally the man in the second chair, mumbling from a mouth made timid by adjacent lather, said: "That was Henry Johnson all right. Why, he always dresses like that when he wants to make a front! He's the biggest dude in town—anybody knows that."

"Chinger!" said Reifsnyder.

Henry was not at all oblivious of the wake of wondering ejaculation that streamed out behind him. On other occasions he had reaped this same joy, and he always had an eye for the demonstration. With a face beaming with happiness he turned away from the scene of his victories into a narrow side street, where the electric light still hung high, but only to exhibit a row of tumble-down houses leaning together like paralytics.

The saffron Miss Bella Farragut, in a calico frock, had been crouched on the front stoop, gossiping at long range, but she espied her approaching caller at a distance. She dashed around the corner of the house, galloping like a horse. Henry saw it all, but he preserved the polite demeanor of a guest when a waiter spills claret down his cuff. In this awkward situation he was simply perfect.

The duty of receiving Mr. Johnson fell upon Mrs. Farragut, because Bella, in another room, was scrambling wildly into her best gown. The fat old woman met him with a great ivory smile, sweeping back with the door, and bowing low. "Walk in, Misteh Johnson, walk in. How is you dis ebenin', Misteh Johnson—how is you?"

Henry's face showed like a reflector as he bowed and bowed, bending almost from his head to his ankles, "Good-evenin', Mis' Fa'gut; good-evenin'. How is you dis evenin'? Is all you' folks well, Mis' Fa'gut?"

After a great deal of kowtow, they were planted in two chairs opposite each other in the living-room. Here they exchanged the most tremendous civilities, until Miss Bella swept into the room, when there was more kowtow on all sides, and a smiling show of teeth that was like an illumination.

The cooking-stove was of course in this drawing-room, and on the fire was some kind of a long-winded stew. Mrs. Farragut was obliged to arise and attend to it from time to time. Also young Sim came in and went to bed on his pallet in the corner. But to all these domesticities the three maintained an absolute dumbness. They bowed and smiled and ignored and imitated until a late hour, and if they had been the occupants of the most gorgeous salon in the world they could not have been more like three monkeys.

After Henry had gone, Bella, who encouraged herself in the appropriation of phrases, said, "Oh, ma, isn't he divine?"

178

IV

A Saturday evening was a sign always for a larger crowd to parade the thoroughfare. In summer the band played until ten o'clock in the little park. Most of the young men of the town affected to be superior to this band, even to despise it; but in the still and fragrant evenings they invariably turned out in force, because the girls were sure to attend this concert, strolling slowly over the grass, linked closely in pairs, or preferably in threes, in the curious public dependence upon one another which was their inheritance. There was no particular social aspect to this gathering, save that group regarded group with interest, but mainly in silence. Perhaps one girl would nudge another girl and suddenly say, "Look! there goes Gertie Hodgson and her sister!" And they would appear to regard this as an event of importance.

On a particular evening a rather large company of young men were gathered on the sidewalk that edged the park. They remained thus beyond the borders of the festivities because of their dignity, which would not exactly allow them to appear in anything which was so much fun for the younger lads. These latter were careering madly through the crowd, precipitating minor accidents from time to time, but usually fleeing like mist swept by the wind before retribution could lay hands upon them.

The band played a waltz which involved a gift of prominence to the bass horn, and one of the young men on the sidewalk said that the music reminded him of the new engines on the hill pumping water into the reservoir. A similarity of this kind was not inconceivable, but the young man did not say it because he disliked the band's playing. He said it because it was fashionable to say that manner of thing concerning the band. However, over in the stand, Billie Harris, who played the snare-drum, was always surrounded by a throng of boys, who adored his every whack.

After the mails from New York and Rochester had been finally distributed, the crowd from the post-office added to the mass already in the park. The wind waved the leaves of the maples, and, high in the air, the blue-burning globes of the arc lamps caused the wonderful traceries of leaf shadows on the ground. When the light fell upon the upturned face of a girl, it caused it to glow with a wonderful pallor. A policeman came suddenly from the darkness and chased a gang of obstreperous little boys. They hooted him from a distance. The leader of the band had some of the mannerisms of the great musicians, and during a period of silence the crowd smiled when they saw him raise his hand to his brow, stroke it sentimentally, and glance upward with a look of poetic anguish. In the shivering light, which gave to the park an effect like a great vaulted hall, the throng swarmed, with a gentle murmur of dresses switching the turf, and with a steady hum of voices.

Suddenly, without preliminary bars, there arose from afar the great hoarse roar of a factory whistle. It raised and swelled to a sinister note, and then it sang on the night wind one long call that held the crowd in the park immovable, speechless. The band-master had been about to vehemently let fall his hand to start the band on a thundering career through a popular march, but, smitten by this giant voice from the night, his hand dropped slowly to his knee, and, his mouth agape, he looked at his men in silence. The cry died away to a wail and then to stillness. It released the muscles of the company of young men on the sidewalk, who had been like statues, posed eagerly, lithely, their ears turned. And then they wheeled upon each other simultaneously, and, in a single explosion, they shouted, "One!"

Again the sound swelled in the night and roared its long ominous cry, and as it died away the crowd of young men wheeled upon each other and, in chorus, yelled, "Two!"

There was a moment of breathless waiting. Then they bawled, "Second district!" In a flash the company of indolent and cynical young men had vanished like a snowball disrupted by dynamite.

V

Jake Rogers was the first man to reach the home of Tuscarora Hose Company Number Six. He had wrenched his key from his pocket as he tore down the street, and he jumped at the spring-lock like a demon. As the doors flew back before his hands he leaped and kicked the wedges from a pair of wheels, loosened a tongue from its clasp, and in the glare of the electric light which the town placed before each of its hose-houses the next comers beheld the spectacle of Jake Rogers bent like hickory in the manfulness of his pulling, and the heavy cart was moving slowly towards the doors. Four men joined him at the time, and as they swung with the cart out into the street, dark figures sped towards them from the ponderous shadows back of the electric lamps. Some set up the inevitable question, "What district?"

"Second," was replied to them in a compact howl. Tuscarora Hose Company Number Six swept on a perilous wheel into Niagara Avenue, and as the men, attached to the cart by the rope which had been paid out from the windlass under the tongue, pulled madly in their fervor and abandon, the gong under the axle clanged incitingly. And sometimes the same cry was heard, "What district?"

"Second."

On a grade Johnnie Thorpe fell, and exercising a singular muscular ability, rolled out in time from the track of the on-coming wheel, and arose, dishevelled and aggrieved, casting a look of mournful disenchantment upon the black crowd that poured after the machine. The cart seemed to be the apex of a dark wave that was whirling as if it had been a broken dam. Back of the lad were stretches of lawn, and in that direction front-doors were banged by men who hoarsely shouted out into the clamorous avenue, "What district?"

At one of these houses a woman came to the door bearing a lamp, shielding her face from its rays with her hands. Across the cropped grass the avenue represented to her a kind of black torrent, upon which, nevertheless, fled numerous miraculous figures upon bicycles. She did not know that the towering light at the corner was continuing its nightly whine.

Suddenly a little boy somersaulted around the corner of the house as if he had been projected down a flight of stairs by a catapultian boot. He halted himself in front of the house by dint of a rather extraordinary evolution with his legs. "Oh, ma," he gasped, "can I go? Can I, ma?"

She straightened with the coldness of the exterior mother-judgment, although the hand that held the lamp trembled slightly. "No, Willie; you had better come to bed."

Instantly he began to buck and fume like a mustang. "Oh, ma," he cried, contorting himself—"oh, ma, can't I go? Please, ma, can't I go? Can't I go, ma?"

"It's half-past nine now, Willie."

He ended by wailing out a compromise: "Well, just down to the corner, ma? Just down to the corner?"

From the avenue came the sound of rushing men who wildly shouted. Somebody had grappled the bell-rope in the Methodist church, and now over the town rang this solemn and terrible voice, speaking from the clouds. Moved from its peaceful business, this bell gained a new spirit in the portentous night, and it swung the heart to and fro, up and down, with each peal of it.

"Just down to the corner, ma?"

"Willie, it's half-past nine now."

VI

The outlines of the house of Dr. Trescott had faded quietly into the evening, hiding a shape such as we call Queen Anne against the pall of the blackened sky. The neighborhood was at this time so quiet, and seemed so devoid of obstructions, that Hannigan's dog thought it a good opportunity to prowl in forbidden precincts, and so came and pawed Trescott's lawn, growling, and considering himself a formidable beast. Later, Peter Washington strolled past the house and whistled, but there was no dim light shining from Henry's loft, and presently Peter went his way. The rays from the street, creeping in silvery waves over the grass, caused the row of shrubs along the drive to throw a clear, bold shade.

A wisp of smoke came from one of the windows at the end of the house and drifted quietly into the branches of a cherry-tree. Its companions followed it in slowly increasing numbers, and finally there was a current controlled by invisible banks which poured into the fruit-laden boughs of the cherry-tree. It was no more to be noted than if a troop of dim and silent gray monkeys had been climbing a grapevine into the clouds.

After a moment the window brightened as if the four panes of it had been stained with blood, and a quick ear might have been led to imagine the fire-imps calling and calling, clan joining clan, gathering to the colors. From the street, however, the house maintained its dark quiet, insisting to a passer-by that it was the safe dwelling of people who chose to retire early to tranquil dreams. No one could have heard this low droning of the gathering clans.

Suddenly the panes of the red window tinkled and crashed to the ground, and at other windows there suddenly reared other flames, like bloody spectres at the apertures of a haunted house. This outbreak had been well planned, as if by professional revolutionists.

A man's voice suddenly shouted: "Fire! Fire! Fire!" Hannigan had flung his pipe frenziedly from him because his lungs demanded room. He tumbled down from his perch, swung over the fence, and ran shouting towards the front-door of the Trescotts'. Then he hammered on the door, using his fists as if they were mallets. Mrs. Trescott instantly came to one of the windows on the second floor. Afterwards she knew she had been about to say, "The doctor is not at home, but if you will leave your name, I will let him know as soon as he comes."

Hannigan's bawling was for a minute incoherent, but she understood that it was not about croup.

"What?" she said, raising the window swiftly.

"Your house is on fire! You're all ablaze! Move quick if—" His cries were resounding, in the street as if it were a cave of echoes. Many feet pattered swiftly on the stones. There was one man who ran with an almost fabulous speed. He wore lavender trousers. A straw hat with a bright silk band was held half crumpled in his hand.

As Henry reached the front-door, Hannigan had just broken the lock with a kick. A thick cloud of smoke poured over them, and Henry, ducking his head, rushed into it. From Hannigan's clamor he knew only one thing, but it turned him blue with horror. In the hall a lick of flame had found the cord that supported "Signing the Declaration." The engraving slumped

183

suddenly down at one end, and then dropped to the floor, where it burst with the sound of a bomb. The fire was already roaring like a winter wind among the pines.

At the head of the stairs Mrs. Trescott was waving her arms as if they were two reeds.

"Jimmie! Save Jimmie!" she screamed in Henry's face. He plunged past her and disappeared, taking the long-familiar routes among these upper chambers, where he had once held office as a sort of second assistant house-maid.

Hannigan had followed him up the stairs, and grappled the arm of the maniacal woman there. His face was black with rage. "You must come down," he bellowed.

She would only scream at him in reply: "Jimmie! Jimmie! Save Jimmie!" But he dragged her forth while she babbled at him.

As they swung out into the open air a man ran across the lawn, and seizing a shutter, pulled it from its hinges and flung it far out upon the grass. Then he frantically attacked the other shutters one by one. It was a kind of temporary insanity.

"Here, you," howled Hannigan, "hold Mrs. Trescott—And stop—"

The news had been telegraphed by a twist of the wrist of a neighbor who had gone to the fire-box at the corner, and the time when Hannigan and his charge struggled out of the house was the time when the whistle roared its hoarse night call, smiting the crowd in the park, causing the leader of the band, who was about to order the first triumphal clang of a military march, to let his hand drop slowly to his knees.

VII

Henry pawed awkwardly through the smoke in the upper halls. He had attempted to guide himself by the walls, but they were too hot. The paper was crimpling, and he expected at any moment to have a flame burst from under his hands.

"Jimmie!"

He did not call very loud, as if in fear that the humming flames below would overhear him.

"Jimmie! Oh, Jimmie!"

Stumbling and panting, he speedily reached the entrance to Jimmie's room and flung open the door. The little chamber had no smoke in it at all. It was faintly illuminated by a beautiful rosy light reflected circuitously from the flames that were consuming the house. The boy had apparently just been aroused by the noise. He sat in his bed, his lips apart, his eyes wide, while upon his little white-robed figure played caressingly the light from the fire. As the door flew open he had before him this apparition of his pal, a terror-stricken negro, all tousled and with wool scorching, who leaped upon him and bore him up in a blanket as if the whole affair were a case of kidnapping by a dreadful robber chief. Without waiting to go through the usual short but complete process of wrinkling up his face, Jimmie let out a gorgeous bawl, which resembled the expression of a calf's deepest terror. As Johnson, bearing him, reeled into the smoke of the hall, he flung his arms about his neck and buried his face in the blanket. He called twice in muffled tones: "Mam-ma! Mam-ma!" When Johnson came to the top of the stairs with his burden, he took a quick step backward. Through the smoke that rolled to him he could see that the lower hall was all ablaze. He cried out then in a howl that resembled Jimmie's former achievement. His legs gained a frightful faculty of bending sideways. Swinging about precariously on these reedy legs, he made his way back slowly, back along the upper hall. From the way of him then, he had given up almost all idea of escaping from the burning house, and with it the desire. He was submitting, submitting because of his fathers, bending his mind in a most perfect slavery to this conflagration.

He now clutched Jimmie as unconsciously as when, running toward the house, he had clutched the hat with the bright silk band.

Suddenly he remembered a little private staircase which led from a bedroom to an apartment which the doctor had fitted up as a laboratory and work-house, where he used some of his leisure, and also hours when he might have been sleeping, in devoting himself to experiments which came in the way of his study and interest.

When Johnson recalled this stairway the submission to the blaze departed instantly. He had been perfectly familiar with it, but his confusion had destroyed the memory of it.

In his sudden momentary apathy there had been little that resembled fear, but now, as a way of safety came to him, the old frantic terror caught him. He was no longer creature to the flames, and he was afraid of the battle with them. It was a singular and swift set of alternations in which he feared twice without submission, and submitted once without fear.

"Jimmie!" he wailed, as he staggered on his way. He wished this little inanimate body at his breast to participate in his tremblings. But the child had lain limp and still during these headlong charges and countercharges, and no sign came from him.

Johnson passed through two rooms and came to the head of the stairs. As he opened the door great billows of smoke poured out, but gripping Jimmie closer, he plunged down through them. All manner of odors assailed him during this flight. They seemed to be alive with envy, hatred, and malice. At the entrance to the laboratory he confronted a strange spectacle. The room was like a garden in the region where might be burning flowers. Flames of violet, crimson, green, blue, orange, and purple were blooming everywhere. There was one blaze that was precisely the hue of a delicate coral. In another place was a mass that lay merely in phosphorescent inaction like a pile of emeralds. But all these marvels were to be seen dimly through clouds of heaving, turning, deadly smoke.

Johnson halted for a moment on the threshold. He cried out again in the negro wail that had in it the sadness of the swamps. Then he rushed across the room. An orange-colored flame leaped like a panther at the lavender trousers. This animal bit deeply into Johnson. There was an explosion at one side, and suddenly before him there reared a delicate, trembling sapphire shape like a fairy lady. With a quiet smile she blocked his path and doomed him and Jimmie. Johnson shrieked, and then ducked in the manner of his race in fights. He aimed to pass under the left guard of the sapphire lady. But she was swifter than eagles, and her talons caught in him as he plunged past her. Bowing his head as if his neck had been struck, Johnson lurched forward, twisting this way and that way. He fell on his back. The still form in the blanket flung from his arms, rolled to the edge of the floor and beneath the window.

Johnson had fallen with his head at the base of an old-fashioned desk. There was a row of jars upon the top of this desk. For the most part, they were silent amid this rioting, but there was one which seemed to hold a scintillant and writhing serpent.

Suddenly the glass splintered, and a ruby-red snakelike thing poured its thick length out upon the top of the old desk. It coiled and hesitated, and then began to swim a languorous way down the mahogany slant. At the angle it waved its sizzling molten head to and fro over the closed eyes of the man beneath it. Then, in a moment, with a mystic impulse, it moved again, and the red snake flowed directly down into Johnson's upturned face.

Afterwards the trail of this creature seemed to reek, and amid flames and low explosions drops like red-hot jewels pattered softly down it at leisurely intervals.

VIII

Suddenly all roads led to Dr. Trescott's. The whole town flowed towards one point. Chippeway Hose Company Number One toiled desperately up Bridge Street Hill even as the Tuscaroras came in an impetuous sweep down Niagara Avenue. Meanwhile the machine of the hook-and-ladder experts from across the creek was spinning on its way. The chief of the fire department had been playing poker in the rear room of Whiteley's cigar-store, but at the first breath of the alarm he sprang through the door like a man escaping with the kitty.

In Whilomville, on these occasions, there was always a number of people who instantly turned their attention to the bells in the churches and school-houses. The bells not only emphasized the alarm, but it was the habit to send these sounds rolling across the sky in a stirring brazen uproar until the flames were practically vanquished. There was also a kind of rivalry as to which bell should be made to produce the greatest din. Even the Valley Church, four miles away among the farms, had heard the voices of its brethren, and immediately added a quaint little yelp.

Dr. Trescott had been driving homeward, slowly smoking a cigar, and feeling glad that this last case was now in complete obedience to him, like a wild animal that he had subdued, when he heard the long whistle, and chirped to his horse under the unlicensed but perfectly distinct impression that a fire had broken out in Oakhurst, a new and rather high-flying suburb of the town which was at least two miles from his own home. But in the second blast and in the ensuing silence he read the designation of his own district. He was then only a few blocks from his house. He took out the whip and laid it lightly on the mare. Surprised and frightened at this extraordinary action, she leaped forward, and as the reins straightened like steel bands, the doctor leaned backward a trifle. When the mare whirled him up to the closed gate he was wondering whose house could be afire. The man who had rung the signal-box yelled something at him, but he already knew. He left the mare to her will.

In front of his door was a maniacal woman in a wrapper. "Ned!" she screamed at sight of him. "Jimmie! Save Jimmie!"

Trescott had grown hard and chill. "Where?" he said. "Where?"

Mrs. Trescott's voice began to bubble. "Up—up—up—" She pointed at the second-story windows.

Hannigan was already shouting: "Don't go in that way! You can't go in that way!"

Trescott ran around the corner of the house and disappeared from them. He knew from the view he had taken of the main hall that it would be impossible to ascend from there. His hopes were fastened now to the stairway which led from the laboratory. The door which opened from this room out

188

upon the lawn was fastened with a bolt and lock, but he kicked close to the lock and then close to the bolt. The door with a loud crash flew back. The doctor recoiled from the roll of smoke, and then bending low, he stepped into the garden of burning flowers. On the floor his stinging eyes could make out a form in a smouldering blanket near the window. Then, as he carried his son towards the door, he saw that the whole lawn seemed now alive with men and boys, the leaders in the great charge that the whole town was making. They seized him and his burden, and overpowered him in wet blankets and water.

But Hannigan was howling: "Johnson is in there yet! Henry Johnson is in there yet! He went in after the kid! Johnson is in there yet!"

These cries penetrated to the sleepy senses of Trescott, and he struggled with his captors, swearing, unknown to him and to them, all the deep blasphemies of his medical-student days. He rose to his feet and went again towards the door of the laboratory. They endeavored to restrain him, although they were much affrighted at him.

But a young man who was a brakeman on the railway, and lived in one of the rear streets near the Trescotts, had gone into the laboratory and brought forth a thing which he laid on the grass.

IX

There were hoarse commands from in front of the house. "Turn on your water, Five!" "Let 'er go, One!" The gathering crowd swayed this way and that way. The flames, towering high, cast a wild red light on their faces. There came the clangor of a gong from along some adjacent street. The crowd exclaimed at it. "Here comes Number Three!" "That's Three a-comin'!" A panting and irregular mob dashed into view, dragging a hose-cart. A cry of exultation arose from the little boys. "Here's Three!" The lads welcomed Never-Die Hose Company Number Three as if it was composed of a chariot dragged by a band of gods. The perspiring citizens flung themselves into the fray. The boys danced in impish joy at the displays of prowess. They acclaimed the approach of Number Two. They welcomed Number Four with cheers. They were so deeply moved by this whole affair that they bitterly guyed the late appearance of the hook and ladder company, whose heavy apparatus had almost stalled them on the Bridge Street hill. The lads hated and feared a fire, of course. They did not particularly want to have anybody's house burn, but still it was fine to see the gathering of the companies, and amid a great noise to watch their heroes perform all manner of prodigies.

They were divided into parties over the worth of different companies, and supported their creeds with no small violence. For instance, in that part of the little city where Number Four had its home it would be most daring for a boy to contend the superiority of any other company. Likewise, in another quarter, where a strange boy was asked which fire company was the best in Whilomville, he was expected to answer "Number One." Feuds, which the boys forgot and remembered according to chance or the importance of some recent event, existed all through the town.

They did not care much for John Shipley, the chief of the department. It was true that he went to a fire with the speed of a falling angel, but when there he invariably lapsed into a certain still mood, which was almost a preoccupation, moving leisurely around the burning structure and surveying it, putting meanwhile at a cigar. This quiet man, who even when life was in danger seldom raised his voice, was not much to their fancy. Now old Sykes Huntington, when he was chief, used to bellow continually like a bull and gesticulate in a sort of delirium. He was much finer as a spectacle than this Shipley, who viewed a fire with the same steadiness that he viewed a raise in a large jack-pot. The greater number of the boys could never understand why the members of these companies persisted in re-electing Shipley, although they often pretended to understand it, because "My father says" was a very formidable phrase in argument, and the fathers seemed almost unanimous in advocating Shipley.

At this time there was considerable discussion as to which company had gotten the first stream of water on the fire. Most of the boys claimed that Number Five owned that distinction, but there was a determined minority who contended for Number One. Boys who were the blood adherents of other companies were obliged to choose between the two on this occasion, and the talk waxed warm.

190

But a great rumor went among the crowds. It was told with hushed voices. Afterwards a reverent silence fell even upon the boys. Jimmie Trescott and Henry Johnson had been burned to death, and Dr. Trescott himself had been most savagely hurt. The crowd did not even feel the police pushing at them. They raised their eyes, shining now with awe, towards the high flames.

The man who had information was at his best. In low tones he described the whole affair. "That was the kid's room—in the corner there. He had measles or somethin', and this coon—Johnson—was a-settin' up with 'im, and Johnson got sleepy or somethin' and upset the lamp, and the doctor he was down in his office, and he came running up, and they all got burned together till they dragged 'em out."

Another man, always preserved for the deliverance of the final judgment, was saying: "Oh, they'll die sure. Burned to flinders. No chance. Hull lot of 'em. Anybody can see." The crowd concentrated its gaze still more closely upon these flags of fire which waved joyfully against the black sky. The bells of the town were clashing unceasingly.

A little procession moved across the lawn and towards the street. There were three cots, borne by twelve of the firemen. The police moved sternly, but it needed no effort of theirs to open a lane for this slow cortege. The men who bore the cots were well known to the crowd, but in this solemn parade during the ringing of the bells and the shouting, and with the red glare upon the sky, they seemed utterly foreign, and Whilomville paid them a deep respect. Each man in this stretcher party had gained a reflected majesty. They were footmen to death, and the crowd made subtle obeisance to this august dignity derived from three prospective graves. One woman turned away with a shriek at sight of the covered body on the first stretcher, and people faced her suddenly in silent and mournful indignation. Otherwise there was barely a sound as these twelve important men with measured tread carried their burdens through the throng.

The little boys no longer discussed the merits of the different fire companies. For the greater part they had been routed. Only the more courageous viewed closely the three figures veiled in yellow blankets.

X

Old Judge Denning Hagenthorpe, who lived nearly opposite the Trescotts, had thrown his door wide open to receive the afflicted family. When it was publicly learned that the doctor and his son and the negro were still alive, it required a specially detailed policeman to prevent people from scaling the front porch and interviewing these sorely wounded. One old lady appeared with a miraculous poultice, and she quoted most damning Scripture to the officer when he said that she could not pass him. Throughout the night some lads old enough to be given privileges or to compel them from their mothers remained vigilantly upon the kerb in anticipation of a death or some such event. The reporter of the Morning Tribune rode thither on his bicycle every hour until three o'clock.

Six of the ten doctors in Whilomville attended at Judge Hagenthorpe's house.

Almost at once they were able to know that Trescott's burns were not vitally important. The child would possibly be scarred badly, but his life was undoubtedly safe. As for the negro Henry Johnson, he could not live. His body was frightfully seared, but more than that, he now had no face. His face had simply been burned away.

Trescott was always asking news of the two other patients. In the morning he seemed fresh and strong, so they told him that Johnson was doomed. They then saw him stir on the bed, and sprang quickly to see if the bandages needed readjusting. In the sudden glance he threw from one to another he impressed them as being both leonine and impracticable.

The morning paper announced the death of Henry Johnson. It contained a long interview with Edward J. Hannigan, in which the latter described in full the performance of Johnson at the fire. There was also an editorial built from all the best words in the vocabulary of the staff. The town halted in its accustomed road of thought, and turned a reverent attention to the memory of this hostler. In the breasts of many people was the regret that they had not known enough to give him a hand and a lift when he was alive, and they judged themselves stupid and ungenerous for this failure.

The name of Henry Johnson became suddenly the title of a saint to the little boys. The one who thought of it first could, by quoting it in an argument, at once overthrow his antagonist, whether it applied to the subject or whether it did not.

> *"Nigger, nigger, never die.*
>
> *Black face and shiny eye."*

Boys who had called this odious couplet in the rear of Johnson's march buried the fact at the bottom of their hearts.

Later in the day Miss Bella Farragut, of No. 7 Watermelon Alley, announced that she had been engaged to marry Mr. Henry Johnson.

<u>XI</u>

The old judge had a cane with an ivory head. He could never think at his best until he was leaning slightly on this stick and smoothing the white top with slow movements of his hands. It was also to him a kind of narcotic. If by any chance he mislaid it, he grew at once very irritable, and was likely to speak sharply to his sister, whose mental incapacity he had patiently endured for thirty years in the old mansion on Ontario Street. She was not at all aware of her brother's opinion of her endowments, and so it might be said that the judge had successfully dissembled for more than a quarter of a century, only risking the truth at the times when his cane was lost.

On a particular day the judge sat in his armchair on the porch. The sunshine sprinkled through the lilac-bushes and poured great coins on the boards. The sparrows disputed in the trees that lined the pavements. The judge mused deeply, while his hands gently caressed the ivory head of his cane.

Finally he arose and entered the house, his brow still furrowed in a thoughtful frown. His stick thumped solemnly in regular beats. On the second floor he entered a room where Dr. Trescott was working about the bedside of Henry Johnson. The bandages on the negro's head allowed only one thing to appear, an eye, which unwinkingly stared at the judge. The later spoke to Trescott on the condition of the patient. Afterward he evidently had something further to say, but he seemed to be kept from it by the scrutiny of the unwinking eye, at which he furtively glanced from time to time.

When Jimmie Trescott was sufficiently recovered, his mother had taken him to pay a visit to his grandparents in Connecticut. The doctor had remained to take care of his patients, but as a matter of truth he spent most of his time at Judge Hagenthorpe's house, where lay Henry Johnson. Here he slept and ate almost every meal in the long nights and days of his vigil.

At dinner, and away from the magic of the unwinking eye, the judge said, suddenly, "Trescott, do you think it is—" As Trescott paused expectantly, the judge fingered his knife. He said, thoughtfully, "No one wants to advance such ideas, but somehow I think that that poor fellow ought to die."

There was in Trescott's face at once a look of recognition, as if in this tangent of the judge he saw an old problem. He merely sighed and answered, "Who knows?" The words were spoken in a deep tone that gave them an elusive kind of significance.

The judge retreated to the cold manner of the bench. "Perhaps we may not talk with propriety of this kind of action, but I am induced to say that you are performing a questionable charity in preserving this negro's life. As near as I can understand, he will hereafter be a monster, a perfect monster, and probably with an affected brain. No man can observe you as I have observed you and not know that it was a matter of conscience with you, but I am afraid, my friend, that it is one of the blunders of virtue." The judge had delivered his views with his habitual oratory. The last three words he spoke with a particular emphasis, as if the phrase was his discovery.

The doctor made a weary gesture. "He saved my boy's life."

"Yes," said the judge, swiftly—"yes, I know!"

"And what am I to do?" said Trescott, his eyes suddenly lighting like an outburst from smouldering peat. "What am I to do? He gave himself for—for Jimmie. What am I to do for him?"

The judge abased himself completely before these words. He lowered his eyes for a moment. He picked at his cucumbers.

Presently he braced himself straightly in his chair. "He will be your creation, you understand. He is purely your creation. Nature has very evidently given him up. He is dead. You are restoring him to life. You are making him, and he will be a monster, and with no mind.

"He will be what you like, judge," cried Trescott, in sudden, polite fury. "He will be anything, but, by God! he saved my boy."

The judge interrupted in a voice trembling with emotion: "Trescott! Trescott! Don't I know?"

Trescott had subsided to a sullen mood. "Yes, you know," he answered, acidly; "but you don't know all about your own boy being saved from death." This was a perfectly childish allusion to the judge's bachelorhood. Trescott knew that the remark was infantile, but he seemed to take desperate delight in it.

But it passed the judge completely. It was not his spot.

"I am puzzled," said he, in profound thought. "I don't know what to say."

Trescott had become repentant. "Don't think I don't appreciate what you say, judge. But—"

"Of course!" responded the judge, quickly. "Of course."

"It—" began Trescott.

"Of course," said the judge.

In silence they resumed their dinner.

"Well," said the judge, ultimately, "it is hard for a man to know what to do."

"It is," said the doctor, fervidly.

There was another silence. It was broken by the judge:

"Look here, Trescott; I don't want you to think—"

"No, certainly not," answered the doctor, earnestly.

"Well, I don't want you to think I would say anything to—It was only that I thought that I might be able to suggest to you that—perhaps—the affair was a little dubious."

With an appearance of suddenly disclosing his real mental perturbation, the doctor said: "Well, what would you do? Would you kill him?" he asked, abruptly and sternly.

"Trescott, you fool," said the old man, gently.

"Oh, well, I know, judge, but then—" He turned red, and spoke with new violence: "Say, he saved my boy—do you see? He saved my boy."

"You bet he did," cried the judge, with enthusiasm. "You bet he did." And they remained for a time gazing at each other, their faces illuminated with memories of a certain deed.

After another silence, the judge said, "It is hard for a man to know what to do."

XII

Late one evening Trescott, returning from a professional call, paused his buggy at the Hagenthorpe gate. He tied the mare to the old tin-covered post, and entered the house. Ultimately he appeared with a companion—a man who walked slowly and carefully, as if he were learning. He was wrapped to the heels in an old-fashioned ulster. They entered the buggy and drove away.

After a silence only broken by the swift and musical humming of the wheels on the smooth road, Trescott spoke. "Henry," he said, "I've got you a home here with old Alek Williams. You will have everything you want to eat and a good place to sleep, and I hope you will get along there all right. I will pay all your expenses, and come to see you as often as I can. If you don't get along, I want you to let me know as soon as possible, and then we will do what we can to make it better."

The dark figure at the doctor's side answered with a cheerful laugh. "These buggy wheels don' look like I washed 'em yesterday, docteh," he said.

Trescott hesitated for a moment, and then went on insistently, "I am taking you to Alek Williams, Henry, and I—"

The figure chuckled again. "No, 'deed! No, seh! Alek Williams don' know a hoss! 'Deed he don't. He don' know a hoss from a pig." The laugh that followed was like the rattle of pebbles.

Trescott turned and looked sternly and coldly at the dim form in the gloom from the buggy-top. "Henry," he said, "I didn't say anything about horses. I was saying—"

"Hoss? Hoss?" said the quavering voice from these near shadows. "Hoss? 'Deed I don' know all erbout a boss! 'Deed I don't." There was a satirical chuckle.

At the end of three miles the mare slackened and the doctor leaned forward, peering, while holding tight reins. The wheels of the buggy bumped often over out-cropping bowlders. A window shone forth, a simple square of topaz on a great black hill-side. Four dogs charged the buggy with ferocity, and when it did not promptly retreat, they circled courageously around the flanks, baying. A door opened near the window in the hill-side, and a man came and stood on a beach of yellow light.

"Yah! yah! You Roveh! You Susie! Come yah! Come yah this minit!"

Trescott called across the dark sea of grass, "Hello, Alek!"

"Hello!"

"Come down here and show me where to drive."

The man plunged from the beach into the surf, and Trescott could then only trace his course by the fervid and polite ejaculations of a host who was somewhere approaching. Presently Williams took the mare by the head, and uttering cries of welcome and scolding the swarming dogs, led the equipage towards the lights. When they halted at the door and Trescott was climbing out, Williams cried, "Will she stand, docteh?"

"She'll stand all right, but you better hold her for a minute. Now, Henry." The doctor turned and held both arms to the dark figure. It crawled to him painfully like a man going down a ladder. Williams took the mare away to be tied to a little tree, and when he returned he found them awaiting him in the gloom beyond the rays from the door.

He burst out then like a siphon pressed by a nervous thumb. "Hennery! Hennery, ma ol' frien'. Well, if I ain' glade. If I ain' glade!"

Trescott had taken the silent shape by the arm and led it forward into the full revelation of the light. "Well, now, Alek, you can take Henry and put him to bed, and in the morning I will—"

Near the end of this sentence old Williams had come front to front with Johnson. He gasped for a second, and then yelled the yell of a man stabbed in the heart.

For a fraction of a moment Trescott seemed to be looking for epithets. Then he roared: "You old black chump! You old black—Shut up! Shut up! Do you hear?"

Williams obeyed instantly in the matter of his screams, but he continued in a lowered voice: "Ma Lode amassy! Who'd ever think? Ma Lode amassy!"

Trescott spoke again in the manner of a commander of a battalion. "Alek!"

The old negro again surrendered, but to himself he repeated in a whisper, "Ma Lode!" He was aghast and trembling.

As these three points of widening shadows approached the golden doorway a hale old negress appeared there, bowing. "Good-evenin', docteh! Good-evenin'! Come in! come in!" She had evidently just retired from a tempestuous struggle to place the room in order, but she was now bowing rapidly. She made the effort of a person swimming.

"Don't trouble yourself, Mary," said Trescott, entering. "I've brought Henry for you to take care of, and all you've got to do is to carry out what I tell you." Learning that he was not followed, he faced the door, and said, "Come in, Henry."

Johnson entered. "Whee!" shrieked Mrs. Williams. She almost achieved a back somersault. Six young members of the tribe of Williams made a simultaneous plunge for a position behind the stove, and formed a wailing heap.

<u>XIII</u>

"You know very well that you and your family lived usually on less than three dollars a week, and now that Dr. Trescott pays you five dollars a week for Johnson's board, you live like millionaires. You haven't done a stroke of work since Johnson began to board with you—everybody knows that—and so what are you kicking about?"

The judge sat in his chair on the porch, fondling his cane, and gazing down at old Williams, who stood under the lilac-bushes. "Yes, I know, jedge," said the negro, wagging his head in a puzzled manner. "Tain't like as if I didn't 'preciate what the docteh done, but—but—well, yeh see, jedge," he added, gaining a new impetus, "it's—it's hard wuk. This ol' man nev' did wuk so hard. Lode, no."

"Don't talk such nonsense, Alek," spoke the judge, sharply. "You have never really worked in your life—anyhow, enough to support a family of sparrows, and now when you are in a more prosperous condition than ever before, you come around talking like an old fool."

The negro began to scratch his head. "Yeh see, jedge," he said at last, "my ol' 'ooman she cain't 'ceive no lady callahs, nohow."

"Hang lady callers'" said the judge, irascibly. "If you have flour in the barrel and meat in the pot, your wife can get along without receiving lady callers, can't she?"

"But they won't come ainyhow, jedge," replied Williams, with an air of still deeper stupefaction. "Noner ma wife's frien's ner noner ma frien's 'll come near ma res'dence."

"Well, let them stay home if they are such silly people."

The old negro seemed to be seeking a way to elude this argument, but evidently finding none, he was about to shuffle meekly off. He halted, however. "Jedge," said he, "ma ol' 'ooman's near driv' abstracted."

"Your old woman is an idiot," responded the judge.

Williams came very close and peered solemnly through a branch of lilac. "Judge," he whispered, "the chillens."

"What about them?"

Dropping his voice to funereal depths, Williams said, "They—they cain't eat."

"Can't eat!" scoffed the judge, loudly. "Can't eat! You must think I am as big an old fool as you are. Can't eat—the little rascals! What's to prevent them from eating?"

In answer, Williams said, with mournful emphasis, "Hennery." Moved with a kind of satisfaction at his tragic use of the name, he remained staring at the judge for a sign of its effect.

The judge made a gesture of irritation. "Come, now, you old scoundrel, don't beat around the bush any more. What are you up to? What do you want? Speak out like a man, and don't give me any more of this tiresome rigamarole."

"I ain't er-beatin' round 'bout nuffin, jedge," replied Williams, indignantly. "No, seh; I say whatter got to say right out. 'Deed I do."

"Well, say it, then."

"Jedge," began the negro, taking off his hat and switching his knee with it, "Lode knows I'd do jes 'bout as much fer five dollehs er week as ainy cul'd man, but—but this yere business is awful, jedge. I raikon 'ain't been no sleep in—in my house sence docteh done fetch 'im."

"Well, what do you propose to do about it?"

Williams lifted his eyes from the ground and gazed off through the trees. "Raikon I got good appetite, an' sleep jes like er dog, but he—he's done broke me all up. 'Tain't no good, nohow. I wake up in the night; I hear 'im, mebbe, er-whimperin' an' er-whimperin', an' I sneak an' I sneak until I try th' do' to see if he locked in. An' he keep me er-puzzlin' an' er-quakin' all night long. Don't know how'll do in th' winter. Can't let 'im out where th' chillen is. He'll done freeze where he is now." Williams spoke these sentences as if he were talking to himself. After a silence of deep reflection he continued: "Folks go round sayin' he ain't Hennery Johnson at all. They say he's er devil!"

"What?" cried the judge.

"Yesseh," repeated Williams, in tones of injury, as if his veracity had been challenged. "Yesseh. I'm er-tellin' it to yeh straight, jedge. Plenty cul'd people folks up my way say it is a devil."

"Well, you don't think so yourself, do you?"

"No. 'Tain't no devil. It's Hennery Johnson."

"Well, then, what is the matter with you? You don't care what a lot of foolish people say. Go on 'tending to your business, and pay no attention to such idle nonsense."

"'Tis nonsense, jedge; but he *looks* like er devil."

"What do you care what he looks like?" demanded the judge.

"Ma rent is two dollehs and er half er month," said Williams, slowly.

"It might just as well be ten thousand dollars a month," responded the judge. "You never pay it, anyhow."

"Then, anoth' thing," continued Williams, in his reflective tone. "If he was all right in his haid I could stan' it; but, jedge, he's crazier 'n er loon. Then when he looks like er devil, an' done skears all ma frien's away, an' ma chillens cain't eat, an' ma ole 'ooman jes raisin' Cain all the time, an' ma rent two dollehs an' er half er month, an' him not right in his haid, it seems like five dollehs er week—"

The judge's stick came down sharply and suddenly upon the floor of the porch. "There," he said, "I thought that was what you were driving at."

Williams began swinging his head from side to side in the strange racial mannerism. "Now hol' on a minnet, jedge," he said, defensively. "'Tain't like as if I didn't 'preciate what the docteh done. 'Tain't that. Docteh Trescott is er kind man, an' 'tain't like as if I didn't 'preciate what he done; but—but—"

"But what? You are getting painful, Alek. Now tell me this: did you ever have five dollars a week regularly before in your life?"

Williams at once drew himself up with great dignity, but in the pause after that question he drooped gradually to another attitude. In the end he answered, heroically: "No, jedge, I 'ain't. An' 'tain't like as if I was er-sayin' five dollehs wasn't er lot er money for a man like me. But, jedge, what er man oughter git fer this kinder wuk is er salary. Yesseh, jedge," he repeated, with a great impressive gesture; "fer this kinder wuk er man oughter git er Salary." He laid a terrible emphasis upon the final word.

The judge laughed. "I know Dr. Trescott's mind concerning this affair, Alek; and if you are dissatisfied with your boarder, he is quite ready to move him to some other place; so, if you care to leave word with me that you are tired of the arrangement and wish it changed, he will come and take Johnson away."

Williams scratched his head again in deep perplexity. "Five dollehs is er big price fer bo'd, but 'tain't no big price fer the bo'd of er crazy man," he said, finally.

"What do you think you ought to get?" asked the judge.

"Well," answered Alek, in the manner of one deep in a balancing of the scales, "he looks like er devil, an' done skears e'rybody, an' ma chillens cain't eat, an' I cain't sleep, an' he ain't right in his haid, an'—"

"You told me all those things."

After scratching his wool, and beating his knee with his hat, and gazing off through the trees and down at the ground, Williams said, as he kicked nervously at the gravel, "Well, jedge, I think it is wuth—" He stuttered.

"Worth what?"

"Six dollehs," answered Williams, in a desperate outburst.

The judge lay back in his great arm-chair and went through all the motions of a man laughing heartily, but he made no sound save a slight cough. Williams had been watching him with apprehension.

"Well," said the judge, "do you call six dollars a salary?"

"No, seh," promptly responded Williams. "'Tain't a salary. No, 'deed! 'Tain't a salary." He looked with some anger upon the man who questioned his intelligence in this way.

"Well, supposing your children can't eat?"

"I—"

"And supposing he looks like a devil? And supposing all those things continue? Would you be satisfied with six dollars a week?"

Recollections seemed to throng in Williams's mind at these interrogations, and he answered dubiously. "Of co'se a man who ain't right in his haid, an' looks like er devil—But six dollehs—" After these two attempts at a sentence Williams suddenly appeared as an orator, with a great shiny palm waving in the air. "I tell yeh, jedge, six dollehs is six dollehs, but if I git six dollehs for bo'ding Hennery Johnson, I uhns it! I uhns it!"

"I don't doubt that you earn six dollars for every week's work you do," said the judge.

"Well, if I bo'd Hennery Johnson fer six dollehs er week, I uhns it! I uhns it!" cried Williams, wildly.

XIV

Reifsnyder's assistant had gone to his supper, and the owner of the shop was trying to placate four men who wished to be shaved at once. Reifsnyder was very garrulous—a fact which made him rather remarkable among barbers, who, as a class, are austerely speechless, having been taught silence by the hammering reiteration of a tradition. It is the customers who talk in the ordinary event.

As Reifsnyder waved his razor down the cheek of a man in the chair, he turned often to cool the impatience of the others with pleasant talk, which they did not particularly heed.

"Oh, he should have let him die," said Bainbridge, a railway engineer, finally replying to one of the barber's orations. "Shut up, Reif, and go on with your business!"

Instead, Reifsnyder paused shaving entirely, and turned to front the speaker. "Let him die?" he demanded. "How vas that? How can you let a man die?"

"By letting him die, you chump," said the engineer. The others laughed a little, and Reifsnyder turned at once to his work, sullenly, as a man overwhelmed by the derision of numbers.

"How vas that?" he grumbled later. "How can you let a man die when he vas done so much for you?"

"'When he vas done so much for you?'" repeated Bainbridge. "You better shave some people. How vas that? Maybe this ain't a barber shop?"

A man hitherto silent now said, "If I had been the doctor, I would have done the same thing."

"Of course," said Reifsnyder. "Any man could do it. Any man that vas

204

not like you, you—old—flint-hearted—fish." He had sought the final words with painful care, and he delivered the collection triumphantly at Bainbridge. The engineer laughed.

The man in the chair now lifted himself higher, while Reifsnyder began an elaborate ceremony of anointing and combing his hair. Now free to join comfortably in the talk, the man said: "They say he is the most terrible thing in the world. Young Johnnie Bernard—that drives the grocery wagon—saw him up at Alek Williams's shanty, and he says he couldn't eat anything for two days."

"Chee!" said Reifsnyder.

"Well, what makes him so terrible?" asked another.

"Because he hasn't got any face," replied the barber and the engineer in duct.

"Hasn't got any face!" repeated the man. "How can he do without any face?"

> "He has no face in the front of his head.
>
> In the place where his face ought to grow."

Bainbridge sang these lines pathetically as he arose and hung his hat on a hook. The man in the chair was about to abdicate in his favor. "Get a gait on you now," he said to Reifsnyder. "I go out at 7.31."

As the barber foamed the lather on the cheeks of the engineer he seemed to be thinking heavily. Then suddenly he burst out. "How would you like to be with no face?" he cried to the assemblage.

"Oh, if I had to have a face like yours—" answered one customer.

Bainbridge's voice came from a sea of lather. "You're kicking because if losing faces became popular, you'd have to go out of business."

"I don't think it will become so much popular," said Reifsnyder.

"Not if it's got to be taken off in the way his was taken off," said another man. "I'd rather keep mine, if you don't mind."

"I guess so!" cried the barber. "Just think!"

The shaving of Bainbridge had arrived at a time of comparative liberty for him. "I wonder what the doctor says to himself?" he observed. "He may be sorry he made him live."

"It was the only thing he could do," replied a man. The others seemed to agree with him.

"Supposing you were in his place," said one, "and Johnson had saved your kid. What would you do?"

"Certainly!"

"Of course! You would do anything on earth for him. You'd take all the trouble in the world for him. And spend your last dollar on him. Well, then?"

"I wonder how it feels to be without any face?" said Reifsnyder, musingly.

The man who had previously spoken, feeling that he had expressed himself well, repeated the whole thing. "You would do anything on earth for him. You'd take all the trouble in the world for him. And spend your last dollar on him. Well, then?"

"No, but look," said Reifsnyder; "supposing you don't got a face!"

XV

As soon as Williams was hidden from the view of the old judge he began to gesture and talk to himself. An elation had evidently penetrated to his vitals, and caused him to dilate as if he had been filled with gas. He snapped his fingers in the air, and whistled fragments of triumphal music. At times, in his progress towards his shanty, he indulged in a shuffling movement that was really a dance. It was to be learned from the intermediate monologue that he had emerged from his trials laurelled and proud. He was the unconquerable Alexander Williams. Nothing could exceed the bold self-reliance of his manner. His kingly stride, his heroic song, the derisive flourish of his hands— all betokened a man who had successfully defied the world.

On his way he saw Zeke Paterson coming to town. They hailed each other at a distance of fifty yards.

"How do, Broth' Paterson?"

"How do, Broth' Williams?"

They were both deacons.

"Is you' folks well, Broth' Paterson?"

"Middlin', middlin'. How's you' folks, Broth' Williams?"

Neither of them had slowed his pace in the smallest degree. They had simply begun this talk when a considerable space separated them, continued it as they passed, and added polite questions as they drifted steadily apart. Williams's mind seemed to be a balloon. He had been so inflated that he had not noticed that Paterson had definitely shied into the dry ditch as they came to the point of ordinary contact.

Afterwards, as he went a lonely way, he burst out again in song and pantomimic celebration of his estate. His feet moved in prancing steps.

When he came in sight of his cabin, the fields were bathed in a blue dusk, and the light in the window was pale. Cavorting and gesticulating, he gazed joyfully for some moments upon this light. Then suddenly another idea seemed to attack his mind, and he stopped, with an air of being suddenly dampened. In the end he approached his home as if it were the fortress of an enemy.

Some dogs disputed his advance for a loud moment, and then discovering their lord, slunk away embarrassed. His reproaches were addressed to them in muffled tones.

Arriving at the door, he pushed it open with the timidity of a new thief. He thrust his head cautiously sideways, and his eyes met the eyes of his wife, who sat by the table, the lamp-light defining a half of her face. "'Sh!" he said, uselessly. His glance travelled swiftly to the inner door which shielded the one bed-chamber. The pickaninnies, strewn upon the floor of the living-room, were softly snoring. After a hearty meal they had promptly dispersed themselves about the place and gone to sleep. "'Sh!" said Williams again to his motionless and silent wife. He had allowed only his head to appear. His wife, with one hand upon the edge of the table and the other at her knee, was regarding him with wide eyes and parted lips as if he were a spectre. She looked to be one who was living in terror, and even the familiar face at the door had thrilled her because it had come suddenly.

Williams broke the tense silence. "Is he all right?" he whispered, waving his eyes towards the inner door. Following his glance timorously, his wife nodded, and in a low tone answered:

"I raikon he's done gone t' sleep."

Williams then slunk noiselessly across his threshold.

He lifted a chair, and with infinite care placed it so that it faced the dreaded inner door. His wife moved slightly, so as to also squarely face it. A silence came upon them in which they seemed to be waiting for a calamity, pealing and deadly.

Williams finally coughed behind his hand. His wife started, and looked upon him in alarm. "Pears like he done gwine keep quiet ternight," he breathed. They continually pointed their speech and their looks at the inner door, paying it the homage due to a corpse or a phantom. Another long stillness followed this sentence. Their eyes shone white and wide. A wagon rattled down the distant road. From their chairs they looked at the window, and the effect of the light in the cabin was a presentation of an intensely black and solemn night. The old woman adopted the attitude used always in church at funerals. At times she seemed to be upon the point of breaking out in prayer.

208

"He mighty quiet ter-night," whispered Williams. "Was he good ter-day?" For answer his wife raised her eyes to the ceiling in the supplication of Job. Williams moved restlessly. Finally he tiptoed to the door. He knelt slowly and without a sound, and placed his ear near the key-hole. Hearing a noise behind him, he turned quickly. His wife was staring at him aghast. She stood in front of the stove, and her arms were spread out in the natural movement to protect all her sleeping ducklings.

But Williams arose without having touched the door. "I raikon he er-sleep," he said, fingering his wool. He debated with himself for some time. During this interval his wife remained, a great fat statue of a mother shielding her children.

It was plain that his mind was swept suddenly by a wave of temerity. With a sounding step he moved towards the door. His fingers were almost upon the knob when he swiftly ducked and dodged away, clapping his hands to the back of his head. It was as if the portal had threatened him. There was a little tumult near the stove, where Mrs. Williams's desperate retreat had involved her feet with the prostrate children.

After the panic Williams bore traces of a feeling of shame. He returned to the charge. He firmly grasped the knob with his left hand, and with his other hand turned the key in the lock. He pushed the door, and as it swung portentously open he sprang nimbly to one side like the fearful slave liberating the lion. Near the stove a group had formed, the terror stricken mother, with her arms stretched, and the aroused children clinging frenziedly to her skirts.

The light streamed after the swinging door, and disclosed a room six feet one way and six feet the other way. It was small enough to enable the radiance to lay it plain. Williams peered warily around the corner made by the door-post.

Suddenly he advanced, retired, and advanced again with a howl. His palsied family had expected him to spring backward, and at his howl they heaped themselves wondrously. But Williams simply stood in the little room emitting his howls before an open window. "He's gone! He's gone! He's gone!" His eye and his hand had speedily proved the fact. He had even thrown open a little cupboard.

Presently he came flying out. He grabbed his hat, and hurled the outer door back upon its hinges. Then he tumbled headlong into the night. He was yelling: "Docteh Trescott! Docteh Trescott!" He ran wildly through the fields, and galloped in the direction of town. He continued to call to Trescott, as if the latter was within easy hearing. It was as if Trescott was poised in the contemplative sky over the running negro, and could heed this reaching voice—"Docteh Trescott!"

In the cabin, Mrs. Williams, supported by relays from the battalion of children, stood quaking watch until the truth of daylight came as a reinforcement and made the arrogant, strutting, swashbuckler children, and a mother who proclaimed her illimitable courage.

XVI

Theresa Page was giving a party. It was the outcome of a long series of arguments addressed to her mother, which had been overheard in part by her father. He had at last said five words, "Oh, let her have it." The mother had then gladly capitulated.

Theresa had written nineteen invitations, and distributed them at recess to her schoolmates. Later her mother had composed five large cakes, and still later a vast amount of lemonade.

So the nine little girls and the ten little boys sat quite primly in the dining-room, while Theresa and her mother plied them with cake and lemonade, and also with ice-cream. This primness sat now quite strangely upon them. It was owing to the presence of Mrs. Page. Previously in the parlor alone with their games they had overturned a chair; the boys had let more or less of their hoodlum spirit shine forth. But when circumstances could be possibly magnified to warrant it, the girls made the boys victims of an insufferable pride, snubbing them mercilessly. So in the dining-room they resembled a class at Sunday-school, if it were not for the subterranean smiles, gestures, rebuffs, and poutings which stamped the affair as a children's party.

Two little girls of this subdued gathering were planted in a settle with their backs to the broad window. They were beaming lovingly upon each other with an effect of scorning the boys.

Hearing a noise behind her at the window, one little girl turned to face it. Instantly she screamed and sprang away, covering her face with her hands. "What was it? What was it?" cried every one in a roar. Some slight movement of the eyes of the weeping and shuddering child informed the company that she had been frightened by an appearance at the window. At once they all faced the imperturbable window, and for a moment there was a silence. An astute lad made an immediate census of the other lads. The prank of slipping out and looming spectrally at a window was too venerable. But the little boys were all present and astonished.

As they recovered their minds they uttered warlike cries, and through a side door sallied rapidly out against the terror. They vied with each other in daring.

None wished particularly to encounter a dragon in the darkness of the garden, but there could be no faltering when the fair ones in the dining-room were present. Calling to each other in stern voices, they went dragooning over the lawn, attacking the shadows with ferocity, but still with the caution of reasonable beings. They found, however, nothing new to the peace of the night. Of course there was a lad who told a great lie. He described a grim figure, bending low and slinking off along the fence. He gave a number of details, rendering his lie more splendid by a repetition of certain forms which he recalled from romances. For instance, he insisted that he had heard the creature emit a hollow laugh.

Inside the house the little girl who had raised the alarm was still shuddering and weeping. With the utmost difficulty was she brought to a state approximating calmness by Mrs. Page. Then she wanted to go home at once.

Page entered the house at this time. He had exiled himself until he concluded that this children's party was finished and gone. He was obliged to escort the little girl home because she screamed again when they opened the door and she saw the night.

She was not coherent even to her mother. Was it a man? She didn't know. It was simply a thing, a dreadful thing.

XVII

In Watermelon Alley the Farraguts were spending their evening as usual on the little rickety porch. Sometimes they howled gossip to other people on other rickety porches. The thin wail of a baby arose from a near house. A man had a terrific altercation with his wife, to which the alley paid no attention at all.

There appeared suddenly before the Farraguts a monster making a low and sweeping bow. There was an instant's pause, and then occurred something that resembled the effect of an upheaval of the earth's surface. The old woman hurled herself backward with a dreadful cry. Young Sim had been perched gracefully on a railing. At sight of the monster he simply fell over it to the ground. He made no sound, his eyes stuck out, his nerveless hands tried to grapple the rail to prevent a tumble, and then he vanished. Bella, blubbering, and with her hair suddenly and mysteriously dishevelled, was crawling on her hands and knees fearsomely up the steps.

Standing before this wreck of a family gathering, the monster continued to bow. It even raised a deprecatory claw. "Doh' make no botheration 'bout me, Miss Fa'gut," it said, politely. "No, 'deed. I jes drap in ter ax if yer well this evenin', Miss Fa'gut. Don' make no botheration. No, 'deed. I gwine ax you to go to er daince with me, Miss Fa'gut. I ax you if I can have the magnifercent gratitude of you' company on that 'casion, Miss Fa'gut."

The girl cast a miserable glance behind her. She was still crawling away. On the ground beside the porch young Sim raised a strange bleat, which expressed both his fright and his lack of wind. Presently the monster, with a fashionable amble, ascended the steps after the girl.

She grovelled in a corner of the room as the creature took a chair. It seated itself very elegantly on the edge. It held an old cap in both hands. "Don' make no botheration, Miss Fa'gut. Don' make no botherations. No, 'deed. I jes drap in ter ax you if you won' do me the proud of acceptin' ma humble invitation to er daince, Miss Fa'gut."

She shielded her eyes with her arms and tried to crawl past it, but the genial monster blocked the way. "I jes drap in ter ax you 'bout er daince, Miss Fa'gut. I ax you if I kin have the magnifercent gratitude of you' company on that 'casion, Miss Fa'gut."

In a last outbreak of despair, the girl, shuddering and wailing, threw herself face downward on the floor, while the monster sat on the edge of the chair gabbling courteous invitations, and holding the old hat daintily to his stomach.

At the back of the house, Mrs. Farragut, who was of enormous weight, and who for eight years had done little more than sit in an armchair and describe her various ailments, had with speed and agility scaled a high board fence.

XVIII

The black mass in the middle of Trescott's property was hardly allowed to cool before the builders were at work on another house. It had sprung upward at a fabulous rate. It was like a magical composition born of the ashes. The doctor's office was the first part to be completed, and he had already moved in his new books and instruments and medicines.

Trescott sat before his desk when the chief of police arrived. "Well, we found him," said the latter.

"Did you?" cried the doctor. "Where?"

"Shambling around the streets at daylight this morning. I'll be blamed if I can figure on where he passed the night."

"Where is he now?"

"Oh, we jugged him. I didn't know what else to do with him. That's what I want you to tell me. Of course we can't keep him. No charge could be made, you know."

"I'll come down and get him."

The official grinned retrospectively. "Must say he had a fine career while he was out. First thing he did was to break up a children's party at Page's. Then he went to Watermelon Alley. Whoo! He stampeded the whole outfit. Men, women, and children running pell-mell, and yelling. They say one old woman broke her leg, or something, shinning over a fence. Then he went right out on the main street, and an Irish girl threw a fit, and there was a sort of a riot. He began to run, and a big crowd chased him, firing rocks. But he gave them the slip somehow down there by the foundry and in the railroad yard. We looked for him all night, but couldn't find him."

"Was he hurt any? Did anybody hit him with a stone?"

"Guess there isn't much of him to hurt any more, is there? Guess he's been hurt up to the limit. No. They never touched him. Of course nobody really wanted to hit him, but you know how a crowd gets. It's like—it's like—"

"Yes, I know."

For a moment the chief of the police looked reflectively at the floor. Then he spoke hesitatingly. "You know Jake Winter's little girl was the one that he scared at the party. She is pretty sick, they say."

"Is she? Why, they didn't call me. I always attend the Winter family."

"No? Didn't they?" asked the chief, slowly. "Well—you know—Winter is—well, Winter has gone clean crazy over this business. He wanted—he wanted to have you arrested."

"Have me arrested? The idiot! What in the name of wonder could he have me arrested for?"

"Of course. He is a fool. I told him to keep his trap shut. But then you know how he'll go all over town yapping about the thing. I thought I'd better tip you."

"Oh, he is of no consequence; but then, of course, I'm obliged to you, Sam."

"That's all right. Well, you'll be down tonight and take him out, eh? You'll get a good welcome from the jailer. He don't like his job for a cent. He says you can have your man whenever you want him. He's got no use for him."

"But what is this business of Winter's about having me arrested?"

"Oh, it's a lot of chin about your having no right to allow this—this—this man to be at large. But I told him to tend to his own business. Only I thought I'd better let you know. And I might as well say right now, doctor, that there is a good deal of talk about this thing. If I were you, I'd come to the jail pretty late at night, because there is likely to be a crowd around the door, and I'd bring a—er—mask, or some kind of a veil, anyhow."

XIX

Martha Goodwin was single, and well along into the thin years. She lived with her married sister in Whilomville. She performed nearly all the house-work in exchange for the privilege of existence. Every one tacitly recognized her labor as a form of penance for the early end of her betrothed, who had died of small-pox, which he had not caught from her.

But despite the strenuous and unceasing workaday of her life, she was a woman of great mind. She had adamantine opinions upon the situation in Armenia, the condition of women in China, the flirtation between Mrs. Minster of Niagara Avenue and young Griscom, the conflict in the Bible class of the Baptist Sunday-school, the duty of the United States towards the Cuban insurgents, and many other colossal matters. Her fullest experience of violence was gained on an occasion when she had seen a hound clubbed, but in the plan which she had made for the reform of the world she advocated drastic measures. For instance, she contended that all the Turks should be pushed into the sea and drowned, and that Mrs. Minster and young Griscom should be hanged side by side on twin gallows. In fact, this woman of peace, who had seen only peace, argued constantly for a creed of illimitable ferocity. She was invulnerable on these questions, because eventually she overrode all opponents with a sniff. This sniff was an active force. It was to her antagonists like a bang over the head, and none was known to recover from this expression of exalted contempt. It left them windless and conquered. They never again came forward as candidates for suppression. And Martha walked her kitchen with a stern brow, an invincible being like Napoleon.

Nevertheless her acquaintances, from the pain of their defeats, had been long in secret revolt. It was in no wise a conspiracy, because they did not care to state their open rebellion, but nevertheless it was understood that any woman who could not coincide with one of Martha's contentions was entitled to the support of others in the small circle. It amounted to an arrangement by which all were required to disbelieve any theory for which Martha fought. This, however, did not prevent them from speaking of her mind with profound respect.

Two people bore the brunt of her ability. Her sister Kate was visibly afraid of her, while Carrie Dungen sailed across from her kitchen to sit respectfully at Martha's feet and learn the business of the world. To be sure, afterwards, under another sun, she always laughed at Martha and pretended to deride her ideas, but in the presence of the sovereign she always remained silent or admiring. Kate, the sister, was of no consequence at all. Her principal delusion was that she did all the work in the up-stairs rooms of the house, while Martha did it down-stairs. The truth was seen only by the husband, who treated Martha with a kindness that was half banter, half deference. Martha herself had no suspicion that she was the only pillar of the domestic edifice. The situation was without definitions. Martha made definitions, but she devoted them entirely to the Armenians and Griscom and the Chinese and other subjects. Her dreams, which in early days had been of love of meadows and the shade of trees, of the face of a man, were now involved otherwise, and they were companioned in the kitchen curiously, Cuba, the hot-water kettle, Armenia, the washing of the dishes, and the whole thing being jumbled. In regard to social misdemeanors, she who was simply the mausoleum of a dead passion was probably the most savage critic in town. This unknown woman, hidden in a kitchen as in a well, was sure to have a considerable effect of the one kind or the other in the life of the town. Every time it moved a yard, she had personally contributed an inch. She could hammer so stoutly upon the door of a proposition that it would break from its hinges and fall upon her, but at any rate it moved. She was an engine, and the fact that she did not know that she was an engine contributed largely to the effect. One reason that she was formidable was that she did not even imagine that she was formidable. She remained a weak, innocent, and pig-headed creature, who alone would defy the universe if she thought the universe merited this proceeding.

One day Carrie Dungen came across from her kitchen with speed. She had a great deal of grist. "Oh," she cried, "Henry Johnson got away from where they was keeping him, and came to town last night, and scared everybody almost to death."

Martha was shining a dish-pan, polishing madly. No reasonable person could see cause for this operation, because the pan already glistened like silver. "Well!" she ejaculated. She imparted to the word a deep meaning. "This, my prophecy, has come to pass." It was a habit.

The overplus of information was choking Carrie. Before she could go on she was obliged to struggle for a moment. "And, oh, little Sadie Winter is awful sick, and they say Jake Winter was around this morning trying to get Doctor Trescott arrested. And poor old Mrs. Farragut sprained her ankle in trying to climb a fence. And there's a crowd around the jail all the time. They put Henry in jail because they didn't know what else to do with him, I guess. They say he is perfectly terrible."

Martha finally released the dish-pan and confronted the headlong speaker. "Well!" she said again, poising a great brown rag. Kate had heard the excited new-comer, and drifted down from the novel in her room. She was a shivery little woman. Her shoulder-blades seemed to be two panes of ice, for she was constantly shrugging and shrugging. "Serves him right if he was to lose all his patients," she said suddenly, in blood-thirsty tones. She snipped her words out as if her lips were scissors.

"Well, he's likely to," shouted Carrie Dungen. "Don't a lot of people say that they won't have him any more? If you're sick and nervous, Doctor Trescott would scare the life out of you, wouldn't he? He would me. I'd keep thinking."

Martha, stalking to and fro, sometimes surveyed the two other women with a contemplative frown.

XX

After the return from Connecticut, little Jimmie was at first much afraid of the monster who lived in the room over the carriage-house. He could not identify it in any way. Gradually, however, his fear dwindled under the influence of a weird fascination. He sidled into closer and closer relations with it.

One time the monster was seated on a box behind the stable basking in the rays of the afternoon sun. A heavy crepe veil was swathed about its head.

Little Jimmie and many companions came around the corner of the stable. They were all in what was popularly known as the baby class, and consequently escaped from school a half-hour before the other children. They halted abruptly at sight of the figure on the box. Jimmie waved his hand with the air of a proprietor.

"There he is," he said.

"O-o-o!" murmured all the little boys—"o-o-o!" They shrank back, and grouped according to courage or experience, as at the sound the monster slowly turned its head. Jimmie had remained in the van alone. "Don't be afraid! I won't let him hurt you," he said, delighted.

"Huh!" they replied, contemptuously. "We ain't afraid."

Jimmie seemed to reap all the joys of the owner and exhibitor of one of the world's marvels, while his audience remained at a distance—awed and entranced, fearful and envious.

One of them addressed Jimmie gloomily. "Bet you dassent walk right up to him." He was an older boy than Jimmie, and habitually oppressed him to a small degree. This new social elevation of the smaller lad probably seemed revolutionary to him.

"Huh!" said Jimmie, with deep scorn. "Dassent I? Dassent I, hey? Dassent I?"

The group was immensely excited. It turned its eyes upon the boy that Jimmie addressed. "No, you dassent," he said, stolidly, facing a moral defeat. He could see that Jimmie was resolved. "No, you dassent," he repeated, doggedly.

"Ho?" cried Jimmie. "You just watch!—you just watch!"

Amid a silence he turned and marched towards the monster. But possibly the palpable wariness of his companions had an effect upon him that weighed more than his previous experience, for suddenly, when near to the monster, he halted dubiously. But his playmates immediately uttered a derisive shout, and it seemed to force him forward. He went to the monster and laid his hand delicately on its shoulder. "Hello, Henry," he said, in a voice that trembled a trifle. The monster was crooning a weird line of negro melody that was scarcely more than a thread of sound, and it paid no heed to the boy.

Jimmie: strutted back to his companions. They acclaimed him and hooted his opponent. Amid this clamor the larger boy with difficulty preserved a dignified attitude.

"I dassent, dassent I?" said Jimmie to him.

"Now, you're so smart, let's see you do it!"

This challenge brought forth renewed taunts from the others. The larger boy puffed out his checks. "Well, I ain't afraid," he explained, sullenly. He had made a mistake in diplomacy, and now his small enemies were tumbling his prestige all about his ears. They crowed like roosters and bleated like lambs, and made many other noises which were supposed to bury him in ridicule and dishonor. "Well, I ain't afraid," he continued to explain through the din.

Jimmie, the hero of the mob, was pitiless. "You ain't afraid, hey?" he sneered. "If you ain't afraid, go do it, then."

"Well, I would if I wanted to," the other retorted. His eyes wore an expression of profound misery, but he preserved steadily other portions of a pot-valiant air. He suddenly faced one of his persecutors. "If you're so smart, why don't you go do it?" This persecutor sank promptly through the group to the rear. The incident gave the badgered one a breathing-spell, and for a moment even turned the derision in another direction. He took advantage of his interval. "I'll do it if anybody else will," he announced, swaggering to and fro.

Candidates for the adventure did not come forward. To defend themselves from this counter-charge, the other boys again set up their crowing and bleating. For a while they would hear nothing from him. Each time he opened his lips their chorus of noises made oratory impossible. But at last he was able to repeat that he would volunteer to dare as much in the affair as any other boy.

"Well, you go first," they shouted.

But Jimmie intervened to once more lead the populace against the large boy. "You're mighty brave, ain't you?" he said to him. "You dared me to do it, and I did—didn't I? Now who's afraid?" The others cheered this view loudly, and they instantly resumed the baiting of the large boy.

He shamefacedly scratched his left shin with his right foot. "Well, I ain't afraid." He cast an eye at the monster. "Well, I ain't afraid." With a glare of hatred at his squalling tormentors, he finally announced a grim intention. "Well, I'll do it, then, since you're so fresh. Now!"

The mob subsided as with a formidable countenance he turned towards the impassive figure on the box. The advance was also a regular progression from high daring to craven hesitation. At last, when some yards from the monster, the lad came to a full halt, as if he had encountered a stone wall. The observant little boys in the distance promptly hooted. Stung again by these cries, the lad sneaked two yards forward. He was crouched like a young cat ready for a backward spring. The crowd at the rear, beginning to respect this display, uttered some encouraging cries. Suddenly the lad gathered himself together, made a white and desperate rush forward, touched the monster's shoulder with a far-outstretched finger, and sped away, while his laughter rang out wild, shrill, and exultant.

The crowd of boys reverenced him at once, and began to throng into his camp, and look at him, and be his admirers. Jimmie was discomfited for a moment, but he and the larger boy, without agreement or word of any kind, seemed to recognize a truce, and they swiftly combined and began to parade before the others.

"Why, it's just as easy as nothing," puffed the larger boy. "Ain't it, Jim?"

"Course," blew Jimmie. "Why, it's as e-e-easy."

They were people of another class. If they had been decorated for courage on twelve battle-fields, they could not have made the other boys more ashamed of the situation.

Meanwhile they condescended to explain the emotions of the excursion, expressing unqualified contempt for any one who could hang back. "Why, it ain't nothin'. He won't do nothin' to you," they told the others, in tones of exasperation.

One of the very smallest boys in the party showed signs of a wistful desire to distinguish himself, and they turned their attention to him, pushing at his shoulders while he swung away from them, and hesitated dreamily. He was eventually induced to make furtive expedition, but it was only for a few yards. Then he paused, motionless, gazing with open mouth. The vociferous entreaties of Jimmie and the large boy had no power over him.

Mrs. Hannigan had come out on her back porch with a pail of water. From this coign she had a view of the secluded portion of the Trescott grounds that was behind the stable. She perceived the group of boys, and the monster on the box. She shaded her eyes with her hand to benefit her vision. She screeched then as if she was being murdered. "Eddie! Eddie! You come home this minute!"

Her son querulously demanded, "Aw, what for?"

"You come home this minute. Do you hear?"

The other boys seemed to think this visitation upon one of their number required them to preserve for a time the hang-dog air of a collection of culprits, and they remained in guilty silence until the little Hannigan, wrathfully protesting, was pushed through the door of his home. Mrs. Hannigan cast a piercing glance over the group, stared with a bitter face at the Trescott house, as if this new and handsome edifice was insulting her, and then followed her son.

There was wavering in the party. An inroad by one mother always caused them to carefully sweep the horizon to see if there were more coming. "This is my yard," said Jimmie, proudly. "We don't have to go home."

The monster on the box had turned its black crepe countenance towards the sky, and was waving its arms in time to a religious chant. "Look at him now," cried a little boy. They turned, and were transfixed by the solemnity and mystery of the indefinable gestures. The wail of the melody was mournful and slow. They drew back. It seemed to spellbind them with the power of a funeral. They were so absorbed that they did not hear the doctor's buggy drive up to the stable. Trescott got out, tied his horse, and approached the group. Jimmie saw him first, and at his look of dismay the others wheeled.

"What's all this, Jimmie?" asked Trescott, in surprise.

The lad advanced to the front of his companions, halted, and said nothing. Trescott's face gloomed slightly as he scanned the scene.

"What were you doing, Jimmie?"

"We was playin'," answered Jimmie, huskily.

"Playing at what?"

"Just playin'."

Trescott looked gravely at the other boys, and asked them to please go home. They proceeded to the street much in the manner of frustrated and revealed assassins. The crime of trespass on another boy's place was still a crime when they had only accepted the other boy's cordial invitation, and they were used to being sent out of all manner of gardens upon the sudden appearance of a father or a mother. Jimmie had wretchedly watched the departure of his companions. It involved the loss of his position as a lad who controlled the privileges of his father's grounds, but then he knew that in the beginning he had no right to ask so many boys to be his guests.

Once on the sidewalk, however, they speedily forgot their shame as trespassers, and the large boy launched forth in a description of his success in the late trial of courage. As they went rapidly up the street, the little boy who had made the furtive expedition cried out confidently from the rear, "Yes, and I went almost up to him, didn't I, Willie?"

The large boy crushed him in a few words. "Huh!" he scoffed. "You only went a little way. I went clear up to him."

The pace of the other boys was so manly that the tiny thing had to trot, and he remained at the rear, getting entangled in their legs in his attempts to reach the front rank and become of some importance, dodging this way and that way, and always piping out his little claim to glory.

XXI

"By-the-way, Grace," said Trescott, looking into the dining-room from his office door, "I wish you would send Jimmie to me before school-time."

When Jimmie came, he advanced so quietly that Trescott did not at first note him. "Oh," he said, wheeling from a cabinet, "here you are, young man."

"Yes, sir."

Trescott dropped into his chair and tapped the desk with a thoughtful finger. "Jimmie, what were you doing in the back garden yesterday—you and the other boys—to Henry?"

"We weren't doing anything, pa."

Trescott looked sternly into the raised eyes of his son. "Are you sure you were not annoying him in any way? Now what were you doing, exactly?"

"Why, we—why, we—now—Willie Dalzel said I dassent go right up to him, and I did; and then he did; and then—the other boys were 'fraid; and then—you comed."

Trescott groaned deeply. His countenance was so clouded in sorrow that the lad, bewildered by the mystery of it, burst suddenly forth in dismal lamentations. "There, there. Don't cry, Jim," said Trescott, going round the desk. "Only—" He sat in a great leather reading-chair, and took the boy on his knee. "Only I want to explain to you—"

After Jimmie had gone to school, and as Trescott was about to start on his round of morning calls, a message arrived from Doctor Moser. It set forth that the latter's sister was dying in the old homestead, twenty miles away up the valley, and asked Trescott to care for his patients for the day at least. There was also in the envelope a little history of each case and of what had already been done. Trescott replied to the messenger that he would gladly assent to the arrangement.

He noted that the first name on Moser's list was Winter, but this did not seem to strike him as an important fact. When its turn came, he rang the Winter bell. "Good-morning, Mrs. Winter," he said, cheerfully, as the door was opened. "Doctor Moser has been obliged to leave town to-day, and he has asked me to come in his stead. How is the little girl this morning?"

Mrs. Winter had regarded him in stony surprise. At last she said: "Come in! I'll see my husband." She bolted into the house. Trescott entered the hall, and turned to the left into the sitting-room.

Presently Winter shuffled through the door. His eyes flashed towards Trescott. He did not betray any desire to advance far into the room. "What do you want?" he said.

"What do I want? What do I want?" repeated Trescott, lifting his head suddenly. He had heard an utterly new challenge in the night of the jungle.

"Yes, that's what I want to know," snapped Winter. "What do you want?"

Trescott was silent for a moment. He consulted Moser's memoranda. "I see that your little girl's case is a trifle serious," he remarked. "I would advise you to call a physician soon. I will leave you a copy of Dr. Moser's record to give to any one you may call." He paused to transcribe the record on a page of his note-book. Tearing out the leaf, he extended it to Winter as he moved towards the door. The latter shrunk against the wall. His head was hanging as he reached for the paper. This caused him to grasp air, and so Trescott simply let the paper flutter to the feet of the other man.

"Good-morning," said Trescott from the hall. This placid retreat seemed to suddenly arouse Winter to ferocity. It was as if he had then recalled all the truths which he had formulated to hurl at Trescott. So he followed him into the hall, and down the hall to the door, and through the door to the porch, barking in fiery rage from a respectful distance. As Trescott imperturbably turned the mare's head down the road, Winter stood on the porch, still yelping. He was like a little dog.

XXII

"Have you heard the news?" cried Carrie Dungen as she sped towards Martha's kitchen. "Have you heard the news?" Her eyes were shining with delight.

"No," answered Martha's sister Kate, bending forward eagerly. "What was it? What was it?"

Carrie appeared triumphantly in the open door. "Oh, there's been an awful scene between Doctor Trescott and Jake Winter. I never thought that Jake Winter had any pluck at all, but this morning he told the doctor just what he thought of him."

"Well, what did he think of him?" asked Martha.

"Oh, he called him everything. Mrs. Howarth heard it through her front blinds. It was terrible, she says. It's all over town now. Everybody knows it."

"Didn't the doctor answer back?"

"No! Mrs. Howarth—she says he never said a word. He just walked down to his buggy and got in, and drove off as co-o-o-l. But Jake gave him jinks, by all accounts."

"But what did he say?" cried Kate, shrill and excited. She was evidently at some kind of a feast.

"Oh, he told him that Sadie had never been well since that night Henry Johnson frightened her at Theresa Page's party, and he held him responsible, and how dared he cross his threshold—and—and—and—"

"And what?" said Martha.

"Did he swear at him?" said Kate, in fearsome glee.

"No—not much. He did swear at him a little, but not more than a man does anyhow when he is real mad, Mrs. Howarth says."

"O-oh!" breathed Kate. "And did he call him any names?"

Martha, at her work, had been for a time in deep thought. She now interrupted the others. "It don't seem as if Sadie Winter had been sick since that time Henry Johnson got loose. She's been to school almost the whole time since then, hasn't she?"

They combined upon her in immediate indignation. "School? School? I should say not. Don't think for a moment. School!"

Martha wheeled from the sink. She held an iron spoon, and it seemed as if she was going to attack them. "Sadie Winter has passed here many a morning since then carrying her schoolbag. Where was she going? To a wedding?"

The others, long accustomed to a mental tyranny, speedily surrendered.

"Did she?" stammered Kate. "I never saw her." ·

Carrie Dungen made a weak gesture.

"If I had been Doctor Trescott," exclaimed Martha, loudly, "I'd have knocked that miserable Jake Winter's head off."

Kate and Carrie, exchanging glances, made an alliance in the air. "I don't see why you say that, Martha," replied Carrie, with considerable boldness, gaining support and sympathy from Kate's smile. "I don't see how anybody can be blamed for getting angry when their little girl gets almost scared to death and gets sick from it, and all that. Besides, everybody says—"

"Oh, I don't care what everybody says," said Martha.

"Well, you can't go against the whole town," answered Carrie, in sudden sharp defiance.

"No, Martha, you can't go against the whole town," piped Kate, following her leader rapidly.

"'The whole town,'" cried Martha. "I'd like to know what you call 'the whole town.' Do you call these silly people who are scared of Henry Johnson 'the whole town'?"

"Why, Martha," said Carrie, in a reasoning tone, "you talk as if you wouldn't be scared of him!"

"No more would I," retorted Martha.

"O-oh, Martha, how you talk!" said Kate. "Why, the idea! Everybody's afraid of him."

Carrie was grinning. "You've never seen him, have you?" she asked, seductively.

"No," admitted Martha.

"Well, then, how do you know that you wouldn't be scared?"

Martha confronted her. "Have you ever seen him? No? Well, then, how do you know you *would* be scared?"

The allied forces broke out in chorus: "But, Martha, everybody says so. Everybody says so."

"Everybody says what?"

"Everybody that's seen him say they were frightened almost to death. Tisn't only women, but it's men too. It's awful."

Martha wagged her head solemnly. "I'd try not to be afraid of him."

"But supposing you could not help it?" said Kate.

"Yes, and look here," cried Carrie. "I'll tell you another thing. The Hannigans are going to move out of the house next door."

"On account of him?" demanded Martha.

Carrie nodded. "Mrs. Hannigan says so herself."

"Well, of all things!" ejaculated Martha. "Going to move, eh? You don't say so! Where they going to move to?"

"Down on Orchard Avenue."

"Well, of all things! Nice house?"

"I don't know about that. I haven't heard. But there's lots of nice houses on Orchard."

"Yes, but they're all taken," said Kate. "There isn't a vacant house on Orchard Avenue."

"Oh yes, there is," said Martha. "The old Hampstead house is vacant."

"Oh, of course," said Kate. "But then I don't believe Mrs. Hannigan would like it there. I wonder where they can be going to move to?"

"I'm sure I don't know," sighed Martha. "It must be to some place we don't know about."

"Well." said Carrie Dungen, after a general reflective silence, "it's easy enough to find out, anyhow."

"Who knows—around here?" asked Kate.

"Why, Mrs. Smith, and there she is in her garden," said Carrie, jumping to her feet. As she dashed out of the door, Kate and Martha crowded at the window. Carrie's voice rang out from near the steps. "Mrs. Smith! Mrs. Smith! Do you know where the Hannigans are going to move to?"

XXIII

The autumn smote the leaves, and the trees of Whilomville were panoplied in crimson and yellow. The winds grew stronger, and in the melancholy purple of the nights the home shine of a window became a finer thing. The little boys, watching the sear and sorrowful leaves drifting down from the maples, dreamed of the near time when they could heap bushels in the streets and burn them during the abrupt evenings.

Three men walked down the Niagara Avenue. As they approached Judge Hagenthorpe's house he came down his walk to meet them in the manner of one who has been waiting.

"Are you ready, judge?" one said.

"All ready," he answered.

The four then walked to Trescott's house. He received them in his office, where he had been reading. He seemed surprised at this visit of four very active and influential citizens, but he had nothing to say of it.

After they were all seated, Trescott looked expectantly from one face to another. There was a little silence. It was broken by John Twelve, the wholesale grocer, who was worth $400,000, and reported to be worth over a million.

"Well, doctor," he said, with a short laugh, "I suppose we might as well admit at once that we've come to interfere in something which is none of our business."

"Why, what is it?" asked Trescott, again looking from one face to another. He seemed to appeal particularly to Judge Hagenthorpe, but the old man had his chin lowered musingly to his cane, and would not look at him.

"It's about what nobody talks of—much," said Twelve. "It's about Henry Johnson."

Trescott squared himself in his chair. "Yes?" he said.

Having delivered himself of the title, Twelve seemed to become more easy. "Yes," he answered, blandly, "we wanted to talk to you about it."

"Yes?" said Trescott.

Twelve abruptly advanced on the main attack. "Now see here, Trescott, we like you, and we have come to talk right out about this business. It may be none of our affairs and all that, and as for me, I don't mind if you tell me so; but I am not going to keep quiet and see you ruin yourself. And that's how we all feel."

"I am not ruining myself," answered Trescott.

"No, maybe you are not exactly ruining yourself," said Twelve, slowly, "but you are doing yourself a great deal of harm. You have changed from being the leading doctor in town to about the last one. It is mainly because there are always a large number of people who are very thoughtless fools, of course, but then that doesn't change the condition."

A man who had not heretofore spoken said, solemnly, "It's the women."

"Well, what I want to say is this," resumed Twelve: "Even if there are a lot of fools in the world, we can't see any reason why you should ruin yourself by opposing them. You can't teach them anything, you know."

"I am not trying to teach them anything." Trescott smiled wearily. "I— It is a matter of—well—"

"And there are a good many of us that admire you for it immensely," interrupted Twelve; "but that isn't going to change the minds of all those ninnies."

"It's the women," stated the advocate of this view again.

"Well, what I want to say is this," said Twelve. "We want you to get out of this trouble and strike your old gait again. You are simply killing your practice through your infernal pigheadedness. Now this thing is out of the ordinary, but there must be ways to—to beat the game somehow, you see. So we've talked it over—about a dozen of us—and, as I say, if you want to tell us to mind our own business, why, go ahead; but we've talked it over, and we've come to the conclusion that the only way to do is to get Johnson a place somewhere off up the valley, and—"

Trescott wearily gestured. "You don't know, my friend. Everybody is so afraid of him, they can't even give him good care. Nobody can attend to him as I do myself."

"But I have a little no-good farm up beyond Clarence Mountain that I was going to give to Henry," cried Twelve, aggrieved. "And if you—and if you—if you—through your house burning down, or anything—why, all the boys were prepared to take him right off your hands, and—and—"

Trescott arose and went to the window. He turned his back upon them. They sat waiting in silence. When he returned he kept his face in the shadow. "No, John Twelve," he said, "it can't be done."

There was another stillness. Suddenly a man stirred on his chair.

"Well, then, a public institution—" he began.

"No," said Trescott; "public institutions are all very good, but he is not going to one."

In the background of the group old Judge Hagenthorpe was thoughtfully smoothing the polished ivory head of his cane.

XXIV

Trescott loudly stamped the snow from his feet and shook the flakes from his shoulders. When he entered the house he went at once to the dining-room, and then to the sitting-room. Jimmie was there, reading painfully in a large book concerning giraffes and tigers and crocodiles.

"Where is your mother, Jimmie?" asked Trescott.

"I don't know, pa," answered the boy. "I think she is up-stairs."

Trescott went to the foot of the stairs and called, but there came no answer. Seeing that the door of the little drawing-room was open, he entered. The room was bathed in the half-light that came from the four dull panes of mica in the front of the great stove. As his eyes grew used to the shadows he saw his wife curled in an arm-chair. He went to her. "Why, Grace." he said, "didn't you hear me calling you?"

She made no answer, and as he bent over the chair he heard her trying to smother a sob in the cushion.

"Grace!" he cried. "You're crying!"

She raised her face. "I've got a headache, a dreadful headache, Ned."

"A headache?" he repeated, in surprise and incredulity.

He pulled a chair close to hers. Later, as he cast his eye over the zone of light shed by the dull red panes, he saw that a low table had been drawn close to the stove, and that it was burdened with many small cups and plates of uncut tea-cake. He remembered that the day was Wednesday, and that his wife received on Wednesdays.

"Who was here to-day, Gracie?" he asked.

From his shoulder there came a mumble, "Mrs. Twelve."

"Was she—um," he said. "Why—didn't Anna Hagenthorpe come over?"

The mumble from his shoulder continued, "She wasn't well enough."

Glancing down at the cups, Trescott mechanically counted them. There were fifteen of them. "There, there," he said. "Don't cry, Grace. Don't cry."

The wind was whining round the house, and the snow beat aslant upon the windows. Sometimes the coal in the stove settled with a crumbling sound, and the four panes of mica flashed a sudden new crimson. As he sat holding her head on his shoulder, Trescott found himself occasionally trying to count the cups. There were fifteen of them.

THE BLUE HOTEL

I

The Palace Hotel at Fort Romper was painted a light blue, a shade that is on the legs of a kind of heron, causing the bird to declare its position against any background. The Palace Hotel, then, was always screaming and howling in a way that made the dazzling winter landscape of Nebraska seem only a gray swampish hush. It stood alone on the prairie, and when the snow was falling the town two hundred yards away was not visible. But when the traveller alighted at the railway station he was obliged to pass the Palace Hotel before he could come upon the company of low clapboard houses which composed Fort Romper, and it was not to be thought that any traveller could pass the Palace Hotel without looking at it. Pat Scully, the proprietor, had proved himself a master of strategy when he chose his paints. It is true that on clear days, when the great trans-continental expresses, long lines of swaying Pullmans, swept through Fort Romper, passengers were overcome at the sight, and the cult that knows the brown-reds and the subdivisions of the dark greens of the East expressed shame, pity, horror, in a laugh. But to the citizens of this prairie town and to the people who would naturally stop there, Pat Scully had performed a feat. With this opulence and splendor, these creeds, classes, egotisms, that streamed through Romper on the rails day after day, they had no color in common.

As if the displayed delights of such a blue hotel were not sufficiently enticing, it was Scully's habit to go every morning and evening to meet the leisurely trains that stopped at Romper and work his seductions upon any man that he might see wavering, gripsack in hand.

One morning, when a snow-crusted engine dragged its long string of freight cars and its one passenger coach to the station, Scully performed the marvel of catching three men. One was a shaky and quick-eyed Swede, with a great shining cheap valise; one was a tall bronzed cowboy, who was on his way to a ranch near the Dakota line; one was a little silent man from the East, who didn't look it, and didn't announce it. Scully practically made them prisoners. He was so nimble and merry and kindly that each probably felt it would be the height of brutality to try to escape. They trudged off over the creaking board sidewalks in the wake of the eager little Irishman. He wore a heavy fur cap squeezed tightly down on his head. It caused his two red ears to stick out stiffly, as if they were made of tin.

At last, Scully, elaborately, with boisterous hospitality, conducted them through the portals of the blue hotel. The room which they entered was small. It seemed to be merely a proper temple for an enormous stove, which, in the centre, was humming with godlike violence. At various points on its surface the iron had become luminous and glowed yellow from the heat. Beside the stove Scully's son Johnnie was playing High-Five with an old farmer who had whiskers both gray and sandy. They were quarrelling. Frequently the old farmer turned his face towards a box of sawdust—colored brown from tobacco juice—that was behind the stove, and spat with an air of great impatience and irritation. With a loud flourish of words Scully destroyed the game of cards, and bustled his son up-stairs with part of the baggage of the new guests. He himself conducted them to three basins of the coldest water in the world. The cowboy and the Easterner burnished themselves fiery-red with this water, until it seemed to be some kind of a metal polish. The Swede, however, merely dipped his fingers gingerly and with trepidation. It was notable that throughout this series of small ceremonies the three travellers were made to feel that Scully was very benevolent. He was conferring great favors upon them. He handed the towel from one to the other with an air of philanthropic impulse.

Afterwards they went to the first room, and, sitting about the stove, listened to Scully's officious clamor at his daughters, who were preparing the mid-day meal. They reflected in the silence of experienced men who tread carefully amid new people. Nevertheless, the old farmer, stationary, invincible in his chair near the warmest part of the stove, turned his face from the sawdust box frequently and addressed a glowing commonplace to the strangers. Usually he was answered in short but adequate sentences by either the cowboy or the Easterner. The Swede said nothing. He seemed to be occupied in making furtive estimates of each man in the room. One might have thought that he had the sense of silly suspicion which comes to guilt. He resembled a badly frightened man.

Later, at dinner, he spoke a little, addressing his conversation entirely to Scully. He volunteered that he had come from New York, where for ten years he had worked as a tailor. These facts seemed to strike Scully as fascinating, and afterwards he volunteered that he had lived at Romper for fourteen years. The Swede asked about the crops and the price of labor. He seemed barely to listen to Scully's extended replies. His eyes continued to rove from man to man.

Finally, with a laugh and a wink, he said that some of these Western communities were very dangerous; and after his statement he straightened his legs under the table, tilted his head, and laughed again, loudly. It was plain that the demonstration had no meaning to the others. They looked at him wondering and in silence.

II

As the men trooped heavily back into the front-room, the two little windows presented views of a turmoiling sea of snow. The huge arms of the wind were making attempts—mighty, circular, futile—to embrace the flakes as they sped. A gate-post like a still man with a blanched face stood aghast amid this profligate fury. In a hearty voice Scully announced the presence of a blizzard. The guests of the blue hotel, lighting their pipes, assented with grunts of lazy masculine contentment. No island of the sea could be exempt in the degree of this little room with its humming stove. Johnnie, son of Scully, in a tone which defined his opinion of his ability as a card-player, challenged the old farmer of both gray and sandy whiskers to a game of High-Five. The farmer agreed with a contemptuous and bitter scoff. They sat close to the stove, and squared their knees under a wide board. The cowboy and the Easterner watched the game with interest. The Swede remained near the window, aloof, but with a countenance that showed signs of an inexplicable excitement.

The play of Johnnie and the gray-beard was suddenly ended by another quarrel. The old man arose while casting a look of heated scorn at his adversary. He slowly buttoned his coat, and then stalked with fabulous dignity from the room. In the discreet silence of all other men the Swede laughed. His laughter rang somehow childish. Men by this time had begun to look at him askance, as if they wished to inquire what ailed him.

A new game was formed jocosely. The cowboy volunteered to become the partner of Johnnie, and they all then turned to ask the Swede to throw in his lot with the little Easterner, He asked some questions about the game, and, learning that it wore many names, and that he had played it when it was under an alias, he accepted the invitation. He strode towards the men nervously, as if he expected to be assaulted. Finally, seated, he gazed from face to face and laughed shrilly. This laugh was so strange that the Easterner looked up quickly, the cowboy sat intent and with his mouth open, and Johnnie paused, holding the cards with still fingers.

Afterwards there was a short silence. Then Johnnie said, "Well, let's get at it. Come on now!" They pulled their chairs forward until their knees were bunched under the board. They began to play, and their interest in the game caused the others to forget the manner of the Swede.

The cowboy was a board-whacker. Each time that he held superior cards he whanged them, one by one, with exceeding force, down upon the improvised table, and took the tricks with a glowing air of prowess and pride that sent thrills of indignation into the hearts of his opponents. A game with a board-whacker in it is sure to become intense. The countenances of the Easterner and the Swede were miserable whenever the cowboy thundered down his aces and kings, while Johnnie, his eyes gleaming with joy, chuckled and chuckled.

Because of the absorbing play none considered the strange ways of the Swede. They paid strict heed to the game. Finally, during a lull caused by a new deal, the Swede suddenly addressed Johnnie: "I suppose there have been a good many men killed in this room." The jaws of the others dropped and they looked at him.

"What in hell are you talking about?" said Johnnie.

The Swede laughed again his blatant laugh, full of a kind of false courage and defiance. "Oh, you know what I mean all right," he answered.

"I'm a liar if I do!" Johnnie protested. The card was halted, and the men stared at the Swede. Johnnie evidently felt that as the son of the proprietor he should make a direct inquiry. "Now, what might you be drivin' at, mister?" he asked. The Swede winked at him. It was a wink full of cunning. His fingers shook on the edge of the board. "Oh, maybe you think I have been to nowheres. Maybe you think I'm a tenderfoot?"

"I don't know nothin' about you," answered Johnnie, "and I don't give a damn where you've been. All I got to say is that I don't know what you're driving at. There hain't never been nobody killed in this room."

The cowboy, who had been steadily gazing at the Swede, then spoke: "What's wrong with you, mister?"

Apparently it seemed to the Swede that he was formidably menaced. He shivered and turned white near the corners of his mouth. He sent an appealing glance in the direction of the little Easterner. During these moments he did not forget to wear his air of advanced pot-valor. "They say they don't know what I mean," he remarked mockingly to the Easterner.

The latter answered after prolonged and cautious reflection. "I don't understand you," he said, impassively.

The Swede made a movement then which announced that he thought he had encountered treachery from the only quarter where he had expected sympathy, if not help. "Oh, I see you are all against me. I see—"

The cowboy was in a state of deep stupefaction. "Say." he cried, as he tumbled the deck violently down upon the board "—say, what are you gittin' at, hey?"

The Swede sprang up with the celerity of a man escaping from a snake on the floor. "I don't want to fight!" he shouted. "I don't want to fight!"

The cowboy stretched his long legs indolently and deliberately. His hands were in his pockets. He spat into the sawdust box. "Well, who the hell thought you did?" he inquired.

The Swede backed rapidly towards a corner of the room. His hands were out protectingly in front of his chest, but he was making an obvious struggle to control his fright. "Gentlemen," he quavered, "I suppose I am going to be killed before I can leave this house! I suppose I am going to be killed before I can leave this house!" In his eyes was the dying-swan look. Through the windows could be seen the snow turning blue in the shadow of dusk. The wind tore at the house and some loose thing beat regularly against the clapboards like a spirit tapping.

A door opened, and Scully himself entered. He paused in surprise as he noted the tragic attitude of the Swede. Then he said, "What's the matter here?"

The Swede answered him swiftly and eagerly: "These men are going to kill me."

"Kill you!" ejaculated Scully. "Kill you! What are you talkin'?"

The Swede made the gesture of a martyr.

Scully wheeled sternly upon his son. "What is this, Johnnie?"

The lad had grown sullen. "Damned if I know," he answered. "I can't make no sense to it." He began to shuffle the cards, fluttering them together with an angry snap. "He says a good many men have been killed in this room, or something like that. And he says he's goin' to be killed here too. I don't know what ails him. He's crazy, I shouldn't wonder."

Scully then looked for explanation to the cowboy, but the cowboy simply shrugged his shoulders.

"Kill you?" said Scully again to the Swede. "Kill you? Man, you're off your nut."

"Oh, I know." burst out the Swede. "I know what will happen. Yes, I'm crazy—yes. Yes, of course, I'm crazy—yes. But I know one thing—" There was a sort of sweat of misery and terror upon his face. "I know I won't get out of here alive."

The cowboy drew a deep breath, as if his mind was passing into the last stages of dissolution. "Well, I'm dog-goned," he whispered to himself.

Scully wheeled suddenly and faced his son. "You've been troublin' this man!"

Johnnie's voice was loud with its burden of grievance. "Why, good Gawd, I ain't done nothin' to 'im."

The Swede broke in. "Gentlemen, do not disturb yourselves. I will leave this house. I will go away because"—he accused them dramatically with his glance—"because I do not want to be killed."

Scully was furious with his son. "Will you tell me what is the matter, you young divil? What's the matter, anyhow? Speak out!"

"Blame it!" cried Johnnie in despair, "don't I tell you I don't know. He—he says we want to kill him, and that's all I know. I can't tell what ails him."

The Swede continued to repeat: "Never mind, Mr. Scully; nevermind. I will leave this house. I will go away, because I do not wish to be killed. Yes, of course, I am crazy—yes. But I know one thing! I will go away. I will leave this house. Never mind, Mr. Scully; never mind. I will go away."

"You will not go 'way," said Scully. "You will not go 'way until I hear the reason of this business. If anybody has troubled you I will take care of him. This is my house. You are under my roof, and I will not allow any peaceable man to be troubled here." He cast a terrible eye upon Johnnie, the cowboy, and the Easterner.

"Never mind, Mr. Scully; never mind. I will go away. I do not wish to be killed." The Swede moved towards the door, which opened upon the stairs. It was evidently his intention to go at once for his baggage.

"No, no," shouted Scully peremptorily; but the white-faced man slid by him and disappeared. "Now," said Scully severely, "what does this mane?"

Johnnie and the cowboy cried together: "Why, we didn't do nothin' to 'im!"

Scully's eyes were cold. "No," he said, "you didn't?"

Johnnie swore a deep oath. "Why this is the wildest loon I ever see. We didn't do nothin' at all. We were jest sittin' here playin' cards, and he—"

The father suddenly spoke to the Easterner. "Mr. Blanc," he asked, "what has these boys been doin'?"

The Easterner reflected again. "I didn't see anything wrong at all," he said at last, slowly.

Scully began to howl. "But what does it mane?" He stared ferociously at his son. "I have a mind to lather you for this, me boy."

Johnnie was frantic. "Well, what have I done?" he bawled at his father.

III

"I think you are tongue-tied," said Scully finally to his son, the cowboy, and the Easterner; and at the end of this scornful sentence he left the room.

Up-stairs the Swede was swiftly fastening the straps of his great valise. Once his back happened to be half turned towards the door, and, hearing a noise there, he wheeled and sprang up, uttering a loud cry. Scully's wrinkled visage showed grimly in the light of the small lamp he carried. This yellow effulgence, streaming upward, colored only his prominent features, and left his eyes, for instance, in mysterious shadow. He resembled a murderer.

"Man! man!" he exclaimed, "have you gone daffy?"

"Oh, no! Oh, no!" rejoined the other. "There are people in this world who know pretty nearly as much as you do—understand?"

For a moment they stood gazing at each other. Upon the Swede's deathly pale checks were two spots brightly crimson and sharply edged, as if they had been carefully painted. Scully placed the light on the table and sat himself on the edge of the bed. He spoke ruminatively. "By cracky, I never heard of such a thing in my life. It's a complete muddle. I can't, for the soul of me, think how you ever got this idea into your head." Presently he lifted his eyes and asked: "And did you sure think they were going to kill you?"

The Swede scanned the old man as if he wished to see into his mind. "I did," he said at last. He obviously suspected that this answer might precipitate an outbreak. As he pulled on a strap his whole arm shook, the elbow wavering like a bit of paper.

Scully banged his hand impressively on the foot-board of the bed. "Why, man, we're goin' to have a line of ilictric street-cars in this town next spring."

"'A line of electric street-cars,'" repeated the Swede, stupidly.

"And," said Scully, "there's a new railroad goin' to be built down from Broken Arm to here. Not to mintion the four churches and the smashin' big brick school-house. Then there's the big factory, too. Why, in two years Romper 'll be a *metropolis*."

Having finished the preparation of his baggage, the Swede straightened himself. "Mr. Scully," he said, with sudden hardihood, "how much do I owe you?"

"You don't owe me anythin'," said the old man, angrily.

"Yes, I do," retorted the Swede. He took seventy-five cents from his pocket and tendered it to Scully; but the latter snapped his fingers in disdainful refusal. However, it happened that they both stood gazing in a strange fashion at three silver pieces on the Swede's open palm.

"I'll not take your money," said Scully at last. "Not after what's been goin' on here." Then a plan seemed to strike him. "Here," he cried, picking up his lamp and moving towards the door. "Here! Come with me a minute."

"No," said the Swede, in overwhelming alarm.

"Yes," urged the old man. "Come on! I want you to come and see a picter—just across the hall—in my room."

241

The Swede must have concluded that his hour was come. His jaw dropped and his teeth showed like a dead man's. He ultimately followed Scully across the corridor, but he had the step of one hung in chains.

Scully flashed the light high on the wall of his own chamber. There was revealed a ridiculous photograph of a little girl. She was leaning against a balustrade of gorgeous decoration, and the formidable bang to her hair was prominent. The figure was as graceful as an upright sled-stake, and, withal, it was of the hue of lead. "There," said Scully, tenderly, "that's the picter of my little girl that died. Her name was Carrie. She had the purtiest hair you ever saw! I was that fond of her, she—"

Turning then, he saw that the Swede was not contemplating the picture at all, but, instead, was keeping keen watch on the gloom in the rear.

"Look, man!" cried Scully, heartily. "That's the picter of my little gal that died. Her name was Carrie. And then here's the picter of my oldest boy, Michael. He's a lawyer in Lincoln, an' doin' well. I gave that boy a grand eddycation, and I'm glad for it now. He's a fine boy. Look at 'im now. Ain't he bold as blazes, him there in Lincoln, an honored an' respicted gintleman. An honored an' respicted gintleman," concluded Scully with a flourish. And, so saying, he smote the Swede jovially on the back.

The Swede faintly smiled.

"Now," said the old man, "there's only one more thing." He dropped suddenly to the floor and thrust his head beneath the bed. The Swede could hear his muffled voice. "I'd keep it under me piller if it wasn't for that boy Johnnie. Then there's the old woman—Where is it now? I never put it twice in the same place. Ah, now come out with you!"

Presently he backed clumsily from under the bed, dragging with him an old coat rolled into a bundle. "I've fetched him," he muttered. Kneeling on the floor, he unrolled the coat and extracted from its heart a large yellow-brown whiskey bottle.

His first maneuver was to hold the bottle up to the light. Reassured, apparently, that nobody had been tampering with it, he thrust it with a generous movement towards the Swede.

The weak-kneed Swede was about to eagerly clutch this element of strength, but he suddenly jerked his hand away and cast a look of horror upon Scully.

"Drink," said the old man affectionately. He had risen to his feet, and now stood facing the Swede.

There was a silence. Then again Scully said: "Drink!"

The Swede laughed wildly. He grabbed the bottle, put it to his mouth, and as his lips curled absurdly around the opening and his throat worked, he kept his glance, burning with hatred, upon the old man's face.

IV

After the departure of Scully the three men, with the card-board still upon their knees, preserved for a long time an astounded silence. Then Johnnie said: "That's the dod-dangest Swede I ever see."

"He ain't no Swede," said the cowboy, scornfully.

"Well, what is he then?" cried Johnnie. "What is he then?"

"It's my opinion," replied the cowboy deliberately, "he's some kind of a Dutchman." It was a venerable custom of the country to entitle as Swedes all light-haired men who spoke with a heavy tongue. In consequence the idea of the cowboy was not without its daring. "Yes, sir," he repeated. "It's my opinion this feller is some kind of a Dutchman."

"Well, he says he's a Swede, anyhow," muttered Johnnie, sulkily. He turned to the Easterner: "What do you think, Mr. Blanc?"

"Oh, I don't know," replied the Easterner.

"Well, what do you think makes him act that way?" asked the cowboy.

"Why, he's frightened." The Easterner knocked his pipe against a rim of the stove. "He's clear frightened out of his boots."

"What at?" cried Johnnie and cowboy together.

The Easterner reflected over his answer.

"What at?" cried the others again.

"Oh, I don't know, but it seems to me this man has been reading dime-novels, and he thinks he's right out in the middle of it—the shootin' and stabbin' and all."

"But," said the cowboy, deeply scandalized, "this ain't Wyoming, ner none of them places. This is Nebrasker."

"Yes," added Johnnie, "an' why don't he wait till he gits *out West*?"

The travelled Easterner laughed. "It isn't different there even—not in these days. But he thinks he's right in the middle of hell."

Johnnie and the cowboy mused long.

"It's awful funny," remarked Johnnie at last.

"Yes," said the cowboy. "This is a queer game. I hope we don't git snowed in, because then we'd have to stand this here man bein' around with us all the time. That wouldn't be no good."

"I wish pop would throw him out," said Johnnie.

Presently they heard a loud stamping on the stairs, accompanied by ringing jokes in the voice of old Scully, and laughter, evidently from the Swede. The men around the stove stared vacantly at each other. "Gosh!" said the cowboy. The door flew open, and old Scully, flushed and anecdotal, came into the room. He was jabbering at the Swede, who followed him, laughing bravely. It was the entry of two roisterers from a banquet-hall.

"Come now," said Scully sharply to the three seated men, "move up and give us a chance at the stove." The cowboy and the Easterner obediently sidled their chairs to make room for the new-comers. Johnnie, however, simply arranged himself in a more indolent attitude, and then remained motionless.

"Come! Git over, there," said Scully.

"Plenty of room on the other side of the stove," said Johnnie.

244

"Do you think we want to sit in the draught?" roared the father.

But the Swede here interposed with a grandeur of confidence. "No, no. Let the boy sit where he likes," he cried in a bullying voice to the father.

"All right! All right!" said Scully, deferentially. The cowboy and the Easterner exchanged glances of wonder.

The five chairs were formed in a crescent about one side of the stove. The Swede began to talk; he talked arrogantly, profanely, angrily. Johnnie, the cowboy, and the Easterner maintained a morose silence, while old Scully appeared to be receptive and eager, breaking in constantly with sympathetic ejaculations.

Finally the Swede announced that he was thirsty. He moved in his chair, and said that he would go for a drink of water.

"I'll git it for you," cried Scully at once.

"No," said the Swede, contemptuously. "I'll get it for myself." He arose and stalked with the air of an owner off into the executive parts of the hotel.

As soon as the Swede was out of hearing Scully sprang to his feet and whispered intensely to the others: "Up-stairs he thought I was tryin' to poison 'im."

"Say," said Johnnie, "this makes me sick. Why don't you throw 'im out in the snow?"

"Why, he's all right now," declared Scully. "It was only that he was from the East, and he thought this was a tough place. That's all. He's all right now."

The cowboy looked with admiration upon the Easterner. "You were straight," he said. "You were on to that there Dutchman."

"Well," said Johnnie to his father, "he may be all right now, but I don't see it. Other time he was scared, but now he's too fresh."

Scully's speech was always a combination of Irish brogue and idiom, Western twang and idiom, and scraps of curiously formal diction taken from the story-books and newspapers, He now hurled a strange mass of language at the head of his son. "What do I keep? What do I keep? What do I keep?" he demanded, in a voice of thunder. He slapped his knee impressively, to indicate that he himself was going to make reply, and that all should heed. "I keep a hotel," he shouted. "A hotel, do you mind? A guest under my roof has sacred privileges. He is to be intimidated by none. Not one word shall he hear that would prejudice him in favor of goin' away. I'll not have it. There's no place in this here town where they can say they iver took in a guest of mine because he was afraid to stay here." He wheeled suddenly upon the cowboy and the Easterner. "Am I right?"

"Yes, Mr. Scully," said the cowboy, "I think you're right."

"Yes, Mr. Scully," said the Easterner, "I think you're right."

V

At six-o'clock supper, the Swede fizzed like a fire-wheel. He sometimes seemed on the point of bursting into riotous song, and in all his madness he was encouraged by old Scully. The Easterner was incased in reserve; the cowboy sat in wide-mouthed amazement, forgetting to eat, while Johnnie wrathily demolished great plates of food. The daughters of the house, when they were obliged to replenish the biscuits, approached as warily as Indians, and, having succeeded in their purpose, fled with ill-concealed trepidation. The Swede domineered the whole feast, and he gave it the appearance of a cruel bacchanal. He seemed to have grown suddenly taller; he gazed, brutally disdainful, into every face. His voice rang through the room. Once when he jabbed out harpoon-fashion with his fork to pinion a biscuit, the weapon nearly impaled the hand of the Easterner which had been stretched quietly out for the same biscuit.

After supper, as the men filed towards the other room, the Swede smote Scully ruthlessly on the shoulder. "Well, old boy, that was a good, square meal." Johnnie looked hopefully at his father; he knew that shoulder was tender from an old fall; and, indeed, it appeared for a moment as if Scully was going to flame out over the matter, but in the end he smiled a sickly smile and remained silent. The others understood from his manner that he was admitting his responsibility for the Swede's new view-point.

Johnnie, however, addressed his parent in an aside. "Why don't you license somebody to kick you down-stairs?" Scully scowled darkly by way of reply.

When they were gathered about the stove, the Swede insisted on another game of High Five. Scully gently deprecated the plan at first, but the Swede turned a wolfish glare upon him. The old man subsided, and the Swede canvassed the others. In his tone there was always a great threat. The cowboy and the Easterner both remarked indifferently that they would play. Scully said that he would presently have to go to meet the 6.58 train, and so the Swede turned menacingly upon Johnnie. For a moment their glances crossed like blades, and then Johnnie smiled and said, "Yes, I'll play."

They formed a square, with the little board on their knees. The Easterner and the Swede were again partners. As the play went on, it was noticeable that the cowboy was not board-whacking as usual. Meanwhile, Scully, near the lamp, had put on his spectacles and, with an appearance curiously like an old priest, was reading a newspaper. In time he went out to meet the 6.58 train, and, despite his precautions, a gust of polar wind whirled into the room as he opened the door. Besides scattering the cards, it dulled the players to the marrow. The Swede cursed frightfully. When Scully returned, his entrance disturbed a cosey and friendly scene. The Swede again cursed. But presently they were once more intent, their heads bent forward and their hands moving swiftly. The Swede had adopted the fashion of board-whacking.

Scully took up his paper and for a long time remained immersed in matters which were extraordinarily remote from him. The lamp burned badly, and once he stopped to adjust the wick. The newspaper, as he turned from page to page, rustled with a slow and comfortable sound. Then suddenly he heard three terrible words: "You are cheatin'!"

Such scenes often prove that there can be little of dramatic import in environment. Any room can present a tragic front; any room can be comic. This little den was now hideous as a torture-chamber. The new faces of the men themselves had changed it upon the instant. The Swede held a huge fist in front of Johnnie's face, while the latter looked steadily over it into the blazing orbs of his accuser. The Easterner had grown pallid; the cowboy's jaw had dropped in that expression of bovine amazement which was one of his important mannerisms. After the three words, the first sound in the room was made by Scully's paper as it floated forgotten to his feet. His spectacles had also fallen from his nose, but by a clutch he had saved them in air. His hand, grasping the spectacles, now remained poised awkwardly and near his shoulder. He stared at the card-players.

Probably the silence was while a second elapsed. Then, if the floor had been suddenly twitched out from under the men they could not have moved quicker. The five had projected themselves headlong towards a common point. It happened that Johnnie, in rising to hurl himself upon the Swede, had stumbled slightly because of his curiously instinctive care for the cards and the board. The loss of the moment allowed time for the arrival of Scully, and also allowed the cowboy time to give the Swede a great push which sent him staggering back. The men found tongue together, and hoarse shouts of rage, appeal, or fear burst from every throat. The cowboy pushed and jostled feverishly at the Swede, and the Easterner and Scully clung wildly to Johnnie; but, through the smoky air, above the swaying bodies of the peace-compellers, the eyes of the two warriors ever sought each other in glances of challenge that were at once hot and steely.

Of course the board had been overturned, and now the whole company of cards was scattered over the floor, where the boots of the men trampled the fat and painted kings and queens as they gazed with their silly eyes at the war that was waging above them.

Scully's voice was dominating the yells. "Stop now? Stop, I say! Stop, now—"

Johnnie, as he struggled to burst through the rank formed by Scully and the Easterner, was crying, "Well, he says I cheated! He says I cheated! I won't allow no man to say I cheated! If he says I cheated, he's a —— ——!"

The cowboy was telling the Swede, "Quit, now! Quit, d'ye hear—"

The screams of the Swede never ceased: "He did cheat! I saw him! I saw him—"

As for the Easterner, he was importuning in a voice that was not heeded: "Wait a moment, can't you? Oh, wait a moment. What's the good of a fight over a game of cards? Wait a moment—"

In this tumult no complete sentences were clear. "Cheat"—"Quit"—"He says"—these fragments pierced the uproar and rang out sharply. It was remarkable that, whereas Scully undoubtedly made the most noise, he was the least heard of any of the riotous band.

Then suddenly there was a great cessation. It was as if each man had paused for breath; and although the room was still lighted with the anger of men, it could be seen that there was no danger of immediate conflict, and at once Johnnie, shouldering his way forward, almost succeeded in confronting the Swede. "What did you say I cheated for? What did you say I cheated for? I don't cheat, and I won't let no man say I do!"

The Swede said, "I saw you! I saw you!"

"Well," cried Johnnie, "I'll fight any man what says I cheat!"

"No, you won't," said the cowboy. "Not here."

"Ah, be still, can't you?" said Scully, coming between them.

The quiet was sufficient to allow the Easterner's voice to be heard. He was repealing, "Oh, wait a moment, can't you? What's the good of a fight over a game of cards? Wait a moment!"

Johnnie, his red face appearing above his father's shoulder, hailed the Swede again. "Did you say I cheated?"

The Swede showed his teeth. "Yes."

"Then," said Johnnie, "we must fight."

"Yes, fight," roared the Swede. He was like a demoniac. "Yes, fight! I'll show you what kind of a man I am! I'll show you who you want to fight!

Maybe you think I can't fight! Maybe you think I can't! I'll show you, you skin, you card-sharp! Yes, you cheated! You cheated! You cheated!"

"Well, let's go at it, then, mister," said Johnnie, coolly.

The cowboy's brow was beaded with sweat from his efforts in intercepting all sorts of raids. He turned in despair to Scully. "What are you goin' to do now?"

A change had come over the Celtic visage of the old man. He now seemed all eagerness; his eyes glowed.

"We'll let them fight," he answered, stalwartly. "I can't put up with it any longer. I've stood this damned Swede till I'm sick. We'll let them fight."

VI

The men prepared to go out-of-doors. The Easterner was so nervous that he had great difficulty in getting his arms into the sleeves of his new leather coat. As the cowboy drew his fur cap down over his ears his hands trembled. In fact, Johnnie and old Scully were the only ones who displayed no agitation. These preliminaries were conducted without words.

Scully threw open the door. "Well, come on," he said. Instantly a terrific wind caused the flame of the lamp to struggle at its wick, while a puff of black smoke sprang from the chimney-top. The stove was in mid-current of the blast, and its voice swelled to equal the roar of the storm. Some of the scarred and bedabbled cards were caught up from the floor and dashed helplessly against the farther wall. The men lowered their heads and plunged into the tempest as into a sea.

No snow was falling, but great whirls and clouds of flakes, swept up from the ground by the frantic winds, were streaming southward with the speed of bullets. The covered land was blue with the sheen of an unearthly satin, and there was no other hue save where, at the low, black railway station—which seemed incredibly distant—one light gleamed like a tiny jewel. As the men floundered into a thigh deep drift, it was known that the Swede was bawling out something. Scully went to him, put a hand on his shoulder and projected an ear. "What's that you say?" he shouted.

"I say," bawled the Swede again, "I won't stand much show against this gang. I know you'll all pitch on me."

Scully smote him reproachfully on the arm. "Tut, man!" he yelled. The wind tore the words from Scully's lips and scattered them far alee.

"You are all a gang of—" boomed the Swede, but the storm also seized the remainder of this sentence.

Immediately turning their backs upon the wind, the men had swung around a corner to the sheltered side of the hotel. It was the function of the little house to preserve here, amid this great devastation of snow, an irregular V-shape of heavily incrusted grass, which crackled beneath the feet. One could imagine the great drifts piled against the windward side. When the party reached the comparative peace of this spot it was found that the Swede was still bellowing.

"Oh, I know what kind of a thing this is! I know you'll all pitch on me. I can't lick you all!"

Scully turned upon him panther fashion. "You'll not have to whip all of us. You'll have to whip my son Johnnie. An' the man what troubles you durin' that time will have me to dale with."

The arrangements were swiftly made. The two men faced each other, obedient to the harsh commands of Scully, whose face, in the subtly luminous gloom, could be seen set in the austere impersonal lines that are pictured on the countenances of the Roman veterans. The Easterner's teeth were chattering, and he was hopping up and down like a mechanical toy. The cowboy stood rock-like.

The contestants had not stripped off any clothing. Each was in his ordinary attire. Their fists were up, and they eyed each other in a calm that had the elements of leonine cruelty in it.

During this pause, the Easterner's mind, like a film, took lasting impressions of three men—the iron-nerved master of the ceremony; the Swede, pale, motionless, terrible; and Johnnie, serene yet ferocious, brutish yet heroic. The entire prelude had in it a tragedy greater than the tragedy of action, and this aspect was accentuated by the long, mellow cry of the blizzard, as it sped the tumbling and wailing flakes into the black abyss of the south.

"Now!" said Scully.

The two combatants leaped forward and crashed together like bullocks. There was heard the cushioned sound of blows, and of a curse squeezing out from between the tight teeth of one.

As for the spectators, the Easterner's pent-up breath exploded from him with a pop of relief, absolute relief from the tension of the preliminaries. The cowboy bounded into the air with a yowl. Scully was immovable as from supreme amazement and fear at the fury of the fight which he himself had permitted and arranged.

For a time the encounter in the darkness was such a perplexity of flying arms that it presented no more detail than would a swiftly revolving wheel. Occasionally a face, as if illumined by a flash of light, would shine out, ghastly and marked with pink spots. A moment later, the men might have been known as shadows, if it were not for the involuntary utterance of oaths that came from them in whispers.

Suddenly a holocaust of warlike desire caught the cowboy, and he bolted forward with the speed of a broncho. "Go it, Johnnie! go it! Kill him! Kill him!"

Scully confronted him. "Kape back," he said; and by his glance the cowboy could tell that this man was Johnnie's father.

To the Easterner there was a monotony of unchangeable fighting that was an abomination. This confused mingling was eternal to his sense, which was concentrated in a longing for the end, the priceless end. Once the fighters lurched near him, and as he scrambled hastily backward he heard them breathe like men on the rack.

252

"Kill him, Johnnie! Kill him! Kill him! Kill him!" The cowboy's face was contorted like one of those agony masks in museums.

"Keep still," said Scully, icily.

Then there was a sudden loud grunt, incomplete, cut short, and Johnnie's body swung away from the Swede and fell with sickening heaviness to the grass. The cowboy was barely in time to prevent the mad Swede from flinging himself upon his prone adversary. "No, you don't," said the cowboy, interposing an arm. "Wait a second."

Scully was at his son's side. "Johnnie! Johnnie, me boy!" His voice had a quality of melancholy tenderness. "Johnnie! Can you go on with it?" He looked anxiously down into the bloody, pulpy face of his son.

There was a moment of silence, and then Johnnie answered in his ordinary voice, "Yes, I—it—yes."

Assisted by his father he struggled to his feet. "Wait a bit now till you git your wind," said the old man.

A few paces away the cowboy was lecturing the Swede. "No, you don't! Wait a second!"

The Easterner was plucking at Scully's sleeve. "Oh, this is enough," he pleaded. "This is enough! Let it go as it stands. This is enough!"

"Bill," said Scully, "git out of the road." The cowboy stepped aside. "Now." The combatants were actuated by a new caution as they advanced towards collision. They glared at each other, and then the Swede aimed a lightning blow that carried with it his entire weight. Johnnie was evidently half stupid from weakness, but he miraculously dodged, and his fist sent the over-balanced Swede sprawling.

The cowboy, Scully, and the Easterner burst into a cheer that was like a chorus of triumphant soldiery, but before its conclusion the Swede had scuffled agilely to his feet and come in berserk abandon at his foe. There was another perplexity of flying arms, and Johnnie's body again swung away and fell, even as a bundle might fall from a roof. The Swede instantly staggered to a little wind-waved tree and leaned upon it, breathing like an engine, while his savage and flame-lit eyes roamed from face to face as the men bent over Johnnie. There was a splendor of isolation in his situation at this time which the Easterner felt once when, lifting his eyes from the man on the ground, he beheld that mysterious and lonely figure, waiting.

"Arc you any good yet, Johnnie?" asked Scully in a broken voice.

The son gasped and opened his eyes languidly. After a moment he answered, "No—I ain't—any good—any—more." Then, from shame and bodily ill he began to weep, the tears furrowing down through the blood-stains on his face. "He was too—too—too heavy for me."

Scully straightened and addressed the waiting figure. "Stranger," he said, evenly, "it's all up with our side." Then his voice changed into that vibrant huskiness which is commonly the tone of the most simple and deadly announcements. "Johnnie is whipped."

Without replying, the victor moved off on the route to the front door of the hotel.

The cowboy was formulating new and un-spellable blasphemies. The Easterner was startled to find that they were out in a wind that seemed to come direct from the shadowed arctic floes. He heard again the wail of the snow as it was flung to its grave in the south. He knew now that all this time the cold had been sinking into him deeper and deeper, and he wondered that he had not perished. He felt indifferent to the condition of the vanquished man.

"Johnnie, can you walk?" asked Scully.

"Did I hurt—hurt him any?" asked the son.

"Can you walk, boy? Can you walk?"

Johnnie's voice was suddenly strong. There was a robust impatience in it. "I asked you whether I hurt him any!"

"Yes, yes, Johnnie," answered the cowboy, consolingly; "he's hurt a good deal."

They raised him from the ground, and as soon as he was on his feet he went tottering off, rebuffing all attempts at assistance. When the party rounded the corner they were fairly blinded by the pelting of the snow. It burned their faces like fire. The cowboy carried Johnnie through the drift to the door. As they entered some cards again rose from the floor and beat against the wall.

The Easterner rushed to the stove. He was so profoundly chilled that he almost dared to embrace the glowing iron. The Swede was not in the room. Johnnie sank into a chair, and, folding his arms on his knees, buried his face in them. Scully, warming one foot and then the other at a rim of the stove, muttered to himself with Celtic mournfulness. The cowboy had removed his fur cap, and with a dazed and rueful air he was running one hand through his tousled locks. From overhead they could hear the creaking of boards, as the Swede tramped here and there in his room.

The sad quiet was broken by the sudden flinging open of a door that led towards the kitchen. It was instantly followed by an inrush of women. They precipitated themselves upon Johnnie amid a chorus of lamentation. Before they carried their prey off to the kitchen, there to be bathed and harangued with that mixture of sympathy and abuse which is a feat of their sex, the mother straightened herself and fixed old Scully with an eye of stern reproach. "Shame be upon you, Patrick Scully!" she cried. "Your own son, too. Shame be upon you!"

"There, now! Be quiet, now!" said the old man, weakly.

"Shame be upon you, Patrick Scully!" The girls, rallying to this slogan, sniffed disdainfully in the direction of those trembling accomplices, the cowboy and the Easterner. Presently they bore Johnnie away, and left the three men to dismal reflection.

VII

"I'd like to fight this here Dutchman myself," said the cowboy, breaking a long silence.

255

Scully wagged his head sadly. "No, that wouldn't do. It wouldn't be right. It wouldn't be right."

"Well, why wouldn't it?" argued the cowboy. "I don't see no harm in it."

"No," answered Scully, with mournful heroism. "It wouldn't be right. It was Johnnie's fight, and now we mustn't whip the man just because he whipped Johnnie."

"Yes, that's true enough," said the cowboy; "but—he better not get fresh with me, because I couldn't stand no more of it."

"You'll not say a word to him," commanded Scully, and even then they heard the tread of the Swede on the stairs. His entrance was made theatric. He swept the door back with a bang and swaggered to the middle of the room. No one looked at him. "Well," he cried, insolently, at Scully, "I s'pose you'll tell me now how much I owe you?"

The old man remained stolid. "You don't owe me nothin'."

"Huh!" said the Swede, "huh! Don't owe 'im nothin'."

The cowboy addressed the Swede. "Stranger, I don't see how you come to be so gay around here."

Old Scully was instantly alert. "Stop!" he shouted, holding his hand forth, fingers upward. "Bill, you shut up!"

The cowboy spat carelessly into the sawdust box. "I didn't say a word, did I?" he asked.

"Mr. Scully," called the Swede, "how much do I owe you?" It was seen that he was attired for departure, and that he had his valise in his hand.

"You don't owe me nothin'," repeated Scully in his same imperturbable way.

"Huh!" said the Swede. "I guess you're right. I guess if it was any way at all, you'd owe me somethin'. That's what I guess." He turned to the cowboy. "'Kill him! Kill him! Kill him!'" he mimicked, and then guffawed victoriously.

256

"'Kill him!'" He was convulsed with ironical humor.

But he might have been jeering the dead. The three men were immovable and silent, staring with glassy eyes at the stove.

The Swede opened the door and passed into the storm, giving one derisive glance backward at the still group.

As soon as the door was closed, Scully and the cowboy leaped to their feet and began to curse. They trampled to and fro, waving their arms and smashing into the air with their fists. "Oh, but that was a hard minute!" wailed Scully. "That was a hard minute! Him there leerin' and scoffin'! One bang at his nose was worth forty dollars to me that minute! How did you stand it, Bill?"

"How did I stand it?" cried the cowboy in a quivering voice. "How did I stand it? Oh!"

The old man burst into sudden brogue. "I'd loike to take that Swade," he wailed, "and hould 'im down on a shtone flure and bate 'im to a jelly wid a shtick!"

The cowboy groaned in sympathy. "I'd like to git him by the neck and ha-ammer him "—he brought his hand down on a chair with a noise like a pistol-shot—"hammer that there Dutchman until he couldn't tell himself from a dead coyote!"

"I'd bate 'im until he—"

"I'd show *him* some things—"

And then together they raised a yearning, fanatic cry—"Oh-o-oh! if we only could—"

"Yes!"

"Yes!"

"And then I'd—"

"O-o-oh!"

VIII

The Swede, tightly gripping his valise, tacked across the face of the storm as if he carried sails. He was following a line of little naked, gasping trees, which he knew must mark the way of the road. His face, fresh from the pounding of Johnnie's fists, felt more pleasure than pain in the wind and the driving snow. A number of square shapes loomed upon him finally, and he knew them as the houses of the main body of the town. He found a street and made travel along it, leaning heavily upon the wind whenever, at a corner, a terrific blast caught him.

He might have been in a deserted village. We picture the world as thick with conquering and elate humanity, but here, with the bugles of the tempest pealing, it was hard to imagine a peopled earth. One viewed the existence of man then as a marvel, and conceded a glamour of wonder to these lice which were caused to cling to a whirling, fire-smote, ice-locked, disease-stricken, space-lost bulb. The conceit of man was explained by this storm to be the very engine of life. One was a coxcomb not to die in it. However, the Swede found a saloon.

In front of it an indomitable red light was burning, and the snow-flakes were made blood color as they flew through the circumscribed territory of the lamp's shining. The Swede pushed open the door of the saloon and entered. A sanded expanse was before him, and at the end of it four men sat about a table drinking. Down one side of the room extended a radiant bar, and its guardian was leaning upon his elbows listening to the talk of the men at the table. The Swede dropped his valise upon the floor, and, smiling fraternally upon the barkeeper, said, "Gimme some whiskey, will you?" The man placed a bottle, a whiskey-glass, and a glass of ice-thick water upon the bar. The Swede poured himself an abnormal portion of whiskey and drank it in three gulps. "Pretty bad night," remarked the bartender, indifferently. He was making the pretension of blindness which is usually a distinction of his class; but it could have been seen that he was furtively studying the half-erased blood-stains on the face of the Swede. "Bad night," he said again.

"Oh, it's good enough for me," replied the Swede, hardily, as he poured himself some more whiskey. The barkeeper took his coin and maneuvered it through its reception by the highly nickelled cash-machine. A bell rang; a card labelled "20 cts." had appeared.

"No," continued the Swede, "this isn't too bad weather. It's good enough for me."

"So?" murmured the barkeeper, languidly.

The copious drams made the Swede's eyes swim, and he breathed a trifle heavier. "Yes, I like this weather. I like it. It suits me." It was apparently his design to impart a deep significance to these words.

"So?" murmured the bartender again. He turned to gaze dreamily at the scroll-like birds and bird-like scrolls which had been drawn with soap upon the mirrors back of the bar.

"Well, I guess I'll take another drink," said the Swede, presently. "Have something?"

"No, thanks; I'm not drinkin'," answered the bartender. Afterwards he asked, "How did you hurt your face?"

The Swede immediately began to boast loudly. "Why, in a fight. I thumped the soul out of a man down here at Scully's hotel."

The interest of the four men at the table was at last aroused.

"Who was it?" said one.

"Johnnie Scully," blustered the Swede. "Son of the man what runs it. He will be pretty near dead for some weeks, I can tell you. I made a nice thing of him, I did. He couldn't get up. They carried him in the house. Have a drink?"

Instantly the men in some subtle way incased themselves in reserve. "No, thanks," said one. The group was of curious formation. Two were prominent local business men; one was the district-attorney; and one was a professional gambler of the kind known as "square." But a scrutiny of the group would not have enabled an observer to pick the gambler from the men of more reputable pursuits. He was, in fact, a man so delicate in manner, when among people of fair class, and so judicious in his choice of victims, that in the strictly masculine part of the town's life he had come to be explicitly trusted and admired. People called him a thoroughbred. The fear and contempt with which his craft was regarded was undoubtedly the reason that his quiet dignity shone conspicuous above the quiet dignity of men who might be merely hatters, billiard markers, or grocery-clerks. Beyond an occasional unwary traveller, who came by rail, this gambler was supposed to prey solely upon reckless and senile farmers, who, when flush with good crops, drove into town in all the pride and confidence of an absolutely invulnerable stupidity. Hearing at times in circuitous fashion of the despoilment of such a farmer, the important men of Romper invariably laughed in contempt of the victim, and, if they thought of the wolf at all, it was with a kind of pride at the knowledge that he would never dare think of attacking their wisdom and courage. Besides, it was popular that this gambler had a real wife and two real children in a neat cottage in a suburb, where he led an exemplary home life; and when any one even suggested a discrepancy in his character, the crowd immediately vociferated descriptions of this virtuous family circle. Then men who led exemplary home lives, and men who did not lead exemplary home lives, all subsided in a bunch, remarking that there was nothing more to be said.

However, when a restriction was placed upon him—as, for instance, when a strong clique of members of the new Pollywog Club refused to permit him, even as a spectator, to appear in the rooms of the organization—the candor and gentleness with which he accepted the judgment disarmed many of his foes and made his friends more desperately partisan. He invariably distinguished between himself and a respectable Romper man so quickly and frankly that his manner actually appeared to be a continual broadcast compliment.

And one must not forget to declare the fundamental fact of his entire position in Romper. It is irrefutable that in all affairs outside of his business, in all matters that occur eternally and commonly between man and man, this thieving card-player was so generous, so just, so moral, that, in a contest, he could have put to flight the consciences of nine-tenths of the citizens of Romper.

And so it happened that he was seated in this saloon with the two prominent local merchants and the district-attorney.

The Swede continued to drink raw whiskey, meanwhile babbling at the barkeeper and trying to induce him to indulge in potations. "Come on. Have a drink. Come on. What—no? Well, have a little one, then. By gawd, I've whipped a man to-night, and I want to celebrate. I whipped him good, too. Gentlemen," the Swede cried to the men at the table, "have a drink?"

"Ssh!" said the barkeeper.

The group at the table, although furtively attentive, had been pretending to be deep in talk, but now a man lifted his eyes towards the Swede and said, shortly, "Thanks. We don't want any more."

At this reply the Swede ruffled out his chest like a rooster. "Well," he exploded, "it seems I can't get anybody to drink with me in this town. Seems so, don't it? Well!"

"Ssh!" said the barkeeper.

"Say," snarled the Swede, "don't you try to shut me up. I won't have it. I'm a gentleman, and I want people to drink with me. And I want 'em to drink with me now. *Now*—do you understand?" He rapped the bar with his knuckles.

Years of experience had calloused the bartender. He merely grew sulky. "I hear you," he answered.

"Well," cried the Swede, "listen hard then. See those men over there? Well, they're going to drink with me, and don't you forget it. Now you watch."

"Hi!" yelled the barkeeper, "this won't do!"

"Why won't it?" demanded the Swede. He stalked over to the table, and by chance laid his hand upon the shoulder of the gambler. "How about this?" he asked, wrathfully. "I asked you to drink with me."

The gambler simply twisted his head and spoke over his shoulder. "My friend, I don't know you."

"Oh, hell!" answered the Swede, "come and have a drink."

"Now, my boy," advised the gambler, kindly, "take your hand off my shoulder and go 'way and mind your own business." He was a little, slim man, and it seemed strange to hear him use this tone of heroic patronage to the burly Swede. The other men at the table said nothing.

"What! You won't drink with me, you little dude? I'll make you then! I'll make you!" The Swede had grasped the gambler frenziedly at the throat, and was dragging him from his chair. The other men sprang up. The barkeeper dashed around the corner of his bar. There was a great tumult, and then was seen a long blade in the hand of the gambler. It shot forward, and a human body, this citadel of virtue, wisdom, power, was pierced as easily as if it had been a melon. The Swede fell with a cry of supreme astonishment.

The prominent merchants and the district attorney must have at once tumbled out of the place backward. The bartender found himself hanging limply to the arm of a chair and gazing into the eyes of a murderer.

"Henry," said the latter, as he wiped his knife on one of the towels that hung beneath the bar-rail, "you tell 'em where to find me. I'll be home, waiting for 'em." Then he vanished. A moment afterwards the barkeeper was in the street dinning through the storm for help, and, moreover, companionship.

The corpse of the Swede, alone in the saloon, had its eyes fixed upon a dreadful legend that dwelt atop of the cash-machine: "This registers the amount of your purchase."

IX

Months later, the cowboy was frying pork over the stove of a little ranch near the Dakota line, when there was a quick thud of hoofs outside, and presently the Easterner entered with the letters and the papers.

"Well," said the Easterner at once, "the chap that killed the Swede has got three years. Wasn't much, was it?"

"He has? Three years?" The cowboy poised his pan of pork, while he ruminated upon the news. "Three years. That ain't much."

"No. It was a light sentence," replied the Easterner as he unbuckled his spurs. "Seems there was a good deal of sympathy for him in Romper."

"If the bartender had been any good," observed the cowboy, thoughtfully, "he would have gone in and cracked that there Dutchman on the head with a bottle in the beginnin' of it and stopped all this here murderin'."

"Yes, a thousand things might have happened," said the Easterner, tartly.

The cowboy returned his pan of pork to the fire, but his philosophy continued. "It's funny, ain't it? If he hadn't said Johnnie was cheatin' he'd be alive this minute. He was an awful fool. Game played for fun, too. Not for money. I believe he was crazy."

"I feel sorry for that gambler," said the Easterner.

"Oh, so do I," said the cowboy. "He don't deserve none of it for killin' who he did."

"The Swede might not have been killed if everything had been square."

"Might not have been killed?" exclaimed the cowboy. "Everythin' square? Why, when he said that Johnnie was cheatin' and acted like such a jackass? And then in the saloon he fairly walked up to git hurt?" With these arguments the cowboy browbeat the Easterner and reduced him to rage.

"You're a fool!" cried the Easterner, viciously. "You're a bigger jackass than the Swede by a million majority. Now let me tell you one thing. Let me tell you something. Listen! Johnnie *was* cheating!"

"'Johnnie,'" said the cowboy, blankly. There was a minute of silence, and then he said, robustly, "Why, no. The game was only for fun."

"Fun or not," said the Easterner, "Johnnie was cheating. I saw him. I know it. I saw him. And I refused to stand up and be a man. I let the Swede fight it out alone. And you—you were simply puffing around the place and wanting to fight. And then old Scully himself! We are all in it! This poor gambler isn't even a noun. He is kind of an adverb. Every sin is the result of a collaboration. We, five of us, have collaborated in the murder of this Swede. Usually there are from a dozen to forty women really involved in every murder, but in this case it seems to be only five men—you, I, Johnnie, old Scully, and that fool of an unfortunate gambler came merely as a culmination, the apex of a human movement, and gets all the punishment."

The cowboy, injured and rebellious, cried out blindly into this fog of mysterious theory: "Well, I didn't do anythin', did I?"

HIS NEW MITTENS

I

Little Horace was walking home from school, brilliantly decorated by a pair of new red mittens. A number of boys were snowballing gleefully in a field. They hailed him. "Come on, Horace! We're having a battle."

Horace was sad. "No," he said, "I can't. I've got to go home." At noon his mother had admonished him: "Now, Horace, you come straight home as soon as school is out. Do you hear? And don't you get them nice new mittens all wet, either. Do you hear?" Also his aunt had said: "I declare, Emily, it's a shame the way you allow that child to ruin his things." She had meant mittens. To his mother, Horace had dutifully replied, "Yes'm." But he now loitered in the vicinity of the group of uproarious boys, who were yelling like hawks as the white balls flew.

Some of them immediately analyzed this extraordinary hesitancy. "Hah!" they paused to scoff, "afraid of your new mittens, ain't you?" Some smaller boys, who were not yet so wise in discerning motives, applauded this attack with unreasonable vehemence. "A-fray-ed of his mit-tens! A-fray-ed of his mit-tens." They sang these lines to cruel and monotonous music which is as old perhaps as American childhood, and which it is the privilege of the emancipated adult to completely forget. "Afray-ed of his mit-tens!"

Horace cast a tortured glance towards his playmates, and then dropped his eyes to the snow at his feet. Presently he turned to the trunk of one of the great maple-trees that lined the curb. He made a pretence of closely examining the rough and virile bark. To his mind, this familiar street of Whilomville seemed to grow dark in the thick shadow of shame. The trees and the houses were now palled in purple.

"A-fray-ed of his mit-tens!" The terrible music had in it a meaning from the moonlit war-drums of chanting cannibals.

At last Horace, with supreme effort, raised his head. "'Tain't them I care about," he said, gruffly. "I've got to go home. That's all."

Whereupon each boy held his left forefinger as if it were a pencil and began to sharpen it derisively with his right forefinger. They came closer, and sang like a trained chorus, "A-fray-ed of his mittens!"

When he raised his voice to deny the charge it was simply lost in the screams of the mob. He was alone, fronting all the traditions of boyhood held before him by inexorable representatives. To such a low state had he fallen that one lad, a mere baby, outflanked him and then struck him in the cheek with a heavy snowball. The act was acclaimed with loud jeers. Horace turned to dart at his assailant, but there was an immediate demonstration on the other flank, and he found himself obliged to keep his face towards the hilarious crew of tormentors. The baby retreated in safety to the rear of the crowd, where he was received with fulsome compliments upon his daring. Horace retreated slowly up the walk. He continually tried to make them heed him, but the only sound was the chant, "A-fray-ed of his mit-tens!" In this desperate withdrawal the beset and haggard boy suffered more than is the common lot of man.

Being a boy himself, he did not understand boys at all. He had, of course, the dismal conviction that they were going to dog him to his grave. But near the corner of the field they suddenly seemed to forget all about it. Indeed, they possessed only the malevolence of so many flitter-headed sparrows. The interest had swung capriciously to some other matter. In a moment they were off in the field again, carousing amid the snow. Some authoritative boy had probably said, "Aw, come on!"

As the pursuit ceased, Horace ceased his retreat. He spent some time in what was evidently an attempt to adjust his self respect, and then began to wander furtively down towards the group. He, too, had undergone an important change. Perhaps his sharp agony was only as durable as the malevolence of the others. In this boyish life obedience to some unformulated creed of manners was enforced with capricious but merciless rigor. However, they were, after all, his comrades, his friends.

They did not heed his return. They were engaged in an altercation. It had evidently been planned that this battle was between Indians and soldiers. The smaller and weaker boys had been induced to appear as Indians in the initial skirmish, but they were now very sick of it, and were reluctantly but steadfastly, affirming their desire for a change of caste. The larger boys had all won great distinction, devastating Indians materially, and they wished the war to go on as planned. They explained vociferously that it was proper for the soldiers always to thrash the Indians. The little boys did not pretend to deny the truth of this argument; they confined themselves to the simple statement that, in that case, they wished to be soldiers. Each little boy willingly appealed to the others to remain Indians, but as for himself he reiterated his desire to enlist as a soldier. The larger boys were in despair over this dearth of enthusiasm in the small Indians. They alternately wheedled and bullied, but they could not persuade the little boys, who were really suffering dreadful humiliation rather than submit to another onslaught of soldiers. They were called all the baby names that had the power of stinging deep into their pride, but they remained firm.

Then a formidable lad, a leader of reputation, one who could whip many boys that wore long trousers, suddenly blew out his checks and shouted, "Well, all right then. I'll be an Indian myself. Now." The little boys greeted with cheers this addition to their wearied ranks, and seemed then content. But matters were not mended in the least, because all of the personal following of the formidable lad, with the addition of every outsider, spontaneously forsook the flag and declared themselves Indians. There were now no soldiers. The Indians had carried everything unanimously. The formidable lad used his influence, but his influence could not shake the loyalty of his friends, who refused to fight under any colors but his colors.

Plainly there was nothing for it but to coerce the little ones. The formidable lad again became a soldier, and then graciously permitted to join him all the real fighting strength of the crowd, leaving behind a most forlorn band of little Indians. Then the soldiers attacked the Indians, exhorting them to opposition at the same time.

The Indians at first adopted a policy of hurried surrender, but this had no success, as none of the surrenders were accepted. They then turned to flee, bawling out protests. The ferocious soldiers pursued them amid shouts. The battle widened, developing all manner of marvellous detail.

Horace had turned towards home several times, but, as a matter of fact, this scene held him in a spell. It was fascinating beyond anything which the grown man understands. He had always in the back of his head a sense of guilt, even a sense of impending punishment for disobedience, but they could not weigh with the delirium of this snow-battle.

II

One of the raiding soldiers, espying Horace, called out in passing, "A-fray-ed of his mit-tens!" Horace flinched at this renewal, and the other lad paused to taunt him again. Horace scooped some snow, moulded it into a ball, and flung it at the other. "Ho!" cried the boy, "you're an Indian, are you? Hey, fellers, here's an Indian that ain't been killed yet." He and Horace engaged in a duel in which both were in such haste to mould snowballs that they had little time for aiming.

Horace once struck his opponent squarely in the chest. "Hey," he shouted, "you're dead. You can't fight any more, Pete. I killed you. You're dead."

The other boy flushed red, but he continued frantically to make ammunition. "You never touched me!" he retorted, glowering. "You never touched me! Where, now?" he added, defiantly. "Where did you hit me?"

"On the coat! Right on your breast! You can't fight any more! You're dead!"

"You never!"

"I did, too! Hey, fellers, ain't he dead? I hit 'im square!"

"He never!"

Nobody had seen the affair, but some of the boys took sides in absolute accordance with their friendship for one of the concerned parties. Horace's opponent went about contending, "He never touched me! He never came near me! He never came near me!"

The formidable leader now came forward and accosted Horace. "What was you? An Indian? Well, then, you're dead—that's all. He hit you. I saw him."

"Me?" shrieked Horace. "He never came within a mile of me——"

At that moment he heard his name called in a certain familiar tune of two notes, with the last note shrill and prolonged. He looked towards the sidewalk, and saw his mother standing there in her widow's weeds, with two brown paper parcels under her arm. A silence had fallen upon all the boys. Horace moved slowly towards his mother. She did not seem to note his approach; she was gazing austerely off through the naked branches of the maples where two crimson sunset bars lay on the deep blue sky.

At a distance of ten paces Horace made a desperate venture. "Oh, ma," he whined, "can't I stay out for a while?"

"No," she answered solemnly, "you come with me." Horace knew that profile; it was the inexorable profile. But he continued to plead, because it was not beyond his mind that a great show of suffering now might diminish his suffering later.

He did not dare to look back at his playmates. It was already a public scandal that he could not stay out as late as other boys, and he could imagine his standing now that he had been again dragged off by his mother in sight of the whole world. He was a profoundly miserable human being.

Aunt Martha opened the door for them. Light streamed about her straight skirt. "Oh," she said, "so you found him on the road, eh? Well, I declare! It was about time!"

Horace slunk into the kitchen. The stove, straddling out on its four iron legs, was gently humming. Aunt Martha had evidently just lighted the lamp, for she went to it and began to twist the wick experimentally.

"Now," said the mother, "let's see them mittens."

Horace's chin sank. The aspiration of the criminal, the passionate desire for an asylum from retribution, from justice, was aflame in his heart. "I—I—don't—don't know where they are." he gasped finally, as he passed his hand over his pockets.

"Horace," intoned his mother, "you are tellin' me a story!"

"'Tain't a story," he answered, just above his breath. He looked like a sheep-stealer.

His mother held him by the arm, and began to search his pockets. Almost at once she was able to bring forth a pair of very wet mittens. "Well, I declare!" cried Aunt Martha. The two women went close to the lamp, and minutely examined the mittens, turning them over and over. Afterwards, when Horace looked up, his mother's sad-lined, homely face was turned towards him. He burst into tears.

His mother drew a chair near the stove. "Just you sit there now, until I tell you to git off." He sidled meekly into the chair. His mother and his aunt went briskly about the business of preparing supper. They did not display a knowledge of his existence; they carried an effect of oblivion so far that they even did not speak to each other. Presently they went into the dining and living room; Horace could hear the dishes rattling. His Aunt Martha brought a plate of food, placed it on a chair near him, and went away without a word.

Horace instantly decided that he would not touch a morsel of the food. He had often used this ruse in dealing with his mother. He did not know why it brought her to terms, but certainly it sometimes did.

The mother looked up when the aunt returned to the other room. "Is he eatin' his supper?" she asked.

The maiden aunt, fortified in ignorance, gazed with pity and contempt upon this interest. "Well, now, Emily, how do I know?" she queried. "Was I goin' to stand over 'im? Of all the worryin' you do about that child! It's a shame the way you're bringin' up that child."

"Well, he ought to eat somethin'. It won't do fer him to go without eatin'," the mother retorted, weakly.

Aunt Martha, profoundly scorning the policy of concession which these words meant, uttered a long, contemptuous sigh.

III

Alone in the kitchen, Horace stared with sombre eyes at the plate of food. For a long time he betrayed no sign of yielding. His mood was adamantine. He was resolved not to sell his vengeance for bread, cold ham, and a pickle, and yet it must be known that the sight of them affected him powerfully. The pickle in particular was notable for its seductive charm. He surveyed it darkly.

But at last, unable to longer endure his state, his attitude in the presence of the pickle, he put out an inquisitive finger and touched it, and it was cool and green and plump. Then a full conception of the cruel woe of his situation swept upon him suddenly, and his eyes filled with tears, which began to move down his cheeks. He sniffled. His heart was black with hatred. He painted in his mind scenes of deadly retribution. His mother would be taught that he was not one to endure persecution meekly, without raising an arm in his defence. And so his dreams were of a slaughter of feelings, and near the end of them his mother was pictured as coming, bowed with pain, to his feet. Weeping, she implored his charity. Would he forgive her? No; his once tender heart had been turned to stone by her injustice. He could not forgive her. She must pay the inexorable penalty.

The first item in this horrible plan was the refusal of the food. This he knew by experience would work havoc in his mother's heart. And so he grimly waited.

But suddenly it occurred to him that the first part of his revenge was in danger of failing. The thought struck him that his mother might not capitulate in the usual way. According to his recollection, the time was more than due when she should come in, worried, sadly affectionate, and ask him if he was ill. It had then been his custom to hint in a resigned voice that he was the victim of secret disease, but that he preferred to suffer in silence and alone. If she was obdurate in her anxiety, he always asked her in a gloomy, low voice to go away and leave him to suffer in silence and alone in the darkness without food. He had known this maneuvering to result even in pie.

But what was the meaning of the long pause and the stillness? Had his old and valued ruse betrayed him? As the truth sank into his mind, he supremely loathed life, the world, his mother. Her heart was beating back the besiegers; he was a defeated child.

He wept for a time before deciding upon the final stroke. He would run away. In a remote corner of the world he would become some sort of bloody-handed person driven to a life of crime by the barbarity of his mother. She should never know his fate. He would torture her for years with doubts and doubts, and drive her implacably to a repentant grave. Nor would Aunt Martha escape. Some day, a century hence, when his mother was dead, he would write to his Aunt Martha, and point out her part in the blighting of his life. For one blow against him now he would, in time, deal back a thousand— aye, ten thousand.

He arose and took his coat and cap. As he moved stealthily towards the door he cast a glance backward at the pickle. He was tempted to take it, but he knew that if he left the plate inviolate his mother would feel even worse.

A blue snow was falling. People, bowed forward, were moving briskly along the walks. The electric lamps hummed amid showers of flakes. As Horace emerged from the kitchen, a shrill squall drove the flakes around the corner of the house. He cowered away from it, and its violence illumined his mind vaguely in new directions. He deliberated upon a choice of remote corners of the globe. He found that he had no plans which were definite enough in a geographical way, but without much loss of time he decided upon California. He moved briskly as far as his mother's front gate on the road to California. He was off at last. His success was a trifle dreadful; his throat choked.

But at the gate he paused. He did not know if his journey to California would be shorter if he went down Niagara Avenue or off through Hogan

Street. As the storm was very cold and the point was very important, he decided to withdraw for reflection to the wood-shed. He entered the dark shanty, and took seat upon the old chopping-block upon which he was supposed to perform for a few minutes every afternoon when he returned from school. The wind screamed and shouted at the loose boards, and there was a rift of snow on the floor to leeward of a crack.

Here the idea of starting for California on such a night departed from his mind, leaving him ruminating miserably upon his martyrdom. He saw nothing for it but to sleep all night in the wood-shed and start for California in the morning bright and early. Thinking of his bed, he kicked over the floor and found that the innumerable chips were all frozen tightly, bedded in ice.

Later he viewed with joy some signs of excitement in the house. The flare of a lamp moved rapidly from window to window. Then the kitchen door slammed loudly and a shawled figure sped towards the gate. At last he was making them feel his power. The shivering child's face was lit with saturnine glee as in the darkness of the wood-shed he gloated over the evidences of consternation in his home. The shawled figure had been his Aunt Martha dashing with the alarm to the neighbors.

The cold of the wood-shed was tormenting him. He endured only because of the terror he was causing. But then it occurred to him that, if they instituted a search for him, they would probably examine the wood-shed. He knew that it would not be manful to be caught so soon. He was not positive now that he was going to remain away forever, but at any rate he was bound to inflict some more damage before allowing himself to be captured. If he merely succeeded in making his mother angry, she would thrash him on sight. He must prolong the time in order to be safe. If he held out properly, he was sure of a welcome of love, even though he should drip with crimes.

Evidently the storm had increased, for when he went out it swung him violently with its rough and merciless strength. Panting, stung, half blinded with the driving flakes, he was now a waif, exiled, friendless, and poor. With a bursting heart, he thought of his home and his mother. To his forlorn vision they were as far away as heaven.

<u>IV</u>

Horace was undergoing changes of feeling so rapidly that he was merely moved hither and then thither like a kite. He was now aghast at the merciless ferocity of his mother. It was she who had thrust him into this wild storm, and she was perfectly indifferent to his fate, perfectly indifferent. The forlorn wanderer could no longer weep. The strong sobs caught at his throat, making his breath come in short, quick snuffles. All in him was conquered save the enigmatical childish ideal of form, manner. This principle still held out, and it was the only thing between him and submission. When he surrendered, he must surrender in a way that deferred to the undefined code. He longed simply to go to the kitchen and stumble in, but his unfathomable sense of fitness forbade him.

Presently he found himself at the head of Niagara Avenue, staring through the snow into the blazing windows of Stickney's butcher-shop. Stickney was the family butcher, not so much because of a superiority to other Whilomville butchers as because he lived next door and had been an intimate friend of the father of Horace. Rows of glowing pigs hung head downward back of the tables, which bore huge pieces of red beef. Clumps of attenuated turkeys were suspended here and there. Stickney, hale and smiling, was bantering with a woman in a cloak, who, with a monster basket on her arm, was dickering for eight cents' worth of some thing. Horace watched them through a crusted pane. When the woman came out and passed him, he went towards the door. He touched the latch with his finger, but withdrew again suddenly to the sidewalk. Inside Stickney was whistling cheerily and assorting his knives.

Finally Horace went desperately forward, opened the door, and entered the shop. His head hung low. Stickney stopped whistling. "Hello, young man," he cried, "what brings you here?"

Horace halted, but said nothing. He swung one foot to and fro over the saw-dust floor.

274

Stickney had placed his two fat hands palms downward and wide apart on the table, in the attitude of a butcher facing a customer, but now he straightened.

"Here," he said, "what's wrong? What's wrong, kid?"

"Nothin'," answered Horace, huskily. He labored for a moment with something in his throat, and afterwards added, "O'ny——I've——I've run away, and—"

"Run away!" shouted Stickney. "Run away from what? Who?"

"From——home," answered Horace. "I don't like it there any more. I——" He had arranged an oration to win the sympathy of the butcher; he had prepared a table setting forth the merits of his case in the most logical fashion, but it was as if the wind had been knocked out of his mind. "I've run away. I——"

Stickney reached an enormous hand over the array of beef, and firmly grappled the emigrant. Then he swung himself to Horace's side. His face was stretched with laughter, and he playfully shook his prisoner. "Come——come——come. What dashed nonsense is this? Run away, hey? Run away?" Whereupon the child's long-tried spirit found vent in howls.

"Come, come," said Stickney, busily. "Never mind now, never mind. You just come along with me. It'll be all right. I'll fix it. Never you mind."

Five minutes later the butcher, with a great ulster over his apron, was leading the boy homeward.

At the very threshold, Horace raised his last flag of pride. "No——no," he sobbed. "I don't want to. I don't want to go in there." He braced his foot against the step and made a very respectable resistance.

"Now, Horace," cried the butcher. He thrust open the door with a bang. "Hello there!" Across the dark kitchen the door to the living-room opened and Aunt Martha appeared. "You've found him!" she screamed.

"We've come to make a call," roared the butcher. At the entrance to

275

the living-room a silence fell upon them all. Upon a couch Horace saw his mother lying limp, pale as death, her eyes gleaming with pain. There was an electric pause before she swung a waxen hand towards Horace. "My child," she murmured, tremulously. Whereupon the sinister person addressed, with a prolonged wail of grief and joy, ran to her with speed. "Mam-ma! Mam-ma! Oh, mam-ma!" She was not able to speak in a known tongue as she folded him in her weak arms.

Aunt Martha turned defiantly upon the butcher because her face betrayed her. She was crying. She made a gesture half military, half feminine. "Won't you have a glass of our root-beer, Mr. Stickney? We make it ourselves."

About Author

Stephen Crane (November 1, 1871 – June 5, 1900) was an American poet, novelist, and short story writer. Prolific throughout his short life, he wrote notable works in the Realist tradition as well as early examples of American Naturalism and Impressionism. He is recognized by modern critics as one of the most innovative writers of his generation.

The ninth surviving child of Methodist parents, Crane began writing at the age of four and had published several articles by the age of 16. Having little interest in university studies though he was active in a fraternity, he left Syracuse University in 1891 to work as a reporter and writer. Crane's first novel was the 1893 Bowery tale Maggie: A Girl of the Streets, generally considered by critics to be the first work of American literary Naturalism. He won international acclaim in 1895 for his Civil War novel The Red Badge of Courage, which he wrote without having any battle experience.

In 1896, Crane endured a highly publicized scandal after appearing as a witness in the trial of a suspected prostitute, an acquaintance named Dora Clark. Late that year he accepted an offer to travel to Cuba as a war correspondent. As he waited in Jacksonville, Florida for passage, he met Cora Taylor, with whom he began a lasting relationship. En route to Cuba, Crane's vessel the SS Commodore sank off the coast of Florida, leaving him and others adrift for 30 hours in a dinghy. Crane described the ordeal in "The Open Boat". During the final years of his life, he covered conflicts in Greece (accompanied by Cora, recognized as the first woman war correspondent) and later lived in England with her. He was befriended by writers such as Joseph Conrad and H. G. Wells. Plagued by financial difficulties and ill health, Crane died of tuberculosis in a Black Forest sanatorium in Germany at the age of 28.

At the time of his death, Crane was considered an important figure in American literature. After he was nearly forgotten for two decades, critics revived interest in his life and work. Crane's writing is characterized by vivid intensity, distinctive dialects, and irony. Common themes involve fear, spiritual crises and social isolation. Although recognized primarily for The Red Badge of Courage, which has become an American classic, Crane is also known for his poetry, journalism, and short stories such as "The Open Boat", "The Blue Hotel", "The Bride Comes to Yellow Sky", and The Monster. His writing made a deep impression on 20th-century writers, most prominent among them Ernest Hemingway, and is thought to have inspired the Modernists and the Imagists.

Biography

Early years

Stephen Crane was born on November 1, 1871, in Newark, New Jersey, to Jonathan Townley Crane, a minister in the Methodist Episcopal church, and Mary Helen Peck Crane, daughter of a clergyman, George Peck. He was the fourteenth and last child born to the couple. At 45, Helen Crane had suffered the early deaths of her previous four children, each of whom died within one year of birth. Nicknamed "Stevie" by the family, he joined eight surviving brothers and sisters—Mary Helen, George Peck, Jonathan Townley, William Howe, Agnes Elizabeth, Edmund Byran, Wilbur Fiske, and Luther.

The Cranes were descended from Jaspar Crane, a founder of New Haven Colony, who had migrated there from England in 1639. Stephen was named for a putative founder of Elizabethtown, New Jersey, who had, according to family tradition, come from England or Wales in 1665, as well as his great-great-grandfather Stephen Crane (1709–1780), a Revolutionary War patriot who served as New Jersey delegate to the First Continental Congress in Philadelphia. Crane later wrote that his father, Dr. Crane, "was a great, fine, simple mind," who had written numerous tracts on theology. Although his mother was a popular spokeswoman for the Woman's Christian Temperance Union and a highly religious woman, Crane wrote that he did not believe "she was as narrow as most of her friends or family." The young Stephen was raised primarily by his sister Agnes, who was 15 years his senior. The family moved to Port Jervis, New York, in 1876, where Dr. Crane became the pastor of Drew Methodist Church, a position that he retained until his death.

As a child, Stephen was often sickly and afflicted by constant colds.

When the boy was almost two, his father wrote in his diary that his youngest son became "so sick that we are anxious about him." Despite his fragile nature, Crane was an intelligent child who taught himself to read before the age of four. His first known inquiry, recorded by his father, dealt with writing; at the age of three, while imitating his brother Townley's writing, he asked his mother, "how do you spell O?" In December 1879, Crane wrote a poem about wanting a dog for Christmas. Entitled "I'd Rather Have –", it is his first surviving poem. Stephen was not regularly enrolled in school until January 1880, but he had no difficulty in completing two grades in six weeks. Recalling this feat, he wrote that it "sounds like the lie of a fond mother at a teaparty, but I do remember that I got ahead very fast and that father was very pleased with me."

Dr. Crane died on February 16, 1880, at the age of 60; Stephen was eight years old. Some 1,400 people mourned Dr. Crane at his funeral, more than double the size of his congregation. After her husband's death, Mrs. Crane moved to Roseville, near Newark, leaving Stephen in the care of his older brother Edmund, with whom the young boy lived with cousins in Sussex County. He next lived with his brother William, a lawyer, in Port Jervis for several years.

His older sister Helen took him to Asbury Park to be with their brother Townley and his wife, Fannie. Townley was a professional journalist; he headed the Long Branch department of both the New-York Tribune and the Associated Press, and also served as editor of the Asbury Park Shore Press. Agnes, another Crane sister, joined the siblings in New Jersey. She took a position at Asbury Park's intermediate school and moved in with Helen to care for the young Stephen.

Within a couple of years, the Crane family suffered more losses. First, Townley and his wife lost their two young children. His wife Fannie died of Bright's disease in November 1883. Agnes Crane became ill and died on June 10, 1884, of meningitis at the age of 28.

Schooling

Crane wrote his first known story, "Uncle Jake and the Bell Handle", when he was 14. In late 1885, he enrolled at Pennington Seminary, a ministry-focused coeducational boarding school 7 miles (11 km) north of Trenton. His father had been principal there from 1849 to 1858. Soon after her youngest son left for school, Mrs. Crane began suffering what the Asbury Park Shore Press reported as "a temporary aberration of the mind." She had apparently recovered by early 1886, but later that year, her son, 23-year-old Luther Crane, died after falling in front of an oncoming train while working as a flagman for the Erie Railroad. It was the fourth death in six years among Stephen's immediate family.

After two years, Crane left Pennington for Claverack College, a quasi-military school. He later looked back on his time at Claverack as "the happiest period of my life although I was not aware of it." A classmate remembered him as a highly literate but erratic student, lucky to pass examinations in math and science, and yet "far in advance of his fellow students in his knowledge of History and Literature", his favorite subjects. While he held an impressive record on the drill field and baseball diamond, Crane generally did not excel in the classroom. Not having a middle name, as was customary among other students, he took to signing his name "Stephen T. Crane" in order "to win recognition as a regular fellow". Crane was seen as friendly, but also moody and rebellious. He sometimes skipped class in order to play baseball, a game in which he starred as catcher. He was also greatly interested in the school's military training program. He rose rapidly in the ranks of the student battalion. One classmate described him as "indeed physically attractive without being handsome", but he was aloof, reserved and not generally popular at Claverack. Although academically weak, Crane gained experience at Claverack that provided background (and likely some anecdotes from the Civil War veterans on the staff) that proved useful when he came to write The Red Badge of Courage.

In mid-1888, Crane became his brother Townley's assistant at a New Jersey shore news bureau, working there every summer until 1892. Crane's first publication under his byline was an article on the explorer Henry M. Stanley's famous quest to find the Scottish missionary David Livingstone in Africa. It appeared in the February 1890 Claverack College Vidette. Within a few months, Crane was persuaded by his family to forgo a military career and transfer to Lafayette College in Easton, Pennsylvania, in order to pursue a mining engineering degree. He registered at Lafayette on September 12, and promptly became involved in extracurricular activities; he took up baseball again and joined the largest fraternity, Delta Upsilon. He also joined both rival literary societies, named for (George) Washington and (Benjamin) Franklin. Crane infrequently attended classes and ended the semester with grades for four of the seven courses he had taken.

After one semester, Crane transferred to Syracuse University, where he enrolled as a non-degree candidate in the College of Liberal Arts. He roomed in the Delta Upsilon fraternity house and joined the baseball team. Attending just one class (English Literature) during the middle trimester, he remained in residence while taking no courses in the third semester.

Concentrating on his writing, Crane began to experiment with tone and style while trying out different subjects. He published his fictional story, "Great Bugs of Onondaga," simultaneously in the Syracuse Daily Standard and the New York Tribune. Declaring college "a waste of time", Crane decided to become a full-time writer and reporter. He attended a Delta Upsilon chapter meeting on June 12, 1891, but shortly afterward left college for good.

Full-time writer

In the summer of 1891, Crane often camped with friends in the nearby area of Sullivan County, New York, where his brother Edmund occupied a house obtained as part of their brother William's Hartwood Club (Association) land dealings. He used this area as the geographic setting for several short stories, which were posthumously published in a collection under the title Stephen Crane: Sullivan County Tales and Sketches. Crane showed two of these works to Tribune editor Willis Fletcher Johnson, a friend of the family, who accepted them for the publication. "Hunting Wild Dogs" and "The Last of the Mohicans" were the first of fourteen unsigned Sullivan County sketches and tales that were published in the Tribune between February and July 1892. Crane also showed Johnson an early draft of his first novel, Maggie: A Girl of the Streets.

Later that summer, Crane met and befriended author Hamlin Garland, who had been lecturing locally on American literature and the expressive arts; on August 17 he gave a talk on novelist William Dean Howells, which Crane wrote up for the Tribune. Garland became a mentor for and champion of the young writer, whose intellectual honesty impressed him. Their relationship suffered in later years, however, because Garland disapproved of Crane's alleged immorality, related to his living with a woman married to another man.

Stephen moved into his brother Edmund's house in Lakeview, a suburb of Paterson, New Jersey, in the fall of 1891. From here he made frequent trips into New York City, writing and reporting particularly on its impoverished tenement districts. Crane focused particularly on The Bowery, a small and once prosperous neighborhood in the southern part of Manhattan. After the Civil War, Bowery shops and mansions had given way to saloons, dance halls, brothels and flophouses, all of which Crane frequented. He later said he did so for research. He was attracted to the human nature found in the slums, considering it "open and plain, with nothing hidden". Believing nothing honest and unsentimental had been written about the Bowery, Crane became determined to do so himself; this was the setting of his first novel. On December 7, 1891, Crane's mother died at the age of 64, and the 20-year-old appointed Edmund as his guardian.

Despite being frail, undernourished and suffering from a hacking cough, which did not prevent him from smoking cigarettes, in the spring of 1892 Crane began a romance with Lily Brandon Munroe, a married woman who was estranged from her husband. Although Munroe later said Crane "was not a handsome man", she admired his "remarkable almond-shaped gray eyes." He begged her to elope with him, but her family opposed the match because Crane lacked money and prospects, and she declined. Their last meeting likely occurred in April 1898, when he again asked her to run away with him and she again refused.

Between July 2 and September 11, 1892, Crane published at least ten news reports on Asbury Park affairs. Although a Tribune colleague stated that Crane "was not highly distinguished above any other boy of twenty who had gained a reputation for saying and writing bright things," that summer his reporting took on a more skeptical, hypocrisy-deflating tone. A storm of controversy erupted over a report he wrote on the Junior Order of United American Mechanics' American Day Parade, entitled "Parades and Entertainments". Published on August 21, the report juxtaposes the "bronzed, slope-shouldered, uncouth" marching men "begrimed with dust" and the spectators dressed in "summer gowns, lace parasols, tennis trousers, straw hats and indifferent smiles". Believing they were being ridiculed, some JOUAM marchers were outraged and wrote to the editor. The owner of the Tribune, Whitelaw Reid, was that year's Republican vice-presidential candidate, and this likely increased the sensitivity of the paper's management to the issue. Although Townley wrote a piece for the Asbury Park Daily Press in his brother's defense, the Tribune quickly apologized to its readers, calling Stephen Crane's piece "a bit of random correspondence, passed inadvertently by the copy editor". Hamlin Garland and biographer John Barry attested that Crane told them he had been dismissed by the Tribune, although Willis Fletcher Johnson later denied this. The paper did not publish any of Crane's work after 1892.

> Such an assemblage of the spraddle-legged men of the middle class, whose hands were bent and shoulders stooped from delving and constructing, had never appeared to an Asbury Park summer crowd, and the latter was vaguely amused.

> — Stephen Crane, account of the JOUAM parade as it appeared in the Tribune.

Life in New York

Crane struggled to make a living as a free-lance writer, contributing sketches and feature articles to various New York newspapers. In October 1892, he moved into a rooming house in Manhattan whose boarders were a group of medical students. During this time, he expanded or entirely reworked Maggie: A Girl of the Streets, which is about a girl who "blossoms in a mud-puddle" and becomes a pitiful victim of circumstance. In the winter of 1893, Crane took the manuscript of Maggie to Richard Watson Gilder, who rejected it for publication in The Century Magazine.

Crane decided to publish it privately, with money he had inherited from his mother. The novel was published in late February or early March 1893 by a small printing shop that usually printed medical books and religious tracts. The typewritten title page for the Library of Congress copyright application read simply: "A Girl of the Streets, / A Story of New York. / —By—/Stephen Crane." The name "Maggie" was added to the title later. Crane used the pseudonym "Johnston Smith" for the novel's initial publication, later telling friend and artist Corwin Knapp Linson that the nom de plume was the "commonest name I could think of. I had an editor friend named Johnson, and put in the "t", and no one could find me in the mob of Smiths." Hamlin Garland reviewed the work in the June 1893 issue of The Arena, calling it "the most truthful and unhackneyed study of the slums I have yet read, fragment though it is." Despite this early praise, Crane became depressed and destitute from having spent $869 for 1,100 copies of a novel that did not sell; he ended up giving a hundred copies away. He would later remember "how I looked forward to publication and pictured the sensation I thought it would make. It fell flat. Nobody seemed to notice it or care for it... Poor Maggie! She was one of my first loves."

In March 1893, Crane spent hours lounging in Linson's studio while having his portrait painted. He became fascinated with issues of the Century that were largely devoted to famous battles and military leaders from the Civil War. Frustrated with the dryly written stories, Crane stated, "I wonder that some of those fellows don't tell how they felt in those scraps. They spout enough of what they did, but they're as emotionless as rocks." Crane returned to these magazines during subsequent visits to Linson's studio, and eventually the idea of writing a war novel overtook him. He would later state that he "had been unconsciously working the detail of the story out through most of his boyhood" and had imagined "war stories ever since he was out of knickerbockers." This novel would ultimately become The Red Badge of Courage.

A river, amber-tinted in the shadow of its banks, purled at the army's feet; and at night, when the stream had become of a sorrowful blackness, one could see across it the red, eyelike gleam of hostile camp-fires set in the low brows of distant hills.

— Stephen Crane, The Red Badge of Courage

From the beginning, Crane wished to show how it felt to be in a war by writing "a psychological portrayal of fear." Conceiving his story from the point of view of a young private who is at first filled with boyish dreams of the glory of war and then quickly becomes disillusioned by war's reality, Crane borrowed the private's surname, "Fleming", from his sister-in-law's maiden name. He later said that the first paragraphs came to him with "every word in place, every comma, every period fixed." Working mostly nights, he wrote from around midnight until four or five in the morning. Because he could not afford a typewriter, he wrote carefully in ink on legal-sized paper, seldom crossing through or interlining a word. If he did change something, he would rewrite the whole page.

While working on his second novel, Crane remained prolific, concentrating on publishing stories to stave off poverty; "An Experiment in Misery", based on Crane's experiences in the Bowery, was printed by the New York Press. He also wrote five or six poems a day. In early 1894, he showed some of his poems or "lines" as he called them, to Hamlin Garland, who said he read "some thirty in all" with "growing wonder." Although Garland and William Dean Howells encouraged him to submit his poetry for publication, Crane's free verse was too unconventional for most. After brief wrangling between poet and publisher, Copeland & Day accepted Crane's first book of poems, The Black Riders and Other Lines, although it would not be published until after The Red Badge of Courage. He received a 10 percent royalty and the publisher assured him that the book would be in a form "more severely classic than any book ever yet issued in America."

In the spring of 1894, Crane offered the finished manuscript of The Red Badge of Courage to McClure's Magazine, which had become the foremost magazine for Civil War literature. While McClure's delayed giving him an answer on his novel, they offered him an assignment writing about the Pennsylvania coal mines. "In the Depths of a Coal Mine", a story with pictures by Linson, was syndicated by McClure's in a number of newspapers, heavily edited. Crane was reportedly disgusted by the cuts, asking Linson:

"Why the hell did they send me up there then? Do they want the public to think the coal mines gilded ball-rooms with the miners eating ice-cream in boiled shirt-fronts?"

Sources report that following an encounter with a male prostitute that spring, Crane began a novel on the subject entitled Flowers of Asphalt, which he later abandoned. The manuscript has never been recovered.

After discovering that McClure's could not afford to pay him, Crane took his war novel to Irving Bacheller of the Bacheller-Johnson Newspaper Syndicate, which agreed to publish The Red Badge of Courage in serial form. Between the third and the ninth of December 1894, The Red Badge of Courage was published in some half-dozen newspapers in the United States. Although it was greatly cut for syndication, Bacheller attested to its causing a stir, saying "its quality [was] immediately felt and recognized." The lead editorial in the Philadelphia Press of December 7 said that Crane "is a new name now and unknown, but everybody will be talking about him if he goes on as he has begun".

Travels and fame

At the end of January 1895, Crane left on what he called "a very long and circuitous newspaper trip" to the west. While writing feature articles for the Bacheller syndicate, he traveled to Saint Louis, Missouri, Nebraska, New Orleans, Galveston, Texas and then Mexico City. Irving Bacheller would later state that he "sent Crane to Mexico for new color", which the author found in the form of Mexican slum life. Whereas he found the lower class in New York pitiful, he was impressed by the "superiority" of the Mexican peasants' contentment and "even refuse[d] to pity them."

Returning to New York five months later, Crane joined the Lantern (alternately spelled "Lanthom" or "Lanthorne") Club organized by a group of young writers and journalists. The Club, located on the roof of an old house on William Street near the Brooklyn Bridge, served as a drinking establishment of sorts and was decorated to look like a ship's cabin. There Crane ate one good meal a day, although friends were troubled by his "constant smoking, too much coffee, lack of food and poor teeth", as Nelson Greene put it. Living in near-poverty and greatly anticipating the publication of his books, Crane began work on two more novels: The Third Violet and George's Mother.

The Black Riders was published by Copeland & Day shortly before his return to New York in May, but it received mostly criticism, if not abuse, for the poems' unconventional style and use of free verse. A piece in the Bookman called Crane "the Aubrey Beardsley of poetry," and a commentator from the Chicago Daily Inter-Ocean stated that "there is not a line of poetry from the opening to the closing page. Whitman's Leaves of Grass were luminous in comparison. Poetic lunacy would be a better name for the book." In June, the New York Tribune dismissed the book as "so much trash." Crane was pleased that the book was "making some stir".

In contrast to the reception for Crane's poetry, The Red Badge of Courage was welcomed with acclaim after its publication by Appleton in September 1895. For the next four months, the book was in the top six on various bestseller lists around the country. It arrived on the literary scene "like a flash of lightning out of a clear winter sky", according to H. L. Mencken, who was about 15 at the time. The novel also became popular in Britain; Joseph Conrad, a future friend of Crane, wrote that the novel "detonated... with the impact and force of a twelve-inch shell charged with a very high explosive." Appleton published two, possibly three, printings in 1895 and as many as eleven more in 1896. Although some critics considered the work overly graphic and profane, it was widely heralded for its realistic portrayal of war and unique writing style. The Detroit Free Press declared that The Red Badge would give readers "so vivid a picture of the emotions and the horrors of the battlefield that you will pray your eyes may never look upon the reality."

Wanting to capitalize on the success of The Red Badge, McClure Syndicate offered Crane a contract to write a series on Civil War battlefields. Because it was a wish of his to "visit the battlefield—which I was to describe— at the time of year when it was fought", Crane agreed to take the assignment. Visiting battlefields in Northern Virginia, including Fredericksburg, he would later produce five more Civil War tales: "Three Miraculous Soldiers", "The Veteran", "An Indiana Campaign", "An Episode of War" and The Little Regiment.

Scandal

At the age of 24, Crane, who was reveling in his success, became involved in a highly publicized case involving a suspected prostitute named Dora Clark. At 2 a.m. on September 16, 1896, he escorted two chorus girls and Clark from New York City's Broadway Garden, a popular "resort" where he had interviewed the women for a series he was writing. As Crane saw one woman safely to a streetcar, a plainclothes policeman named Charles Becker arrested the other two for solicitation; Crane was threatened with arrest when he tried to interfere. One of the women was released after Crane confirmed her erroneous claim that she was his wife, but Clark was charged and taken to the precinct. Against the advice of the arresting sergeant, Crane made a statement confirming Dora Clark's innocence, stating that "I only know that while with me she acted respectably, and that the policeman's charge was false." On the basis of Crane's testimony, Clark was discharged. The media seized upon the story; news spread to Philadelphia, Boston and beyond, with papers focusing on Crane's courage. The Stephen Crane story, as it became known, soon became a source for ridicule; the Chicago Dispatch in particular quipped that "Stephen Crane is respectfully informed that association with women in scarlet is not necessarily a 'Red Badge of Courage' ".

A couple of weeks after her trial, Clark pressed charges of false arrest against the officer who had arrested her. The next day, the officer physically attacked Clark in the presence of witnesses for having brought charges against him. Crane, who initially went briefly to Philadelphia to escape the pressure of publicity, returned to New York to give testimony at Becker's trial despite advice given to him from Theodore Roosevelt, who was Police Commissioner at the time and a new acquaintance of Crane. The defense targeted Crane: police raided his apartment and interviewed people who knew him, trying to find incriminating evidence in order to lessen the effect of his testimony. A vigorous cross-examination took place that sought to portray Crane as a man of dubious morals; while the prosecution proved that he frequented brothels, Crane claimed this was merely for research purposes. After the trial ended on October 16, the arresting officer was exonerated, and Crane's reputation was ruined.

Cora Taylor and the Commodore shipwreck

None of them knew the color of the sky. Their eyes glanced level and were fastened upon the waves that swept toward them. These waves were of the hue of slate, save for the tops, which were of foaming white, and all of the men knew the colors of the sea.

— Stephen Crane, "The Open Boat"

Given $700 in Spanish gold by the Bacheller-Johnson syndicate to work as a war correspondent in Cuba as the Spanish–American War was pending, the 25-year-old Crane left New York on November 27, 1896, on a train bound for Jacksonville, Florida. Upon arrival in Jacksonville, he registered at the St. James Hotel under the alias of Samuel Carleton to maintain anonymity while seeking passage to Cuba. While waiting for a boat, he toured the city and visited the local brothels. Within days he met 31-year-old Cora Taylor, proprietor of the downtown bawdy house Hotel de Dream. Born into a respectable Boston family, Taylor (whose legal name was Cora Ethel Stewart) had already had two brief marriages; her first husband, Vinton Murphy, divorced her on grounds of adultery. In 1889, she had married British Captain Donald William Stewart. She left him in 1892 for another man, but was still legally married. By the time Crane arrived, Taylor had been in Jacksonville for two years. She lived a bohemian lifestyle, owned a hotel of assignation, and was a well-known and respected local figure. The two spent much time together while Crane awaited his departure. He was finally cleared to leave for the Cuban port of Cienfuegos on New Year's Eve aboard the SS Commodore.

The ship sailed from Jacksonville with 27 or 28 men and a cargo of supplies and ammunition for the Cuban rebels. On the St. Johns River and less than 2 miles (3.2 km) from Jacksonville, Commodore struck a sandbar in a dense fog and damaged its hull. Although towed off the sandbar the following day, it was beached again in Mayport and again damaged. A leak began in the boiler room that evening and, as a result of malfunctioning water pumps, the ship came to a standstill about 16 miles (26 km) from Mosquito Inlet. As the ship took on more water, Crane described the engine room as resembling "a scene at this time taken from the middle kitchen of hades." Commodore's lifeboats were lowered in the early hours of the morning on

January 2, 1897 and the ship ultimately sank at 7 a.m. Crane was one of the last to leave the ship in a 10-foot (3.0 m) dinghy. In an ordeal that he recounted in the short story "The Open Boat", Crane and three other men (including the ship's Captain) foundered off the coast of Florida for a day and a half before trying to land the dinghy at Daytona Beach. The small boat overturned in the surf, forcing the exhausted men to swim to shore; one of them died. Having lost the gold given to him for his journey, Crane wired Cora Taylor for help. She traveled to Daytona and returned to Jacksonville with Crane the next day, only four days after he had left on the Commodore.

The disaster was reported on the front pages of newspapers across the country. Rumors that the ship had been sabotaged were widely circulated but never substantiated. Portrayed favorably and heroically by the press, Crane emerged from the ordeal with his reputation enhanced, if not restored, after the battering he had received in the Dora Clark affair. Meanwhile, Crane's affair with Taylor blossomed.

Three seasons of archaeological investigation were conducted in 2002-04 to examine and document the exposed remains of a wreck near Ponce Inlet, FL conjectured to be that of the SS Commodore. The collected data, and other accumulated evidence, finally substantiated the identification of the Commodore beyond a reasonable doubt.

Greco-Turkish War

Despite contentment in Jacksonville and the need for rest after his ordeal, Crane became restless. He left Jacksonville on January 11 for New York City, where he applied for a passport to Cuba, Mexico and the West Indies. Spending three weeks in New York, he completed "The Open Boat" and periodically visited Port Jervis to see family. By this time, however, blockades had formed along the Florida coast as tensions rose with Spain, and Crane concluded that he would never be able to travel to Cuba. He sold "The Open Boat" to Scribner's for $300 in early March. Determined to work as a war correspondent, Crane signed on with William Randolph Hearst's New York Journal to cover the impending Greco-Turkish conflict. He brought along Taylor, who had sold the Hotel de Dream in order to follow him.

On March 20, they sailed first to England, where Crane was warmly received. They arrived in Athens in early April; between April 17 (when Turkey declared war on Greece) and April 22, Crane wrote his first published report of the war, "An Impression of the 'Concert' ". When he left for Epirus in the northwest, Taylor remained in Athens, where she became the Greek war's first woman war correspondent. She wrote under the pseudonym "Imogene Carter" for the New York Journal, a job that Crane had secured for her. They wrote frequently, traveling throughout the country separately and together. The first large battle that Crane witnessed was the Turks' assault on General Constantine Smolenski's Greek forces at Velestino. Crane wrote, "It is a great thing to survey the army of the enemy. Just where and how it takes hold upon the heart is difficult of description." During this battle, Crane encountered "a fat waddling puppy" that he immediately claimed, dubbing it "Velestino, the Journal dog". Greece and Turkey signed an armistice on May 20, ending the 30-day war; Crane and Taylor left Greece for England, taking two Greek brothers as servants and Velestino the dog with them.

Spanish–American War

After staying in Limpsfield, Surrey, for a few days, Crane and Taylor settled in Ravensbrook, a plain brick villa in Oxted. Referring to themselves as Mr. and Mrs. Crane, the couple lived openly in England, but Crane concealed the relationship from his friends and family in the United States. Admired in England, Crane thought himself attacked back home: "There seem so many of them in America who want to kill, bury and forget me purely out of unkindness and envy and—my unworthiness, if you choose", he wrote. Velestino the dog sickened and died soon after their arrival in England, on August 1. Crane, who had a great love for dogs, wrote an emotional letter to a friend an hour after the dog's death, stating that "for eleven days we fought death for him, thinking nothing of anything but his life." The Limpsfield-Oxted area was home to members of the socialist Fabian Society and a magnet for writers such as Edmund Gosse, Ford Madox Ford and Edward Garnett. Crane also met the Polish-born novelist Joseph Conrad in October 1897, with whom he would have what Crane called a "warm and endless friendship".

Although Crane was confident among peers, strong negative reviews of the recently published The Third Violet were causing his literary reputation to dwindle. Reviewers were also highly critical of Crane's war letters, deeming them self-centered. Although The Red Badge of Courage had by this time gone through fourteen printings in the United States and six in England, Crane was running out of money. To survive financially, he worked at a feverish pitch, writing prolifically for both the English and the American markets. He wrote in quick succession stories such as The Monster, "The Bride Comes to Yellow Sky", "Death and the Child" and "The Blue Hotel". Crane began to attach price tags to his new works of fiction, hoping that "The Bride", for example, would fetch $175.

As 1897 ended, Crane's money crisis worsened. Amy Leslie, a reporter from Chicago and a former lover, sued him for $550. The New York Times reported that Leslie gave him $800 in November 1896 but that he'd repaid only a quarter of the sum. In February he was summoned to answer Leslie's claim. The claim was apparently settled out of court, because no record of adjudication exists. Meanwhile, Crane felt "heavy with troubles" and "chased to the wall" by expenses. He confided to his agent that he was $2,000 in debt but that he would "beat it" with more literary output.

Soon after the USS Maine exploded in Havana Harbor on February 15, 1898, under suspicious circumstances, Crane was offered a £60 advance by Blackwood's Magazine for articles "from the seat of war in the event of a war breaking out" between the United States and Spain. His health was failing, and it is believed that signs of his pulmonary tuberculosis, which he may have contracted in childhood, became apparent.With almost no money coming in from his finished stories, Crane accepted the assignment and left Oxted for New York. Taylor and the rest of the household stayed behind to fend off local creditors. Crane applied for a passport and left New York for Key West two days before Congress declared war. While the war idled, he interviewed people and produced occasional copy.

In early June, he observed the establishment of an American base in Cuba when Marines seized Guantánamo Bay. He went ashore with the Marines, planning "to gather impressions and write them as the spirit moved." Although he wrote honestly about his fear in battle, others observed his calmness and composure. He would later recall "this prolonged tragedy of the night" in the war tale "Marines Signaling Under Fire at Guantanamo". After showing a willingness to serve during fighting at Cuzco, Cuba, by carrying messages to company commanders, Crane was officially cited for his "material aid during the action".

He continued to report upon various battles and the worsening military conditions and praised Theodore Roosevelt's Rough Riders, despite past tensions with the Commissioner. In early July, Crane was sent to the United States for medical treatment for a high fever. He was diagnosed with yellow fever, then malaria. Upon arrival in Old Point Comfort, Virginia, he spent a few weeks resting in a hotel. Although Crane had filed more than twenty dispatches in the three months he had covered the war, the World's business manager believed that the paper had not received its money's worth and fired him. In retaliation, Crane signed with Hearst's New York Journal with the wish to return to Cuba. He traveled first to Puerto Rico and then to Havana. In September, rumors began to spread that Crane, who was working anonymously, had either been killed or disappeared. He sporadically sent out dispatches and stories; he wrote about the mood in Havana, the crowded city sidewalks, and other topics, but he was soon desperate for money again. Taylor, left alone in England, was also penniless. She became frantic with worry over her lover's whereabouts; they were not in direct communication until the end of the year. Crane left Havana and arrived in England on January 11, 1899.

Death

Rent on Ravensbrook had not been paid for a year. Upon returning to England, Crane secured a solicitor to act as guarantor for their debts, after which Crane and Taylor relocated to Brede Place. This manor in Sussex, which dated to the 14th century and had neither electricity nor indoor plumbing, was offered to them by friends at a modest rent. The relocation appeared to give hope to Crane, but his money problems continued. Deciding that he could no longer afford to write for American publications, he concentrated on publishing in English magazines.

Crane pushed himself to write feverishly during the first months at Brede; he told his publisher that he was "doing more work now than I have at any other period in my life". His health worsened, and by late 1899 he was asking friends about health resorts. The Monster and Other Stories was in production and War Is Kind, his second collection of poems, was published in the United States in May. None of his books after The Red Badge of Courage had sold well, and he bought a typewriter to spur output. Active Service, a novella based on Crane's correspondence experience, was published in October. The New York Times reviewer questioned "whether the author of 'Active Service' himself really sees anything remarkable in his newspapery hero."

In December, the couple held an elaborate Christmas party at Brede, attended by Conrad, Henry James, H. G. Wells and other friends; it lasted several days. On December 29 Crane suffered a severe pulmonary hemorrhage. In January 1900 he'd recovered sufficiently to work on a new novel, The O'Ruddy, completing 25 of the 33 chapters. Plans were made for him to travel as a correspondent to Gibraltar to write sketches from Saint Helena, the site of a Boer prison, but at the end of March and in early April he suffered two more hemorrhages. Taylor took over most of Crane's correspondence while he was ill, writing to friends for monetary aid. The couple planned to travel on the continent, but Conrad, upon visiting Crane for the last time, remarked that his friend's "wasted face was enough to tell me that it was the most forlorn of all hopes."

On May 28, the couple arrived at Badenweiler, Germany, a health spa on the edge of the Black Forest. Despite his weakened condition, Crane continued to dictate fragmentary episodes for the completion of The O'Ruddy. He died on June 5, 1900, at the age of 28. In his will he left everything to Taylor, who took his body to New Jersey for burial. Crane was interred in Evergreen Cemetery in what is now Hillside, New Jersey.

Fiction and poetry

Style and technique

Stephen Crane's fiction is typically categorized as representative of

Naturalism, American realism, Impressionism or a mixture of the three. Critic Sergio Perosa, for example, wrote in his essay, "Stephen Crane fra naturalismo e impressionismo," that the work presents a "symbiosis" of Naturalistic ideals and Impressionistic methods. When asked whether or not he would write an autobiography in 1896, Crane responded that he "dare not say that I am honest. I merely say that I am as nearly honest as a weak mental machinery will allow." Similarities between the stylistic techniques in Crane's writing and Impressionist painting—including the use of color and chiaroscuro—are often cited to support the theory that Crane was not only an Impressionist but also influenced by the movement. H. G. Wells remarked upon "the great influence of the studio" on Crane's work, quoting a passage from The Red Badge of Courage as an example: "At nightfall the column broke into regimental pieces, and the fragments went into the fields to camp. Tents sprang up like strange plants. Camp fires, like red, peculiar blossoms, dotted the night.... From this little distance the many fires, with the black forms of men passing to and fro before the crimson rays, made weird and satanic effects." Although no direct evidence exists that Crane formulated a precise theory of his craft, he vehemently rejected sentimentality, asserting that "a story should be logical in its action and faithful to character. Truth to life itself was the only test, the greatest artists were the simplest, and simple because they were true."

Poet and biographer John Berryman suggested that there were three basic variations, or "norms", of Crane's narrative style. The first, being "flexible, swift, abrupt and nervous", is best exemplified in The Red Badge of Courage, while the second ("supple majesty") is believed to relate to "The Open Boat", and the third ("much more closed, circumstantial and 'normal' in feeling and syntax") to later works such as The Monster. Crane's work, however, cannot be determined by style solely on chronology. Not only does his fiction not take place in any particular region with similar characters, but it varies from serious in tone to reportorial writing and light fiction. Crane's writing, both fiction and nonfiction, is consistently driven by immediacy and is at once concentrated, vivid and intense. The novels and short stories contain poetic characteristics such as shorthand prose, suggestibility, shifts in perspective and ellipses between and within sentences. Similarly, omission plays a large part in Crane's work; the names of his protagonists are not commonly used and sometimes they are not named at all.

Crane was often criticized by early reviewers for his frequent incorporation of everyday speech into dialogue, mimicking the regional accents of his characters with colloquial stylization. This is apparent in his first novel, in which Crane ignored the romantic, sentimental approach of slum fiction; he instead concentrated on the cruelty and sordid aspects of poverty, expressed by the brashness of the Bowery's crude dialect and profanity, which he used lavishly. The distinct dialect of his Bowery characters is apparent at the beginning of the text; the title character admonishes her brother saying: "Yeh knows it puts mudder out when yes comes home half dead, an' it's like we'll all get a poundin'."

Major themes

Crane's work is often thematically driven by Naturalistic and Realistic concerns, including ideals versus realities, spiritual crises and fear. These themes are particularly evident in Crane's first three novels, Maggie: A Girl of the Streets, The Red Badge of Courage and George's Mother. The three main characters search for a way to make their dreams come true, but ultimately suffer from crises of identity. Crane was fascinated by war and death, as well as fire, disfigurement, fear and courage, all of which inspired him to write many works based on these concepts. In The Red Badge of Courage, the main character both longs for the heroics of battle but ultimately fears it, demonstrating the dichotomy of courage and cowardice. He experiences the threat of death, misery and a loss of self.

Extreme isolation from society and community is also apparent in Crane's work. During the most intense battle scenes in The Red Badge of Courage, for example, the story's focus is mainly "on the inner responses of a self unaware of others". In "The Open Boat", "An Experiment in Misery" and other stories, Crane uses light, motion and color to express degrees of epistemological uncertainty. Similar to other Naturalistic writers, Crane scrutinizes the position of man, who has been isolated not only from society, but also from God and nature. "The Open Boat", for example, distances itself from Romantic optimism and affirmation of man's place in the world by concentrating on the characters' isolation.

While he lived, Stephen Crane was denominated by critical readers a realist, a naturalist, an impressionist, symbolist, Symboliste, expressionist and ironist; his posthumous life was enriched by critics who read him as nihilistic, existentialist, a neo-Romantic, a sentimentalist, protomodernist, pointilliste, visionist, imagist and, by his most recent biographer, a "bleak naturalist." At midcentury he was a "predisciple of the New Criticism"; by its end he was "a proto-deconstructionist anti-artist hero" who had "leapfrogged modernism, landing on postmodernist ground." Or, as Sergio Perosa wrote in 1964, "The critic wanders in a labyrinth of possibilities, which every new turn taken by Crane's fiction seems to explode or deny."

One undeniable fact about Crane's work, as Anthony Splendora noted in 2015, is that Death haunts it; like a threatening eclipse it overshadows his best efforts, each of which features the signal demise of a main character. Allegorically, "The Blue Hotel," at the pinnacle of the short story form, may even be an autothanatography, the author's intentional exteriorization or objectification, in this case for the purpose of purgation, of his own impending death. Crane's "Swede" in that story can be taken, following current psychoanalytical theory, as a surrogative, sacrificial victim, ritually to be purged.

Transcending this "dark circumstance of composition," Crane had a particular telos and impetus for his creation: beyond the tautologies that all art is alterity and to some formal extent mimesis, Crane sought and obviously found "a form of catharsis" in writing. This view accounts for his uniqueness, especially as operative through his notorious "disgust" with his family's religion, their "vacuous, futile psalm-singing". His favorite book, for example, was Mark Twain's Life on the Mississippi, in which God is mentioned only twice—once as irony and once as "a swindle." Not only did Crane call out God specifically with the lines "Well then I hate thee / righteous image" in "The Black Riders" (1895), but even his most hopeful tropes, such as the "comradeship" of his "Open Boat" survivors, make no mention of deity, specifying only "indifferent nature." His antitheism is most evident in his characterization of the human race as "lice clinging to a space-lost bulb," a climax-nearing speech in "The Blue Hotel," Ch. VI. It is possible that Crane utilized religion's formal psychic space, now suddenly available resulting from the recent "Death of God", as a milieu for his compensative art.

Novels

Beginning with the publication of Maggie: A Girl of the Streets in 1893, Crane was recognized by critics mainly as a novelist. Maggie was initially rejected by numerous publishers because of its atypical and true-to-life depictions of class warfare, which clashed with the sentimental tales of that time. Rather than focusing on the very rich or middle class, the novel's characters are lower-class denizens of New York's Bowery. The main character, Maggie, descends into prostitution after being led astray by her lover. Although the novel's plot is simple, its dramatic mood, quick pace and portrayal of Bowery life have made it memorable. Maggie is not merely an account of slum life, but also represents eternal symbols. In his first draft, Crane did not give his characters proper names. Instead, they were identified by epithets: Maggie, for example, was the girl who "blossomed in a mud-puddle" and Pete, her seducer, was a "knight". The novel is dominated by bitter irony and anger, as well as destructive morality and treacherous sentiment. Critics would later call the novel "the first dark flower of American Naturalism" for its distinctive elements of naturalistic fiction.

Written thirty years after the end of the Civil War and before Crane had any experience of battle, The Red Badge of Courage was innovative stylistically as well as psychologically. Often described as a war novel, it focuses less on battle and more on the main character's psyche and his reactions and responses in war. It is believed that Crane based the fictional battle in the novel on that of Chancellorsville; he may also have interviewed veterans of the 124th New York Volunteer Infantry Regiment, commonly known as the Orange Blossoms, in Port Jervis, New York. Told in a third-person limited point of view, it reflects the private experience of Henry Fleming, a young soldier who flees from combat. The Red Badge of Courage is notable in its vivid descriptions and well-cadenced prose, both of which help create suspense within the story. Similarly, by substituting epithets for characters' names ("the youth", "the tattered soldier"), Crane injects an allegorical quality into his work, making his characters point to a specific characteristic of man. Like Crane's first novel, The Red Badge of Courage has a deeply ironic tone which increases in severity as the novel progresses. The title of the work is ironic; Henry wishes "that he, too, had a wound, a red badge of courage", echoing a wish to have been wounded in battle. The wound he does receive (from the rifle butt of a fleeing Union soldier) is not a badge of courage but a badge of shame.

The novel expresses a strong connection between humankind and nature, a frequent and prominent concern in Crane's fiction and poetry throughout his career. Whereas contemporary writers (Ralph Waldo Emerson, Nathaniel Hawthorne, Henry David Thoreau) focused on a sympathetic bond on the two elements, Crane wrote from the perspective that human consciousness distanced humans from nature. In The Red Badge of Courage, this distance is paired with a great number of references to animals, and men with animalistic characteristics: people "howl", "squawk", "growl", or "snarl".

Since the resurgence of Crane's popularity in the 1920s, The Red Badge of Courage has been deemed a major American text. The novel has been anthologized numerous times, including in the 1942 collection Men at War: The Best War Stories of All Time, edited by Ernest Hemingway. In the introduction, Hemingway wrote that the novel "is one of the finest books of our literature, and I include it entire because it is all as much of a piece as a great poem is."

Crane's later novels have not received as much critical praise. After the success of The Red Badge of Courage, Crane wrote another tale set in the Bowery. George's Mother is less allegorical and more personal than his two previous novels, and it focuses on the conflict between a church-going, temperance-adhering woman (thought to be based on Crane's mother) and her single remaining offspring, who is a naive dreamer. Critical response to the novel was mixed. The Third Violet, a romance that he wrote quickly after publishing The Red Badge of Courage, is typically considered as Crane's attempt to appeal to popular audiences. Crane considered it a "quiet little story." Although it contained autobiographical details, the characters have been deemed inauthentic and stereotypical. Crane's second to last novel, Active Service, revolves around the Greco-Turkish War of 1897, with which the author was familiar. Although noted for its satirical take on the melodramatic and highly passionate works that were popular of the nineteenth century, the novel was not successful. It is generally accepted by critics that Crane's work suffered at this point due to the speed which he wrote in order to meet his high expenses. His last novel, a suspenseful and picaresque work entitled The O'Ruddy, was finished posthumously by Robert Barr and published in 1903.

Short fiction

Crane wrote many different types of fictional pieces while indiscriminately applying to them terms such as "story", "tale" and "sketch". For this reason, critics have found clear-cut classification of Crane's work problematic. While "The Open Boat" and "The Bride Comes to Yellow Sky" are often considered short stories, others are variously identified.

In an 1896 interview with Herbert P. Williams, a reporter for the Boston Herald, Crane said that he did "not find that short stories are utterly different in character from other fiction. It seems to me that short stories are the easiest things we write." During his brief literary career, he wrote more than a hundred short stories and fictional sketches. Crane's early fiction was based in camping expeditions in his teen years; these stories eventually became known as The Sullivan County Tales and Sketches. He considered these "sketches", which are mostly humorous and not of the same caliber of work as his later fiction, to be "articles of many kinds," in that they are part fiction and part journalism.

The subject matter for his stories varied extensively. His early New York City sketches and Bowery tales accurately described the results of industrialization, immigration and the growth of cities and their slums. His collection of six short stories, The Little Regiment, covered familiar ground with the American Civil War, a subject for which he became famous with The Red Badge of Courage. Although similar to Crane's noted novel, The Little Regiment was believed to lack vigor and originality. Realizing the limitations of these tales, Crane wrote: "I have invented the sum of my invention with regard to war and this story keeps me in internal despair."

The Open Boat and Other Tales of Adventure (1898) contains thirteen short stories that deal with three periods in Crane's life: his Asbury Park boyhood, his trip to the West and Mexico in 1895, and his Cuban adventure in 1897. This collection was well received and included several of his most critically successful works. His 1899 collection, The Monster and Other Stories, was similarly well received.

Two posthumously published collections were not as successful. In August 1900 The Whilomville Stories were published, a collection of thirteen stories that Crane wrote during the last year of his life. The work deals almost exclusively with boyhood, and the stories are drawn from events occurring in Port Jervis, where Crane lived from the age of six to eleven. Focusing on small-town America, the stories tend toward sentimentality, but remain perceptive of the lives of children. Wounds in the Rain, published in September 1900, contains fictional tales based on Crane's reports for the World and the Journal during the Spanish–American War. These stories, which Crane wrote while desperately ill, include "The Price of the Harness" and "The Lone Charge of William B. Perkins" and are dramatic, ironic and sometimes humorous.

Despite Crane's prolific output, only four stories--"The Open Boat", "The Blue Hotel", "The Bride Comes to Yellow Sky", and The Monster— have received extensive attention from scholars. H. G. Wells considered "The Open Boat" to be "beyond all question, the crown of all his work", and it is one of the most frequently discussed of Crane's works.

Poetry

Many red devils ran from my heart

And out upon the page.

They were so tiny

The pen could mash them.

And many struggled in the ink.

It was strange

To write in this red muck

Of things from my heart.

— Stephen Crane

Crane's poems, which he preferred to call "lines", are typically not given as much scholarly attention as his fiction; no anthology contained Crane's verse until 1926. Although it is not certain when Crane began to write poetry seriously, he once said that his overall poetic aim was "to give my ideas of life as a whole, so far as I know it". The poetic style used in both of his books of poetry, The Black Riders and Other Lines and War is Kind, was unconventional for the time in that it was written in free verse without rhyme, meter, or even titles for individual works. They are typically short in length; although several poems, such as "Do not weep, maiden, for war is kind", use stanzas and refrains, most do not. Crane also differed from his peers and poets of later generations in that his work contains allegory, dialectic and narrative situations.

Critic Ruth Miller claimed that Crane wrote "an intellectual poetry rather than a poetry that evokes feeling, a poetry that stimulates the mind rather than arouses the heart". In the most complexly organized poems, the significance of the states of mind or feelings is ambiguous, but Crane's poems tend to affirm certain elemental attitudes, beliefs, opinions and stances toward God, man and the universe. The Black Riders in particular is essentially a dramatic concept and the poems provide continuity within the dramatic structure. There is also a dramatic interplay in which there is frequently a major voice reporting an incident seen ("In the desert / I saw a creature, naked, bestial") or experienced ("A learned man came to me once"). The second voice or additional voices represent a point of view which is revealed to be inferior; when these clash, a dominant attitude emerges.

Legacy

In four years, Crane published five novels, two volumes of poetry, three short story collections, two books of war stories, and numerous works of short fiction and reporting. Today he is mainly remembered for The Red Badge of Courage, which is regarded as an American classic. The novel has been adapted several times for the screen, including John Huston's 1951 version. By the time of his death, Crane had become one of the best known writers of his generation. His eccentric lifestyle, frequent newspaper reporting, association with other famous authors, and expatriate status made him somewhat of an international celebrity. Although most stories about his life tended toward the romantic, rumors about his alleged drug use and alcoholism persisted long after his death.

By the early 1920s, Crane and his work were nearly forgotten. It was not until Thomas Beer published his biography in 1923, which was followed by editor Wilson Follett's The Work of Stephen Crane (1925–1927), that Crane's writing came to the attention of a scholarly audience. Crane's reputation was then enhanced by faithful support from writer friends such as Joseph Conrad, H. G. Wells and Ford Madox Ford, all of whom either published recollections or commented upon their time with Crane. John Berryman's 1950 biography of Crane further established him as an important American author. Since 1951 there has been a steady outpouring of articles, monographs and reprints in Crane scholarship.

Today, Crane is considered one of the most innovative writers of the 1890s. His peers, including Conrad and James, as well as later writers such as Robert Frost, Ezra Pound and Willa Cather, hailed Crane as one of the finest creative spirits of his time. His work was described by Wells as "the first expression of the opening mind of a new period, or, at least, the early emphatic phase of a new initiative." Wells said that "beyond dispute", Crane was "the best writer of our generation, and his untimely death was an irreparable loss to our literature." Conrad wrote that Crane was an "artist" and "a seer with a gift for rendering the significant on the surface of things and with an incomparable insight into primitive emotions". Crane's work has proved inspirational for future writers; not only have scholars drawn similarities between Hemingway's A Farewell to Arms and The Red Badge of Courage, but Crane's fiction is thought to have been an important inspiration for Hemingway and his fellow Modernists. In 1936, Hemingway wrote in The Green Hills of Africa that "The good writers are Henry James, Stephen Crane, and Mark Twain. That's not the order they're good in. There is no order for good writers." Crane's poetry is thought to have been a precursor to the Imagist movement, and his short fiction has also influenced American literature. "The Open Boat", "The Blue Hotel", The Monster and "The Bride Comes to Yellow Sky" are generally considered by critics to be examples of Crane's best work.

Several institutions and places have endeavored to keep Crane's legacy alive. Badenweiler and the house where he died became something of a tourist attraction for its fleeting association with the American author; Alexander Woollcott attested to the fact that, long after Crane's death, tourists would be directed to the room where he died. Columbia University Rare Book and Manuscript Library has a collection of Crane and Taylor's personal correspondence dating from 1895 to 1908. Near his brother Edmund's Sullivan County home in New York, where Crane stayed for a short time, a pond is named after him. The Stephen Crane House in Asbury Park, New Jersey, where the author lived with his siblings for nine years, is operated as a museum dedicated to his life and work. Syracuse University has an annual Stephen Crane Lecture Series which is sponsored by the Dikaia Foundation.

Columbia University purchased much of the Stephen Crane materials held by Cora Crane at her death. The Crane Collection is one of the largest in the nation of his materials. Columbia University had an exhibit: 'The Tall Swift Shadow of a Ship at Night': Stephen and Cora Crane, November 2, 1995 through February 16, 1996, about the lives of the couple, featuring letters and other documents and memorabilia. (Source : Wikipedia)

NOTABLE WORKS

NOVELS

Maggie: A Girl of the Streets, 1893.

The Red Badge of Courage, 1895.

George's Mother, 1896.

The Third Violet, 1897.

Active Service, 1899.

Crane, Stephen and Robert Barr. The O'Ruddy, 1903.

The Black Riders and Other Lines, 1895.

The Open Boat and Other Tales of Adventure, 1898

War is Kind, 1899

The Monster and Other Stories, 1899

Wounds in the Rain, 1900

Great Battles of the World, 1901

The O'Ruddy, 1903

SHORT STORY COLLECTIONS

The Little Regiment and Other Episodes from the American Civil War, 1896.

The Open Boat and Other Tales of Adventure, 1898.

The Monster and Other Stories, 1899.

Whilomville Stories, 1900.

Wounds in the Rain: War Stories, 1900.

Great Battles of the World, 1901.

The Monster,1901.

Last Words, 1902.

POETRY COLLECTIONS

The Black Riders and Other Lines, 1895.

War is Kind, 1899.

UNFINISHED WORKS

Sources report that following an encounter with a male prostitute in the spring of 1894, Crane began a novel on the subject entitled Flowers of Asphalt. He reportedly abandoned the project and the manuscript has never been recovered.

CPSIA information can be obtained
at www.ICGtesting.com
Printed in the USA
LVHW050043271020
669864LV00014B/209